Lynne Graham was born in Northern Ireland and has been a keen romance reader since her teens. She is very happily married, to an understanding husband who has learned to cook since she started to write! Her five children keep her on her toes. She has a very large dog, who knocks everything over, a very small terrier, who barks a lot, and two cats. When time allows, Lynne is a keen gardener.

Louise Fuller was once a tomboy who hated pink and always wanted to be the Prince—not the Princess! Now she enjoys creating heroines who aren't pretty push-overs but strong, believable women. Before writing for Mills & Boon she studied literature and philosophy at university, and then worked as a reporter on her local newspaper. She lives in Tunbridge Wells with her impossibly handsome husband Patrick and their six children.

Also by Lynne Graham

His Cinderella's One-Night Heir

Billionaires at the Altar miniseries

The Greek Claims His Shock Heir
The Italian Demands His Heirs
The Sheikh Crowns His Virgin

Also by Louise Fuller

Kidnapped for the Tycoon's Baby
Surrender to the Ruthless Billionaire
Revenge at the Altar
Demanding His Secret Son

Passion in Paradise collection

Consequences of a Hot Havana Night

Discover more at millsandboon.co.uk.

THE GREEK'S SURPRISE CHRISTMAS BRIDE

LYNNE GRAHAM

PROOF OF THEIR ONE-NIGHT PASSION

LOUISE FULLER

MILLS & BOON

First Published in Great Britain 2019
by Mills & Boon, an imprint of HarperCollins*Publishers*
1 London Bridge Street, London, SE1 9GF

The Greek's Surprise Christmas Bride © 2019 by Lynne Graham

Proof of Their One-Night Passion © 2019 by Louise Fuller

ISBN: 978-0-263-27367-0

MIX
Paper from
responsible sources
FSC® C007454

This book is produced from independently certified FSC™ paper
to ensure responsible forest management.
For more information visit www.harpercollins.co.uk/green.

Printed and bound in Spain
by CPI, Barcelona

THE GREEK'S SURPRISE CHRISTMAS BRIDE

LYNNE GRAHAM

CHAPTER ONE

Leo Romanos, billionaire shipping heir, woke up at dawn with four children in his enormous bed.

He had freaked out the first time it had happened, bought pyjamas for the first time ever and hired a twenty-four-hour, round-the-clock rota of nannies.

But the nanny rota wasn't working. His late sister's traumatised kids still got out of bed in the middle of the night and slunk into his, and they brought the babies as well.

It was a wonder that *he* wasn't traumatised, Leo reflected in wonderment. Five-year-old Popi had ten-month-old Theon tucked in her arms, and three-year-old Sybella had two-year-old Cosmo clasped next to her. His nephews and nieces weren't happy, weren't secure—in spite of all his efforts to make a home for them.

And for their benefit alone Leo was willing, finally, to make the ultimate sacrifice. He would take a wife prepared to be a mother to his four inherited children.

His father and stepmother had refused to take charge of their grandkids and had signed over their guardianship to Leo, his stepmother insisting that his father was too old for the task. And, in truth, Leo hadn't appreciated the extent of the challenge he was taking on.

He had assumed that the nannies would enable him to return to his normal life: workaholic hours followed by the occasional party or dinner, and regular visits to his very sexy mistress. Only somehow it wasn't working out that way. Leo's wonderfully smooth and self-indulgent life had gone to hell when his five-year-old niece had sobbed as if her heart was breaking because he'd said he wouldn't be home for dinner.

Guilt and more guilt had dogged him in spades ever since.

The children needed more than he was capable of giving them—which meant he had to step up, take a wife, and give the kids a mother who would do all the things he didn't want to do and keep them happy while allowing him an uninterrupted night of sleep.

He suppressed a groan, knowing exactly where he would head to find that wife. Six years ago he had been offered a bride from the Livas family—a practical dynastic marriage which would have ended the competition between the two shipping companies, amalgamated them and made him the heir to both empires. The alliance had offered him an enormous profit and tremendous prospects and the proposed bride had been a beauty...

But even so he had hesitated. Leo had loved his freedom and still did, and the potential bride had hinted at a dangerous desire for his fidelity and he had baulked at that tripwire and backed off fast.

Leo had been raised in the belief that marriage was for business, property and heirs, all that sort of legal stuff. There was no room in marriage for the adventurous sex and variety which Leo considered to be an absolute essential of life, so he had stepped back. But four troubled, needy children crawling into his bed made him far less exacting in his expectations. As far as he knew, Elexis Livas was still on the market and suddenly he was willing to consider a deal...

Isidore Livas met him in his Athens office, a very traditional setting, far removed from Leo's very contemporary place of business in the City of London. He was quick to inform Leo that his daughter, Elexis, was on the brink of an engagement and no longer available. Leo suppressed a sigh, not of disappointment because his current mistress was considerably sexier than Elexis; however, he had warmed to the concept of marrying her because she was vaguely familiar to him.

'However, I have a granddaughter,' Isidore admitted grudgingly, surprising Leo with that information. 'As I'm sure you're aware, my son went off the rails...'

Leo nodded, for the world and his wife were aware that Julian Livas, product of his father's first marriage, had taken to drugs and drink and manic bad behaviour from an early age. He had died in his twenties from his excesses. Isidore had Elexis later in life, with his second wife.

'Two months ago, I learned to my surprise that Julian *did* have a child with a woman in London. He didn't marry the woman concerned, so my grandchild was born out of wedlock,' Isidore revealed with old-fashioned distaste. 'Letty is twenty-four and single. You can still become my heir if you take her as a bride... I have no one else, Leo. Elexis's chosen husband is a television presenter with no interest in taking over my business, and I would very much like to retire.'

'And this… Letty?' Leo questioned with a frown, for he considered it an ugly name.

The older man grimaced. 'You couldn't compare her to Elexis. She's plain and plump but she'd marry you like a shot because she needs money for her family.'

'Plain and plump' didn't exactly thrill Leo either. He mightn't want a wife for entertainment in the bedroom but, understandably, he wanted a presentable woman. His black brows drew together in complete puzzlement. 'Why aren't *you* helping her family?'

The expression on Isidore's thin face shuttered. 'She approached me for help but, as far as I'm concerned, if my son wasn't prepared to marry her mother, I shouldn't be expected to provide for their child, now that the girl's an adult.'

'And yet you're willing to make this girl your heiress,' Leo remarked wryly.

'*If* she marries you. That's different. She has Livas blood in her veins and I will accept her then. But she's lowborn,' Isidore murmured broodingly. 'She doesn't speak Greek. She has not been raised with our traditions and you may not find that palatable. She works as a care assistant in a home for the elderly.'

Leo's brain could not even encompass the concept of a wife who worked in so humble a capacity. Born with the proverbial silver spoon in his mouth to a family who had enjoyed wealth for generations, he had no experience whatsoever of what it was like to be born poor. 'In your opinion is your granddaughter likely to be the maternal type?'

'If you can judge her by the way she fights and

argues in favour of her siblings' welfare, I would say so...'

Leo was frowning again. 'Siblings? Julian had *more* than one child with her mother?'

'No. Only Letty is Julian's child. Her mother had the two younger boys with another man,' Isidore clarified with compressed lips. 'I gather that relationship didn't last either and now the mother is ill or disabled or something.'

'Tell Letty what I have to offer and send her to me,' Leo advised with all the arrogance of his wealthy forebears. 'I am willing to marry her if I find her acceptable but, for the children's sake, she *must* be a good woman.'

An unexpected laugh erupted from Isidore, startling the older man almost as much as it startled Leo, who had always viewed Isidore as humourless. 'Leo...what would *you* know about *good* women?'

Faint colour accentuated the high exotic slant of Leo's cheekbones and he lifted a brow and nodded in grudging acknowledgement of that accurate question. Even so, he was very conscious of his duty towards his nephews and nieces and he was determined not to land them with a nasty stepmother, such as he had had to endure. In truth, however, he knew much more about calculating, cruel and greedy women than he knew about the other type.

On his flight back to London, Leo decided to look into Letty and have her investigated but was instead forced to have her late father's history explored because Isidore had neglected to give him Letty's surname. By the time he arrived back in London, a file awaited him and the information within was unexpectedly interesting. Juliet, known as Letty, Harbison was a much more thought-provoking bride-to-be than her socialite Aunt Elexis had ever been. Leo's rarely roused curiosity was stimulated.

Unaware of the high-flying plans afoot for her future, Letty stared at the loan shark on their doorstep. 'You're breaking the law,' she told him sharply. 'You are not allowed to harass and intimidate your debtors.'

'I'm entitled to ask for my money,' he told her fiercely, a thin little man in a crumpled suit, another man, unshaven and thuggish in shape, poised behind him, his sidekick, Joe, who had attempted to thump her little brother for trying to stand up to him on his last visit. He had backed off when Letty wielded the cricket bat she kept behind the door.

'You'll have your payment as soon as I get paid, just like last month and the month before,' Letty responded, squaring her shoulders, honey-blonde hair caught up in a ponytail bouncing with the movement, her green eyes clear and steady. 'I can't give you what I don't have.'

'A little bird told me you have rich relations.'

An angry flush illuminated Letty's creamy skin as she wondered if one of her brothers had let that dangerous cat out of the bag. 'I asked. He wouldn't help.'

'He might help soon enough if you was unlucky enough to have an…accident,' Joe piped up ungrammatically, baring crooked teeth in a smile that was a grimace of threat.

'But if I were to have an accident, you wouldn't be getting any money at all,' Letty pointed out flatly and closed the door swiftly, seeing no advantage to continuing the dialogue.

'Rich relations', she thought wryly, thinking back to her one meeting with her Greek grandfather, when he had visited London on business. A cold, unfriendly man more hung up on the reality that she was illegitimate rather than showing any genuine interest in her actual existence. No, contacting Isidore Livas had been a dead end. She had soon worked out that no rescue bid would be coming from him. He had shaken her off like the poor relation she was.

While her mother, Gillian, hobbled painfully round the tiny kitchen of their council flat on crutches and tried to tidy up, Letty made a cheap but nutritious evening meal for her family. Her two brothers sat at the table in the living room, both of them engaged in homework. Tim was thirteen and Kyle was nine. Letty considered her half-brothers marginally less useless than she considered the rest of the world's men.

There were no towering heroes in Letty's depressing experience of men. Her father, Julian, had been a handsome, irresponsible lightweight, incapable of fighting his addictions to toxic substances. He had lived with her mother and her only once and for a brief period, after a more than usually successful stay in a rehab facility, but within months he had fallen off the wagon again and that had been the last Letty had seen of him.

Yet, tragically, meeting Julian Livas had derailed her mother's entire life. Gillian had been a middle-class schoolgirl at the exclusive co-educational boarding school where she had met Julian. A teenage pregnancy had resulted and when Gillian had refused to have a termination her parents had thrown her out and washed their hands of her. Letty had always respected the hard struggle Gillian had faced, simply to survive as a young mother. As a single parent, Gillian had subsequently trained as a nurse and life had been stable until Gillian fell in love again.

Letty grimaced as she thought of her stepfather, Robbie, a steady worker and a likeable man but, underneath the surface show of decency and reliability, a hopeless womaniser. When Gillian could no longer live with his lies and deceptions, they had had to move on and inevitably their standard of living had gone downhill with the divorce. In his own way, Robbie had been as feckless as her father, although he did maintain a stable relationship with his two sons.

Letty had worked very hard at school, determined that she would never have to rely on a man for support. And what good had it done her? she asked herself ruefully. It had given her a scholarship to a top sixth form college and the chance to study medicine at Oxford but, within a few years, just as Letty was starting to stretch her wings into independence and the promise of a satisfying career, misfortune had rolled back in and her family had needed her back at home to bring in a living wage.

She had been three years into her medical degree when Gillian's worsening arthritis had forced her to give up work and live on benefits. Undaunted, Gillian had retrained as a drug and alcohol counsellor, who could work from a wheelchair, but all it took was a broken lift in their tower apartment block—and it was frequently out of order—and she was trapped indoors and unable either to work or to earn. That one very bleak Christmas, when Letty was in the fifth year of her course, Gillian had got involved in the murky un-

derworld of unsecured loans and had fallen into debt
as the interest charges mushroomed.

Letty rode into work on the elderly motorbike she
had restored. Parking her bike and securing it, she
walked into the Sunset Home for the Elderly, where
she worked as the permanent night shift manager. She
was on a good salary and had no complaints about her
working conditions or colleagues. She had every intention of completing her medical studies as soon as
it was possible but, right at that moment, that desired
goal seemed worryingly distant. Her mother was too
frail to be left alone with two active boys until she received the double hip replacement she needed. Sadly,
the waiting lists for free treatment were too long and
private surgery was unaffordable. In the short term,
more accessible accommodation would have much improved Gillian's lot and her ability to work but the large
debt that she had accrued with that iniquitous loan had
to be cleared before moving could even be considered.

As Letty changed out of bike leathers into work
garb, her phone started ringing and she answered it
swiftly, always fearful of her mother having suffered
a fall, which would exacerbate her condition. But it
wasn't one of her brothers calling to give her bad news,
it was, amazingly, her grandfather.

'If you're willing to do whatever it takes to help your
family, Leo is the man to approach. I will text you the
phone number. Furthermore, if you were to reach an
agreement with Leo, I will invite you into my home
and introduce you to Greek society,' the older man informed her loftily in the tone of someone who believed
he was offering her some great honour.

'Er…right. Thanks for that,' Letty responded ruefully, wondering why her grandfather would think that she was interested in being introduced to Greek society and what sort of agreement he believed she could reach with this guy, Leo, that was likely to benefit her or her family. Maybe the older man wasn't as cold a fish as she had assumed, and he was genuinely trying to help her. She was too much of a cynic for a wannabe doctor, she scolded herself, she really had to start trying harder to see the good in human beings.

The next morning, before she headed home to bed after her shift, she took out the number and phoned it.

'VR Shipping,' a woman answered.

'My name is Letty Harbison. I have to make an appointment with someone called Leo?'

'If you will excuse me for a moment…' the woman urged.

Letty groaned at the sound of voices fussing in the background. Was this Leo likely to offer her better paid employment? He was obviously a businessman in an office environment. When she got home, she would look him up online, although she would need more than his first name to accomplish that, she reflected wearily.

'Mr Romanos will see you at ten this morning at his London office.' The woman then read out the address of his building.

'I'm sorry, I'm a night shift worker and it would need to be a little later in the day,' Letty began apologetically.

'Mr Romanos will not be available later. He is a very busy man.'

Letty rolled her eyes. 'Ten will be fine,' she conceded, reasoning that it was only sensible to check the man out because her grandfather *could* genuinely be attempting to do her a good turn. *And pigs might fly*, her inner cynic sniped as she remembered the single cup of black coffee she had enjoyed in the fancy restaurant where she had met her father's father for the first time for a twenty-minute chat which had consisted of his barked questions and her laboured replies.

It had been a painful meeting because she had truly hoped that there would be some sense of family connection between them, but there had been nothing, only an older man, evidently still very bitter about his only son's early death. Even worse, any reference Letty had made to her family's problems had only seemed to increase her grandfather's contempt for her and her mother and brothers.

Dragging herself out of the recollection of that disheartening conversation, she checked the time and suppressed another groan. There was no way on earth she could get home, freshen up and change and then catch the bus to make that appointment in time. Oh, to heck with that, she thought in sudden rebellion, she would attend the appointment as she was, in her bike leathers, and explain that she had just left work and had nothing else to wear. After calling her mother to warn her that she would be late back, Letty climbed back on her bike.

'Have you a parcel?' the receptionist asked Letty on her arrival in the building.

'No, I have an appointment with Mr Leo... Romanos, is it? At ten,' she recited uncertainly because she had been so drowsy when she had made that initial call that her concentration and powers of recall were not operating with their usual efficiency.

The top floor receptionist's eyes rounded as she took in Letty in her biker leathers because she was a gossip and, according to the grapevine, Leo Romanos had unexpectedly cancelled a very important meeting to clear a last-minute space for a female visitor. The usual lively speculation about his sex life had duly erupted in a frenzy. Only, sadly, Letty did not fit the bill because Leo was a living legend for his taste in beautiful women, who were invariably models or socialites, spiced with the occasional actress. Nobody looking at Letty could possibly have placed her in any of those categories.

Letty sank down on a squashy and very comfortable sofa in the reception area and the exhaustion she suffered by never ever getting enough rest simply engulfed her in a drowning tide. Her sleepy eyes executed one last final sweep of the ultra-modern, very luxurious floor of offices and wonderment assailed her. Why on earth had her grandfather sent her to such a place? Yes, she had the usual office skills but she seriously doubted they would be on a par with the kind of commercial skills employees needed to have in a business environment. Even worse, she was dressed all wrong, had only just managed to get out of the lift before being asked if she had brought the pizzas someone was awaiting. She had been mistaken for a takeaway delivery person.

'Your ten o'clock appointment is asleep in Reception,' one of Leo's assistants informed him.

Asleep? *Theos*…how was she contriving to sleep on the brink of potentially meeting her future husband? It did not occur to Leo that Isidore Livas would have been foolish enough to send his granddaughter to see him without that all-important proposal having being outlined in advance. He hadn't expected to meet her quite so quickly, however, had assumed it would take at least a week to set up such a meeting. He was allowing the necessary time for Letty to make whatever effort she could to look her best to meet the expectations of a billionaire seeking a bride.

Leo strode out to Reception, disconcerting everyone, turning every head, and then he saw her, lying full length along the sofa, very nearly merging with the black upholstery in her leathers. Leather? Why was she dressed from top to toe in leather and wearing chunky motorbike boots?

Bemused, Leo came to a halt and stared down at her, noticing the long messy ponytail, so long it almost brushed the floor. She had long honey-blonde hair. All the Livas tribe were some shade of blonde, he recalled abstractedly as his roaming attention mounted the curve of a lush pouting derrière sleekly outlined by leather and a long slender thigh. Her face was pillowed on her hand, sleep-flushed, her lips full and pink. She wasn't very tall. In fact she was short in stature, another Livas trait. She might be lucky to reach his chest, even in high heels. But she wasn't plain and she certainly wasn't plump. She was simply wonderfully curved in all the right feminine places and only a man with a wife and a daughter the size and shape of toothpicks could have deemed Letty plump, Leo reflected wryly. Involuntarily, he was still staring because he wanted to know what lay below the leather jacket she had zipped up tight and he was ridiculously tempted to scoop her up and just carry her into his office. Courtesy, however, would be the wiser choice and Leo was usually wise.

'Letty…' Leo intoned in his deep dark drawl. 'Letty…'

Theos, he hated that name, which was more suited to an Edwardian kitchen maid and Juliet was so much prettier. *He* would call her Juliet.

Letty shifted position and her lashes fluttered as she forced her unwilling body back to wakefulness when all it wanted to do was sleep. She began to push herself up on her arm and her eyes widened on the man poised at the end of the sofa. He was so disconcerting a vision that she blinked, expecting him to vanish like the illusion he had to be. But he stayed steady, a very tall, lean and powerful figure, garbed in a business suit so exquisitely tailored to his exact physique that he looked like a model, a male supermodel who would have looked more at home with the backdrop of a vast yacht behind him.

He had black cropped hair, razor-edged cheekbones and a perfect nose and mouth. As for the eyes, well, Letty, who never went into raptures, could've gone into raptures over those dark deep-set eyes glimmering with rich honey accents and framed by ridiculously long lashes. Letty wasn't even surprised that she was staring, she, who never stared at a man, unless it was in an attempt to intimidate him. He was an outrageously beautiful male specimen and quite dazzlingly noticeable.

He stretched down a hand. 'I'm Leo Romanos,' he informed her with quiet hauteur.

She couldn't wait to look him up online and find out all about him, although it was clear that he shared her grandfather's arrogance even if he wore it differently. Leo Romanos, she sensed, was a man accustomed to having others leap to do his bidding and he took it quite for granted. Isidore Livas, however, didn't project quite the same level of expectation and intimidation, and felt the need to frown and pitch his voice louder to make a similar impression.

'Letty Harbison...' Letty said, belatedly recalling her manners, heated embarrassment momentarily claiming her as she realised she had been sleeping full length along the sofa in a public place. Then, in common with most junior doctors, Letty could've fallen asleep standing up on one leg, particularly after several sessions spent observing, fetching and carrying in a busy emergency unit.

'Is there somewhere I could...freshen up?' she asked, evading that shrewd dark gaze of his, her defences kicking in because she had stared at him—she didn't *stare* at men and didn't feel comfortable with the fact that she had stared at him.

He indicated the cloakroom behind the waiting area and she shot upright, learning that he was even taller than she had suspected and surprised even more to learn that there *were* men around who could make her feel positively small and dainty.

She vanished into the cloakroom at speed, grimacing when she caught her pink and tousled reflection. In an effort to tidy her hair she tugged off her hairband and it snapped, leaving her with a wealth of honey-blonde tresses spilling untidily over her shoulders. She cursed and threw her head back to shift her mane of hair down her back before unzipping and removing her jacket because she was much too hot. She washed her hands, briefly wished she had brought a lipstick with her and suppressed the idle thought again. It would take more than a dash of lipstick to make her look like an efficient and elegant office worker in VR Shipping, where even the receptionist resembled a Miss World contender.

'This way, please...' another employee greeted her when she emerged. 'I'll show you to Mr Romanos's office. Would you like some coffee?'

'Yes, thank you,' Letty responded warmly, thinking that coffee, which she rarely drank, might wake her up because, after that short burst of sleep, her brain cells felt as though they were drowning in sludge. 'I take it black, no sugar.'

Leo had a vague unrealistic hope that Juliet would reappear looking rather more conventional and even wearing a little make-up and carting a bag of some kind like a normal woman. Instead, she came through the door, carrying her jacket with her hair loose. And what hair it was, Leo marvelled, watching the luxuriant honey-blonde strands flick against her shapely hips as she turned to shut the door behind her. She spun back, eyes as green as fresh ferns in sunlight, alert and questioning now, and she gripped her jacket even closer to her chest, as though she was trying to conceal the undeniably magnificent swell of her breasts below the plain black T-shirt she wore.

Leo liked curvy women, but he loved the female breast in all sizes and, as she settled down in the chair set in front of his desk, he was enchanted by the very slight bounce of her bosom as she sat down. Natural curves, he was convinced, not bought and paid for, shaped by some talented surgeon. Encountering her gaze, Leo went as hard as a rock and it shocked him, sincerely shocked him, because *that* didn't happen to him any more in public. He strode around his desk to take a seat, disconcerted by that juvenile response to a woman who was fully clothed, bare of make-up and, so far, not even a little flirtatious or suggestive.

His assistant entered with a tray of coffee and poured it.

'I don't usually drink coffee, but I need it to wake me up this morning,' Letty admitted with a rueful smile that lit up her oval face. 'I apologise for not being more smartly dressed but I only finished work at eight and there wasn't time to go home and change and get back here in time.'

'Why the biker leathers?'

'I use a motorbike to get around. It's cheap to run and perfect for getting through rush hour traffic,' Letty explained, sipping the coffee she held between her cupped hands. 'I don't know why my grandfather insisted that I should come and see you. Do you have some sort of work that I could do? A job to offer?'

Leo froze, belatedly registering that Isidore had not done the footwork for him. 'I have a proposition that you may wish to consider.'

'Did Isidore mention that I'm in need of money?' Letty had to force herself to ask, her creamy skin turning pink with self-consciousness.

'Your grandfather asked you to call him Isidore?' Leo remarked in surprise.

'Oh, he didn't invite me to call him anything,' Letty parried with rueful amusement. 'To be frank, he didn't want to acknowledge the relationship.'

'That must've been a disappointment,' Leo commented wryly.

'Not really. I wasn't expecting a miracle but, considering that my father never paid any child support, it's not as though I've cost that side of my family anything over the years,' she responded quietly. 'My mother has always been very independent but right now that's not possible for her, so I've had to step in…'

'Which is where I enter the equation from your point of view,' Leo incised. 'Your grandfather wants to amalgamate his shipping firm with mine and retire, leaving me in charge. For me, the price of that valuable alliance is that I marry you.'

A pin-drop silence fell.

'You would have to marry *me* to get his shipping business?' Letty exclaimed in disbelief. 'I've never heard anything so outrageous in my life! I knew he was an out-of-date old codger, but I didn't realise he was *insane*!'

'Then I must be insane too,' Leo acknowledged smoothly. 'Because I am willing to agree to that deal, although I also have more pressing reasons for being currently in need of a wife…'

Letty felt disorientated and bewildered. 'You *need* a wife?' she almost whispered, wondering why there wasn't a stampede of eager women pushing her out of their path to reach him and then suppressing that weird and frivolous thought, irritated by her lapse in concentration.

'Six months ago, my sister and her husband died in a car crash. I am attempting to raise their four children. I need a wife to help me with that task,' Leo spelt out succinctly.

'*Four*…children?' Letty gasped in consternation.

'Aged five and under.' Leo decided to give her all the bad news at once. 'The baby was a newborn, who was premature at birth. Ben and Anastasia were on the way to pick him up and finally bring him home from the hospital when they were killed.'

In the stretching heavy silence, Letty blinked in shock. 'How tragic...'

'Yes, but rather more tragic for their children, with only me to fall back on. They need a mother figure, someone who's there more often. I work long hours and I travel as well. The set-up that I have at the moment is not working well enough for them.'

Letty shrugged a slight fatalistic shoulder. 'So, you make sacrifices. You change your lifestyle.'

'I have already done that. Bringing in a wife to share the responsibility makes better sense,' Leo declared in a tone of finality as though only he could give an opinion in that field.

'And you and my grandfather, who doesn't really *want* to be my grandfather,' Letty suggested with a rueful curve to her soft mouth, 'somehow reached the conclusion that *I* could be that wife?'

'You are Isidore's only option, his sole available female relative. His daughter's about to get engaged.'

'So, my Aunt Elexis wasn't ready to snap you up,' Letty observed.

Leo compressed his wide sensual mouth at her slightly mocking intonation. 'Isidore first approached me on her behalf six years ago. I said no.'

'You said no,' Letty echoed weakly, struggling without success to get into the thought patterns of rich Greeks, prepared to marry purely to unite their companies and families.

'I'm only willing to marry now to benefit the children,' Leo told her.

'But marriage is a lot more intimate in nature than an agreement to raise children together,' Letty pointed out.

Leo lounged fluidly back in his chair. 'In our case, it would be *less* intimate. Sex wouldn't be involved. I would satisfy my needs elsewhere.'

Letty turned bright red and she didn't know why. After all, she knew everything there was to know about the mechanics of sex, hormones and physical needs, even if she did lack actual experience. 'So, you wouldn't require sex from your wife?' she checked, not quite sure she could credit that.

'No. I keep a mistress for that purpose. It's more convenient,' Leo informed her without shame or an ounce of embarrassment.

Letty shook her head as if to clear it. Possibly it was to convince herself that this unusual conversation between her and a man she had met only minutes earlier was actually taking place. 'Well,' she breathed thoughtfully, 'you've told me what you would be getting out of such a marriage—another shipping company, presumably greater wealth, a dutiful mother to your sister's children and the continuing freedom to sleep with whomever you like. That's a lot.'

Leo surveyed her with dark golden eyes and slowly smiled, his chiselled dark features more appealing than ever. 'It is…'

'I can see why the arrangement would appeal to you. But what would *I* be getting out of it?' Letty asked gently.

And she thought, *I'm not asking that—seriously I'm not. I can't possibly be considering such a crazy proposition from a man I don't even know! An unscrupulous, immoral man at that, one who prefers a mis-*

tress to a wife in his bed and makes no bones about it either! Absolutely and utterly shameless in his honesty.

Leo studied her, wishing he could read her better, but the smooth oval of her face was unrevealing. Indeed, they could have been discussing something as bland as the weather.

'Let me tell you the benefits of becoming my wife,' Leo urged in that husky accented drawl of his, which was both exotic and sensual.

CHAPTER TWO

'I DON'T KNOW how important money is to you,' Leo remarked deadpan.

'When you don't have money, but you need it, it's *very* important,' Letty countered with a toss of her head and a lift of her chin because she was telling the truth and didn't care if he judged her for it.

Leo rose from his seat and spread his lean brown hands in an expressive gesture that was wonderfully fluid. 'If you marry me, you will be able to have anything that you want. I am a very rich man,' he told her bluntly. 'I assume that you would want to organise private surgery for your mother and find a safer place for your family to live. You will also want the thugs, who are harassing your mother for payment of her loan, dealt with. Those are the difficulties that I can easily settle on your behalf. Only you can tell me what else you would want.'

Letty was astonished by how much he already knew about her life and her family's problems. 'Where did you get all that information? From Isidore?'

'From a very discreet investigation agency. I had to know exactly who you were before I could consider allowing you near the children,' Leo pointed out without a shade of remorse.

Annoyed by his invasion of her privacy and yet simultaneously understanding his reasons for doing so, Letty was bemused. 'And what did you think that you learned about me?' she prompted.

'That you put family loyalty over personal ambition and that no one you have worked with or studied with or enjoyed a friendship with has anything bad to say about you,' Leo recounted levelly. 'I was very impressed and immediately keen to meet you. Such fine qualities are rare.'

Not entirely untouched by that accolade, Letty coloured and watched him move restlessly across the room. He drew her eyes to him, no matter how hard she tried to look away. He had an intensity to him she had not met with in a man before. Leo Romanos was so much *more*. He emanated physical energy in an aura of power. A very strong character, a mover and shaker, a pretty dominant personality, but it would be a dominance laced with intelligence and control. Emotional, *very* emotional—she had seen that emotion flashing in his eyes when he'd referred to his late sister and the children in his care. When he was in a bad mood, she imagined people walked on eggshells around him. Women, she imagined, fell in the aisles around him, stunned by the raw sexual charisma he exuded.

And no, she was not impervious to his masculine appeal, she conceded ruefully. She doubted that many women were impervious to Leo and she was no different, her attention veering involuntarily to the pull of fabric across his long muscular thighs as he moved, the swell of his broad chest below his shirt as he breathed, the muscles there evident. Even fully clothed he was a disturbingly physical man, who would always attract attention and admiration.

'You talk about acquiring a wife much like you're shopping for a fine wine,' she commented quietly. 'It's not the same.'

'Isn't it? I can purchase the finest wine at the highest price and I still may not like the taste of it,' he fenced smoothly.

'I consider marriage to be,' Letty murmured levelly, 'a sacred bond between two people.'

'Yes, you are a practising Christian.' Leo acknowledged that detail, shifting his expressive hands again. 'But you are practical as well and you must know that sex causes a lot of grief in relationships. Take the sex out of the marriage and you have a working, reasonable partnership.'

'And an unfaithful husband,' Letty chipped in, again inwardly denying that she was having such a dialogue with him while wondering how she could possibly be intrigued by his attitude.

Leo shrugged a wide shoulder. 'Is that so important in the grand scheme of things? It's not as though you're in love with me. It's not even as though you know me.'

Letty's head was beginning to ache with the stress of the meeting to which she had walked in totally unprepared. She was too tired to think with clarity and her mind was increasingly awash with irrelevant but seductive images, such as her mother able to walk again, her brothers attending a less crowded and tough school and being able to eat what they liked, rather than what was cheapest. Lack of money, she registered unhappily, controlled their lives, limited it and removed all the choices. But the escape that Leo Romanos was offering carried risks as well.

'I've been up almost twenty-four hours,' Letty admitted. 'I need to sleep to process all this.'

Leo swung back to her, spectacular dark golden eyes locking to her. 'But you're *not* saying no out of hand,' he breathed with satisfaction.

'A drowning swimmer doesn't reject a lifebelt unless it comes anchored to a crocodile,' Letty responded wryly.

'I'm not a crocodile,' Leo told her.

'You have strong aggressive instincts,' Letty informed him.

'I am not violent…in *any* way,' Leo intoned, looking shaken that she might suspect otherwise.

'But who knows what damage you could do in other ways?' Letty fielded as she rose from her chair. 'Right now, I'm going home to bed.'

'You're too tired to bike it back,' Leo stated. 'I will have you driven home and one of my security team will return your motorbike for you.'

'I'm not into bossy men, Leo,' Letty warned him.

'I am considering your welfare,' he parried.

'My welfare is not your business.'

'*Yet…*'

'It's childish to always need to have the last word,' Letty said as she reached the door.

'So, that's why you're having it, is it?' Leo gibed, disconcerting her and pulling the door open for her with a smooth civility that she found equally surprising.

He escorted her all the way to the lift, the eyes of his employees swivelling in their direction. He stabbed the call button at the same time as he settled a business card into her hand. 'My number. Let me know if you're prepared to move forward with this. If you are, I will collect you on Saturday morning at ten and introduce you to the children,' he announced.

Letty turned exasperated eyes onto his chest and then tilted her head back to study his lean strong face and the resolve etched there. 'I don't know how I feel but there is only a one in ten chance that I will agree! I don't want to get married. I'm not ready to be a mother...and I *loathe* promiscuous men!'

'I would take issue with that word,' Leo framed, his strong jawline clenching hard. 'But we will not discuss that insult in a public place.'

Breathing in deep to prevent herself from snapping back at him, Letty stepped into the lift. 'Goodbye, Leo. It's been...interesting.'

The most bloody frustrating woman he had ever met! Leo strode back to his office, his brain buzzing at top speed. So stubborn, so rigid. How dare she label him promiscuous? He was not and never had been promiscuous. Yes, there had been many women in his bed over the years, but he was thirty-one years old and a certain level of experience was natural. He was prepared to concede that keeping a mistress was a little less common but he never stayed with the same woman for longer than three months and while she was in his life, the arrangement was exclusive. He hadn't had a one-night stand since he was a teenager and even then he hadn't slept around.

Isidore's granddaughter was fiercely intelligent though, not a woman to be pushed into a premature decision…but coaxed? Leo didn't know how to coax a woman because he had never had to make that much effort with a member of her sex, but he also knew that he had just met a woman he would be satisfied to call his wife. As far as he was concerned the deal was made and only the date needed to be set. She didn't have a choice, did she? Her life had been overwhelmed by family difficulties and, much as he admired her loyalty, it annoyed him that she had swerved from her own agenda and had allowed her mother's foolish decisions and misfortunes to restrict her.

Letty rode home and Leo need not have worried that exhaustion would make her a less than cautious rider. Leo had set off a chain reaction inside her head. Out of his presence, she could think again, see possibilities and spot the issues he had overlooked. What about *her* sex life? Was she expected to keep a male version of a mistress somewhere? Or was she supposed to cross her legs like the virgin she was and get by without sex?

In truth, Letty didn't know if she would ever want sex with a man. Being a high achiever had never helped her social life. The more she had shone at school, the fewer friends she'd had and she had been christened a nerd and a geek. University and competing with her peers had provided a different learning curve but no boyfriend had ever contrived to make Letty want more than kisses and companionship. All of them had wanted more from her than she was prepared to give because she had always put her studies first. She had once toyed with the idea of just having sex with someone purely to find out what it was like, but she wasn't sufficiently curious and was too cynical to expect fireworks from the experience, so she had retained her ignorance and her innocence.

A man like Leo, however, would have made her want more and would have incited her curiosity. She knew that instinctively and it made her wary of him. He made her feel vulnerable and she didn't like that either. He was too clever as well, too clever to be trusted. Had she had more respect for her grandfather, she would've asked his opinion of Leo Romanos but Isidore Livas was scarcely a disinterested observer and she could not put her faith in him. Presumably her grandfather wanted this alliance to go ahead and he was equally keen for Leo to become his heir. Letty had no doubt that Leo was a blazing success in the business world.

When she arrived home, her mother needed painkillers and she went back out again to collect the prescription. The painkillers were highly addictive and that worried her, for her mother had been on them for quite some time. While she was out, she bought food for dinner and when she returned for the second time her mother was standing rapt in front of the table, on which sat a gorgeous bouquet of flowers, delivered in a vase and ready for display.

'For you…' the older woman said with warm appreciation, turning to study her flushed daughter with curiosity. 'You've been keeping secrets. Who's Leo?'

Letty grabbed the card. It just said 'Leo', but that was all it needed to say.

'Leo?' she repeated, her mouth running dry. 'He's one of the residents' relatives at the care home,' she fibbed in desperation.

'Is he young?' Gillian pressed.

'Yes, and good-looking.'

'Well, don't freeze this one out, the way that you do when men show an interest in you,' her mother urged worriedly. 'Be nice to this one.'

'Mum, I'm only twenty-four. I've got plenty of time to meet someone. Stop worrying about me,' Letty said wryly, giving the older woman a hug. 'I'm off to bed.'

She had hoped to climb into bed and go out like a light but her mind had other ideas: visions of her mother restored to mobility and no longer reliant on painkillers, her family in a home in a decent area with furniture that wasn't worn and shabby and the boys clad in the sports gear of their dreams. Seductive images, she conceded ruefully, cursing Leo Romanos for tempting her before grabbing her laptop to look him up online.

The Greek billionaire, the shipping heir, consummate tycoon…giver of flowers, charming when he wanted to be.

Also a womaniser, she reminded herself, discovering a whole slew of images in which Leo appeared in company with various women but all of them were identikit brunettes. It seemed he had a type and his type was tall, curvy dark-haired women. Of what interest was that to her? Why was she even looking? Scolding herself, Letty returned to trying to sleep while attempting not to recall that Christmas was only just round the corner and that the coming festivities would be just as cheerless as the last.

Christmas was impossible to do on a strict budget and, what with the loan payments due every month and keeping up with the household bills, there was no room for treats or extras. Her brothers were still children and it was hard for them to do without what other boys their age took for granted. If she married Leo, a persuasive little voice whispered inside her head, she could give her family a fantastic Christmas. All their worries would disappear, wouldn't they?

Of course, *she* would be taking on a whole fresh set of worries, striving to meet Leo's high expectations of a wife and mother to four orphans, but if her family was happy and secure, did that really matter? She was good at coping with challenges, in fact the tougher a project was, the harder she worked to complete it. She did her best work under pressure…and Leo would put her under pressure, she had no doubt of that.

Letty pillowed her weary head on her hand and stretched out. Obviously, she would have to deliberate on his proposition because nothing more promising was likely to come her way. If she said no, she would be condemning her family and herself to their current lifestyle for the next few years, at least. That was depressing but it was a fact. Her moral scruples were in conflict with her practical nature. There were too many unknowns for her to reach a decision. What would happen when she wanted a child? Or *he* did? And how long was he expecting the marriage to last? And what about the medical studies she wanted to take up again?

That Thursday evening, thinking longingly of her approaching weekend off, Letty performed her usual round of the patients, checking who was settled, who might need the attentions of the doctor on call later on, while stopping to speak to regular visitors, who wanted information about their relatives or had requests to make. She returned to her office to take her break at eleven and on her path through the quiet reception area she was shaken to see Leo.

In the sleek cashmere overcoat and red silk scarf he wore over a dark suit teamed with a gold silk tie, he looked exactly like the legendary international business mogul he was. His dark carnal beauty flooded her with mesmerising force and momentarily she felt boneless and her knees wobbled, butterflies careening frantically in the pit of her stomach. Letty froze in reaction, disconcertingly aware of her hair in an unglamorous bun and the plain green nursing-type tunic and trousers she wore with a logo badge on her collar.

'Time for a break?' Leo murmured calmly. 'You look tired.'

'It's been a busy week,' she muttered, colliding warily with glittering dark golden eyes, her breath snagging in her throat.

'I have coffee and tea out in my car... You didn't phone,' he censured.

Her cheeks warmed and she gave a little shake of her shoulders, unsure what to say because she hadn't made her mind up yet and didn't want to admit that. In her own head she was a very decisive person but there were too many unknowns attached to Leo Romanos. 'I haven't made up my mind yet,' she admitted grudgingly.

'Then discuss your concerns with me over tea. It'll be very civilised and no doubt we can pretend we're not sitting in a car park,' Leo pointed out.

Letty went to inform her next in command that she was taking her break outside. A big black and unbelievably long and glossy limousine sat double parked.

'Why are you here?' she prompted as his driver

pulled open the door of the car for them and stood to attention as though they were royalty.

'I won't introduce you to the children unless I know you're planning to go ahead. I've never brought a woman home to meet them before and they've had enough upsets in their lives.'

Letty suppressed a sigh as he pressed a button and an incredibly well-stocked refreshment bar complete with refrigerator, hot water and china swung out. The limo was massive and the upholstery was palest pearl grey leather. Her seat was comfier than her bed and, keen to busy her restless hands, Letty selected a cup and a teabag from the wide variety available in a small drawer and added hot water.

'Would you like anything?' she enquired politely.

'No. I've just had dinner,' he responded with an impatient sigh.

Letty sipped her Earl Grey tea and reluctantly glanced at him, encountering the devastating eyes that she would've preferred to avoid, hating his effect on her. He was a force of nature, his temperament lava-hot and dangerous. 'I've spotted four major stumbling blocks to your proposition,' she admitted, her heart suffering a sudden thud as he tensed and his stunning golden eyes narrowed.

'Four?' he stressed in disbelief.

'Yes, you really haven't thought this marriage idea through thoroughly enough,' Letty informed him gently. 'What happens when you decide you would like a child?'

'I've already got four of them. That's not going to happen at any time in the near future,' Leo contended dismissively.

'Unfortunately, I don't have as big a window of fertility as you will have,' Letty pointed out quietly. 'I am likely to want a child of my own some time in the next ten years. I don't want to leave it too long and risk missing my chance to become a mother.'

Leo frowned, level black brows pleating. 'So, we use a laboratory and give you what you want when you want. I don't see a problem.'

Letty noted that he wasn't suggesting that they consider sex for her to conceive, not that she would've agreed to that while he was sleeping with other women, but it really bothered her to recognise the faint sense of disappointment rising inside her. Disappointment allied with curiosity, she acknowledged ruefully. He made her curious in a treacherous way. Letty was not in the habit of looking at a man and thinking of sex but Leo made her think of sex, wonder what it would be like, wonder what it would be like *with him*. And in that thought progression lay one very good reason why she shouldn't marry Leo Romanos.

Her breasts were peaking inside her bra, her thighs pressing together in reaction to the dull ache that was infiltrating her. She couldn't possibly marry a man who awakened her long dormant sensuality but who planned to break his marital vows on a weekly basis, for all she knew even on a daily basis. It would be a recipe for low self-esteem and unhappiness because she would feel rejected.

'That's two stumbling blocks dealt with,' Leo proclaimed briskly. 'What are the other two?'

'As soon as possible I would like to return to studying medicine,' Letty admitted.

'Why not? When I told you that I wanted a wife to

be a mother to my sister's children, I didn't mean to suggest that I expected you to become a stay-at-home wife. I employ an ample staff to take care of the children on a day-to-day basis. You would be free to return to your studies,' he assured her levelly. 'I am not an unreasonable man, Juliet.'

'Don't call me that... I've always been Letty.'

'I don't like the name,' Leo declared calmly. 'To me, you will always be Juliet and I don't know how it ever got shortened into something as ugly as Letty.'

'My mother called my father, Julian, Jules and, although she named me for him, she could never stand to call me Juliet because it made her think of him. That's how I became Letty.'

'But you're not a Letty, you're a Juliet,' Leo told her stubbornly.

Letty shrugged a shoulder in dismissal. She had no intention of changing her name back to please him. Having drunk her tea, she set the cup back tidily on the cabinet top. 'I have to get back to work.'

'You still haven't told me the fourth stumbling block,' Leo protested, dark glittering eyes full of frustration pinned to her.

'My sex life,' Letty said bluntly, abhorring the heat she could feel warming her cheeks.

'Your...sex life?' Leo demanded as if those two words were an incompatible combination. 'You won't have one, unless it's with me.'

In the act of climbing out of the car, Letty came to a sudden halt and scornful green eyes slammed back into his. 'That won't be happening as long as you have other interests in your life,' she assured him tartly. 'And while I'm not currently in a hurry to have a sex life, I imagine the time will come when I feel differently.'

Leo was transfixed. It was a major obstacle and he hadn't foreseen it. In fact, he had been so wrapped up in his own selfish desire to maintain his usual lifestyle and boundaries that he had utterly ignored the obvious. Obviously, Juliet would have the same needs as he did. He wasn't one of those outdated men who believed that women had a smaller appetite for the physical pleasures of life. But the thought of *his* wife getting into bed with another man, the thought of another man touching and enjoying what Leo instinctively saw as *his* property alone, genuinely appalled him. He paled below his bronzed skin. It was hypocrisy, complete hypocrisy, and he knew it and sealed his wide sensual mouth closed before he said something he knew he should not say. That feat of control established, he breathed again.

'We'll discuss that on Saturday,' Leo informed her with finality, knowing he had less than forty-eight hours in which to come up with a miraculous alternative that would prevent her from seeking sexual satisfaction outside their marriage.

'I thought you might say that,' Letty confided, a wry little smile curving her generous mouth. 'I can't believe you didn't think of that angle.'

And with that final mocking little sally, Letty walked back into the nursing home, her head held high while Leo tried to work out how the hell she had contrived to become the very first woman to turn the tables on him.

CHAPTER THREE

ON THE SATURDAY MORNING, Leo travelled up in the smelly lift of the tower block. It was not a salubrious experience but meeting his future bride's family as soon as possible was essential to the smooth running of his plans. He had dressed down for the occasion in jeans, deeming that appropriate attire for informal weekend wear and children, even though he rarely wore casual clothing.

Letty was stunned when the knock on the door disclosed Leo himself because she had been expecting his chauffeur or one of the bodyguards she had seen hovering at a discreet distance in the care home car park to come upstairs and collect her. And there he stood, all sleek and dark and sophisticated in a cashmere sweater in a soft oatmeal shade that accentuated his bronzed skin tone, designer jeans outlining his long powerful legs and narrow hips, teamed with the less subtle hint of a slim eye-wateringly expensive watch at a masculine wrist which suggested that he came from a class of society far removed from her own.

'Leo!' she heard herself say abruptly, taut with disconcertion and discomfiture at being faced with him sooner than she had expected.

'I believe it's time that I met your family,' Leo told her smoothly.

Letty froze, further taken aback, faint colour running up into her cheeks. 'Er... I...'

'Not something we can avoid,' Leo declared, cool and outrageously serene at the prospect.

It made Letty wonder what it took to unnerve Leo Romanos and once she found out she knew she would use it against him in punishment.

And little more than two minutes later he was dominating their tiny living room with his broad-shouldered height and positive buckets of charm. He accepted a cup of black coffee and engaged her mother in conversation. He came up with an entirely fictitious old lady whom he supposedly visited at the care home from time to time, a former employee of his father's who had been kind to him as a boy.

'Letty... I thought *you* said that Leo was related to...'

'Your daughter and I kept on bumping into each other in the corridor late at night. She doesn't always listen well,' Leo proclaimed forgivingly.

Dear heaven, he could act, and he lied like a trooper without a soupçon of evasiveness or unease, Letty registered in consternation, seeing that she would have to sharpen her skills to have any hope of ever outwitting Leo. And that quickly she appreciated that she was already thinking as though she was planning to marry him and that shook her because so many of her misgivings had still to be settled and she wasn't a woman who acted on impulse.

It had been years since she had seen her mother smile so much and he'd even coaxed some attention out of her brothers by showing them a nifty trick with the video game they were engaged in continuing to play in spite of their mother's strictures.

Leo perused his bride-to-be in the lift. She was the right type: he could feel it in his bones even though she was not at all the kind of wife he had once dimly envisaged. Clad only in worn jeans and a black roll-neck sweater, she still somehow contrived to hold his attention. Her hair was braided at the front and long and loose at the back, tiny tendrils curling round her classic oval face, those wide sea-green eyes welded warily to him. There was no flesh on show and he wasn't used to that. He was accustomed to seeing everything a woman had to offer at a glance and inexplicably that covered-up look of hers, that modest mode of dress inflamed him. It made him look closer and turn away slightly from her as the hum of unwelcome arousal pulsed at his groin.

The full sweep of her breasts and the curvaceous swell of her derrière still swam before his inner eye and that lingering image vexed him. He didn't fantasise, he didn't *imagine* women naked. That was a teenage boy trait or the mark of an unsuccessful lover and even as a boy Leo had been skilled at getting what he wanted from the opposite sex. He didn't have to fantasise; he generally only had to show interest in a woman to know that satisfaction would be easily obtained. Yet one glance at Juliet in any garb and he was speared by sheer lust, wanting to touch, wanting to taste, wanting to ride to satisfaction between those slender thighs.

And yet she was the *one* woman whom he should be determined not to take. But maybe that was the secret of her appeal, he reasoned in frustration—the knowledge that she was out of bounds and forbidden. Maybe sex had become too easy, too available to fully engage his libido. Maybe what he really needed was some sort of diversion to direct his energy elsewhere. Clearly his current mistress was past her sell-by date and no longer able to attract him. That was what was wrong with him, he decided in a stark burst of relief; he had simply got bored with the current woman in his bed.

Letty barely breathed in the lift because the edgy atmosphere unsettled her. She focused on the dark shadow of stubble outlining Leo's strong jaw, the clenching of the muscles there, the sheer tension he emanated. Her breasts expanded as she snatched in a shuddering breath and stepped out into the foyer. The lace of her bra chafed her nipples and, as Leo clamped a guiding hand to her spine to urge her out of the building, she was engulfed in a wave of his scent, an achingly appealing medley of designer cologne and raw masculinity. Instantly, she stiffened, aware of the spurt of heat low in her pelvis and the uncomfortably damp sensation that followed. Annoyed that her body was betraying her with reactions she didn't want, she gritted her teeth. She couldn't afford to be attracted to Leo. It would be like walking through a minefield without any form of protection and she would be setting herself up for emotional damage.

After all, nobody knew better than Letty what it was like for a woman to love an unfaithful man. She had watched her mother with her stepfather, standing on the sidelines while Gillian suppressed her suspicions and accepted her husband's lies when he was late home or when phone calls came he couldn't explain or which he wouldn't answer around his family. The lies and evasions had been endless, and her mother had *wanted* to believe the lies because she loved Robbie and she hadn't wanted to credit the ugly truth that he had other women in his life.

But it wouldn't be like that with Leo, a cool inner voice reminded her soothingly. Leo wasn't prepared to lie. Leo preferred to be open and honest about his sexual preferences. He thought sex caused a lot of grief in marriage and that unusual outlook made Letty wonder how he had grown up and what his parents' relationship had been like. What experiences had taught Leo to think that way? Certainly, he didn't associate sex with the warmer emotions. It might even be true that he preferred sex without emotion getting involved at all, she reasoned. The more she thought about what motivated Leo, the more annoyed she became with herself for wondering and questioning everything about him as though he were some source of fascination. Of interest certainly, not fascination, she assured herself circumspectly. She wasn't that much of an idiot, was she?

'You're a very good liar,' she remarked in a brittle voice as the limousine drove off.

'We have to roll out an acceptable back story for your family's sake,' Leo fielded without skipping a beat. 'Unless, of course, you plan to tell them the truth—that you're only prepared to marry me for my money?'

In receipt of that stinging challenge, Letty shot him an outraged glance, green eyes sparking fire. 'Of course I'm not going to tell them that! It would break my mother's heart if she knew how I'm thinking and feeling right at this moment!'

'So, we're fortunate that I'm a good dissembler then,' Leo responded with satisfaction. 'But you need to work on being more convincing. At this point, a few lovelorn glances in my direction would be a good idea.'

'I don't *do* lovelorn!' Letty snapped, wanting to slap him hard enough for that teasing smile to die on his lips. 'I mean, why would I?'

'Because we don't have time to waste on a long engagement. I want the wedding to take place as soon as possible.'

'But I haven't agreed.'

'You're on the brink. You don't have any other options and you know that our marriage makes sense,' Leo countered with infuriating conviction.

Letty didn't appreciate the reminder that she had no other options. She felt as though she had tried to spread her wings, only for him to drag her cruelly back to solid earth again. Unfortunately, he was right: she was going to marry a man she didn't know on terms that appalled her because, from what she knew, the good that that marriage would bring far outweighed the bad. She could help her family and, in so doing, pay back some of the loving support and encouragement she had received from them over the years. And hadn't she long understood that most major gains in life entailed major sacrifices as well?

'I'm still thinking it over,' Letty fielded, her cheeks pink with annoyance, her eyes bright as she encountered dark golden eyes fringed with spiky black lashes that remained resolutely unimpressed by her stubborn response.

Mercifully the car was already pulling in to park. She gazed out at the frontage of the most magnificent mansion she had ever seen outside a movie. Her eyes wide, it felt entirely normal to stare at the rows of gleaming windows and the porticoed entrance which once would have sheltered guests climbing out of carriages drawn by horses. '*This* is where you live...or was this your sister's house?' she queried.

'It's mine. I sold my sister's townhouse and stored the contents.'

'That must've been disruptive for the children...to lose their home and their parents at pretty much the same time.'

Leo sighed, long brown fingers flexing as he spread his hands. 'I'm not a saint. I've given up a lot, but I wasn't prepared to give up my home as well. There's a lot more space here too and four kids and a bunch of nannies take up an enormous amount of space. My sister didn't have nannies. She was a devoted mother, determined to do everything herself.'

'She was younger than you...right?'

'Five years younger. Our mother died bringing her into the world,' Leo confided. 'Although my father remarried soon afterwards, we didn't have a happy family life as children. Ana met her husband, Ben, young and they were both crazy about kids. A large contented family was Ana's dream.'

Letty picked up on the slight hoarseness of his voice. He had loved his sister and he missed her, regretting that the younger woman had not survived to live her dream.

'I'm doing my best with Ana's kids but it's not working out well,' Leo admitted stiffly.

'It's only been six months since they lost their parents. It takes a long time for a wound like that to heal,'

Letty said gently as she slid out of the car, suddenly feeling seriously *under*dressed for her grand surroundings.

The hall was huge, with a marble floor and a grand staircase with a wrought iron balustrade. A massive painting dominated the landing, a portrait of a beautiful smiling brunette. Leo urged her into a drawing room that was so opulent it took her breath away. The décor was country house stylish with wallpaper that looked hand-painted, capacious velvet sofas and a massive fireplace but there was a definite contemporary edge to the sculpture in the window embrasure and the glass tables. Absolutely no allowance had been made in the room for a family with young children, she realised wryly. It was an elegant showpiece room for adults and had the air of a space rarely used.

'Unc' Leo!' a childish voice trilled.

Letty spun in time to see a small dark-haired child break free of a uniformed nanny's hold and rush across the room to embrace Leo's legs.

'Letty, this is Popi,' Leo announced as a smaller child bounded over to greet him, another little girl in a princess net outfit. 'And this little minx is Sybella.'

The other nanny settled the baby in her arms down on the carpet with some toys and the little boy tugged his hand loose of hers and moved closer.

'Cosmo!' Popi hissed, grabbing his hand as she moved over to station him and herself behind her baby brother.

'Cosmo and Theon,' Leo completed with a frown as he dismissed the hovering pair of nannies with a quiet word.

Letty absorbed Popi's defensive stance with her siblings and understood. As the eldest, Popi had taken on the role of protecting her younger siblings and Letty was perceived as a threat. She went down on her knees in front of the baby, who gave her the most adorable wide gummy smile of welcome, unaffected by his sister's disapproval. He held up his arms to be lifted and Letty couldn't resist the invitation, but she was very much aware of Popi's dismay.

'I'll just sit here,' she promised, gathering up Theon and settling into a seat beside the little girl. 'You stay close in case he wants you.'

'He won't. He's just a baby. He doesn't even know who you are,' Popi fired back at her, unhappy at her baby brother's friendliness.

'*Popi...*' Leo's intervention was clipped and cool and the little girl stiffened and dropped her head. 'What did we talk about over breakfast?'

'It's fine,' Letty interposed gently. 'Change is always threatening.'

'I don't want a new mother,' Popi whispered chokily.

'I'm Letty and you can call me that. Nobody can take the place of your mother,' Letty said softly, shooting Leo a warning glance when his lips parted as though he was on the brink of firmly disagreeing with that statement. 'But I do hope that when you get to know me we can be friends.'

'I have lots of friends,' Popi told her.

'It never hurts to have one more,' Letty contended calmly as Theon clutched at her and went in for a kiss. She kissed him back, looked into his big dark trusting eyes and felt her heart literally thump because he was adorable.

Cosmo sidled over and leant back against her knee

while he ran a plastic car over the arm of her chair. He ignored Popi's calls to return to her side. Sybella clutched at Leo's jeans and then ran over to twirl in her princess dress and be admired. Popi stood alone, frozen in the centre of the rug, and her expression of loss and anxiety almost broke Letty's heart.

'Would you like to show me your bedrooms?' Letty asked, eager to leave that awkward moment behind as she stood up, cradling Theon on her hip. The minute the baby laid eyes on his uncle, he lifted his arms out and lurched in his direction instead.

'Show you toys…' Sybella offered, dancing and hopping on one leg like a tiny brightly coloured flamingo.

Upstairs they went, with Popi trailing reluctantly in their wake. Letty now understood Leo's concern about his sister's children. Popi was so busy trying to parent and protect her siblings that she couldn't relax and simply be a child. It was equally obvious that Leo was the children's place of safety, but possibly he wasn't around enough to make them feel secure.

Letty strolled through a set of superb bedrooms crammed with toys. She was taken aback to note that even in Popi's room there were no photographs of the children's late parents and she mentioned that oversight in surprise to Leo.

'I thought it was kinder not to remind them but there'll be photo albums in the stuff I put into storage,' he replied.

'I think they should all have a photo. I also think that if you have a bedroom large enough and could bear the disruption,' Letty whispered, 'they could all sleep in the same room…just for a little while. I think it would help Popi relax more.'

It was a simple suggestion and not one Leo had considered. He hoisted his niece into his arms and asked her if she would like to share a room with her sister.

Popi beamed. 'Oh, yes, it would be just like home then…'

'You used to share with Sybella,' he recalled.

'Yes, but here in *this* house I'd like the boys too… I need to look after them,' Popi told him, silencing Leo with that assurance.

Watching Juliet adjust the gauzy wings on Sybella's fairy outfit and seeing the toddler come running back with a necklace she wanted to put on as well, however, Leo was content. He had brought the baby whisperer home, a kind and practical woman who would take the time and effort to work out what would make the children feel happy and safe in his house.

Lunch was served in a grand dining room. The same nannies appeared beforehand to whisk the children away. Evidently the children did not share their uncle's meals.

'For a first meeting that went very well,' Leo proclaimed with satisfaction as the first course was delivered. His black hair was ruffled by Theon's clutching hands, his stubborn jawline darkly stubbled, outlining the surprisingly full outline of his wide sensual mouth. As Letty looked, a tightness across her chest and butterflies dancing in her stomach, Leo glanced up, spearing her with narrowed dark golden eyes enhanced by thick black lashes. Those eyes were stunning, strikingly compelling, and heat flamed through her body without warning. She had to drop her attention back to her plate to gather herself again.

'It'll take time for the children to get to know and

trust me,' she pointed out, trying not to openly sali-
vate at the sight of the tiny savoury tart and salad on
the plate in front of her. 'Don't set the bar too high.'

'Unlike the nannies, who have come and gone, for
most of them don't want the responsibility of *four*
charges,' Leo stated wryly, 'you will be a constant
in the children's lives and that security is what they
need most.'

It struck her that she had already given unspoken
agreement to the marriage he had suggested and that
shook her. That wasn't how she operated. Even so, the
children had touched her heart and Leo had already
gone ahead and informed them that she was his intended wife. Consequently, backing out now wasn't really a viable prospect, particularly when Leo had boldly
reminded her that he was her *only* option. *Suck it up*,
she urged herself impatiently. By marrying Leo, she
could put her family's life back on track and, eventually, she would be able to return to studying medicine.
In any case, how could she possibly refuse an offer
that would put her mother back on her own two feet?

'All right, so I'm marrying you, but we still haven't
discussed that final stumbling block I raised at our last
meeting,' Letty reminded him resolutely. 'Going into
this, we both need to know exactly where we stand.'

Leo breathed in deep, knowing he couldn't afford to
tell her exactly how he felt about having a wife with a
sex life separate from his own, a wife who slept with
other men whenever she chose, an equal partner in
every way to himself. He had never contemplated taking a wife who would enjoy such freedom and he honestly didn't think he could live with that concept. 'I

suggest that we play that by ear. Why do we have to have a game plan?'

'Rules agreed in advance ensure that things run more smoothly,' Letty told him.

'I'm more a spontaneous kind of guy,' Leo quipped. 'I don't believe that everything can be laid out in black and white before we even know what it will be like to share our lives.'

There was a certain amount of sense in that statement but Letty preferred rules. Rules, as she saw them, prevented misunderstandings and provided firm boundaries. 'I prefer black and white.'

'You're unlikely to get that with me,' Leo admitted simply.

'I disagree. I think you'll want a prenup and other safeguards before we marry,' Letty dared. 'Or am I wrong?'

Leo tensed, recognising that he was dealing with an astute woman. 'No, on that score you are correct. But financial arrangements fall into a very different category. Financial rules and safety measures are only common sense.'

Letty ate with appetite because everything on her plate was a treat. She told herself off for eating the dessert, reminding herself that she would have to work it off at the gym.

'Do you want your grandfather to stage and foot the bill for our wedding?' Leo enquired levelly over the coffee cups. 'He has already made that suggestion.'

Letty almost choked on her coffee. 'Has he indeed? Very generous of him, I'm sure!' she exclaimed, biting back further uncharitable words but only with difficulty. 'He wouldn't help us when we *really* needed his help, but if I'm doing what he wants suddenly he's ready to open his wallet. Sorry, that sounds bitter.'

'But understandable. I had to give you the choice, but I would prefer to organise everything for us,' Leo admitted quietly. 'Your grandfather would probably want to stage the wedding in Greece, which wouldn't suit either of us very well.'

A little embarrassed at having spoken so freely, Letty merely swallowed hard and nodded because travelling to Greece for a wedding certainly wouldn't suit her or her family. Her head was swimming a little from the awareness that she was discussing wedding arrangements with a man she had only met that week. It felt surreal.

'I will be inviting friends and business connections,' Leo declared. 'You, of course, will have your own guest list and I imagine your grandfather will also have names he wishes to put forward.'

'There won't be many on my list. We don't have any other near relatives living and only a few close friends worthy of an invitation.'

'What about your mother's parents?'

'They died years ago without ever having forgiven her for bringing me into the world,' Letty stated with a grimace. 'My maternal grandmother was in her forties when she had Mum and, like my grandfather, Mum's parents viewed my birth as a social embarrassment.'

'Thankfully, few are as judgemental these days,' Leo observed, reaching into his pocket to withdraw a small jewellery box and passing it to her without ceremony. 'It would please me if you wore this. In so far as it is possible for your family's benefit and that of the children, we should behave as though this is a regular relationship.'

Letty lifted the lid on a magnificent solitaire diamond ring and gasped in complete surprise. 'Gosh! You want me to wear an engagement ring?'

Leo lifted and dropped a shoulder as if to suggest that, regardless of his polite assurance that her wearing the ring would please him, he was, in fact, quite indifferent. 'I think your mother would appreciate the conventional touches, particularly when we are getting married so quickly.'

Letty slid the ring onto her finger, relieved that it fitted, her face warming with colour. 'How soon do you expect the wedding to take place?' she asked apprehensively.

'Within a couple of weeks.'

Letty was aghast at that short time frame. *'But—'*

'Now that we've agreed on how to move forward, why would we waste time?' Leo incised. 'I would appreciate it if you tried to spend some time with the children between now and then.'

'Of course. I only have to give a week's notice at work,' Letty mumbled, flustered by the fast pace of events and feeling more than a little overwhelmed by the prospect of marrying Leo, even though it wouldn't be a normal marriage, no matter how hard they tried to pretend otherwise.

'I'll organise a list of surgeons for you so that you can have your mother booked in for the procedure she requires. I would also suggest that you look at a list of properties I have available to choose accommodation that would suit your mother and brothers better than your current home,' Leo added. 'My lawyers will contact you with regard to the legalities of our agreement. Unfortunately, I'll be in Greece over the next few days handling the amalgamation of your grandfather's company with mine. If you need to contact me, you have my number.'

Letty breathed in deep and slow to steady herself. All of a sudden she was seeing that her world was about to be turned inside out and that while the end result might be a great improvement, it would also be even more challenging than she had expected.

'Er… I hate to mention it,' she muttered uncomfortably as she considered her family's most pressing problem and the state of sleepless anxiety that same problem kept her mother in. 'That loan—'

Leo studied her, dark golden eyes hardening to a bright diamond glitter. 'That will be dealt with *without* your input. It will be settled, and those men will never bother you or your family again,' he swore. 'You will also have a security team protecting you from now on.'

'For goodness' sake!' Letty began in disbelief.

'And a car and driver to take you wherever you want to go,' Leo completed as if she hadn't spoken. 'I want you to be safe. I don't want to take the risk of anything happening to you. On our wedding day you will become my wife and Isidore Livas's heiress and such precautions are, sadly, necessary in the world that we live in.'

'I disagree,' Letty protested.

'You don't have to agree with me. As of today, I am taking full responsibility for your safety and that of your family. You will no longer need to keep a cricket bat behind the front door,' Leo informed her grimly. 'Anyone who threatens you now will have *me* to deal with!'

'Careful, Leo,' Letty murmured after she had got her breath back, her eyes colliding with his shimmering angry appraisal. 'Your crocodile instincts are showing…'

Leo expelled his breath in a hiss. 'The sight of that cricket bat incensed me,' he admitted grudgingly. 'I will not have you living in fear any longer.'

CHAPTER FOUR

'HE'S A LITTLE like a magician,' Gillian Harbison contended as she looked out dreamily at the little garden of the ground floor apartment she had moved into the day before. 'Leo, I mean. He just waves his magic wand and suddenly your wildest dreams come true.'

'That's Leo.' Letty studied her mother, seated in her wheelchair by the patio doors that led out into the garden. The lines of stress and tension had eased on the older woman's face. She was booked in for surgery at a private clinic the day after the wedding. Her sons would be staying with their father until she was back on her feet again and her best friend was moving in with her to support her during her recovery. The bright modern flat with three bedrooms and more space than Gillian had enjoyed in years was simply the icing on the cake. It was the moment when Letty accepted that any sacrifice had to be worthwhile when it made her nearest and dearest so much happier.

That was why she had bitten her tongue and surrendered to almost every demand that Leo had made of her. Accepting his generosity without complaint or protest, not to mention his insistence on security precautions, was a key challenge for her independent soul but seeing her family blossom in response was her reward. Furthermore, she couldn't pretend to be a loving bride and fight with Leo at the same time, particularly when she was currently only able to fight with him on the phone, for Leo had been in Greece longer than he had expected. He had uncovered suspect financial practices in her grandfather's company that required his immediate attention.

Letty had visited the children every day since Leo's departure. She would go over in the afternoon, share an evening meal with them and then stay until bedtime. The night before, Popi had given her a hug after she had read her and Sybella a bedtime story. Slowly but surely the barriers were coming down as Letty became more familiar to the children. Since she had handed in her notice at work she had been incredibly busy, dealing with the wedding planner, shopping for a wedding gown and coordinating the million and one things that she now had to do. That had included searching for outfits for the children to wear at the wedding and dealing politely but firmly with her grandfather's demand that *he* play a bigger part in the ceremony. Isidore Livas had been keen to walk her down the aisle but Letty's mother was fulfilling that role in her wheelchair, having already confided that it would be the proudest moment of her life.

'So, what are you wearing for the hen do tonight?' Gillian asked with a smile.

Letty hadn't wanted a hen party, but her friends and former work colleagues did and it had felt mean to deny them the chance of a good night out because once she had mentioned her plans to Leo, he hadn't scrupled to organise that for her as well. He had obtained entry for all of them to a VIP section in an exclusive nightclub where their entertainment and their drinks would be free and, much as Letty had resented him taking over, she hadn't had the heart to rain on everyone else's parade.

'We're all wearing denim shorts,' Letty revealed with a grimace. 'I haven't worn shorts since the summer before university and I had to buy a new pair because I've expanded since then. We'll freeze.'

'Not with a limo ferrying you round,' her mother said quietly. 'Letty…you're only young once. Enjoy it. You don't get a rerun when you realise what you've missed out on. Go out and have a good time tonight with your friends.'

'I will. I promise.' Letty bent down to hug the older woman, annoyed that she had put a troubled furrow between her brows.

'You are so lucky to have found Leo. I couldn't be happier for you,' Gillian confided. 'He takes such an interest in all of us. I just don't understand why you haven't already moved into his home… I mean, you're trekking back and forth to his house every day and I can manage fine on my own.'

Letty had coloured at her mother's natural assumption that she was already sleeping with Leo. 'Leo and I will be together soon enough… It's only forty-eight hours until the wedding,' she pointed out.

'And you *do* love him, don't you?' Gillian pressed anxiously. 'His wealth and those looks of his haven't turned your head too much? Because neither of those things will keep you together if you don't love him.'

'Mum… I realise that I'm not the world's most demonstrative person but believe me,' Letty urged with as much conviction as she could muster. 'I *love* him! It was practically love at first sight.'

Lust at first sight, she adjusted with an inner wince of embarrassment as she dried her hair in the new bedroom that would only be hers until the wedding. She hated lying to her mother, but she didn't have a choice. And she felt guilty because she wasn't seeing the children that evening. The chaos of moving to a new apartment and the hen party organised for the same night hadn't left her a moment to call her own, even though Leo had sent professional house movers to smooth the way. The sheer speed at which Leo accomplished things still shook her.

Money talked, she thought ruefully—money *definitely* talked. Her grandfather had been positively warm when he called to congratulate her on her decision to marry Leo. He was elated at the prospect of his retirement from business, although, from a couple of stray comments he had made, she also suspected that he regretted that Letty, rather than his adored daughter, her Aunt Elexis, was to be the bride.

Letty rarely touched alcohol. When tensions were high in her mother and stepfather's marriage, Robbie had resorted to drink and the scenes and arguments that had resulted had put Letty off alcohol. At least her stepfather had never been violent, she conceded, seated with her friends and feeling ridiculous in her fake tiara and bridal sash. In truth she felt like the spectre at the feast. Her companions were having a whale of a time, but Letty was much too conscious that she wasn't a *true* bride on the brink of marrying a man that she loved and it not only made her sad but also made her thoroughly irritated with her oversensitivity.

In response, she decided to have a few drinks and within an hour she was contriving to laugh naturally at the silly sex jokes that usually made her stiffen up, painfully aware of her own ignorance in practice. An hour after that, she was game for taking a turn on the pole on the podium, following the example of her two university friends, who were better at letting their hair down than she was. The three of them had attended pole-dancing classes for several years, relishing the strength, skill and flexibility they had gained from the experience.

Leo was travelling home from the airport when Darius phoned him. He had grown up with Darius, whose father had been *his* father's bodyguard, and there was no one he trusted more to look after Letty. Yes, he had given way on the name because she refused to answer to Julie or Juliet or any other diminutive. And her opposition on that score had intrigued him because women rarely challenged Leo and, once he had got to know Letty, her name had mysteriously grown to fit her.

'How's the party going?' Leo enquired with amusement against the backdrop of loud thumping music.

'Your bride is having a blast,' Darius replied. She's waiting her turn to pole-dance. I tried to head her off because it's a little too public here but she's…well, she's her own woman.'

Leo came off the phone, struggling to even picture Letty on a pole. At worst she would hurt herself, at best she would embarrass herself. He groaned out loud and raked an impatient hand through his black cropped hair. He had assumed she was too sensible to get involved in any kind of mischief and he most certainly didn't want her photographed for posterity doing anything that would mortify her in daylight. Without hesitation, he told his driver to head to the club. 'She's her own woman,' Darius had said tactfully, meaning that Letty was as stubborn as a mule and had dismissed his attempt to dissuade her.

Theos. Well, she wasn't going to dismiss him as easily, Leo reflected with resolve, springing out of the car, leaving his own security team struggling to follow him at the same speed. He strode through the club and up the stairs to the VIP section, with a hasty gesture dismissing the manager who came running to attend him. It was *his* club and he knew it like the back of his hand. Unlike his father and Isidore, Leo had diversified, refusing to rely on shipping as his sole means of profit and that more liberal approach to business had served him well in the entertainment industry, in the hotel trade and in property development.

At the top of the stairs, only vaguely aware of Darius approaching him, Leo came to a sudden unrehearsed halt, transfixed by the sight of Letty spinning effortlessly round the pole, blonde mane of hair flying as she dipped and flipped upside down and then went off into a handspring that took his breath away.

Certainly, she wasn't going to embarrass herself, he conceded in shock, his attention locking to the tight denim defining her curvaceous hips and the extension of one long shapely leg that revealed a creamy stretch of inner thigh. Her chest heaved below the light top she wore, the firm swell of her breasts pushing against the fabric as she sucked in oxygen, her tiny waist and flat stomach revealed as the top lifted. It was the most erotic thing Leo had ever seen and there was nothing visually arousing that some woman somewhere, some time hadn't already treated him to.

'So, how are you planning to handle this diplomatically?' Darius prompted with unhidden curiosity.

'Like a caveman,' Leo admitted thickly, fighting the nagging pulse of arousal with the greatest difficulty because lust was surging through him in a volatile wave.

He strode through the crush, forcing everyone to yield to let him past, and pounced on Letty without hesitation. He lifted her before she could get a hold on the pole again and walked back to the table Darius indicated to sit down in the midst of the chattering women with Letty sprawled across his lap.

'I'm Leo,' he said cheerfully.

'This is a girls' night out,' one of the women told him tartly.

'Letty's tired,' Leo murmured, rearranging his bride like the floppy rag doll she resembled when her legs threatened to slide off him again.

'Leo…' Letty looked up at him with a sunny laid-back smile.

Letty wasn't tired: she was drunk.

'I'm taking you home.'

'Party pooper,' she mumbled, burying her face in his neck. 'You need a shave but gosh, you do smell amazing…'

Disconcerted, Leo grinned.

'Letty never drinks. We egged her on,' someone said.

'We wanted her to have fun.'

Leo gazed down at her, long brown fingers brushing her tousled hair off her brow. 'Did you have a good time?'

Letty made an admirable effort to sit up without the support of his arm. 'I had a fabulous time,' she told her companions with careful diction. 'Thank you all for coming.'

'I'm dizzy,' she complained on the stairs.

'Of course you are,' Leo assured her.

'I'm not drunk.'

'Only well-refreshed,' Leo incised.

'I don't want to go home like this.'

'I'm taking you home with me,' Leo told her smoothly. 'It's too late to phone your mother.'

'I'll text her. She won't sleep until I'm home or she's heard from me.' Letty sighed, pulling out her phone and discovering that she was all fingers and thumbs and that it was a battle to focus.

While she texted she swayed and Leo breathed in deep and slow. She was a vision, honey-blonde hair tangled and falling round her, crystal tiara lurching to one side, green eyes myopic in their intensity, her classic profile taut with concentration.

When she had finished, Leo scooped her off her feet and she exclaimed, 'I can walk perfectly well!'

'Not in those heels you can't,' Leo assured her as he settled her into the limousine, relieved that no paparazzi had been awaiting them outside. 'Imagine if you broke an ankle—'

'And then we couldn't get married!' Letty pointed out. 'Let me go back and break an ankle before we make the biggest mistake of our lives!'

'I don't make big mistakes,' Leo intoned, recognising the hint of panic in her wide gaze before stretching across her to grab the seat belt and secure it firmly around her, the fingers of one lean brown hand brushing against a slender thigh as he did so. 'All you're suffering from is an attack of cold feet.'

* * *

Letty shivered, goosebumps breaking out at that fleeting and entirely accidental touch. She looked up into smouldering dark golden eyes and her breath was held suspended in her throat for a long timeless moment. Close up, his eyes were stunning, an absolutely riveting mixture of tawny shades and those lashes made her weak at the knees. The portrait of the beautiful brunette on the landing in his house was of his late mother. The resemblance between mother and son was arresting, particularly around the eyes. She wondered what his father looked like because, having had a glimpse of Leo's mother, she wasn't at all surprised that Leo had the flawless beauty of a dark angel.

'Besides, I'd take you even with a broken ankle,' Leo told her huskily. 'Popi says you read much better stories than I do.'

'Sybella likes the same one over and over again but Popi needs more stimulation,' Letty muttered unevenly, oxygen seesawing in and out of her lungs as though she had been running because, that close to Leo's raw masculinity, she felt weak and breathless. 'And Cosmo only listens if you put pictures of cars or trains in front of him.'

Leo studied her flushed face, the languorous fresh green eyes welded to his, and he tensed and shifted in his seat, disturbingly aware of how aroused he was by her. The sight of her, so relaxed and confiding, was incredibly sexy. He was striving very hard not to relive those few staggering moments when he had seen her twirling round that pole with fluid grace and a sensuality that had taken him wholly by surprise.

'I'd listen if you were on that pole,' Leo muttered in a driven undertone. 'Sexiest show I ever saw.'

Letty frowned at him, her disapproval palpable. 'It was exercise, Leo. I went to classes for years and found it a great way of keeping fit and strong. It's not sexy, except to a certain type of man.'

'You *were* sexy,' Leo told her before she could christen him a pervert.

Her eyes widened because no man had ever given her that label before and it knocked her off balance. She had always been the sensible, practical one in her circle of friends, the one who looked after her mates and guarded the drinks and the handbags. She didn't know *how* to be sexy, had occasionally envied those to whom it came naturally but had ultimately decided that she was happier having her brains.

'*Incredibly* sexy,' Leo purred, threading a straying strand of hair back behind one small ear. 'But if you dance like that again in a public place…well, you won't like my reaction. I don't want other men perving over your body like that.'

Leo was so close that her head swam. Her throat tightened and her mind went blank and her chest heaved as she pulled in as deep a breath as she could manage. 'I don't think you should be saying that to me.'

Leo's hand came up to curve to her cheekbone. 'It's said. It was the truth. Don't argue with the truth.'

'But it sounded possessive, territorial,' Letty whispered in troubled rebuke.

'I'm not possessive,' Leo muttered thickly as his head lowered. 'But I probably am territorial. I can't change who I am to fit some perfect male blueprint.'

'Not asking, not expecting perfection,' she mumbled, mesmerised by the golden glitter of his eyes on hers and the trail of fireworks sparking off somewhere deep down inside her.

One hand wound into her hair to turn her face, the other curving to her spine to ease her closer.

And then his mouth came down on hers with a fierce lancing urgency that took Letty by storm. His tongue tangled with hers and it was as if every kiss she had ever dreamt of was being delivered all at once. He tasted of mint and brandy. With that first little taste, the power of his demanding mouth was on hers, pausing to stroke her lips wider apart and nibble seductively on the lower lip before invading the moist interior of her mouth for a second time. His explosive passion sent her spinning with her heartbeat thundering in her ears and her body flushing and heating in reaction. He was very passionate, teasing one moment, carnally sensual the next. Her fingers speared into his dark hair, delving into the thickness, marvelling at how silky it was.

Her other hand braced on a long muscular thigh to hold herself steady. She wanted more—for the first time ever with a man, she *wanted* more. A stampede of angry elephants wouldn't have dragged her out of Leo's powerful hold. Her fingers trailed down his neck and clawed into his jacket, her heart racing, the very blood in her veins on fire with a hunger that hurt. Every sensitive spot on her body seemed to ache and throb. In a sudden movement, she released her seat belt with jittery fingers and clambered clumsily over him, needing to be closer, needing that full body contact to settle her racing pulse.

Taken aback by that change in attitude from the most buttoned-up bride a man had probably ever contemplated marrying, Leo absolutely froze for a split second. He knew he couldn't do anything because only alcohol had released her inhibitions. He knew she would never forgive him if he took advantage of her. But he also knew that a rejection of any kind when she had made the first move would bury him deeper than Australia because he knew women. At the same time, he was fiercely aroused and sheet lightning couldn't have prevented the groan that escaped him when she ground down on him in a basic approach that was shockingly effective. As her pelvis pressed down on his, Leo was electrified by hunger.

'Leo…' Letty pronounced with distinct satisfaction as she studied him, pale soft hands cradling his cheekbones, fingertips gently smoothing the skin.

Leo thought she was waiting for him to do something, and he had sworn he would do nothing, so he was entirely unprepared for Letty to lean back where she perched on him and tug off her crop top, revealing the scorchingly lush swell of her breasts in an unexpectedly pretty embroidered bra. He had expected serviceable white cotton. A slight shudder ran through him as he contemplated those pale full mounds of flesh and he closed his hands to her hips in protest—hands somehow sliding down over those pert swells to flirt with the hem of her shorts. Shorts—Letty in short shorts— he thought in abstracted wonderment, fighting for the control he lacked.

'I thought you'd be all over me like a rash,' Letty confided hoarsely, big green eyes wide with surprise and innocence. 'I thought you were a player…but maybe *I just don't do it for you.*'

In desperation, Leo kissed her with urgent force and

she ground down on him again, dredging a grudging groan of appreciation from his wide muscular chest as his fingertips grazed the soft silky skin of her inner thighs in an attempt to hold her still and prevent her from teasing him further. The tip of a finger slid beneath the hem and learned the damp silky welcome of her there and a breathless moan parted her lips beneath his and Leo was lost in the magic of her response. In all his life Leo had never been in such a state of excitement over so little and his control broke.

Letty was in a heaven without boundaries, her body seduced and sensation seducing her. Nothing had ever felt so physically good to her before, no previous experience had ever lit her up like a star from the inside out. *He* was touching her and she liked it, dear heaven, she liked it, indeed *loved* how with every mesmerising skim of those clever fingers she shivered and shook on the edge of something she didn't know but had somehow always secretly craved. Her hips were moving of their own accord, little sounds brimming beneath the erotic pressure of his mouth still on hers. And then suddenly the pressure tightening in her pelvis became unbearable and she was flying sky-high and inwardly screaming from the sheer glory of sexual delight that engulfed her.

Well, now you've done it, a snide little voice announced to Leo inside his swimming head. He shifted Letty into a more comfortable position until a faint little snore that brought a grin to his taut mouth warned him that fate had taken care of the problem for him. He would put her to bed and say nothing, make his usual dawn start at the office and thereafter act as though nothing had happened. Ignore, ignore, he urged himself firmly. She had called him a player and, in terms of what he estimated to be her level of experience, perhaps she saw that as an apt label, even if it wasn't.

Leo was perplexed when he settled Letty down on a guest room bed and removed her shoes only, before spreading a quilt over her. What was it about her that turned him on so hard and fast? He behaved like a sex-starved teenager with Letty and, while it was true that he was currently between mistresses and without a woman in his life, no other woman had ever made him lose focus and control as he had in the car with her. Hunger and need had overwhelmed him and he didn't like it. In retrospect, he didn't like that *at all*. Leo was careful never to lose control, never to want a woman *too* much. He wouldn't risk falling in love with the wrong woman, as his father had with his vindictive stepmother, who had loathed Leo purely because he truly knew what a slut she was, one who had tried to climb into her stepson's bed when he was twenty-one…

Loving the wrong woman could blind a man to his family's needs and make him weak and treacherous. It had happened to Leo's father, Panos Romanos. He had married a much younger woman. Katrina had wed him only for his wealth and had never loved him back. That marriage had slowly but surely destroyed Leo's family. As soon as she could, his sister Ana had fled that unhappy background and married far too young, desperate to create a happy family life. Leo, less vulnerable than his sibling, had merely decided that sex and marriage should always remain separate entities. He didn't need to love a wife to be a good husband, he only needed to like and respect and care for her. But then, had it not been for Ana's four needy children, he might never have married at all, he acknowledged grimly.

Letty wakened with a splitting headache. A hangover, she registered in dismay, sitting up in bed and noticing the glass of water and the painkiller set on the cabinet beside her. She reached for both with a groan, her brain a swirl of tangled images. She had got on that pole in public, she recalled in dismay and embarrassment, and then she recalled kissing Leo…and more.

Dear heaven, in the grip of urges stronger and more primal than she had ever dreamt existed, she had flung herself at him like a nymphomaniac, she recalled in horror. She had an image of peeling off her crop top and throwing it. And she remembered every second of what had followed with shuddering accuracy. Her sense of humiliation was so intense that she moaned out loud with self-loathing. How could she have done that? How could she have behaved like that?

He had been aroused too. She shifted in the bed, a mortifying heat warming her pelvis at the knowledge that she had had that effect on him. But she needn't be feeling like some wildly sexy seductress, she censured herself bitterly. Just about any man would've been put in that state by what *she* had been doing. It was certainly not a compliment to her personal attractions, such as they were. She wanted to blame him for what had happened but knew it would be unfair when she had offered so much encouragement. She couldn't imagine how she would ever look Leo in the eye again, which wasn't good when it was their wedding day in less than twenty-four hours.

It was a huge relief to go downstairs in her embarrassing shorts and discover that Leo had left for the office hours before. Popi's giggles at her appearance were somehow healing, the little girl's innocence soothing, and by the time Letty had cuddled Theon, set Cosmo's cars out in a line for him and done Sybella's hair in a princess style adorned with the bridal tiara from the night before, Letty was well on the road to recovery and telling herself that she was too sensitive, too naïve…

Leo, however, was having a difficult morning. No matter how hard he tried to shut it out and regain his usual deep concentration, he kept on remembering the feel and look of Letty on his lap in the limo and the taste of her on his lips. He was fantasising about a woman he had sworn he would leave untouched, he acknowledged grimly. A woman who set him on fire. A woman who had broken down his disciplined barriers and subjected him to a long, hot, sleepless night craving what he couldn't have. He had chemistry with Letty to a level that inflamed him. But he was not ready to embrace anyone's *sacred bond*.

Those two words said it all to Leo. He was not and would never be a one-woman man. Look at what that obsession for Katrina, his stepmother, had done to his spineless father! It had brought his father low, blinding the older man to his beloved's flaws.

And while Leo agonised and regretted, with a series of curses that he was rarely driven to use because sexual frustration was new to him, the solution finally came and it was stunningly simple. His brain had thrown out the obvious answer.

He blinked, the lush black lashes that enthralled Letty shooting up, a glow of satisfaction and relief warming the tawny depths of his eyes... *Of course*— the only answer that made sound practical sense and it would surely appeal to Letty as much as it appealed to him.

CHAPTER FIVE

SEATED IN HER CHAIR, Gillian flipped open the jewellery box that had been delivered and gasped out loud. 'Oh, my word, Letty... Come here and see!'

Letty rustled over in her bridal gown and was almost blinded by the flashing white fire of the diamond tiara, earrings and necklace laid out in the wide velvet-lined box. She flipped up the note enclosed in the box, in which Leo informed her that the set had belonged to his mother and he would be pleased if she wore the pieces. 'A little extravagant for me,' she began uncertainly.

'Nonsense, this is going to be a big fancy wedding attended by a lot of well-heeled people,' her mother told her roundly. 'And when a man hands over the family heirlooms *before* the wedding, you say "Thank you very much indeed" and wear them!'

Letty reddened and lifted out the tiara to anchor it into the thick mass of her upswept hair. Unlike the fake one she had worn on her hen night, it fixed in with ease. Adorned in the diamonds, she studied herself in the mirror, her hands trembling a little as her fingers dropped from attaching the last earring. In truth she barely recognised herself. She had had her hair and make-up done earlier that day at a local salon but, because she didn't own a full-length mirror, she could only see herself from the waist up.

Even so, she still cherished the image she had seen when she'd picked her dress from the designer studio Leo had instructed the wedding planner to escort her to. It was a simply glorious dress and she had fallen for it before it had even been removed from the hanger. It reminded her of an Edwardian tea dress except it was much more finely tailored, the styling accentuating her small waist and smoothing over the generous breasts and hips she preferred to conceal. Except when you got the goods out for Leo, a snide little voice reminded her at the optimum wrong moment because she had been training herself very thoroughly to totally bury and disremember that little incident in the limousine.

After all, Leo had been around the block a few times and he was not innocent. Since she had not seen him since then, he evidently wanted to overlook that wanton little episode and so did she, so *forget*, she instructed herself impatiently. In terms of their agreement, what was a meaningless little kerfuffle in a car to do with anything?

The previous week, Letty had signed a prenuptial document that ran to many pages of impenetrable legalese. But she had read and digested and ensured that she understood every word of it because she wasn't the kind of woman who signed anything on trust. She had *agreed* that Leo's infidelity would not be grounds for a divorce and that clause had had a sobering effect on her because it etched his future betrayal in stone for her. No sacred bond on offer from Leo, she recalled cynically. If their marriage did break down, however, she would retain some access to the children and a financial settlement that ran to lottery win figures. Nothing whatsoever was being left to chance in their marriage. In addition, she would have to have a child fathered by Leo for her baby to qualify for the Romanos name and inheritance.

Literally tormented by nerves, Letty climbed out of the limousine, winter sunshine glittering over the beautiful beaded lace on her gown and firing up the diamonds. She had never felt so self-conscious in her life and only the sight of her mother and Jenna, her closest friend from university, waiting with the children in the church porch settled her down again.

Popi and Sybella were resplendent in dresses that matched the bridesmaid, Jenna's, the little girls twirling with pleasure in their floaty skirts and chattering while Cosmo, quite indifferent to his smart little outfit and any sense of occasion, was clambering all over a stone bench. Leo had been amazed that she wanted to include the children in the bridal party while Letty had seen their inclusion as a necessity. While Leo might be too empathetically dim to appreciate the fact that what they were really trying to achieve with their marriage was the creation of a *new* family to make his nieces and nephews feel secure, Letty was not.

The walk down the aisle in the big packed church full of staring strangers disturbed Letty because she was uncomfortable being the cynosure of attention. She kept her hand resting lightly on her mother's shoulder and focused on Leo, utterly, effortlessly and flawlessly gorgeous, awaiting her at the altar. If only it had been their *real* wedding, she found herself thinking and she flushed, hastily squashing that foolish notion, assuming that all the frilly trappings of the day were confusing her. Certainly, Leo in a morning suit was a sight to behold with his sleek dark angel beauty, his perfect features bronzed and composed, those dark eyes steady and serious, not softened or bright with the love he might have felt for a genuine bride. Inwardly, Letty swore at the tenor of her thoughts.

'You look fantastic,' Leo told her as she reached the altar.

Of course, he had to say something like that, it was expected of him, and it was almost as if someone had yelled 'Showtime!' in Letty's ear. She switched on her approximation of a bright bridal smile because Leo had made it clear that their agreement was private, and the rest of the world were to be left to believe that they were a normal couple. As if she would ever have captured a guy with Leo's looks and wealth in the *real* world, Letty found herself thinking with helpless cynicism, reckoning that it was little wonder that people were curious and staring while they wondered how she had contrived such a miraculous feat.

The beautiful words of the ceremony were something she tried not to dwell on or feel even slightly bitter about because, all else aside, this was *not* how Letty had once vaguely imagined her wedding day would be: with a groom by her side who loved and cared for her as she cared for him, a true partnership of hearts and souls. She reminded herself sternly of the benefits that the wedding had already brought to her family and would bring to Leo's orphaned nieces and nephews. It was foolish to crave some starry-eyed ideal, she told herself firmly, because that craving was a fantasy—a fantasy that Leo would definitely never deliver.

'*Diávolos...*' Leo whispered the curse in her ear as

they progressed back down the aisle. 'That's the worst bit over.'

Letty laughed. Yes, that sentiment was very much Leo. He had as much sensitivity as a brick thrown at a window. Airy, feminine, finer feelings about weddings were foreign to him. Cosmo clutched at her skirts and she bent down and lifted him up, pressing a kiss to his troubled little face. 'You don't like the crowds, do you?' she gathered, holding him close, enjoying the sweet baby smell he still retained.

'I warned you that this might be too much for them,' Leo declared.

'They need the memory of being part of this,' Letty told him gently and only then registered that she was having her first conversation with Leo since that shameful little episode in the limousine. Her face warmed but she buried the recollection deep again. She had been brazen and silly and she had embarrassed herself, but that was human and it would be pointless to punish herself about something she could not change.

Leo was hoisting Sybella to his shoulder when a tall, slender blonde in a blue dress approached them. 'What on earth are your nannies doing, Leo?' she demanded imperiously. 'The kids should be out of sight and out of mind at such an occasion.'

Reluctant to offend a stranger, Letty swallowed back a sharp retort.

'We *want* them with us today,' Leo stated smoothly in direct contradiction of his words to Letty only seconds earlier. 'Katrina, meet Letty… Letty, this is my father's wife, Katrina.'

Grateful then that she hadn't snapped out a tart response, Letty absorbed the reality that Leo's stepmother, Katrina, was much younger than she had expected and English into the bargain. She smiled.

But the pretty blonde wasn't even bothering to look her way. Indeed, all her attention, her curiously *avid* attention, was for Leo. 'I just can't believe the size of the sacrifice you're making for those kids…actually getting married,' she said in an incredulous tone. 'Your father and I were astonished.'

Katrina's very blue eyes were locked on Leo, her fascination with him so strong it was tangible. Dear heaven, his stepmother was in love with him, Letty registered with shocked distaste. Luckily the photographer wanted a few shots at that point and Katrina was forced to back off while the nannies reclaimed the children. In the crush around the porch steps she watched a white-haired older man with a hint of Leo's cast of feature join Katrina, undoubtedly his father.

'I didn't realise your stepmother was much closer to your age than your father's,' Letty admitted simply on the drive to the hotel where the reception was being staged.

Leo compressed his lips. 'She's fourteen years older than me. She was twenty when my father married her. I was six. Ana was a baby. After her arrival in our lives I don't have one good memory of my childhood. She doesn't like kids, but she wanted one of her own to cement her position in the family. When she failed to conceive, she resented Ana and me even more.'

'She doesn't resent you now,' Letty pointed out, not being a woman to ignore a controversial topic, in spite of the warning signs that Leo's harsh diction and grim expression put out. 'In fact I'd say she's in love with you.'

Leo's big shoulders tensed and his teeth gritted

but he said nothing, deeming it a topic better left untouched.

'No comment?' Letty looked at him in disbelief. 'I suggest that your stepmother is in love with you and you have nothing to say at all?'

'I wouldn't call it love,' Leo countered between clenched teeth, feeling that he had no choice other than to be honest about the situation since Letty was too astute to be fooled and left ignorant. 'Katrina began flirting with me when I was sixteen and by the time I was twenty-one she was trying to seduce me!'

'Oh, my goodness!' Letty exclaimed with shocked distaste, registering that she had had to pressure him to surrender that truth about his father's wife because naturally such a sordid secret must have put a huge burden on Leo. 'Did you tell your father?'

'Of course not… It would have destroyed him!' Leo framed harshly. 'He adores her. Whatever faults I have, I am at least loyal and I care about my father even though he has been pretty hopeless as a parent. Katrina, however, disgusts me.'

'I shouldn't have pried,' Letty muttered ruefully, watching the anger she had ignited fade from his taut, lean dark features while noting the pain he was striving to bury about his disturbing past. 'But I sort of felt I had to know the family background so that I didn't put my foot in it.'

'Don't worry. We won't see much of either of them. My father and Katrina live in New York,' Leo informed her. 'He's devoted to her. Whatever she wants, she gets. I remember a huge row many years ago about the diamond set you're wearing. Katrina wanted them but they belonged to my mother and her jewellery was left to her children in her will. Katrina couldn't get past the law.'

'Is that why I'm wearing it today?'

'Only one of the reasons. You're my wife. You're a Romanos now and you are entitled to wear my mother's diamonds.'

'You've never told me anything about your mother either,' Letty remarked.

'I have few memories of her. She died having Ana. In those days, we lived on her family's island… My mother was an heiress from a far wealthier family than my father,' Leo stated wryly. 'Ios, the island, now belongs to me, along with everything else that was my mother's. Her inheritance was protected by an unbreakable family trust. Katrina was not best pleased to marry my father and learn that he wasn't as rich a man as she had naively assumed.'

'Serves her right if that's all she cared about,' Letty said roundly.

'I've always believed that she was his mistress before she was his wife. My mother may have died before her time, but I suspect that if she had lived my father would have divorced her for Katrina because he was and still *is* besotted with her.'

'There must be a huge age gap between them.'

'Twenty-odd years.'

Letty raised a brow but knew that it worked for some couples even though it clearly hadn't worked for Leo's father and stepmother. 'I wonder if your mother knew your father had a mistress.'

Leo took the easy way out of that unanswerable question by shrugging a broad shoulder, but his expression was grim, belying that show of casual acceptance. 'It's how the marriages in my family have always worked. Marriage is for children, inheritance, property protection. It's got very little to do with sex.'

Letty blinked. 'Maybe for very rich people,' she qualified uneasily and then she finally wondered in dawning dismay if possibly he was into some sort of kink that the average wife was unlikely to deliver. That prospect hadn't occurred to her before but, the more she thought about it, the more she thought that to be a possible explanation for his instinctive mental separation of sex and marriage.

After all, there had to be some very good reason why he thought that way. Ancestors with mistresses being an accepted way of life for the men? The stepmother from hell? The stepmother who had been his father's mistress? An unrepentantly unfaithful father, who must have hurt his mother? Wasn't that a more probable truth? That Leo suffered from that clichéd view of women as either angels or whores? A belief system that had been born in the early death of his mother and the arrival of a shamelessly unscrupulous stepmother?

'I know you don't understand my attitude,' Leo commented, startling her with that perception. 'We'll discuss it over dinner tonight.'

Letty was disconcerted by that suggestion, not having expected Leo to be so open on such topics. Ironically, in spite of her curiosity, she was in no hurry to hear his views, preferring to stuff the whole thorny question of his marital infidelity under a large mental rock and leave it buried there. What she didn't know couldn't unsettle her, after all. Ignorance would be preferable.

They arrived at the hotel. Letty drank champagne, greeted a never-ending line of guests, exchanged pleasantries and smiled. Her aunt, Elexis, her grandfather's daughter, cornered Letty when she emerged from the cloakroom after a quick touch-up of her make-up. Elexis was as thin as a playing card and a very attractive woman with a chic blonde bob.

'You look very like photos I've seen of your father, Julian,' the blonde commented on the subject of her late half-brother. 'Did you ever even get to meet him?'

Letty chose to ignore the rather offensive tone of that question.

'Several times when I was a child. My mother had an on-off relationship with him in the early years, before she realised that he would never settle down and stay clean,' Letty admitted quietly. 'But he was her first love and it was hard for her to step away from him.'

'You sound like a romantic. Leo won't like that,' Isidore's daughter proclaimed.

Letty simply smiled. 'I believe that you're getting married in the spring,' she said, keen to change the subject because she felt a little awkward about the fact that Leo had, years earlier, considered marrying Elexis.

'Yes, I can't wait. Anatole adores me,' Elexis told her smugly. 'You see, *I* wanted more from Leo than he was willing to give me. I wanted fidelity and I know for a fact that he's not willing to pledge that.'

'How do you know?' Letty asked in as mild a tone as she could manage.

'His current mistress is a guest at your wedding… and *you* didn't know?' Elexis queried in unkind surprise. 'Mariana Santos—that's her over there with the lady in the lime-green hat. Mariana, Spain's most acclaimed supermodel.'

'Fancy that…' Letty said noncommittally, determined not to react although she had felt the blood draining out of her face as her aunt spoke. Even before the brittle blonde had dropped her bombshell about Leo's mistress, Letty had suspected from her tart defensive tone that Elexis had wanted Leo much more than he had ever wanted her and that her ego had been stung by his walking away from her. The blonde's final words made that reality clear.

As Elexis drifted off, seemingly happy to have stuck the knife in Leo's bride, Letty's attention strayed towards Mariana Santos, a gorgeous brunette with a curvier figure than was usual for a model, her hourglass shape artfully revealed by a turquoise dress with a plunging neckline. Her tummy curdled and she glanced away, annoyed that Leo could be that insensitive. If Elexis knew the identity of his current lover, others had to know as well and it was disrespectful, at the very least, to include such a woman on the guest list. It was not that she felt jealous or possessive of Leo, Letty assured herself as she lifted her chin, a combative glint in her green eyes, it was simply a question of what was right and appropriate.

She looked away from the voluptuous model again, reminding herself that Leo's sex life was none of her business. Even so, the awareness that he had invited his lover to their wedding stung like salt on an open wound. *Get over yourself*, she told herself sternly. The wedding ring on her finger had never been intended as a promise that Leo belonged to her in any way. Their marriage was a fake steadily turning into a farce, she ruminated. So far, she had met Leo's infatuated stepmother, the jealous and spiteful Elexis and now she had Mariana Santos covertly sending the bridegroom a look of burning longing.

Leo had a toxic effect on women, she decided. A little taste of Leo and it seemed women tended to become strongly attached to him and then pine for him. Her nose wrinkled and she thanked her lucky stars that she was not so easily impressed. If that was true, why was she stressing about his obvious compelling attraction in the eyes of *other* women? It shouldn't bother her, should it? She should be able to ignore those other women and not care. Letty swallowed hard, unable to fathom her own reactions and annoyed that the indifference she needed to project towards Leo with regard to his extra-marital interests was nowhere to be found. If she was annoyed, *why* was she annoyed?

That thorny question occupied her brain throughout the reception that followed. It swept her through the wedding speeches and her mother's brief tribute, which brought tears to her daughter's eyes. She strayed into a polite conversation with Leo's father, Panos, and her own grandfather, who it seemed was in a rather glum mood because Leo had recently uncovered some financial irregularities within his company, which Isidore felt he should've discovered for himself.

'Leo's got fantastic financial ability,' Panos Romanos contended with a clear pride in his son's abilities that warmed Letty towards the older man.

'Oh, I'm not denying that,' Isidore responded. 'Our businesses couldn't be in stronger hands than his.'

Leo spanned a lean hand across Letty's stiff spine. 'It's time for us to open the dancing,' he murmured softly in her ear. 'One more hour and then we're out of here.'

Letty twisted her head, eyes wide with surprise. 'Only an hour... Where are we going?'

'Ios...the island,' Leo told her as he urged her on to the dance floor, wondering why she was pulling back from him to ensure a large space separated them.

'But we can't *both* leave the children!' Letty exclaimed.

'They're coming too,' Leo soothed, long brown fingers smoothing down her arms in a curiously caressing motion that sent the oddest little shiver shooting down her taut spinal cord. 'The kids, the nannies, the whole shebang... Happy now?'

'But I didn't do any packing for them and they probably need new clothes *and*—' she began in bemusement.

'That's why I employ staff. It's all taken care of for us,' Leo soothed, lowering his dark head, tawny eyes ablaze with gold below the lights, enhanced by the black lace frame of his lashes. 'And once we arrive I will finally have you all to myself, *yineka mou*.'

Letty stared up at him in confusion, questioning why he would make such a statement and ducking her head to peer around him to see if there was someone nearby for whom he might be putting on an act. Why else would he say such a thing? Coincidentally, Mariana Santos was only a couple of feet away, dancing in the arms of another man, and Letty received a frozen look from the brunette, who had clearly been watching the bridal couple closely. Of course she was, Letty reflected ruefully. Leo was much more Mariana's property than he would ever be his wife's but in public he would pretend otherwise. She marvelled that Mariana had attended the wedding to watch her lover becoming the husband of another woman.

Indeed, so busy was Letty's brain that when Leo kissed her she didn't even see it coming. One minute she was wondering what it was like to be a mistress… and the next? Leo was crushing her parted lips under his with an urgency that shocked her rigid, all that explosive passion of his smouldering and burning through her cool front and smashing it to broken pieces. She swayed, knees turning weak, the sudden pulse of answering heat low in her pelvis a treacherous self-betrayal.

It was just one little kiss and she swiftly tugged free of him and grabbed the back of a convenient chair to steady herself. For a split second she had been shattered by an urgent desire to flatten Leo to the nearest horizontal surface and have her way with him so thoroughly that he would never look at another woman again. And that dangerous thought stayed with her as she recovered from his sensual onslaught. Physically she was fine but mentally she was in another place, she recognised unhappily. He had only kissed her as part of the wedding show. Possibly he had kissed her too because Mariana was nearby, and he intended to make some sort of statement.

But as Letty went upstairs to the room where she was to change, she was much more bothered by her own response to Leo. There was the lust she evidently couldn't suppress and *that* thought she had succumbed to in the same moment…an utterly pathetic and inappropriate desire to have Leo all to herself. In other words, while she was thinking with disdain of all the other women still caught in the trap of craving Leo's blazingly sexual energy, *she* was no better and had absolutely no reason to feel even slightly superior…

CHAPTER SIX

IN THE BIG villa sited on the hill above the bay, Leo grabbed Letty's hand when she would have followed the children and the nannies upstairs. 'No, they've had enough of your attention for one day. Those kids were a nightmare to travel with,' he said with a decided wince.

'*Because*,' Letty replied with emphasis, 'they were overtired and overexcited and the journey totally disrupted their routine.'

'Sometimes schedules have to be disrupted,' Leo countered lazily, tugging her inexorably back to the entrance door and the darkness outside, which had prevented her from seeing much of the island as they flew in on a helicopter. 'This was a special day and you wanted to share it with them. The downside of that decision was their exhaustion.'

Letty nodded, silently conceding that but more curious about where he was trying to take her. 'Where on earth are we going?'

Leo recalled the flight out to Greece and the cross crying, continual demands and screaming from the children and gritted his teeth. Parenting was tougher than he had ever imagined but he was adapting because he hadn't once contemplated leaving his nieces and nephews behind in London. Instead he had come up with a compromise for their honeymoon that would give Letty and him some much-needed space. Not for the first time that day his head spun with a definite sense of wonderment at the commitment he was about to make—one he had never anticipated. It was a huge step for him and he was still marvelling at the awareness that such an idea had even occurred to him.

'There's a guest cottage on the beach. We're staying there.'

'But we have to be here with the children,' Letty began afresh.

Leo froze and turned back to her. 'I am delighted that you have already become so fond of the children,' he admitted truthfully. 'But it would be good if you could concentrate...*occasionally*...on my needs.'

Her lashes fluttered in sheer bewilderment. 'But why would I want to do that?' she whispered as he urged her into the beach buggy awaiting them outside the villa.

'We'll discuss that over dinner,' Leo assured her smoothly as the driver took off down a sloping trail.

Why on earth would he ask her to concentrate on him and his needs? Letty was utterly bewildered. Did he see that as some fundamental rule for an award-winning wife? Was she supposed to be considering *his* comfort 'occasionally' more than the well-being and security of the children? That was very possible, she conceded with a faint sigh of relief that she had finally grasped what he was driving at in his expectations of her. Really, sometimes, Leo was *hopeless* at communication! She supposed it was a reasonable request that she not put the kids first in every case and allow that now and again, much as Leo clearly loved the children and rejoiced in a wealth of nannies, he would appreciate some adult freedom and peace. In any case, she resolved, she could get up early in the morning and join the children for breakfast.

'So, what's this guest cottage all about?' she asked as they climbed out of the buggy and had their luggage offloaded and carried into the substantial natural stone building sited on the edge of the beach.

'My mother liked to paint and it was originally built as an art studio. Katrina renovated it and used it for guests. She had a great need to eradicate anything that reminded her that she was my father's *second* wife,' he stated grimly. 'Strictly speaking, any changes to the properties here were illegal because even as a child the island was mine but, realistically, I was never going to prosecute my father.'

'I suppose you would've liked to inherit it as your mother left it,' Letty gathered quietly, picking up on Leo's innate protectiveness when it came to anything relating to his mother's memory. 'But you knew your father couldn't stand up to Katrina's more forceful character.'

'In a nutshell,' Leo agreed as the door to the softly lit interior was opened and the luggage was piled in and carted upstairs. 'Dad's a wimp when it comes to Katrina.'

In silence Letty raised a brow, able to recognise how much Leo despised his father's weakness when it came to Katrina and belatedly grasping that over the years he had come to regard his dead mother as a complete saint and a wronged woman.

The accommodation might not have been in the

state which Leo would have preferred to inherit but it was contemporary and very stylish and, in Letty's humble opinion, quite beautiful, with floor-deep windows overlooking the sea and the shore. The table at the far end was already set for a candlelit meal. She wondered who was providing the food and then heard noises of activity emanating from what appeared to be a kitchen to the rear. She was relieved not to have to cook because she was tired and she doubted that Leo, raised with attentive staff from birth, even knew how to switch on a kettle. He genuinely had grown up in a different world from hers.

'Have I time to freshen up?' Letty asked, already halfway up the spiral staircase.

'Yes. I could use a shower too,' Leo admitted, following her.

At the top of the staircase, Letty gazed in astonishment at the huge bedroom. Only *one* bedroom? Only *one* bed? Surely not? She slowly turned and watched Leo calmly stripping off his suit jacket and yanking off his tie as if she were invisible. She bent down to open a case and extracted a change of clothing, wondering if they were only to dine at the guest cottage and sleep up at the house, but there was something awfully like a statement about the fresh flowers on display and what looked like herbs or something scattered across the fancy silk cover on the bed. Of course, the staff would assume it was a normal marriage with a normal wedding night, Letty conceded, quelling her unease as Leo got naked right in front of her as if that too was quite normal.

Maybe he assumed that because she was training as a doctor she had few inhibitions about the human body, but Letty was shy, sexually inexperienced, and the sight of Leo's lean, bronzed and very muscular physique naked brought her out in goosebumps of awareness. She hastened into the bathroom, considered locking the door and then abandoned the concept because she wasn't a child or a frightened teenager, was she? He could use the shower—she could *share* the facilities, couldn't she?

In haste she used the shower, scared the door would open but it didn't, and then, in even greater haste, she donned a blue cotton maxi dress that she had bought with her own money to relax in. Leo's credit cards had purchased all the wedding finery as if money were no object and she supposed to him it wasn't. But expressing that little bit of independence had helped her come to terms better with the prospect of a new moneyed lifestyle which she hoped to become used to one small step at a time because spending was still so foreign to her. She had never had money to spend freely, had always had to live on a strict budget. She unwound her hair from its elaborate upswept bridal style and massaged her stiff neck muscles before walking out to the bedroom again.

Leo was out on the balcony beyond the bedroom, still stark naked and nonchalant as he gazed out to sea. Her breath feathered in her throat. He was like… *perfect*—she selected the word inwardly, her cheeks burning. A flawless pinup for an anatomy lesson. No longer need she wonder at the attachment women developed for him. Clothed, he was a very sexy box of tricks. Unclothed, he was undeniably gorgeous, every honed powerful line of him revealed.

'You're very shy…' Leo breathed in apparent surprise when her flushed face met his and she glanced hurriedly away again, terrified her thoughts were showing in her expression. 'I'm sorry... I didn't think—'

He was more sensitive than she had given him credit for, Letty acknowledged, and she smiled. 'No harm done. We're supposed to be married. I'm sure there'll be occasions when we have to share...er...stuff.'

'We *are* married,' Leo reminded her as if she might forget.

'I'll see you downstairs,' Letty breezed with determination, mortified by the reality that she was behaving like a shrinking violet simply because he had undressed. Naturally, he wouldn't have been expecting that, probably having assumed that she had had a man or two in her bed, and she wasn't going to admit that she was a virgin because there was no reason for her to share such an irrelevant fact with him.

Unsurprisingly, Leo was accustomed to experienced women—women who probably stared and mentally oohed and aahed over his magnificent body. Modesty wasn't a skill he had ever needed to learn, and he had, she strongly suspected, few inhibitions in the bedroom. As she sat down at the exquisitely set table, she smiled to herself. She needed to practise being less hidebound and conventional around Leo.

Leo came down again, garbed in jeans and a black shirt and still barefoot, black hair damp from the shower. He had shaved though, the dark stubble that had started to noticeably shadow his strong jawline gone. His lean, darkly arresting features held her gaze and only when she registered that she was staring did she hurriedly look away and address herself to the food now being brought to the table.

'It feels so weird being waited on all the time,' she confided.

'You won't mind it once you return to your studies,' Leo forecast. 'By the way, how is that going?'

'Hopefully, I'll be able to take up my studies again in London next year,' Letty told him cheerfully. 'I didn't have time to get in more than my application before the wedding and there'll be interviews and probably refresher classes and various hurdles to get past before I can start back. I'm lucky my academic record is good.'

There was no luck about it, Leo reflected wryly, wondering why she was so diffident about her achievements. Letty was extremely clever, had been top of her class in just about every subject at Oxford and had won several awards during her time there.

'Let's drink to that,' Leo suggested, nudging her untouched glass with his own. 'Go on, a couple of glasses isn't likely to have a dangerous effect on you.'

Letty coloured to the roots of her hair, knowing that both of them were recalling that encounter in the limousine after her hen party. Leo read her well: he had guessed that she was nervous of alcohol now.

She snatched up her glass and sipped. 'So, you said we had something to discuss... I seem to recall,' she managed to say, relieved that she had stopped squirming and blushing like a teenager over that episode in the car.

'Ne...yes,' Leo translated for her as he subsided into Greek and seemed to hesitate as he searched for words, which was sufficiently unlike him to command her full attention and etch a frown between her fine brows. 'It relates to our future as a couple...'

'Yes, I'm sure there must be lots of little things we still have to iron out,' Letty conceded with innate practicality.

'This is not a *little* thing,' Leo contradicted, studying her with dark golden eyes that were pure golden enticement in the candlelight.

'Oh?' Letty prompted, sipping her wine assiduously, irritated that Leo had guessed how she felt about alcohol after the virtual assault she had mounted on him. She pinned her attention to her plate and worked through the delicious first course and a silence that stretched much longer than she had expected.

Finally, Letty looked up again to catch Leo still studying her as though she were a complete mystery to him in some way. 'You were saying?'

Leo breathed in deep and threw back his handsome dark head, his eyes gleaming. 'I don't think I'll ever enter "sacred bond" territory in the manner that you meant,' he murmured smoothly. 'But I have reached the conclusion that it would only be practical for us to at least have a go at making this a *real* marriage.'

Letty literally froze with her glass halfway to her mouth. 'A *real* marriage?' she exclaimed.

'A marriage in which we have sex,' Leo specified with unashamed clarity.

Letty breathed in so deep she was surprised that she didn't spontaneously combust into flames of outrage. 'You have a mistress,' she reminded him tartly.

Leo didn't bat a single eyelash. 'Not currently.'

'That's a lie!' Letty shot back at him. 'Elexis pointed Mariana out to me at the wedding.'

A dark frown formed on Leo's lean strong face. 'That was spiteful,' he breathed with visible annoyance. 'But I'm not lying. I was last with Mariana *before* I met you and I finished with her *after* I met you.'

'Which is…what? All of four short weeks ago?' Letty sniped, unimpressed. 'So, why was she at our wedding?'

'She wasn't invited. She came with a male guest who *was*,' Leo clarified. 'I was irritated when I saw her too.'

Letty recognised the truth when she was hearing it and absolved Leo of inappropriate behaviour because, evidently, Mariana Santos had become old history. Not that that had the slightest cooling effect on her growing anger. That Leo could simply sit there and just proclaim that they should 'have a go' at being married as if it were a casual takeaway meal he could sample at will shocked her to the core.

The main course was brought out and Letty started eating again, although she was barely able to chew and swallow because she was so very angry with him.

'You have nothing to say to my suggestion?' Leo finally pressed in frustration.

'Nothing you'd want to hear,' Letty assured him curtly, pushing her plate away and lifting her glass because she needed a vat of wine, she told herself, to deal with Leo, who was twisty and manipulative and clever and utterly unaccustomed to any form of rejection from a woman.

'Allow me to decide that,' Leo urged.

Letty leapt out of her chair with her glass in one hand, unable to sit still any longer, and she crossed the room to stand by the patio doors. 'We signed a legal agreement in which I agreed to overlook your infidelity,' she reminded him stubbornly. 'Now you want something else from me, something completely different.'

Leo sprang upright. 'I want *you*, so kill me for it!' he urged with sardonic bite, spreading his arms and splaying his expressive hands as part of the gesture.

'You'll want me for all of five minutes!' Letty told him tartly.

'I last longer than five minutes,' Leo assured her, refusing to take that comeback seriously.

And at that provocative sally something Letty had never felt before erupted inside her like a volcano spewing lava. It could only have been described as hissing, spitting rage. She flung what remained of her wine at him. 'You bastard!' she launched at him as the clear liquid splashed his face. 'I trusted you to keep your word but now you're trying to move the goalposts, which is totally unfair to me. And over what? *Sex?*' Letty grimaced in dismissal of that paltry motivation. 'Just because you're between mistresses? What else would suddenly make me so irresistible?'

'It's not like that,' Leo delivered harshly. 'I wanted you the first time I met you and I fought it. Now we're married and it doesn't make sense for me to go out and look for another mistress when the only woman I want right now is *my* wife.'

'Don't you dare call me *your* wife!' Letty fired back at him hotly. 'I married you to be a mother to your sister's children and that was all you asked of me. I'm entitled to receive the agreement I signed up to and the terms I legally approved. You are *not* entitled to demand anything more from me. Is that clear?'

Shocked, Leo scrutinised her, registering that her passion that night in the limo should have forewarned him that she could have a much more tempestuous nature than he had initially appreciated.

'Yes, I can see you're shattered by that news. You know *why*, Leo? Women are too easy for you. Today, in the space of a few short hours, I had Mariana, Katrina and my Aunt Elexis all drooling over you and hating me for marrying you.'

'Is that my fault?' Leo asked with the first hint of anger he had shown. 'Is it my fault that two women I have never been intimate with lust after me? Am I supposed to apologise for that? Clearly, it annoyed you, *but—*'

'I didn't say it annoyed me,' Letty bit out in haste, recognising that she had hit the wall with that comment because it really wasn't fair to blame *him* for being gorgeous and rich and highly desirable to other women. 'What annoys me is that with clear forethought and planning you brought me here to a house with *one* bed and *one* bedroom in expectation of a positive answer!'

'*Theé mou*…there's nothing positive about your attitude,' Leo acknowledged grimly, his lean dark face set in forbidding lines. 'In fact, everything you think about yourself and my interest in you and our marriage is incredibly negative in tone. I didn't mention my intentions *before* the wedding because I had to stay in Greece until shortly before it and it was scarcely a subject I could tackle on the phone.'

'Whatever!' Letty waved an angrily dismissive hand and hauled open the patio doors to walk down onto the sand, desperate for some fresh air and the space to think after that incredibly volatile rush of rage that had so disconcerted her, never mind him.

'It's dark out there!' Leo asserted in warning from behind her.

Letty swung her head back, her honey-blonde mane fluttering in the cool breeze, green eyes gleaming like sea glass polished by the surf. 'I'm not thinking of going for a swim!'

She stomped along the beach, powered by anger, frustration and a whole host of other emotions she could not immediately neatly label and identify. *How dare he?* She grimaced. Leo would always *dare*. Leo didn't respect boundaries and assumed every woman was available should he show interest. But, even if that had been his experience, he shouldn't assume the same thing about *her*!

And then that mortifying incident in the limo returned to haunt her and she groaned out loud because she had given him very willing signals that night, making it obvious that she was attracted to him. Perhaps it wasn't quite so shocking that Leo had expected a positive response from her when she had already given him that much encouragement.

She hitched up her skirt as her heels sank into the sand and, with a muttered curse, bent down to flip off her shoes and walk barefoot, her shoes dangling in one hand.

Slowly, her breathing steadied and her heartbeat stopped thumping madly in her ears. Mariana was no longer his mistress and her departure from the scene had created a vacancy, which Leo hoped to fill with her. It was a practical proposition from a man who clearly saw sex as a need that had to be met. She didn't think that he attached much more importance to sex than that or that he was offering to throw anything more lasting into the mix. Yet the suggestion that they make their marriage the real deal was *still* light years removed from what he had originally proposed. And that made Letty intensely curious to know what it was about her which had brought about that amazing change in attitude.

It was about her—it truly *was* about her. Leo had the hots for her and a choked little giggle erupted in the back of her throat, making her feel remarkably like a teenager again. She raised her brows and continued walking, although her pace had slowed. In the sense that Leo was highly desirable in his own right, his interest made her feel ridiculously flattered but, in another sense, it offended her. If they had sex, and she was honest enough to admit to herself that she was physically willing, where did they go from there? That was the *big* question.

Back at the beach house, Leo tossed back a brandy and paced, wondering where he had gone wrong in his approach because Letty had gone up in flames and that had never happened with a woman before, most definitely not when he was trying to show a woman attention. Was she still so locked into that 'sacred bond' viewpoint that she could not see past it to appreciate that there were other kinds of relationships that functioned perfectly well without twinned souls and romance and all the rest of that nonsense? Leo reasoned impatiently. In a sudden movement, he set down the glass and strode down onto the sand.

Registering that she was cold, for an October night on a Greek island was not that warm with a breeze blowing, Letty had started walking back towards the house. Seeing Leo's tall powerful figure approaching in the moonlight, she sighed and wondered what she was going to say to him.

'I am not an unreasonable woman,' she told him before he reached her. 'If we make this a real marriage, where do we go from there?'

'I don't have a crystal ball,' Leo told her succinctly.

'No, but you do have to think deeply about what you're doing,' Letty countered. 'And I've yet to be convinced that you *do* think that much when it comes to women.'

'*Theé mou...*' Leo ground out.

'You would have to promise to be faithful,' Letty informed him ruefully. 'But you said you couldn't do that.'

'No, I said I didn't want to risk breaking a *promise* of fidelity,' Leo qualified. 'That was what that clause in the prenup meant.'

'That still won't work for me. Either you're mine or you're not mine. There's no halfway house option on offer.'

Surprisingly, Leo felt amusement lick up through his dark mood of dissatisfaction. 'You drive a hard bargain.'

'But you expected that from me,' she guessed.

A wolfish grin slanted Leo's wide sensual mouth and he jerked his chin in acknowledgement. 'If I am with you, I will be with no other woman,' he intoned. 'If I am not content with that, however—'

Shivering, Letty lifted a determined hand to silence him. '*No*, you don't get to qualify it with me. It's either yes or no; you're all in or all out, no escape clauses, no excuses. But that's not all I have to say. Are you viewing this marriage as a temporary aberration or as something that could have a future?'

Leo expelled his breath in audible frustration, his lean dark features taut as he started unbuttoning his shirt. 'I don't know the answer to that.'

'I don't want to enter into a "try before you buy" scenario, Leo. I'm worth more than that,' Letty assured him, throwing her head high, her honey-blonde tresses blowing in the breeze, her clear gaze reflecting the light bouncing off the sea. 'I won't come cheap or easy. I'll make demands. I'll have expectations. I have no idea how a mistress behaves but I would imagine that if a woman is dependent on a man's continuing interest she has to refrain from demands and expectations.'

Leo slid fluidly out of his shirt and draped it round her in a gesture that startled her. 'You're cold,' he said simply.

'I assumed it would be warmer,' she admitted as he closed an arm around her to walk her back towards the beach house. 'But my winter clothes would be too warm.'

'I'll take you shopping,' Leo told her calmly. 'So, *yineka mou*, if I'm now yours, what next have you in store for me?'

Letty chuckled. 'I was rather hoping you'd take the lead there. I haven't had sex before.'

Halfway into the house again, Leo stopped dead and turned to look at her with startled dark golden eyes. 'You mean—?'

'Yes. No experience at all,' she admitted with an uneasy shrug.

Leo was frowning. 'But why?'

'Wasn't interested enough to bother before. Clearly,' Letty murmured with hot cheeks, '*you* float my boat, which is very apt for a shipping tycoon.'

Leo laughed with rich appreciation and swept her towards the stairs. 'I can't wait to get you into that bed,' he admitted frankly. 'Since that night in the car, you've been playing a leading role in all my fantasies.'

Warmth filtered into Letty's chilled body at the concept of figuring in Leo's fantasies. She guessed that it was the unexplored sensual side of her nature which enjoyed that admission of his and then she drew in a stark breath, wondering how he would react when he realised that she was a perfectly ordinary young woman with no box of bedroom tricks with which to amuse a sophisticate. Would he stay faithful then? She swallowed hard on her insecurities, censuring herself for holding such a low opinion of her own powers of attraction. Maybe sex was just sex to Leo and he didn't look for bells and whistles as well, but it was hard to credit that a practised lover couldn't offer much more than she could.

'Leo…' she began anxiously.

'Stop fretting, Letty,' Leo urged with his glimmering smile. 'Don't spoil the moment. I will also be sure to discreetly break the news to your grandfather that you came to me pure as the driven snow. That will set him back on his heels and teach him to respect you more.'

'Leo, for goodness' sake!' Letty broke in, mortified by the idea.

'No, you should be proud rather than apologetic or embarrassed,' her bridegroom told her with conviction as he closed a hand over hers to tug her inexorably up the stairs. 'I haven't been with a virgin since my own first experience. I was sixteen and in the grip of first love. It was a demoralising episode.'

'Why?' Letty asked starkly.

'She was lying—she wasn't a virgin, and within the space of a week she was bedding one of my friends,' Leo confided with a sardonic slant to his lean dark features. 'Following on from my dysfunctional relationship with my stepmother, who was already giving me the come-on, it soured my outlook on women. I promised myself that I'd never fall in love again and I turned my back on the sentimental stuff. It was the most sensible move I ever made.'

Letty put that little fact along with the other stuff she had garnered about Leo's background: the licentious and vindictive stepmother he had endured in his infatuated father's hasty second marriage, the mother he barely remembered, the disillusionment provided by his first love. Grief and hurt and distaste had made him distrustful and pessimistic and his experiences as an adult had only reinforced that outlook. Yet, at the same time, he loved his nephews and nieces enough to surrender his freedom in an attempt to give them a happier and more secure life. There were two sides to Leo, Letty acknowledged, a loving side and a dark cynical side, and she wondered which side would take precedence in their marriage.

A practical sexless marriage about to become a *real* marriage. The shock of realisation that she was about to embark on that challenge shrilled through her taut length and jolted her because she was taking a risk on Leo, and Letty generally avoided risks. And Leo was a *huge* risk, a man only prepared to accept the concept of fidelity at the point of a gun. In a tempest of doubt, Letty turned pale and flicked at one of the dried flowers scattered across the silky bedspread.

'What are these?'

'Rosemary.' Leo shrugged. 'An ancient Greek belief in the power of rosemary to enhance fertility.'

'I thought rosemary was for remembrance,' Letty muttered uncertainly. 'But I suppose I should mention that I'm not on the pill.'

Leo laughed with rich appreciation, dark golden eyes alight with amusement. 'With four little children up in that house on the hill, that's not a risk I will take…unless, of course, you ask me to.'

Letty coloured. 'Er…no, thanks, not just yet.'

'Relax,' Leo purred, enclosing her taut body in the circle of his arms. 'You don't have to worry about stuff like that. I will take care of everything.'

Letty bridled at that assurance, her fierce independent spirit rebelling. 'I take care of myself, Leo,' she said drily.

Leo quirked an ebony brow. 'Not any more. That's my department now.'

'We'll see,' Letty muttered.

'No, we won't,' Leo contradicted, long brown fingers knotting into the breeze-blown tangle of her hair to tug her head back as he crushed her parted lips under his, every ounce of mastery in his erotic repertoire powering that kiss.

CHAPTER SEVEN

HEATED ARGUMENT WAS swirling in Letty's busy brain and then she was pierced by heat of a different kind.

A long shiver snaked through her and she trembled, desire like a living flame flaring low in her belly. She didn't understand her response or the sudden dimming of rational thought and, being Letty, she struggled to comprehend how her physical response could overwhelm her mental reactions. And in that moment of disconcerted stasis Leo tangled his tongue with hers, skated it over the roof of her mouth and her legs literally went weak. Ultimately that didn't matter because he was already leaning her up against him for support while tugging down the straps on her maxi dress and letting it fall to the floor.

Eyes fluttering in dismay, Letty found herself lying back on the bed with no clear awareness of how she had arrived there. She gazed up at Leo worriedly, painfully sober, painfully aware of the size of her bare breasts, which had always been larger and more noticeable than she was comfortable with, but then bosomy women ran in the family genes and she hadn't got a choice in the matter.

'Theé mou...' Leo groaned with unashamed appreciation. 'You have gorgeous breasts.'

Taken aback, Letty peered down at her attributes in bewilderment as Leo curved what could only be described as reverent hands to the bountiful swell of her breasts, shaping and moulding them, fingers grazing the stiffened peaks, lingering to rub the sensitive tips and provoke a breathy gasp from her lips as an arrow of heat ran down to her pelvis. Leo liked her body, Leo accepted her as she was, and a whole slice of her anxiety fell away in that moment. He closed his mouth to a tender pink nipple and she jerked in surprise, unprepared for the pulsing ache stirring at the heart of her body.

A sensual daze cocooned her as a tightening sensation banded her womb, her hips pushing up for relief as he teased a swollen bud with the edge of his teeth and moved hungrily to the other. Answering heat sizzled through her quivering body before the slowly heightening delight just seemed to explode deep down inside her, sending streamers of multi-coloured fire darting through every nerve-ending she possessed and dragging a cry from deep in her throat. Stray convulsions of pleasure continued to tug at her as she flung her head back in reaction, her honey-blonde mass of hair spreading across the pillows in a silken tangle.

'You're very sensitive there, *meli mou*,' Leo murmured with satisfaction, long fingers gently brushing an almost painfully tender pink nipple. 'I love that.'

Letty lifted a hand to frame one high cheekbone, utterly mesmerised by the smouldering blaze of his dark golden eyes. Her other hand curved to a bare bronzed shoulder with a new sense of intimacy that pleased her almost as much as it unnerved her. She liked the feel of his hot smooth skin and that was fine, perfectly acceptable as long as she accepted that that physical connection was as much as she could allow herself to feel for him.

'What are you thinking about?' Leo demanded with a disconcerted frown.

'Nothing, nothing at all,' Letty fibbed, lashes veiling her eyes as she drew herself up to put her lips against his again and he took the bait with alacrity, kissing her breathless while her restive hands roved over the smooth taut muscles of his spine to inch down into the waistband of his jeans to tug him closer still.

'There's so much more for us to discover,' Leo murmured huskily, darting a trail of kisses down the slope that ran from her ear to her shoulder, singling out sensitive spots that even she had not known she possessed and reawakening the hunger he had briefly sated.

Somewhere during that moment, her last garment disappeared but she was much more preoccupied by the line of kisses Leo was tracing down over her midriff to the honeyed, throbbing core of her. She closed her eyes tight, surrendering control for the first time ever, knowing that the more aroused she was, the easier her introduction to sex would be. Before very long, she was no longer capable of such practical reflections and her body was writhing without her at the controls.

Excitement began to build in waves that climbed higher and higher. He slid a finger into her and toyed with the slick damp flesh between her slender thighs. Desire engulfed her in a sharp flood of impatience and frustration. She couldn't stay still—she couldn't stay still long enough to catch her breath and her heart was racing, perspiration breaking out on her skin as the heat mushroomed up from her pelvis and made her fingernails claw into his luxuriant hair.

'Just do it!' she told him fiercely. 'I'm not expecting rainbows and unicorns!'

'Which is why we're doing it my way,' Leo countered with ferocious amusement.

With difficulty, Letty overcame a mortifying sense of being out of her depth and hating that almost as much as she loved what he was doing to her. Being in bed with Leo was one of the biggest learning experiences of her life, teaching her how much she had underestimated the power of desire to seduce. In a daze and still on the crest of an almost unbearable high of physical responsiveness, she watched Leo reach for protection and roll back to thrust his jeans out of his path with something less than the cool and control she had expected from him.

And then he came back to her with a hungry demanding urgency that taught her that, regardless of his patience, he was every bit as fiercely aroused as she was. He rearranged her with deft hands, scored an expert fingertip over the throbbing bud and triggered a breath-stealing climax that blew her away seconds before he angled his lean hips and filled her in one smooth motion. The sharp stab of pain was lost in a welter of other sensations that consumed her and within seconds he was tilting her up to drive in deeper with restrained thrusts.

He groaned something in Greek but Letty was way beyond asking him to translate, far too concentrated as she was on the eddying pulse of pleasure picking up pace with his every fluid movement. She arched up with a long gasping sigh to greet the wildly sensual and satisfying slam of his body into hers and the all-consuming excitement fired her afresh. He shifted to sink into her receptive core from another angle and grind down on her and her body ignited like oil thrown on a bonfire, tightening and burning and flying into renewed release.

Afterwards she wasn't quite sure what planet she was on, even if she was actually present with her own body because she felt weirdly insubstantial and detached from the world. She was drained, exhausted but somehow happy in a way she had never known before. For the first time ever she didn't feel alone, and the arms she had linked round Leo stayed in place until he pulled away, rolling off the bed to stride into the bathroom. Safe sex, she reminded herself. Of course the practicalities would disrupt the aftermath.

'Did you catch a distant glimpse of even one tiny rainbow?' Leo murmured huskily as he strode back to the bed.

'The whole sky was full of them,' Letty whispered, suddenly feeling self-conscious, which struck her as ridiculous after the intimacy they had shared. She had known Leo for only a month and already he had turned her inside out and upside down, she conceded worriedly.

Leo came down on the bed beside her again and it occurred to her that everything that had transpired between them had been entirely one-sided. Her face burned with guilt and embarrassment because she had been selfish. Sex was supposed to be a two-way activity and she had barely participated.

An unholy grin slashed his wide sensual mouth as he looked down at her. 'I could swear I saw a unicorn,' he teased.

And Letty shook free of her insecurities and laughed,

responding to the charisma Leo emitted at every turn. Certainly, he knew how to dispel an awkward moment.

'I'd love a rerun,' Leo confided. 'But I know that right now that wouldn't be very comfortable for you.'

Hot colour washed Letty's cheeks and she turned her face into the pillow and curled up. 'I'm exhausted,' she agreed ruefully because she was. Not only had it been a very long day full of stresses and strains but also her relationship with Leo had shifted into dramatically new territory and she wasn't yet sure how she felt about that.

'Sleep,' Leo urged lazily.

Letty would have enjoyed a bath to relax in but that would've entailed getting out of bed naked and crossing the room in front of Leo and she wasn't quite ready for that amount of exposure. He had given her a great deal of pleasure and presumably had taken pleasure in her. Or was it merely a matter of gaining sexual release for Leo? It was better not to dress harsh facts up, she told herself; it would be wiser to remain realistic.

But the knowledge that that was the sensible way to behave didn't prevent Letty from wishing that he would close an arm around her and show her some affection and discovering that need, that craving, inside her chilled her blood. There was no point seeking more from a male who had spelt out the reality that he didn't want or need more, that indeed a bloodless convenient marriage that included sex was the current summit of his ambitions.

At the same time, she ruminated, that prenup agreement she had signed would have to be updated and changed to reflect the major alteration that had taken place in their relationship. Letty looked forward to that.

Even when she had believed that she and Leo would never have a normal marriage, it had gone against the grain to sign any document that sanctioned his infidelity. On that soothing thought of what she viewed as an innate wrong being righted, she went to sleep.

When the phone beside the bed rang in the early hours, Letty, inured to wake-up calls and early rising, answered it immediately before it could disturb Leo. It was one of the nannies. Popi had had a bad dream and was inconsolable. Letty crept out of bed and rustled in her suitcase for sensible clothes before allowing herself a last glance at Leo as he slept in a lazy sprawl that had left her sleeping on the far edge of the bed. She smiled as she hurriedly brushed her hair. Even asleep Leo looked gorgeous, a rumpled sheet barely covering his bronzed and muscular length, his black hair and his stubbled jawline very dark against the pale bedding. She brushed her teeth, regretted that she dared not waste time taking a shower and padded out of the beach house to be greeted by Darius, who looked equally tired at the wheel of the beach buggy that would take her up to the villa.

Popi had got herself really worked up and it took time to calm her, and her sobs had wakened Sybella, who curled up at the foot of the bed once Letty arrived and quietly went back to sleep. Letty rocked Popi until she had recovered enough to make herself understood and then it all came flooding out: the argument she had had with her mother the night of the accident, her fear that her bad behaviour could have somehow caused the tragedy. Letty soothed her with the truth that nothing could've changed events that fatal night and the assurance that her loving mother would've understood her daughter's disappointment at not being allowed to accompany her parents to the hospital to collect her baby brother and bring him home for the first time.

Leo woke at dawn and sat up, surprised to find himself in an empty bed and then furious, stalking into the shower to cool off before pulling on jeans and a shirt. Letty would be with the children, he knew that, but he also knew that they needed to spend alone time as a couple and if she couldn't even go a few hours without checking in with the kids, how were they going to get to know each other? Righteously annoyed, Leo left the beach house and found Darius seated bleary-eyed with lack of sleep on a chair on the veranda.

'Popi had a nightmare,' Darius told him. 'The nanny phoned before I could advise her not to.'

'Go to bed, Darius. You don't need to be on call twenty-four-seven here on the island,' Leo responded ruefully.

'I stayed up to try and prevent you from shooting yourself in the foot,' his oldest friend admitted ruefully.

'And how am I going to do that?'

'You have to share her with the kids and you're accustomed to women who make *you* the centre of their world,' Darius remarked warily.

'There speaks the father,' Leo quipped, for Darius had three children.

Darius stood up and grimaced. 'Children change the dynamics of things,' he said wryly.

Leo knew all about how the arrival of children changed life, but it still bothered him that Darius had stayed out of bed to intercept him before he confronted Letty for sneaking off before their wedding night was even over. Did he seem that intolerant? Was he, in fact, spoiled by too many women who had unquestioningly put him first? Was he suffering from wounded pride? After all, why was he concerned in any way? Everything had gone according to plan and the sex, the marital sex, had been superlative. Letty was also the one and only woman who had ever been his alone and he liked that; indeed he was surprised by how much he had revelled in being the first.

As Leo appeared at the door of his nieces' bedroom, Popi held a finger to her lips, urging his silence. Letty was fast asleep on the little girl's bed with Sybella tucked in at her back. Leo smiled and crossed the room to lift his bride gently off the bed and carry her down the corridor to his bedroom, where he settled her down on the big bed and, as an afterthought, tugged up a throw to toss over her.

Letty stirred, opening drowsy green eyes to take in his vibrant presence.

'Go back to sleep. We're heading out shopping later and you'll need your energy.'

Her smooth brow furrowed. 'Shopping?'

'You need clothes,' Leo reminded her.

'I should tell you about Popi's nightmare first.'

'*Later...*' Leo stressed. 'She's quite happy now.'

Letty subsided back against the pillows.

'I also thought we could consider consulting the island doctor. You may deem it safer to take the contraceptive pill,' Leo framed with caution.

'Yes…that would be a good idea,' Letty conceded, thinking that the last thing they needed was an unplanned pregnancy but that, in time, she would probably want to have her own baby. A family of five and a career and Leo into the bargain? She almost rolled her eyes at that enormous challenge. Other women coped though and so would she and she could hardly complain when she would have all the help she needed on the home front.

By that afternoon, they were walking into a designer atelier in Athens, where Leo was received like returning royalty. That started her thinking that Leo was disturbingly knowledgeable about where to buy expensive female clothing. The thought made her uncomfortable because it reminded her of her many predecessors. She swallowed hard, conceding that, for a womaniser, such familiarity went with the territory.

She was disconcerted to recognise her aunt, Elexis Livas, in conversation with a fawning assistant, a tall, voluptuous brunette by her side. The brunette instantly gave Leo her attention, throwing him a lingering look and a flirtatious smile before breaking away from Elexis to say, 'I wasn't expecting to see you here today, Leo. Elexis has been telling me all about the wedding.'

'Letty…' Leo murmured smoothly. 'Dido Bakas… How's the theatre run going?'

'Brilliantly!' Dido exclaimed, resting a hand on Leo's sleeve with the familiarity of a lover. 'You should try to make the show before it closes. I'd love to see you in the audience.'

Letty felt invisible. The other woman had ignored her extended hand and continued to focus solely on Leo.

'Sadly, I'm a little too busy right now,' Leo parried as Elexis joined them.

'I can't believe you're out and about the day after the wedding,' Elexis commented, shooting Letty an amused look as if it were a mortification for a bridegroom to be seen in public so soon after the wedding.

'Letty doesn't enjoy shopping, so I'm here to do it for her,' Leo said lightly. 'Excuse me. We have a private viewing organised and we're running a little late.'

'Are you sure you can't make it to my engagement party on Saturday?' Elexis pressed, big brown eyes pinned to Leo as though he hung the moon.

'Unfortunately, we have a prior engagement,' Leo countered. 'My new nightclub is opening up in Athens on Saturday.'

Elexis looked pained. 'But I thought that was next week.'

'I moved it forward. Saturday is Letty's birthday... It seemed fitting to change the date,' Leo suggested lazily, spreading his hand across Letty's taut spine and guiding her towards the woman waiting to welcome them.

'How did you know it was my birthday?' Letty whispered.

'Marriage licence,' Leo told her as they were ushered into a large showroom, shown to seats and offered champagne.

'And you moved the opening date forward?' Letty questioned in disbelief. 'Because of *my* birthday?'

'You're my wife. It seemed appropriate, even if it did cast the organisers into a loop.'

'And we're attending this event together?' Letty prompted.

'Even I would not leave you alone to celebrate your birthday,' Leo chided as models began to stroll out of the changing rooms behind the small catwalk and strut their stuff. It was an entertaining show, but Letty was

intimidated by the height and slenderness of the models and could not picture her more ordinary self wearing such elegant, exclusive garments.

Leo, however, had no such inhibitions. He signalled
the designer and indicated the outfits he preferred,
seemingly impervious to the reality that she was very
different in shape from the models and would not look
the same.

An assistant escorted her into a changing room to
be measured and within a very short space of time she
was trying on clothes and the tailor was taking note
of the adjustments to be made. A rack of lingerie was
brought to her to try on next.

Her phone buzzed while she was striving not to
think about Dido, who was clearly an ex of Leo's. It
was a text from Leo.

Come out and model the lingerie for me.

Letty was aghast at that suggestion, and the thought
of displaying herself that way for Leo made her grow
uncomfortably hot. Wide-eyed and flushed, she studied her reflection in the mirror. She was wearing a
very pretty bra and briefs combination in pale blue.
The bra fitted much better than the bras she usually
wore. In fact, it seemed that she had been wearing the
wrong size for years.

What's made you so shy?

And Letty went pink. It was as if the wretched man
was inside her head, rooting about and forcing her insecurities into the light of day.

In her head was an image of Elexis, pencil-thin in tangerine, and Dido, curvy but still skinny in all the right places with long legs. Letty was different, shorter and rounder, but she was *still* the woman Leo wanted, the woman he had made passionate love to the night before.

Only love had had nothing to do with it, she reminded herself ruefully. Even so, bodies came in all shapes and sizes and she did not like to acknowledge that she had a poor body image or low self-esteem. It was *just*… Her brow furrowed until she understood herself better. It occurred to her, for the very first time, that she *was* actually quite shy but that the need to focus on other people throughout her life had blinded her to that truth. And the women around Leo, the women he had actually been with, seemed so ridiculously beautiful that she was intimidated and shrank from the comparisons.

Enough was enough, Letty decided on the back of that lowering thought, stepping out of the changing room with a sway to her hips and an angle to her chin. And Leo, sprawled in his chair looking bored and clearly not expecting her, sat up with a jerk, stunned by her response to his challenge. And Letty liked that reaction; she liked it very much. She strolled across to the table and lifted her champagne to sip it, gloriously aware that Leo could not take his spectacular dark golden eyes from her.

'So, basic is what turns you on,' Letty murmured with a rueful sigh.

'Pretty much,' Leo admitted, his attention welded to that wondrous hourglass shape of hers and the swell of her breasts.

'At least that's fairly normal,' Letty conceded, em-powered by the reality that Leo, basic or otherwise, was visibly aroused. 'At one stage early on I did wonder if you were insisting on keeping a mistress because you were into some sort of kink—'

Leo almost choked on his champagne and hurriedly set down the glass. *'Kink?'* he stressed, his gorgeous eyes bright with disbelief.

'It was a fair enough assumption when I didn't know you,' Letty parried, cool as a cucumber now. 'Want to see anything else?'

'Surprise me again… You keep *on* doing that,' Leo breathed, studying her with intense dark golden eyes. 'I didn't think you'd have the nerve to come out.'

Letty sashayed back to the changing room wear-ing a grin she wouldn't have shown him for a million pounds. She emerged again in a black set ornamented with shocking pink lace and Leo lounged back in his chair to enjoy the show.

'You do realise that I'm likely to jump you in the limo after this?' he murmured thickly.

'Promises…promises,' Letty countered with a roll of her green sea glass eyes and with more daring than she had known she possessed.

'I can't wait that long,' Leo breathed, striding into the changing room in her wake and catching her into his arms before she could guess his intention.

'You can't…*here*!' Letty gasped, thoroughly dis-concerted as he backed her up against the wall, pin-ning her hands to either side of her and caging her in with his lean powerful body. Yet looking up into the smouldering heat of his eyes, she found his dominance outlandishly sexy.

'Nobody will disturb us,' Leo murmured huskily. 'I only need a little taste of you.'

His mouth crashed down on hers and she strained helplessly against him, a flood of hunger released instantly. He hitched one of her legs up and ground against her and her awareness of his arousal mounted a thousandfold and sent fireworks shooting through her pelvis. His tongue tangled with hers and a low moan escaped her, an ache forming between her taut thighs. He released her hands and glided his fingertips lightly down her ribcage, making her shiver convulsively. Her heart was racing so fast she could hardly catch her breath, and then he touched her where she most needed to be touched and she thought she would spontaneously combust from the surge of tingling tormenting sensation at her core.

Her eyes flicked open on the mirror behind Leo and a belated awareness of where they were engulfed her. She pushed her palms against his chest and looked up at him, hot and flushed and damningly conscious of how much she wanted him.

'Not here,' she muttered tautly.

His body screaming for release, Leo snatched in a ragged breath. He should never have left the island, he recognised, because he couldn't keep his hands off her. That hadn't happened to him with a woman in more years than he could count, and he didn't want it to happen with her. Control was important to Leo. Anything excessive in any aspect of his life set up warning markers he heeded. His father loved his stepmother obsessively and it had meant that the older man made some very bad decisions. Not that Leo was afraid that he could be falling in love—no, far from it. He almost smiled at the idea, knowing himself to be too battle-hardened by far to be prone to that weakness. On the other hand, obsessive lust was dangerous as well.

'We'll get back to Ios,' Leo agreed. 'I'll have the rest of your new wardrobe sent out to the island for you to choose from there.'

Letty seemed transfixed by the idea and her eyes widened. 'I'll get dressed.'

'Yes, that would be sensible,' Leo murmured as if he had never asked her to model the lingerie for him or, indeed, had followed her into the changing room.

Letty was restive in the limo that returned them to the airport because Leo had withdrawn from her. Because she had said no? She didn't think so. She suspected Leo had also succumbed to a moment of temptation and taking account of their surroundings had reined back his desire for her. But she knew he had an apartment in Athens and he didn't suggest heading there and he didn't approach her in the limo either.

Finally, shortly before they reached the airport, she asked him a question that had been playing heavily on her mind. 'I've been wondering...' she began tautly. 'When will you be changing the terms in the prenuptial contract I signed?'

Dark brows pleating, Leo frowned at her in apparent astonishment. 'Why would I do that?'

'Because everything between us has changed,' Letty pointed out simply. 'This is not the detached marriage we originally agreed, and I do not accept your right to be unfaithful now.'

That assurance fell into a bottomless pit of silence.

Leo's dark gaze was hooded and cool. His jawline clenched hard. 'We'll discuss it later, although I should warn you that we have different viewpoints.'

Letty swallowed hard, not liking the sound of that for she couldn't imagine what he could think they *could* have to discuss in the circumstances. He had radically changed the terms of their marriage and she had rights too...*didn't she?*

CHAPTER EIGHT

LETTY REFUSED TO be intimidated by Leo's forbidding coolness on the flight back to the island and she was surrounded by the children when they walked into the big house. Popi, as lively as though that nightmare had never happened, wanted to know where they had been, what they had done, what they had bought. Cosmo had a car to show her. Sybella was lugging around a doll almost as big as she was and Theon just held out his arms to her, always eager for a cuddle.

'We're dining at the beach house,' Leo decreed, unable to hang onto his reserve with Sybella trying to climb up him as if he were a tree.

'Yes,' Letty agreed. 'Later. I'll see the children to bed first…if that's all right with you?'

Leo studied her, a muscle pulling at the edge of his taut jaw. His spectacular bone structure was visible beneath his bronzed skin, his dark golden eyes bright with a glint of impatience. And anger? Well, if he was angry, too bad, Letty reasoned. The prenup stuff had to be dealt with, whether he liked it or not. He jerked his chin in acknowledgement of her plans and swung round, bending to let Sybella slide down from his arms. 'I'll catch up with some work.'

* * *

Why did she want to mess around with the prenup? he was asking himself grimly. It was there as a safeguard, nothing more. Could she already be contemplating divorcing him? Why the urgency? Had he made a crucial mistake choosing Letty as a wife? Why should she hang around, playing mother to four kids who weren't her own, when she could be living the life of a millionaire, free and clear? A dark brooding expression set his lean strong features hard. Why had he been so sure that she was different from other women? Money, after all, was the most persuasive power on the planet for many, many people. It made them turn their back on moral scruples. Yet the children were already attached to Letty, and Popi was finally behaving more like a little girl without the worries of the world weighing down her tiny shoulders.

Nothing was going quite as Leo had planned and he hated that. For a start, he was aware that he had underestimated the importance of the woman he had married and the value of the role she would play in his life. His sex drive had got in the way of pragmatism and possibly put everything else at risk, which was crazy, he acknowledged broodingly. Letty had warned him that she would make demands and have expectations and he hadn't really listened. His sole focus had been on getting her into bed and, even worse, it *still* was. He hadn't counted on wanting Letty as much as he did. Somewhere in the back of his mind he had wondered if a couple of weeks of her would sate him and if he would then eventually return to his former way of life…

Letty resolved to encourage Leo to get more involved with the children's bedtime routine but acknowledged that perhaps today wasn't the right day to make that suggestion. Turning a sophisticated tycoon into a get-down-and-dirty father would be a project and a half, she reflected, but his nieces and nephews did need more than the occasional hug from him.

The children all tucked up, Letty sped down to the beach house with Darius at the wheel of the buggy. He told her about his wife and children who lived on Ios, admitting that his wife refused to move because her family was there, and he travelled a great deal with Leo.

Arriving at the beach house, Letty hurtled upstairs for the shower she was desperate to enjoy. Her suit-cases had been unpacked and she rifled through the slender collection of clothes hung for her, recognising that she had seriously misjudged the number of outfits she would need. Of course, that wasn't likely to be a problem once she picked out new clothes. Selecting a flouncy skirt and cotton sweater, she went for a shower and broke out her even smaller collection of cosmet-ics. A lick of mascara, a touch of blusher and clear lip gloss and she was done. She scrutinised her reflection as she blow-dried her hair.

There was no point in kidding herself that she could compete in the looks department with women like Dido and Mariana. They were dark, she was fair. They were tall, she was short. They were well-groomed and so-phisticated, she was more the girl next door, put to-gether in a hurry and on a wing and a prayer. Would *he* even notice if she put on nail varnish? It would get chipped when she was messing about with the kids. What on earth was that man doing to her priorities? Why she was looking so critically at herself? Why was she only seeing flaws? Well, how was she to help doing so? Right now, she seemed to be continually meeting women like Elexis or Katrina panting for Leo's interest, or exes like Dido and Mariana, more than ready for a sexual rerun with him!

And possibly she had always lacked confidence in herself, she acknowledged for the first time, hiding behind the needs of her family and putting them first. In a sense that attitude and intensive study had provided a shield between her and the world, but that shield was gone now that she was with Leo.

Leo awaited her downstairs, a balloon glass of brandy between his fingers. Just seeing him stopped her dead in her tracks. His luxuriant black hair was still damp and, like her, he had changed, the exquisitely cut designer suit he had worn earlier now replaced by narrow black pants and a white linen shirt left open at the neck.

'A drink?' he enquired.

'Something soft if you have it.' Letty knew that she needed to keep her head clear for the conversation they had to have.

'We don't need drama twenty-four hours into our marriage,' Leo murmured with measured cool. 'You're not giving us a fair crack of the whip.'

Letty paled and stiffened, annoyed by his attitude. 'This is not drama.'

Leo shifted a shoulder in a fluid shrug of brazen disagreement, lean muscles flexing beneath his shirt, and she dragged her attention away from him again, embarrassed by her need to savour him like a starstruck teenager. There would never be another Leo in her life. That went without saying. But she also knew that if their relationship was to have any chance of survival, she had to fight for that chance and ensure that he understood that she was serious.

'In the prenup there was a clause relating to your freedom to sleep with whomever you chose and that not being grounds for divorce,' she reminded him doggedly.

His shrewd gaze widened a little and lingered. 'That was the deal.'

'*Was* being the operative word,' Letty stressed. 'That *was* the deal until *you* changed it last night, when I understood that you are now prepared to commit to this marriage. If that is the case, why do you *still* need that clause?'

'Commitment is a rather strong word,' Leo countered, sipping his brandy. 'In fact, it gives me chills. I've never been committed to anybody but my family.'

'I'm supposed to be your family now,' Letty pointed out stiffly as he passed her a drink.

'Committing to a woman is a tall order. I said I was willing to *try* being married.'

'And I said I wouldn't be part of a "try before you buy" experiment!' Letty riposted in sudden anger. 'This isn't a fluid situation, Leo. You can't keep on changing the terms. You don't want to commit? You don't want to promise fidelity?'

'No. I don't want to hear either of those words,' Leo admitted harshly, thinking of his father's devotion to Katrina and her constant betrayal of his trust, not to mention the many other infidelities he had witnessed in both sexes over the years. 'I will promise not to lie to you. I will promise never to go behind your back. But the best I can do on the fidelity front is to promise that I will always be honest. As I said once before, I can't foretell the future.'

Letty felt as if she had been crushed against a brick wall and suddenly she was reeling with a sense of betrayal. Had she misunderstood him the night before? Surely she had been plain about what *she* wanted and needed? Her oval face tightened, her eyes veiling. 'You know what? That's fine, Leo…' she said limply, turning with relief as the first course of their meal arrived and using the hiatus to take a seat at the beautifully set table.

Leo's tension evaporated. He had been expecting all sorts of things from her other than what he had received. She was still hung up on the fidelity stuff, still striving to idealise their marriage into some perfect picture, but she wasn't thinking of divorce. He refused to label the sensation strongly reminiscent of relief travelling through him. Obviously, he was grateful that she had staying power for the children's sake. But she was still wilfully misunderstanding him, he reasoned in exasperation. It wasn't as though he had any plans to cheat on Letty; he simply preferred complete honesty because he was a cynic about the promises of fidelity that people blithely made and then broke.

Letty shook out her napkin with a flourish, slight colour slowly returning to mantle her cheeks. 'As I said, that's fine. You do what you need to do. But you have to accept that I have certain requirements as well. If you're not prepared to have that clause eliminated from the prenup, then you're clearly not prepared to make a concrete commitment to our marriage. Sorry, did I use that nasty word again?' she said as his arrogant head came up, dark eyes ablaze with gold challenge.

'Letty…' Leo began.

Letty faked a greater interest than she truly felt in her tiny portion of red pepper, feta and olive frittata. In fact, hungry as she was, she was feeling nauseous about the situation she was in and crushingly, horribly *hurt*. As if Leo's refusal to commit was a personal rejection.

'You're making far too much of that clause.'

'I saw it being deleted from the agreement as a pledge, as proof that you were serious in your intentions.'

'I *am* serious in my intentions!' Leo snapped back at her in frustration. 'I said I would *try*.'

Letty leant back in her chair, the delicious bite of pie turning to ashes in her dry mouth. 'And that's not enough for me. We're at a crossroads here. I suggest that we agree to differ, rather than argue a non-negotiable point and—'

Leo thrust away his plate untouched, his dark golden eyes mirroring his turbulent emotions. Letty was putting him through the mill and he hadn't expected that, but this time around he didn't mistake his sense of reprieve for anything other than what it was. 'That would be sensible,' he conceded.

Letty sighed. 'You didn't let me finish, Leo. For us both to be happy in this relationship, we have to compromise. But, since I can't share a bed with a man I can't trust, you will have to embrace your sexual freedom…and we'll never discuss this thorny and distasteful subject again.'

Leo was shattered. He certainly hadn't seen *that* offer coming. He breathed in deep and slow. 'That's not a reasonable compromise, Letty.'

'I can't be reasonable about everything,' Letty said quietly. 'We're compromising. You're getting what you want.'

'*How?* I want *you*!' Leo slung back at her wrathfully, the temper he controlled rigidly breaking free.

'Not as much as you want a get-out clause for when you get bored with me,' Letty qualified without a shade of expression. 'That's how it is. I'm not going to quarrel with you about it.'

'No!' Leo rasped, expelling his breath and thrusting his hands down to rise from his seat, a deep sense of injustice powering him. 'You're only kicking me out of the marital bed for a sin I haven't committed yet!'

'*Yet.*' Letty stressed his use of that word. 'You see, in your mind you're still a free man, *not* a married man. Even worse, you view yourself as a man who cannot be faithful. I would have to be a very stupid woman not to steer clear of that accident waiting to happen… and I'm not stupid, Leo.'

Tied into knots by her words and his own and infuriated by her tranquil attitude when he was ready to punch holes in walls, Leo scrutinised his wife with outraged, dark as jet eyes, faint colour scoring his hard cheekbones. 'I'll have your stuff moved back up to the main house immediately.'

'There's no rush,' Letty told him uneasily.

Leo ate with appetite, even offered occasional conversation. To give him his due, he didn't brood or give her the silent treatment. Letty, however, was under no illusion that what still powered him was anger: he was determined to keep his freedom and she wanted to take it away. There was no possible conciliation between such far-removed objectives. Maybe he needed time and space to consider those facts before he would be willing to acknowledge the good sense of leaving sex out of their marriage. That was what he had first wanted and what she had been happy to accept, but then he had changed his mind and decided he wanted her...and fatally, foolishly, she had decided to give him a chance.

Why? She wanted to box her own ears for her stupidity. She had taken a risk on him, but he had quickly brought her crashing down to earth again.

Her luggage was discreetly carted out while they finished their meal with coffee. It was all very civilised but Letty still felt as though she were the one being kicked out and when Darius drove her back up to the main house his diplomatic silence warned her that, like the rest of the staff, he also knew that the brief honeymoon was over and Letty was mortified by Leo's intransigence and his disinterest in what other people might think. Evidently the pretence that theirs was a normal marriage was already over.

Tears leaked out of the corners of Letty's eyes and stung her quivering cheeks that night as she lay in her new bed. She wouldn't let herself sob or grieve for what had proved to be an empty illusion. She was hurt and she acknowledged that while also acknowledging that she had already become far too attached to Leo in spite of his ferocious stubbornness. She was doing the sensible thing in protecting herself, she told herself.

Leo couldn't sleep. He paced the bedroom floor, trying to pin down the exact moment when everything had gone pear-shaped. It was the first time in his life that that had happened to him with a woman. He was accustomed to calling all the shots, to having exactly what he wanted but Letty didn't work that way. She wanted pledges, sacred bonds, all the rest of that nonsense, he fumed in measured annoyance as he fought a growing sense of injustice.

He couldn't imagine being faithful all his life to one woman. But his overriding belief remained that he did not want to *hurt* Letty or any other woman! As he suspected his mother must often have been hurt by his father's infidelities. Leo had never in his life cheated on any woman, choosing to be honest when he knew he wanted to move on, had never had a desire to have more than one woman at a time in his life.

None of his ancestors, his grandfather or his father, had pledged fidelity. Even so, as far as he knew, his father had always been slavishly faithful to his step-mother, Katrina. But that was only because his father, weak and pathetic man that he was, worshipped the ground that Katrina walked on. And look where that had got the older man: a wife who was well known for her extra-marital affairs! No, he certainly wasn't ready to follow that unpleasant and humiliating example as a blueprint for his future, he assured himself squarely, while stamping firmly down on the knowledge at the back of his mind that Letty wasn't that sort of woman.

Letty had given him one fantastic night and he would have to be content with that. He studied the bed that they had shared and gritted his teeth. He wanted her, he wanted her there now, *ached* just at the thought of reliving that pleasure. But he would get over that, the sneaky type of sexual infatuation she had some-how plunged him into. Because he had been her first? Was that the secret of her intense attraction for him? He didn't know; he only knew he felt angry, frustrated and frazzled and most unlike himself and he *hated* it— absolutely bloody hated it!

* * *

The following morning, all the clothes and accessories arrived for Letty to try on and consider and she was trying to decide between two black cocktail dresses when Leo entered the room with a small warning knock that made her spin round in dismay, the zip she had been struggling with still open and exposing her bare back.

'I'll call your maid.'

Letty laughed. 'No, now you're here…you can make yourself useful. Are you still taking me to that club opening on Saturday?'

Leo raised an ebony brow, clearly surprised that she had assumed that he might have changed his mind on that score. 'Is it still your birthday on Saturday? Then yes, but don't pick a black dress. You need something *more*…' He rifled through the rack of clothes and dragged out a scarlet dress that she wouldn't have considered in a thousand years for her wardrobe. It was stretchy, glittery, low-necked and low-backed, in short everything she avoided.

'Er…no…' She didn't want to hurt his feelings when he was trying to help. 'That's a little daring for me. I mean, look at that neckline.'

'I'm a man—of course I'm looking at the neckline,' Leo reasoned. 'You've got a terrific figure. Wear colours and show it off.'

Letty flushed. 'I'll try it on and see,' she conceded, still doubtful but knowing that that accolade from him would make her more than consider wearing it. Was she a people-pleaser? Or a Leo-pleaser? She only knew that she craved his admiration, which was childish and rather unfair to him when she had refused to sleep with him again.

Leo lifted the house phone and spoke in Greek. 'I've called your maid. Use the staff. That's what they're here for,' he urged.

Letty grimaced. 'It'll take a while for me to get used to having staff around but I'll work on it... OK?'

'OK.' Leo studied her with a totally unreadable expression but his dark golden eyes were alight and she felt that scrutiny make her nipples peak inside her bra and force her to press her thighs together on the ache that stirred in her pelvis.

Of course she was still attracted to him and *that* was going to happen, she reminded herself, but eventually she would get a handle on such responses, wouldn't she? And, under all the surface sophistication, he was a really decent guy, she acknowledged. He wasn't holding spite. He wasn't fretting or doing anything to make her uncomfortable because she had made a decision that he disagreed with and that was a pretty special ability in such a strong and volatile man, wasn't it? But the real problem was, she reckoned, as she watched him leave the room, tall and dark and totally, breathtakingly gorgeous, that the situation they were in would be much easier for her if he behaved badly and made her hate him a little more.

Over the remainder of the week Leo continued to confound her innately low expectations of the male sex. He joined her for a rather windblown picnic on the beach with the children and played ball with Cosmo, who shrieked with excitement and hugged his uncle's knees as if he would never let him go. He read a bedtime story to Popi and even tried a few baby-animal-lost-in-the-jungle noises that made both Popi and Sybella go off into whooping giggles. He was making an effort to spend more time with the children and without being asked or encouraged, finally admitting to her when they were talking about it afterwards that on his own he had felt swamped by the kids and their attention had felt too full-on for him to handle.

Recognising that she was in the mood to offer him sex just for pleasing her, Letty took herself off safely to bed early that night. She also stopped lingering over dinner in the evening when he joined her at the house and made absolutely no comment when he too abandoned the beach house and moved back into his usual room across the corridor from hers. They were discovering a new and *better* way to be with each other, she told herself—friends, partners, whatever anyone wanted to call it. She had wanted more but had had to settle for less, which she could live with perfectly well, she reasoned, noting the dark golden intensity of Leo's eyes with what she assured herself was only academic interest.

The day of the club opening rolled up and Letty spent the afternoon getting ready for her first social appearance as Leo's wife. She was keen to look the part. Her maid did her hair for her, straightening it into a luxuriously conditioned smooth blonde mane and Letty knew that it had never looked that good in her life before. She had ordered cosmetics online and boned up on eye shadow application and she made a major effort there too, before donning the scarlet dress and sliding her feet into the sort of very high heels she had always laughed about. All for Leo, a snide little voice whispered at the back of her head and she ignored the voice, telling herself that presenting herself polished up occasionally was only what her position as Leo's wife demanded.

As she had promised, Letty stepped into the girls' bedroom to show them her dress.

'You look pretty, Mummy Letty,' Popi pronounced, bouncing on top of her bed in her pyjamas and failing to notice how Letty momentarily froze at that designation, tears burning the back of her eyes at the compliment.

'Mummy Letty,' Sybella repeated obediently.

Leo watched Letty come downstairs and immediately regretted choosing the dress because she looked fantastic and incredibly sexy in it and he was tempted enough without the sight of her superb breasts showcased in red and her shapely legs on show. The pulse at his groin which rarely quit around Letty kicked up into a dull throb and he ground his teeth together.

'You look amazing,' Leo murmured hoarsely. 'But you forgot your jewellery…'

'I have my rings on.'

He urged her into his office and opened a big wooden box, full of smaller boxes and a tangled array of other gold and jewels untidily stored. 'My mother's collection. It's all yours to wear now. I would suggest the rubies with that dress.'

Letty stood still as Leo attached a ruby pendant to her throat and handed her earrings to put on. When he was this close and she could smell the wonderfully familiar scent of him she felt light-headed and she gulped in steadying air as she donned the earrings. Leo handed her a gold watch.

'My goodness,' she muttered uneasily. 'I'll look like a Christmas tree.'

'No, you'll look like a Romanos wife...*my* wife,' Leo completed with distinct pride as he removed a ruby and diamond bangle from its protective box and watched her slide it over her hand.

Letty allowed him to escort her out to the helicopter waiting for them before sharing with him that Popi had called her 'Mummy Letty'.

'That's wonderful!' Leo exclaimed with his brilliant flashing smile before he lifted her into the helicopter. 'They've accepted you.'

Letty thought it was rather more of a first step on that road but she didn't deflate him. Loving the children had come as easily to her as loving her own family. Her mother had made a really good recovery from her surgery and was no longer in pain. The boys were back home from their father's as well and everyone was missing her. Popi started back to school after half-term the following week, so she would be back in London soon enough, she reminded herself wryly.

Infinity, Leo's new club in Athens, was surrounded by paparazzi and Leo strode down the red carpet between the crash barriers restraining the crowds, past the surge of flashing cameras and shouted questions, quite unbothered by the attention, while Letty was tempted to pull her hem down to her ankles and haul her neckline up to her chin but didn't have sufficient fabric to achieve either wish.

As she joined Leo at a crowded table of well-wishers, she asked him if his father had arrived yet and he rolled his eyes at the question. 'No, it'll be another no-show on his part. He often makes promises he doesn't keep,' he admitted wryly.

Leo's cynical attitude to his father's failures in the

paternal field made Letty feel sad for him because *her* mother had always been reliable. His insecure background had most definitely damaged Leo's ability to trust either himself or anyone else but she knew he wouldn't appreciate that information.

As Letty's gaze fell on a familiar face at a nearby table, she stiffened and interrupted Leo to hiss, 'What's Dido doing here? Is she one of your *special* guests?'

Leo froze. 'No, but she's a famous actress. I imagine she got a free ticket from the organisers. The more celebrities that attend, the more headlines the event garners,' he countered drily, closing a hand over hers to guide her over to a more secluded table in the corner.

As she sat down a waiter arrived with a tray carrying a birthday cake and another with a bottle of champagne.

'Happy birthday, Letty,' Leo murmured as the cake was ceremonially sliced and the champagne was uncorked to froth down into glasses. 'I had a gift bought for you, but it no longer seemed appropriate so I had to get creative. As an alternative gift, I'm signing that apartment your mother and brothers are living in over to them,' he said quietly. 'Owning the property will give them a greater feeling of security.'

'Oh, Leo, that's so…*so* generous of you!' Letty gasped and hauled him into a hug, painfully aware of how rigid he remained in her hold and quickly drawing back with the sense that she had crossed a boundary she should've respected. 'But what did you originally buy me?' she prompted, hopelessly curious on that score.

'It was an eternity ring.' Leo grimaced. 'I returned it.'

Disappointment filled her because it had been a personal present and an eternity ring from Leo, the studiously free man, would have been a very satisfying item to wear.

As she fumbled for the right words with which to respond, Dido slid into the seat beside Leo. 'Leo, just the man I've been needing to see!' she carolled in English, before shifting into Greek.

Letty strove to be polite and contrived to drain a glass of champagne and even munch on a slice of cake while Dido, once again, ignored her presence. But by the time her glass was refreshed such restraint was becoming a challenge and anger was stirring like green fire in her gaze because the other woman had, very rudely, broken in on a private moment.

'Get rid of her,' she bit out in Leo's ear. *'Or I will!'*

Leo shot her a startled appraisal and then rose from the table to effectively bring the conversation to an end. 'Excuse me,' he murmured smoothly, long brown fingers capturing Letty's to raise her by his side. 'My wife and I are in the midst of celebrating her birthday...'

CHAPTER NINE

'DON'T YOU EVER, for as long as you live, address me like that again!' Leo launched at Letty in a furious undertone as he tugged her up the spiral staircase in the corner and flung open a door into an office, already occupied by an older man.

'Sorry, Dmitri... I need a private space,' said Leo, and the other man quickly vacated the room to leave them alone.

'I am fed up with your ex-girlfriends swarming like piranha fish around us!' Letty sliced back at Leo. 'They're everywhere we go, demanding your attention!'

Leo regarded her, his anger mysteriously ebbing from his bright golden gaze. 'You're a jealous, possessive woman, *yineka mou*,' he declared, utterly disconcerting Letty as she squared up to him with angrily clenched fists. 'And that is remarkable behaviour from a woman who told me to embrace my sexual freedom and kicked me out of bed!'

'I did *not* kick you out of bed!' Letty fired back at him, still trying to work out when she had lost the plot to the extent that she had blamed Leo for Dido's rudeness and persistence and had literally snarled at him. Her cheeks went red. 'But I am not jealous either.'

Leo stalked forward, crowding her back against the desk. 'You *were* jealous,' he persisted with the most curious edge of satisfaction stamped on his lean, darkly handsome features. 'So, how are you planning to handle me being with these other women you want me to sleep with?'

'Like a trooper!' Letty threw back at him. 'It wouldn't mean anything to me. I'm tough.'

'You may be tough,' conceded Leo, framing her hectically flushed face with two big hands. 'But you *are* a lousy liar! You want me and you don't want to share me. I wouldn't want to share you either because you're mine—'

'Oh, take a hike with the property claim!' Letty advised with acid bite. 'I don't belong to you in any way!'

'Let me *show* you then,' Leo growled, rough and low, crushing her mouth under his with such insistence that her knees went weak, all the fiery intensity that was Leo powering his passionate assault on her tender mouth.

With the unfamiliar knowledge that her temper was out of control, Letty's mind was a whirling turmoil of contrasting reactions. She wanted to slap him but she wanted to kiss him back too, and the liquid heat pooling in her pelvis wouldn't let her push him away. Instead she traded kiss for kiss, hard and fierce and so necessary to her in her current mood that she could not have restrained that desperate need hurtling up through her.

And suddenly Leo was settling her down on the desk, long fingers smoothing up her inner thighs to yank with force at her knickers. And Letty was shocked but *not* outraged, hunger for him driving her, ensuring that she too unconditionally craved the drivingly urgent invasion of his body into hers. She yanked at his tousled black hair as he endeavoured to don protection while she ran her greedy hands below his shirt, over the smooth flexing muscles shifting below her every caress.

'You're driving me insane!' Leo rasped in a tone of raw arousal, his eyes blazing like polished gold ingots set between sweeping black lashes.

He sank into the slick wet welcome of her body with an uninhibited groan of appreciation. The desk creaked under that very physical onslaught. Her body jolted, hot sweet delight laced with savage excitement making her heart hammer and her blood race. With every sinuous twist of his lithe hips he hammered the exact spot inside her that maximised her pleasure. The pressure inside her built and built until it surged up through her in a wild white-knuckle climax that made her cry out his name.

'Would this be the right or the wrong moment to say thank you for sharing your birthday with me?' Leo murmured huskily above her head, still panting to catch his breath from his exertions.

As Leo righted his clothing, Letty leapt off the desk like a scalded cat and discovered her legs were too wobbly to hold her upright. 'It was the champagne,' she muttered between clenched teeth.

'One glass? Even you are not that much of a lightweight. No, finally accept that we have crazy good chemistry together,' Leo asserted without remorse.

And why was she looking for remorse from him? she asked herself fiercely. Of course he had no regrets, having just comprehensively proved that he could break down her barriers and persuade her to do what she had sworn *not* to do. A guilty sense of having failed her own standards afflicted Letty.

'*So* good it's off the charts,' Leo grated, hauling her into his arms, striving to hang onto the advantage he had gained. 'The sex ban isn't going to work for us.'

Letty froze as he brushed her tumbled hair back from her woodenly self-contained face to look down at her. 'It *has* to work,' she parried with an edge of desperation because she didn't know who she was any more, what she was trying to do, why she had let herself down to such an extent, and then she gazed up into Leo's stunning eyes and reeled at the beauty of them set in that lean strong face of his.

In that instant, the stark realisation that in the matter of a few short weeks she had become deeply attached to Leo shattered her. She *loved* him. Of course she found it a challenge to step back and deny what her own mind and body longed to have, that intimate connection which might have been essentially meaningless to a male of Leo's experience and habits, but which meant a great deal more to her. No longer could she deny or wilfully misunderstand the powerful feelings he inspired in her. Earlier, he had been right, and she had been wrong. She *was* jealous of his tribe of exes and admirers. She didn't like seeing him with another woman, didn't like watching another woman command his attention. How petty was that?

Yet being with Leo made her feel stronger, more confident, more individual in more ways than she had words to describe. That was the positive side to loving him while she mentally shook her head over the foolishness that accompanied those same feelings. She had lost her temper over pushy Dido, had been intolerant and idiotically possessive. So, he was right and she was wrong. If this was how she truly felt, how could she ever contrive to live with the knowledge that Leo was having sex with other women? Suddenly she felt as though she had backed herself into a corner and she didn't know how to get out of it again.

'Compromise is not the end of the world,' Leo murmured huskily, pressing an abstracted kiss against her furrowed brow, uncomfortably aware that that clever brain of hers was turning like a clock and probably not in his favour. 'Eventually we'll understand what works best for us. It's too soon to make major decisions about our direction right now.'

Letty gritted her teeth. She was too proud to appreciate Leo being generous enough to offer her a face-saving excuse. 'We'll see,' she muttered flatly. 'We should return to our table.'

Leo fished a comb out of his jacket and tidied her hair and suggested she fix her lipstick. She had never felt as ashamed of herself as she did at that moment when she registered that her inexperience in relationships had sent her rushing down the wrong path. It was an effort to return to the crowds downstairs and smile and chat as though nothing whatsoever had happened while her body still hummed and pulsed from Leo's rawly masculine possession. He had won his point but he wasn't crowing in triumph and she supposed she should be grateful for small mercies.

When they arrived back on the island it was very late and when Darius greeted Leo in Greek and spoke words that etched a look of astonishment on Leo's lean strong face, Letty was sprung out of her drowsiness.

'What's happened?'

'Apparently my father arrived here with a suitcase during the evening. Darius seems to think he's broken up with Katrina, but I find that long-desired event very hard to credit,' Leo mused with a curled lip.

As they entered the hall, Letty headed towards the stairs.

'Where are you going?' Leo questioned.

'I thought that you and your father would appreciate privacy,' Letty said uncertainly. 'I mean, if he's in the midst of a personal crisis...'

'My father and I don't have private or personal conversations,' Leo parried drily, and he closed a hand round hers to turn her back in the direction of the main reception room. 'A wife as a third party is very welcome. Panos can get very emotional.'

The distaste with which Leo admitted that truth about his father spoke volumes to Letty. Leo evidently respected men who concealed their feelings more, but Letty considered that attitude archaic.

As they entered the room the older man leapt to his feet and greeted his son in a flood of distraught Greek, which made Letty wish very much that she had made it up the stairs because it didn't feel right to her to be present at such a meeting when she barely knew Leo's father. Leo replied to him in Greek and in what sounded like a bracing tone but whatever he said etched an expression of grief-stricken horror on Panos's face and he fell back down on the sofa and sobbed as though his heart would break.

'What on earth did you say?' Letty whispered.

'That she's been having affairs for over twenty years,' Leo murmured in an undertone.

'Is that how you would normally comfort some-one who's just had their heart broken?' Letty snapped back in disbelief that Leo had chosen that particular moment to drop even worse news on his father about his estranged wife.

'No, but it is essential that he understands *right now* that her betrayal is not an isolated episode which he can forgive or overlook,' Leo proffered without shame.

'I disagree,' said Letty, approaching the older man and ordering some tea and supper for him before sit-ting down beside him to offer him the compassion that his son appeared to lack.

Yes, even at that point she grasped that Leo and his late sister had suffered as children at his stepmother's unmaternal hands and that, as adults, they and even Ana's children had been shoved out of their father's life at Katrina's behest. And Katrina had even tried to get Leo into bed. She fully understood that Katrina was a nasty corrupt woman, but she also understood that Panos Romanos genuinely loved her and was en-titled to sympathetic support from his son, who was, aside of the children, his only surviving family. And what she saw was that Leo was not prepared to offer that support because he despised his father's ongoing attachment to Katrina and the evidence of his grief over the loss of her.

Leo was aware that Letty thought he was being cruel but he knew better. He was being cruel to be kind. Now that Katrina's infidelity was out in the open, it was time to be honest rather than offer empty consolations. Watching his father grip both of Letty's hands and sob out English words, Leo rolled his eyes and walked out of the room. How could he have a father with so little control over his emotions? He cringed inwardly at the thought of ever allowing a woman to bring him down that low. It was shameful, utterly shameful for a man to be so infatuated with a woman that he thought his life was at an end because she had betrayed him. Leo assured himself that he would never descend to such a level of weakness. He didn't *need* any woman and he never would, and seeing his father in such a state only reinforced that warning.

By the time Letty finally contrived to persuade Panos that he needed to go to bed and sleep, it was almost dawn and he had told her the whole story of his two marriages from start to finish. She wished Leo had stayed for those revelations because they might have made him a little less judgemental. If there was one thing she could do for Leo, it would be to persuade him to talk to his father about Leo's mother and what their marriage had been like because Leo had put his mother on a saint's pedestal at the age of six and had made a lot of wrong assumptions about his father. Unfortunately, Leo would probably be very resistant to the idea that there were two sides to every story.

When she entered the bedroom she had been using it was disconcerting for her to meet Leo walking out of the bathroom with only a towel linked round his lean hips. 'Why are you in here?' she queried wearily, too worn out by her hours of comforting Panos to voice it as anything more than a fleetingly curious question.

'We are not sleeping apart any more,' Leo informed her. 'How is he?'

Letty stopped dead. 'Do you actually *care*? I mean, you just walked out and left me with him!' she said bitterly.

'I've been waiting for over twenty years for Katrina to be exposed as the monster she is,' Leo countered unapologetically. 'Her infidelity was widely known. She made my father a laughing stock and the only reason I didn't intervene and tell him the truth about her sooner was that she made him happy and I didn't want to be the messenger. Forgive me if I find it too much of a challenge to cry crocodile tears over the reality that she's now going to become his ex-wife.'

'You need to talk to your father about his marriage to your mother. You need to hear what that was like.'

'Who the hell do you think you are to drag my mother into this sordid situation?' Leo launched at her, wholly taken aback by that advice.

'Someone who, thanks to your walk-out tonight, knows rather more than I feel I should about your background,' Letty observed heavily. 'Seriously, Leo. You need to get over yourself and talk to your dad.'

Leo stiffened defensively. 'It's not a matter of getting over myself—'

'No, it's a matter of setting aside your prejudice and taking a fresh look at old history—'

'You could simply just tell me what he told you,' Leo stated impatiently.

'No. It's not my business,' Letty said succinctly. 'It's father and son stuff. And now I'm going to bed and I'm going to sleep for hours.'

Leo was transfixed by that little conversation while cursing Letty's sense of honour in feeling that it was not her place to share such stuff with him second-hand because he had never had a personal chat with his father in his entire life and he wasn't looking forward to the prospect. How would he even approach such a challenge? Curiosity, however, was pulling at him.

'Letty's wonderful,' his father assured him over lunch, when he came downstairs. 'An amazing woman. So kind and thoughtful and loving. You're very lucky.'

Leo ordered coffee on the veranda and sat down there with his father for the first time in many years. Panos still looked worn, his eyes bloodshot, his weathered face still puffy from his distress the night before. Leo was seriously hoping that he didn't start crying again because he didn't think he would cope very well with that but, now that the truth about Katrina was finally out, he was learning that he *did* feel more sympathetic towards his father's plight than he had ever imagined he would.

Panos explained how, having missed his flight to Athens, he had returned unexpectedly to the hotel, where he had discovered Katrina in bed with one of Leo and Letty's wedding guests. Leo nodded and answered his father's questions about why he had remained silent for so long about Katrina's affairs. Leo gave him the honest answer and went on to ask the kind of questions about his mother that it had never even occurred to him to ask before. And what he learned then rocked his world and his perceptions about his family. He discovered then that he *could* handle the tears shining in the older man's eyes. He discovered that those tears didn't seem so weak once he was better aware of Panos's experiences. He also appreciated that he owed his bride enormous gratitude for pushing him into that long-overdue dialogue with his only surviving parent.

For that reason, when Letty finally reappeared, surrounded by leaping, jumping kids and with Theon tucked securely on one hip, Leo experienced one of those increasingly rare moments when he wished there were no children in his life because he wanted Letty all to himself and he couldn't have her. Even his father gravitated straight to her as though drawn by the magnet of her warmth and smiles. Leo wanted those smiles all to himself, he registered in surprise at that acknowledgement.

Over dinner, Letty rifled through the letters that had arrived that day for her and extracted one that provoked a huge grin from her. 'I've got an interview next week,' she told him.

Leo frowned. 'For what?'

'To return to medical school,' Letty replied happily. 'I've applied for entrance for next year because I thought the kids and I should have the rest of this year to bond.'

Leo wondered when *he* would get the chance to bond with her and then questioned why he was having such a weird thought when they were already married. 'I'm sure they'll rearrange the interview for you,' he commented.

Letty frowned. 'There's no need to rearrange it. Popi returns to school next week, so it all dovetails perfectly.'

'Popi can return to London with one of the nannies and the rest of the kids while you stay on here. I have meetings in Athens next week,' Leo pointed out equably, certain he had found the perfect solution.

Letty wrinkled her nose. 'Oh, that won't do. We

can't separate the children and Popi shouldn't be in that huge house alone.'

'Alone with a domestic staff of at least ten people,' Leo slotted in drily, wishing yet again that Letty didn't place literally everyone else's needs ahead of his. '*I* want you to stay here with me next week.'

Letty opened and closed her mouth a couple of times and then encountered her father-in-law's curious gaze and opted to remain silent. She would talk to Leo in private, *fight* with him without an audience because she had not the slightest doubt that it would be a fight when Leo spoke in that *my way or the highway* measured tone.

'Leo…?' she murmured from the office doorway once the children were in bed and his father had gone down to the village to catch up with old friends.

Leo frowned down at his laptop and then glanced up, immediately thinking how incredibly beautiful she was, even in worn jeans and a sweater. Maybe it was the appeal of *au naturel* to a man who had never had that option with a woman before, he reasoned absently. There was faint colour in her cheeks and with her hair tumbling round her shoulders just a little messily she still contrived to look amazingly appealing to his eyes, and thinking about that wildly sensual little encounter in his manager's office made him instantly hard.

'Yes?' His voice emerged huskily.

'I have to return to London next week and I'm taking all the kids as well,' Letty told him bluntly.

Leo frowned. 'But I'd prefer you to remain here with me.'

Letty drew in a deep breath. 'Leo…you married me to be a mother figure to the children, so please allow me to occasionally know what's best for them. Popi would be upset to be parted from her sister and brothers and I want to attend that interview, *not* rearrange it. Don't forget that my right to return to studying medicine is in our prenup.'

All of a sudden Leo could feel his usually very even and controlled temper threatening to go nuclear on him. He realised that it was her reference to that wretched prenuptial agreement that set him off, not to mention his father's disturbing revelations about his marriage to Leo's mother. Had the document been sitting in front of him at that moment he would have ripped it to shreds. 'Does that mean you can't compromise?' he pressed in a curt undertone.

'I won't compromise when it comes to being straight about what the children need,' Letty countered squarely. 'I'm sorry, that's not something that can be or should be negotiated.'

Leo released his breath on a long slow hiss and vaulted upright. Stunning dark golden eyes locked to her like grappling hooks. 'We're newly married. I am *trying* to be reasonable here!' he bit out in a harsh undertone. 'I want you to make what I want a priority— your *main* priority.'

Letty suppressed a sigh and cursed all the very many willing-to-please women who had worked tirelessly together to imbue Leo, the ultimate Greek tycoon, with such an outdated set of values. 'This time I'm going to say no because the children are still too vulnerable to suffer separation or too much disruption…but another time, when they are better adjusted to their life with us, I *will* try to accommodate your wishes.'

Leo ground his teeth together. He totally understood

her reasoning, even sympathised, but they had been married only a week and had spent very little time together. Now they would be apart another week and soon after that he had a trip to the US planned. Exactly when was he going to find time to *be* with his wife? Surely that should be of crucial importance to her too because without a functioning marriage, where would the children be then?

Feeling very dissatisfied with Leo's reaction, Letty went off to dig out a book and read while striving to put that exchange behind her and not brood. She had to be reasonable, she instructed herself. She was dealing with a pretty spoilt and selfish man, who was still learning to deal with the changes children brought to life. Leo wasn't likely to turn into a gilded saint overnight and her constantly reminding him that the kids had to come first seemed to be a particular goad. She wondered why that was when he had only married her to be their substitute mother.

She was tossing and turning, sleepless and still trying to fathom the mystery that was Leo's tangled and contradictory thought processes, when Leo slid into bed beside her, startling her. 'I thought you were still working,' she commented.

'No. I need to make the most of my wife while she's still here and available,' Leo told her, stripping her out of her silky nightgown with ruthless efficiency.

Rather exciting efficiency, Letty conceded, pulses picking up speed, heart pounding before his mouth even enclosed hers. She lifted up to him, wildly enthralled by the lean, hard muscular length of him pressing down on her. She was learning so much about herself that her head was spinning, registering that even when Leo set her teeth on edge she continued to crave him and was reassured now rather than annoyed to find herself still an object of desire. She loved him so much, she thought passionately, small fingers smoothing caressingly over his satin-smooth broad shoulders and up into his silky hair. There was no rhyme or reason to it but Leo was *it* for her, the summit of her dreams, her most insane fantasies and the key to her happiness and accepting that reality unnerved her a little.

'Get with the programme,' Leo breathed, gazing down at her with eyes that glittered jet black in the moonlight. 'You're a thousand miles away inside your head.'

'How do you know that?' Letty asked with a look of guilt.

'Because you're the only woman who has ever treated me like that and it is *not* a compliment,' he murmured ruefully.

'Well, maybe I'm disconnecting because you're always in control,' Letty suggested, planting her hands against his chest and sending him flat on the mattress beside her because she was embarrassed by the truth that she had floated away inside her anxious thoughts.

Letty revelled in Leo's surprise and she chuckled. 'So lie back and think of Greece like Victorian women used to do—'

Obligingly, Leo stretched, naked and bronzed and awesomely attractive, all lithe and sexy and willing to be seduced. Letty grinned down at him. 'Now, I warn you I may be a little clumsy at first, but practice is crucial,' she pointed out.

Leo lay back and surveyed the wonder that was Letty, who never ever did anything the way he expected and, as he was discovering, it was an extraordinarily fascinating quality in a woman. He had been seduced by women to whom sex was an art form, but every stroke of Letty's uncertain fingers, every tiny enthusiastic kiss from her generous mouth had an infinitely stronger effect on him. And whether it was the medical training or the truth that he had married a superbly sensual woman, it was the sexiest hour he had ever enjoyed, and he told her so afterwards.

'Nonsense,' she told him, a little crossly because he had stopped her at what she considered to be a crucial point and before he could climax and she felt cheated.

Leo spread her out across the bed. 'Now it's my turn.'

He found her ready, *aching* for him, and he plunged and she gasped in delight at the sheer rush of sensation flaring and flaming through her needy body. She wanted more and he gave her more until containing that pleasure became too much and she rose against him with a keening cry as sweet gratification flooded her in an unstoppable rush.

'You will miss me when you're in London, *meli mou*,' Leo pronounced with satisfaction.

And Letty saw no good reason to deny the truth because sometimes that was just the way the cookie crumbled. 'Yes, but life throws you lemons occasionally when you really want peaches.'

Leo laughed out loud in appreciation and held her close because he was already thinking of round two.

And she lay there, feeling unexpectedly secure and happy, thinking *I can do this*.

CHAPTER TEN

LEO WATCHED IN near disbelief as his father climbed into the helicopter with the children, the nannies and Letty: *he* was going to London too.

Letty had invited Panos, pointing out to Leo that the grandkids were a great source of distraction for the older man and that, apparently, *he* enjoyed Christmas shopping. And, seemingly, she planned to be doing a great deal of shopping, even though it was only November and Christmas had never started for Leo before Christmas Eve, when a last-minute dash settled all his requirements.

'But I've got so many people to buy for now and no credit limit!' Letty had enthused with starry eyes and not a hint of the greed Leo was accustomed to seeing in a woman's face. He knew that Letty was already imagining the pleasure she could give to others with her gifts and he frowned at that oddity and yet smiled at the same time.

Even so, his entire family abandoning him sucked, Leo conceded grimly. Like rats leaving a sinking ship, they had left him alone, the wagons circling Letty as though she were a bonfire on a winter's day. A text arrived on his phone and he glanced down at it, his jawline hardening as he recognised that he had a small problem from his more eventful past that required handling…and not with gracious tact either.

In the week that followed, Leo had a great deal to think about because he was still coming to terms with what his father had confessed about his marriage to Leo's mother, Athena. Having his assumptions about both parents so brutally rearranged had shaken Leo, reminding him that he had been a clueless six-year-old when his mother, Athena, died, giving birth to his sister, Ana.

Athena had been an extremely wealthy heiress, an only child of the Romanos dynasty with an authoritarian widowed father. Part of the marriage settlement had entailed Panos's agreement to assume the Romanos name on the marriage. On their wedding night Athena had admitted that she had only married Panos because her father had threatened to disinherit her in favour of his nephew if she did not marry and have a child. She had also disclosed the truth that, having been abused as a little girl by a long-dead uncle, she had no interest in sex but would engage in it solely to conceive as she too longed to have a child of her own. Leo's father had been urged to seek sexual pleasure elsewhere by his bride.

Learning those facts had utterly transformed Leo's image of his father, whom he had long tended to view rather as a fortune-hunting adulterous gigolo who had taken advantage of a naïve heiress. Ironically, if anything, it was his *father* who had suffered rejection from the woman he'd loved and who had continued to love the troubled woman until she died.

Katrina had come *after* Athena's death, *not* before, as Leo had always believed and his father, overwhelmed to find himself apparently wanted and loved at last, had fallen fast and hard and had swiftly remarried, hoping for a more normal marriage. By the end of that admission, Leo had sympathised with the older man, understanding, as Panos did not, that he had been targeted by Katrina, who had assumed he was much richer than he truly was. The family trust had ensured that Athena's children inherited virtually everything that had been hers, limiting his father to only an ongoing income from the estate while he was raising his two children and, after that, a considerably smaller income.

In short, Leo was suffering a great deal of regret when it came to his father. Panos had been stitched up in the marriage settlement by Leo's wily grandfather, duped into his first marriage and had then fallen madly in love with a mercenary and unscrupulous woman. Yet Leo had never reached out to the older man and had never offered him financial help, had, effectively, never done anything but judge on false premises and found Panos wanting. That awareness sat on his conscience like a giant weight and he would have liked to discuss it with Letty, only she wasn't there and the wretched house echoed with her absence...

In contrast to Leo, Letty, *initially*, had a wonderful time back in London. She enjoyed a most successful interview relating to her return to medical school and was assured of her place the following year. Her mother was slowly becoming fully mobile again and it had transformed her life. She was ready to return to being the active, interested parent whom Letty recalled from her younger years and she was quite overpowered by Leo's generous signing over of the lovely apartment, where she was now living in comfort. It was a challenge for Gillian to grasp the extent of the Romanos wealth but a visit to her daughter's marital home in London helped to dispel her misapprehension that her son-in-law had spent money he couldn't afford to spend on her.

Her half-brothers, on the other hand, had converted to their new lifestyle with an enthusiasm that was slightly embarrassing to Letty, but the sight of Leo's games room in the mansion provoked them into excited whoops of rare teenage enthusiasm. Assured that her family's future was now rosy beyond belief from what it had been only weeks earlier, Letty could only be happy at what her marriage had achieved for those she loved.

Panos, meanwhile, had found a compassionate listener in her mother, Gillian, because both of them had suffered the misery of having an unfaithful partner. At the same time, Panos, having recovered from the first shock of Katrina's betrayal, was already moving on and was very much occupied getting to know the grandchildren that Katrina had rigorously kept him apart from to finally become a loving grandfather to his daughter's orphaned offspring. He had also admitted to Letty that his new closeness to Leo meant a great deal to him because Leo's reserve had kept him at a distance for years.

In the meantime, Letty was resisting Popi's pleas to put up Christmas decorations in November, so excited was the little girl at the prospect of the festive season. Apparently, her late mother, Ana, had always done so and Letty was tempted but stood firm on the point until Gillian shoved a gossip page under her nose

when they were having coffee one morning, ten days
after her return to London.

'I think it's sickening what these journalists try to
do to rich men like Leo!' Letty's mother opined in disgust. 'There he is, having a business lunch or a meal
with a friend, and they try to make it into something
sordid just to get a story!'

Letty glanced down at the black and white photo
of Leo caught in profile, smiling at the woman on the
other side of the table, and her breath caught in her
throat because it was Dido, the beautiful actress who
had pursued Leo with such relentless interest on the
two occasions when she had met her.

'She's an old flame,' she said and for her mother's
benefit she forced her shoulders into a careless shrug
and smiled, keen to hide that she felt as though someone had just planted a knife in her heart. She understood from her mother's face that she was genuinely
worried that her daughter had married a man who slept
around, just as her ex-husband had.

'*Oh...*' Gillian responded uncomfortably, searching
her daughter's expression for any sign of concern. 'But
you don't think *that*—?'

'No, of course not!' That was when Letty's previ-
ously unexercised acting ability really kicked in and
she contrived to laugh to reassure the older woman.
'*Not* Leo,' she declared firmly. 'He's not like Robbie
in any way.'

'I didn't think so,' Gillian agreed with clear relief
on her daughter's behalf. 'You wouldn't stand for that.'

'No, I wouldn't,' Letty fibbed with a frog in her
throat and a fierce attempt to hold back the shocked
tears stinging the back of her eyes as she thought about

that prenuptial agreement and Leo's determination to keep it in place.

Well, Leo had *warned* her, hadn't he? Really, why was she so shocked by what had been written in the stars, never mind imposed in legal terms, even *before* they'd married?

Panos wandered in to join the women and Letty took the opportunity to make an excuse and leave the older couple chatting. Inside her chest she could feel her heart cracking down the middle and she went into the bathroom she had been naively expecting to share with Leo as a couple, closed the door and broke down into sobbing misery.

She would allow herself thirty minutes in which to grieve the loss of hope and faith which she had just endured. Leo had been with Dido and no way could she credit that it had been innocent when she was aware that the actress was so desperate to regain his interest. Dido was the sort of woman always ready to pounce on an available man and, evidently, Leo *was* still available. He had been unfaithful to her, exactly as she had feared. *Deal with it*, she told herself fiercely…but *how*?

She needed to protect herself, needed to be strong and, ironically, being with Leo, living with Leo and challenging him *had* made her stronger, she acknowledged wryly. She was tough as old boots, she told herself; she could do it.

After all, nothing had gone the way she had expected in their marriage. First, they had been in agreement that their marriage would be sexless and then Leo had changed his mind and changed her mind as well. She had then swung back on the defensive once she'd appreciated that Leo was still not willing to surrender his freedom to sleep with whomever he chose. For the space of a week they had been extremely polite to each other, but that week had concluded with her breaking her promise to herself that he *had* to remain faithful and she was now thinking of that thoroughly wanton joining on the office desk of Leo's new club. Recalling that episode her face burned, and it burned even more when she looked back on the sensual indulgence of that last week she had spent on the island with Leo.

They had been like rabbits, she thought shamefacedly, her entire body tightening and heating in acknowledgement of her own weakness. *She* hadn't been able to keep her hands off him. It was not as though Leo had been sex-starved at the time of her departure, it was not as though there were any kind of excuse for his meeting up with Dido again. Maybe there *was* such a thing as sex addiction, the celebrity excuse for misbehaviour, but the suggestion of rehabilitation wasn't one she felt equal to tackling with Leo. He would probably just laugh, she reflected, stricken, because evidently he saw sexual freedom as one of life's necessities and he was determined not to live any other way.

And that was the guy she had *knowingly* married and fallen crazily in love with, she reminded herself with dogged honesty. He had been upfront on the fidelity score from the very beginning.

Her head was starting to ache and she checked herself in the mirror, appalled to see how red her nose was and how swollen her eyes were from her giving way so freely to her distress. Yes, thirty minutes of self-pity was all she would allow herself for hadn't she agreed to the marriage? And wasn't she very happy with what that marriage had achieved for her family?

Yes, she was.

And if she divorced Leo she would lose the children and she loved them too. Occasional access to Popi, Sybella, Cosmo and Theon would not compensate any of them for such a brutal severance. The children would suffer, and she did not have an automatic right to write off their need for her as a mother simply because marriage to Leo was turning out to be more of a nightmare than she had innocently foreseen.

Life wasn't that simple, she acknowledged ruefully. The innocents in her family and his would be hurt by her departure from Leo's life. If she broke up with Leo, her mother would want to sell the apartment she lived in and return the money to him because that was the sort of woman she was. Accepting such a massive gift from a member of her family, as Leo currently was, was one thing but retaining it as the proceeds of a very short-lived marriage would strike Gillian as something else entirely.

So, she had to be tough and adapt to being married to an adulterous husband, didn't she? She would *stay* married to Leo. She would hide her hurt and act as if everything in the garden was rosy and wonderful because only then could she keep everybody around her happy.

Her eyes misted again just when she was managing to use concealer on her eyes and she blinked rapidly. On one level she didn't want to live like that but just then she didn't feel she had much of a choice unless she was prepared to destroy everything that their marriage had achieved...

And just as Panos had required a distraction from his depressed thoughts about his broken marriage,

Letty registered that she needed one too. Leo phoned her every day and while, only hours ago, she had been longing for his arrival in London, now she was considering it fortunate that it would be a couple of weeks before he returned. His absence would give her time to come to terms with his infidelity in whatever way she could, and she had to stop loving and missing him as well because that was an even worse recipe for disaster and she would have to live in a continual state of being hurt and disillusioned.

So, step one in her own necessary emotional rehabilitation, she told herself in her mirror reflection, was to *stop* loving Leo, step back, *look after herself...* That was the sensible approach.

By the time she was descending the stairs it was lunchtime, Leo's father and her mother were still chatting and Popi was home from school, proudly displaying a homemade Christmas card with drawings of her family that made Letty crack up in genuine appreciation. Ana's children were learning to see her and Leo as their family unit and she was proud of that achievement and resolved not to damage it with what she told herself would be selfish oversensitivity. She would cope with his infidelity because she was tough, she reminded herself doggedly, but she wouldn't continue to sleep with him. They would have the convenient marriage he had first wanted while she devoted herself to raising the children and completing her studies. That way she would preserve her dignity and her strength.

As for the distraction she sensed she currently needed while she came to terms with the effective end of her intimacy with Leo, she decided to go for an over-the-top Christmas to delight the children and keep herself busy. Christmas was going to start in November for them, just as it had when they had still had their birthparents. And she was going to buy a family dog and buy a present for Leo, even though he didn't deserve one. Yes, she would be treating him perfectly normally by the time he flew back from the US, doubtless having sampled various other female bodies during his time away from her, she told herself sourly. He would not even suspect that anything was amiss with her. She would be solid steel and calm and quite unbothered by what she had discovered…

Leo arrived home on the first day of December and so unrecognisable was his home he almost walked straight out of the door again. A scruffy terrier rushed up to him, sniffed him thoroughly and then retreated to bark as though he were an intruder. That was odd enough, but the transformation of the entrance hall could only put him in mind of a Christmas grotto gone mad. There was not an inch of space left because everywhere he looked there were glittering trees, giant stuffed reindeer and elves, stockings and tinsel and holly and decorations. A log fire roared in the grate of a fireplace that had never been lit before. He had vague memories of his sister's house during the festive season but even his kid sister, bless her heart, hadn't gone for anything quite so magnificent or…extreme.

Leo smiled though, registering that Letty treated Christmas as an explosion of glitter and good cheer, which was probably exactly what the children loved. He did notice the absence of mistletoe though, just as he noticed that the warm welcome he had subconsciously expected from his wife was missing. At that point the children came rushing downstairs and he was greeted with all the enthusiasm he could've wished for, attended by cries of 'Unc' Leo' and 'Daddy Leo', because evidently the children hadn't yet made up their minds what to call him.

Of course, all his conversations with Letty on the phone had somehow always turned into conversations about the children. No matter how hard he had tried to take those talks in a more personal direction, he had been redirected to discussing his nephews and nieces. The whole time he was away he had felt starved of Letty, as if she was a presence that could only be pinned down and enjoyed when she was face to face with him. He had sensed the difference in her attitude towards him; he did not consider himself an imaginative man and it bothered him, seriously disturbed his usual rock-solid assurance with women. Something was badly wrong with Letty and that brought him out in a cold sweat of anxiety that he had never experienced before.

'Where's Letty?' he asked with a rather fake smile when his father and mother-in-law appeared in the doorway of the drawing room.

'She had to rush out for something and she took Theon with her,' Gillian imparted anxiously. 'I did warn her that she might miss you but she's got *so* into this Christmas stuff—'

'It's wonderful that she has,' Leo commented, not having failed to notice that he had three happy kids bouncing and chattering at his side when only months earlier they had all been subdued and tense. 'How are you doing, Dad?'

'Oh, I'm feeling much more myself,' Panos Romanos assured him with a grin and a hand that Leo noted, surprisingly, had been anchored on Gillian's slim hip. 'Friends and family, that's what my life is all about now.'

Bit more than friends, Leo reckoned by the very sociable way the older couple kept on exchanging glances. 'I'm disappointed Letty's not here,' he admitted. 'I mean, I've been gone for weeks and—'

The front door opened, and Letty blew in with the baby clamped to one hip. 'Leo, I'm so sorry I wasn't here!' she carolled because their respective parents were standing there as an audience and she didn't want either of them to suspect that anything was amiss between her and Leo.

Passing over Theon to the nanny at the foot of the stairs, whereupon he wailed like a banshee in protest, Letty stripped off her coat and gloves and feasted her attention on Leo. Still absolutely gorgeous, clad in a cashmere overcoat on top of one of his exquisitely well-fitted business suits, he *still* took her breath away. That was a disappointment, she allowed, because she had tried to make him less sexy in her recollections, worked hard at trying to make herself less vulnerable. But there he stood and even travel-worn and badly in need of a shave, stubble outlining his wide sensual mouth and somehow accentuating his fantastic bone structure and oh, those eyes... Well, they certainly weren't the windows of the soul, she scolded herself. His eyes were spectacular but they had to carry a hint of an innately manipulative and secretive personality, she instructed herself. After all, this was the man she had spent pretty much most of a week in bed with, striving to be the sensual woman every man was supposed to want and crave…and where had it got her?

Well, he had given her a great deal of sexual satisfaction and then he had still gone on to get into bed with other women. Oh, yes, she was convinced that there had been *more* than that encounter with Dido, for the opportunities to flirt and seduce for a man of Leo's looks and wealth probably came up everywhere he went, particularly when he was travelling. This was a guy she literally could not trust out of her sight, she reminded herself sternly.

'So, how was your trip?' Letty asked Leo with an interest that even he could see was false, for she was not a good dissembler and her expressive face was a dead giveaway.

'Like every other trip.'

What the hell had he done? Leo was asking himself in frustration, striving to think of something he might have said on the phone that could have brought about such a change in her. She had left Ios acting warm and confiding and caring and all of a sudden that was gone. He watched in disbelief as Letty sped upstairs, clearly keen to leave him behind, and that was the final straw that broke his control and sent him stalking up the stairs in her wake.

Letty was locked in the bathroom, frantically washing and rewashing her hands, unaware that she was doing it while she struggled to work out how she was supposed to deal with Leo, now that he was back in the house.

She had decorated the whole house for Christmas. There were trees everywhere but the bedrooms. They now had George the dog, a rescue animal with more bad habits than a criminal. George chewed everything from shoes to rugs. He stole food. He tried to get into bed with the children. Much like Leo, George had no boundaries but, unlike Leo, he was very loving. Leo would totally freak out if he knew she was comparing him, even in passing, with a homeless animal, she conceded, finally drying her hands and pulling herself together, although the tendency to cry over the pain she was suppressing still hovered over her like a threatening black cloud. It had been easier to pretend to be happy when Leo was absent. Now that he was back it was a huge challenge for her.

'Letty!' A sharp knock sounded on the door and she froze like a burglar caught in the act of theft before swallowing hard and opening the door.

'Sorry… I'm sure you want a shower,' she said in a brittle tone.

'No, surprisingly enough,' Leo murmured with only the merest hint of sarcasm, 'I wanted to see my wife.'

Halfway to the bedroom door to leave, Letty stilled. *'Oh?'* she said, spinning reluctantly back.

'Luckily for me, you are a lousy actress,' Leo continued tautly, subjecting her to a feverishly intense scrutiny. 'I'm not blind, Letty. What's wrong? Obviously there's something wrong because you've *changed.'*

Letty lost colour and stiffened, wondering how on earth he had so quickly registered that change on her part while she had flattered herself with the belief that she was treating him as she always had.

'We've always been honest with each other,' Leo bit out harshly in the dragging silence that had fallen between them.

'I saw a newspaper photo of you having lunch with

Dido,' Letty framed flatly, accusingly, failing utterly to hold back that tone of condemnation. 'I didn't require anything else to know that you'd returned to your former way of life.'

'*Theé mou*, Letty,' Leo growled. 'I'm not guilty of that cardinal error. I lunched with Dido, no argument on that score. For a long time I've been a theatre angel. I back stage productions that are likely to be successful. That's how I first met Dido years ago. She was a very good investment.'

'Investment?' Letty echoed with raised brows and a frown. 'I think your ties were rather more intimate than that.'

'*Were* being the correct word. Eight years ago, Letty, and there has been no sexual intimacy between us since that ended after an affair that lasted a couple of months,' Leo clarified. 'Dido, who is fiercely ambitious, chases me purely for my wealth in the hope of persuading me to invest in her next stage production. But, to be frank, I only had lunch with her in the first place to tell her to back off with the texts and the allegedly accidental meetings and the pretence that we were once a couple. We were never a couple. We were never close…and that's the truth.'

Letty clamped her hands together because they were trembling, and she didn't want him to notice that humiliating fact. 'I'm not sure I can believe—'

'I'm afraid you *have* to because I will not accept that one stupid photo can come between you and me!' Leo countered in a raw undertone.

'No…' Letty made an almost clumsy movement with one hand to express her continuing tension. 'What came between us was your insistence on retaining your freedom as a married man, which meant that naturally when I saw you in company with Dido, I assumed—'

Leo cast off his coat and dug a hand into the inner pocket of his suit jacket to withdraw a folded document. 'Our prenuptial agreement with that clause removed. You have to sign it too with a witness before it's legal but please note the date when I signed…'

Her throat tight, her brow indented with uncertainty as she accepted the document and rifled through it to check that the that offensive clause had genuinely been removed and not simply rephrased and slipped in someplace else. He had signed it within a day of her leaving the island, which was a surprise.

As Letty sat down at the foot of the bed to read it all properly, Leo's mouth quirked with appreciation. 'You're never going to take me on trust, are you?'

'Probably not,' she agreed, setting the prenuptial contract down beside her on the bed and adding, 'So… I have to ask…what led to this sudden change of heart. I mean, I know that only a few days before you signed that you were still vehemently insisting that you had to keep that freedom.'

Put on the spot that directly, Leo grimaced. 'Finding out what my father went through, married to my mother, had an enormous effect on me. It knocked me for six,' he confessed with faint embarrassment. 'I have ignored him pretty much all my life because I held onto unfair assumptions about his character but, when I really thought about it, my resentment came down to his inability to control Katrina and the way she treated my sister and me as children. I blamed him for that because *he* married her. Now I appreciate that he had no idea what was going on in his own home because she never treated us badly when he was around.'

Letty nodded. 'You had a real heart to heart with him, didn't you?' she pressed.

'And I have you to thank for that because without your intervention I would have gone on with the same mind-set.' He sighed with regret. 'Now I have the father I always wanted but didn't appreciate. Katrina being gone from our lives makes that possible.'

'Does he *know*…? I mean, about Katrina coming on to you as well?' Letty enquired with a grimace of distaste.

'Yes. There had to be total honesty from both of us. He was devastated when I told him, but I think it also helped him to accept that Katrina never loved him the way he believed she did and, in a sense, it drew a line under all the rest of it,' he completed grimly. 'I notice that his state of mind is much improved since I last saw him.'

'Yes, Mum and he are great buddies,' Letty re-marked. 'I understand everything that you're sharing with me but I still don't understand why you finally decided to remove that clause from the agreement. Just to please me? To lull me into a false sense of security? Why?'

'Do you believe me about Dido? She was after my financial backing, not me personally,' Leo stated in frustration. 'She's very persistent, and I realised that it would take a personal meeting and a blunt refusal to get her to back off. She's so vain that she couldn't see that flattery and flirtation weren't going to get her anywhere with me, particularly after she had offended my wife. That's what that lunch was about.'

Letty nodded, wryly amused at that 'offended my wife', thrown in as if it was a fact of life that Leo should object to such a sin. 'Yes, I believe that the lunch was innocent,' she conceded, feeling a great rolling wave of wounded pain evaporating from her stiff body as she sat there. 'So, according to you, you're going to be faithful now…or are you still in the *trying* to be faithful phase?' she asked suspiciously.

'No, I'm all yours, *entirely* yours,' Leo stressed, a faint smile lightening the lingering strain etched around his wide sensual mouth. 'For good.'

Letty frowned. *'For good?'* she queried in astonishment.

'You're not grasping what I'm trying to tell you here, *yineka mou*,' Leo lamented. 'A gorgeous blonde in biker leathers came into my office and blew my whole life apart in the space of a day. Within a week I was more fascinated by her than any woman I have ever met. Within two weeks I was so hot for her I was performing mental acrobatics to persuade her into being mine, *really* mine…but I hadn't quite come to terms with what I was signing up for. That was my mistake. I came at you like a bull in a china shop *before* I had thought it all through.'

'Are you talking about me?' Letty whispered uncertainly.

'Letty, who the hell else would I be talking about?' he groaned, crouching down in front of her. 'When I said I'm yours for good, I was telling you that I fell head over heels in love with you like a stupid teenager.'

Her lashes fluttered up on wide green eyes as she studied him fixedly. 'Like a very bright but emotionally stunted teenager,' she parried.

'I knew you would put another spin on it...so to try romance with an unromantic and very practical woman and me being a man who has never tried that before either,' Leo admitted ruefully, 'I bought *this*...'

In a state of disbelief at Leo telling her that he had fallen in love with her, Letty watched as he threaded a diamond eternity ring on her finger next to her wedding band. 'Is that the one I *didn't* get for my birthday?' she asked uneasily.

'No, it's an entirely new and much more expensive one and this time it truly expresses what I feel—that I've got to have you for ever,' Leo confessed.

'Oh...' Letty was speechless, plunged in the misery of believing she was being forced to welcome home an unfaithful husband and then sent shooting back up to heights she had never dared to even dream of, before being told that she was loved. Leo *loved* her. It felt as if she was living a dream, a dizzy impossible girlish dream, and she burst into floods of tears, her self-control destroyed.

'*Theós mou*...what did I say?' Leo exclaimed, vaulting back upright again and hauling her up into the circle of his arms.

'I'm just so h-happy!' Letty sobbed into his shoulder. 'I was worried you were a sex addict rather than a player and I didn't think you'd consider therapy—'

'Listen to me for once. I was never a player. I never did one-night stands. I picked one woman and would be with her for a couple of months...a mistress, rather than a lover, though,' Leo hastened to explain.

'But why...*mistresses*?' Letty demanded, struggling to get the stupid, far too emotional, tears back under control because she knew he had to think she was crazy to react like that to a declaration of love.

'Think about it, Letty. I never knew love. When I was still pretty young my grandfather informed me that I would be expected to marry but that the men in my family always had mistresses. It was what he called "a tidy solution". He had one. I assumed my father had one, although he assures me he didn't. It seemed normal not to want to get involved, other than sexually, with a woman. My mother's love is the vaguest, most distant memory. My stepmother had no time for me and I soon understood that she didn't love my father either,' he explained. 'Although Panos tried to be affectionate I backed away from it because Katrina was worse if Ana or I took my father's attention away from her. I didn't know what love was. I didn't know what it felt like...'

'And what does it feel like?' she asked her volatile husband.

'Like living in a storm where everything's magnified and little things assume too much importance,' he groaned. 'When we were on the island it wasn't that I resented the time you spent with the kids, it was that I wanted more of you myself and it wasn't working out that way. Only when you were gone did I appreciate how confused I was, how everything seemed different with you and I didn't understand why until I had the space to think it through.'

'And decided that it was love? Are you sure?' Letty, ever the doubter, questioned.

Leo laughed with unholy amusement as he gazed down into her anxious face. 'Nobody was more shocked than I was to appreciate that I loved you, but then you're a pretty special woman so it's not really that surprising. You didn't want me for my money, except to help your family. You didn't want me for my body.'

'And where did you get that idea?' Letty asked as she began unbuttoning his shirt with alacrity.

'Yes, but it's not only for sex, is it?' Leo studied her. 'Although, if it is, I'm not strong enough to say no, you can't have me until you return my feelings…but do you think you could…*eventually*?'

Not impervious to the vulnerability in his stunning gaze, Letty pretended to ponder and then said, 'Truth is… I started falling in love with you that first day in your office too. There was just something about you and, apart from the commitment phobia, I liked everything else about you a lot.'

'You…*did*? You didn't show it.'

'Obviously I tried to hide the fact that I found you attractive when you told me you were suggesting a platonic marriage,' Letty pointed out. 'But somehow that inappropriate attraction just kept on getting stronger, which is why I probably succumbed on our wedding night.'

'And then I wrecked it all again within hours.' Leo sighed. 'I'm sorry, sincerely sorry that I kept on flip-flopping all over the place like a stranded fish on the shore. I didn't know what I wanted at that point, apart from you, and my brain was still fighting with this concept of sacred bonds.'

'Are you ever likely to let me forget that phrase?' Letty teased as he shed his jacket and his shirt and dragged her down on the bed with him, solely to hold her close, both arms wrapped tightly and possessively round her while she continued to contemplate her glittering eternity ring with satisfaction.

'Probably not. It doesn't feel sacred to me, but then I'm too earthy for that kind of attitude,' Leo murmured apologetically. 'But when you're not there, everything feels uncomfortable and lonely and depressing. When did you see that photo of Dido and me lunching?'

'The first week we were apart,' she said with regret.

'I knew something was wrong, but I didn't want to broach it on the phone. Didn't it cross your mind that only a man in love phones you at least three times a day?'

'Nope... I've no experience of men in love,' she reminded him. 'Oh, Leo, I've been such an idiot—and so unhappy without you.'

'Well, you're truly stuck with me now,' Leo proclaimed with unashamed approval. 'And, what's more, we're likely to have an enormous family because we are going to want to have children of our own, aren't we?'

'You mean, you're actually comfortable with that idea?' Letty asked in wonderment.

'The more the merrier,' Leo assured her. 'I really love the kids. I know I'm selfish sometimes when it comes to you, but I really like having them in our life.'

'That's good because it's likely to be years before you get a baby from me. I want to finish my training first,' Letty informed him gently.

'Enough talking and enough warnings...' Leo covered her mouth with his in a long drugging kiss before breaking free to add, 'We need some mistletoe downstairs. I want to watch my father trying to manoeuvre your mother under it.'

Letty rolled her eyes. 'It's a friendship, Leo…nothing else.'

'Want to make a bet?' Leo was convinced that, whether either party appreciated it or not, their respective parents were getting attached to each other and it was no surprise to Leo that, having finally been exposed to a normal middle-aged and kind-hearted woman, his father was attracted to her after so many years living with a brittle fashion queen many years his junior, who made constant demands for luxuries the older man could rarely afford to provide.

'No, I don't do bets,' Letty told him circumspectly, circling his beautiful mouth with her own, nipping at his lower lip the way he had taught her because, yes, she was a very fast learner in some departments. 'Allow me, though, to know my own mother better than you do…and she said, "Never ever again, that's me done," after divorcing Robbie.'

'You haven't a romantic bone in your body, Letty,' Leo groaned.

'I'll put up the mistletoe for *our* benefit,' she promised. 'Goodness knows, I've got every other Christmas extra on display.'

'Yes, I liked the giant reindeer and the elves.'

'You mightn't like them when you see what they cost.'

'I don't care. It all looks fantastic, like a real home, and I've never had that before,' he told her huskily as he began to snake down the zip on her dress by tiny increments.

'You're breaking my heart, Leo…and being far too cool and subtle—just rip it off!' Letty told him cheer-

fully. 'I love you enough to forgive you anything…
Well, just about…not other women—'

'I've got you, and I don't need anyone else. I love
you more than I ever thought I could love anyone.'

Letty stretched luxuriantly, every romantic bone in
her body that she denied twanging to that announce-
ment but, true to her determination not to get slushy,
she told him he was wearing too many clothes and it
was remarkable how fast he got out of them.

EPILOGUE

SIX YEARS LATER, Letty walked round her London home arm in arm with her mother to check that everything was in place for the important guest they were expecting. It was Christmas Eve and her grandfather, Isidore Livas, was coming to share the big day with them—and that was a development she could never have foreseen years earlier.

'I think Isidore assumed that the mother of his son's child was another disreputable druggie and downgraded all of us accordingly,' Gillian opined, her thoughts in the same place about the older man's coolness on first meeting Letty. 'Once he met me, once he realised how young I was when I gave birth to you, he changed his tune…and then you had Kristo, and a great-grandchild was the perfect gift as far as he's concerned.'

'Yes, he is amazingly attached to Kristo,' Letty conceded, racing across the hall to prevent her son from trying to climb one of the stuffed elves.

At two years of age, Leo and Letty's first child was a livewire, always into everything. George, elderly now, lay in his basket and feebly wagged his tail as they went past.

'Kristo!' Popi called as she came clattering down

the stairs with Sybella on her heels. 'Give Mummy some peace—'

'Your brother doesn't know the meaning of that word,' Letty remarked, watching Popi—at the age of eleven very much a young lady now—impose order on her son. Sybella still loved to dress up and perform, and Letty couldn't help wondering if she would eventually enter the entertainment world. Cosmo was a wannabe scientist, always doing little experiments and peering through a toy microscope.

Embarrassing as it was for a doctor to admit, however, Kristo had been an unplanned surprise package in their lives. In the midst of changing contraception, Letty had discovered that she was pregnant and had thought that it could not have happened at a worse time because she had been facing her final exams. Now she felt guilty for having thought that because Kristo, so much Leo's son, with his beautiful dark eyes and the Livas blond hair, had brought her and Leo so much joy. He had also brought Isidore hotfoot to London with a train set because apparently her unhappy Aunt Elexis was still having problems conceiving.

'Come on, Kristo,' Theon, a laidback and sturdy little boy, said to his kid brother with pity as the toddler pouted. 'We'll watch cartoons.'

'They grow up so fast. You'll probably be planning another soon, I imagine,' Letty's mother commented fondly.

'Maybe next year,' Letty responded with amusement because she lived a frantically busy life and, even six years after marrying Leo, she was still doing some form of training for her work as a GP, the hours she worked in the surgery being the best fit for their life.

Of course, she couldn't have achieved what she had without supportive staff and she knew she was blessed. Five children were a challenge but she wouldn't have had it any other way because she and Leo revelled in the rough and tumble nature of their big family and the warm love that linked them all. Panos marrying her mother the previous year had only extended the family circle. It had taken much longer for the older couple to get together than her husband had believed it would, but Panos's divorce from Katrina had been dragged out and bitterly contested. Still, Leo had spotted the first signs of mutual interest between Panos and Gillian far quicker than Letty had, but then that was classic Leo.

He was shrewd, quick to size up people, even faster at guessing their next step, which was probably why everything he touched in business seemed to turn to gold. He had even recently got his father involved as a director in a project, pretty much, she surmised, to ensure the older man could have a decent income without feeling it was charity. Her husband's relationship with his father was now close and caring.

'Why did you invite Isidore anyway?' her mother asked.

'I think he's quite lonely. Elexis is a bit of a cold fish and doesn't seem to visit him much.'

They wandered into the games room where her half-brothers, Tim and Kyle, were playing video games. Tim was at university now, Kyle studying for GCSEs, both of them well-adjusted and hardworking. Letty often thought back to that very first day she had met Leo and all the very many positives which had flowed from their marriage. It was the icing on the cake that

Leo adored her, supported her and still thought she was somehow special.

For the first year of their marriage she had feared he would suddenly shake off such feelings and appreciate that she was really pretty ordinary but, mercifully, that hadn't happened. Leo's love had all the longevity she had craved, and she was incredibly happy with him.

They spent a lot of the summer on the island of Ios, where the children enjoyed the kind of freedom they couldn't safely have anywhere else. Kristo had been conceived on Ios at the beach cottage where they always went when they wanted to relax alone and he was named for Leo's late grandfather, an honour that went with the proviso that Leo promised never ever to tell their son that marriage and sex were separate entities and mistresses were normal for a Romanos man.

Leo breezed through the door, laden with parcels and bags, and was surrounded by children and even the dog, who made the effort to leave his basket for Leo's benefit. He smiled at Gillian and asked if she and Panos were still joining them for dinner with Isidore that evening. 'We need the support. He's a chilly personality.'

'But we're working on him!' Letty laughed, grabbing Leo's hand as he deposited his bags on a bench seat. 'Come here, you... I've missed you!' she exclaimed, winding her arms round his neck.

'We're not under the mistletoe,' Leo carped.

'As if that would stop you!' Letty told him as Gillian melted discreetly out of the front door, where her husband awaited her.

'They're being *gross*,' Cosmo complained with an eight-year-old's disgust for parents who larked about.

'No, we're taking our kisses *upstairs*,' Leo declared, dragging Letty by the hand towards them.

Popi said something sharp to Cosmo and an argument erupted but Letty still walked away, knowing that she needed stolen moments with Leo and that she had to take them when she could. 'So, what's in all the bags?' she asked curiously.

'Just a few last-minute purchases. I love buying you stuff because you never buy it for yourself.'

'Excuse me?' Letty lifted a brow. 'I bought a very expensive designer dress last week for that dinner you had.'

'Yes…that's what I mean. There has to be an excuse or a special occasion for you to spend, so I do it for you,' Leo intoned with the greatest good cheer as he pulled a diamond pendant out of his pocket and proceeded to fasten it round her neck on the landing.

The sizeable diamond glittered white fire below the lights and she reached up and kissed him, wondering where he thought she was going to wear it because she dressed very sensibly and simply for work and didn't flash her opulent lifestyle.

'You can wear it in bed,' Leo told her as if she had spoken her thoughts out loud. 'That'll make you feel really decadent.'

'No, it's *you* who makes me feel decadent,' Letty confessed, hauling him closer by his tie and reaching up for his mouth, all surging impatience and unhidden hunger for his touch.

And Leo really loved that boldness of hers, the knowledge that she was as hot for him as he was for her and that these days she did make him a priority. They were kissing as they stumbled into their bedroom, madly, passionately kissing and heading in the general direction of the bed.

'Golly…when's Isidore arriving?' she struggled to recall. 'We can't be in bed when—'

'Yes, we can be. I'll have the door shut in his face if he interrupts us,' Leo asserted, gorgeous dark golden eyes welded to her flushed oval face.

'That wouldn't be very hospitable.'

'If he comes between me and my wife, he's unwelcome,' Leo growled, spreading her back on the bed like a feast to be savoured. 'Because I love my wife.'

'And you're insanely oversexed!'

Leo ran a lazy hand through her silky hair where it flowed across the pillows. 'I haven't heard you complaining,' he commented with a blazing smile.

'And I'm not,' Letty confided, a fingertip tracing the line of his sensual mouth, loving confidence in her eyes. 'You make me so happy, Leo. I love you so much.'

* * * * *

PROOF OF THEIR ONE-NIGHT PASSION

LOUISE FULLER

To Georgia.
For endlessly listening to my rants and for
sending me cheering photos of chickens and rabbits.
All my love. X

CHAPTER ONE

Rubbing her eyes, Lottie Dawson drew the curtain back and gazed out of her bedroom window. The garden was in darkness, but she could hear the steady patter of the rain, and in the glow of the night light the glass was speckled with fat blobs of water.

Yawning, she glanced over at the clock beside her bed.

It was only five-thirty a.m., an unpleasant hour at most times of the year, but particularly so on a cold, wet November day in rural Suffolk. But for once her eleven-month-old daughter's early-morning routine was an advantage. Today they were going to London, and she actually needed to get up.

Turning round, she glanced over to where Sóley was standing in her cot, her blonde curls flattened against her head, her mouth clamped around the edge of her teddy bear.

As Lottie walked towards her she held up her fat little arms and began dancing on the spot.

'Hi.' Leaning forward, she lifted her daughter up, pressing her body close.

Her heart swelled. She was so beautiful, so perfect. Born in December, on the shortest day of the year, she had been as golden and welcome as the unseasonal sun that had come out to celebrate her birth and inadvertently suggested her name.

'Let's go get you some milk,' she murmured, inhaling the clean, sweet smell of her daughter's skin.

Downstairs, she switched the light on in the kitchen and frowned. A frying pan sat in the sink and the remains of a bacon sandwich were congealing on a plate on the crumb-strewn table. Beside it stood an open tool box and a tattoo gun.

Lottie gritted her teeth. She loved living with her brother Lucas, and he was brilliant with Sóley, but he was six foot four, and it sometimes felt that their tiny cottage wasn't big enough for him—especially as his idea of domesticity was taking his boots off to sleep.

Tutting under her breath, she shifted Sóley's weight to her hip. 'Look at all this mess Uncle Lucas has made,' she said softly, gazing down into her daughter's wide blue eyes.

There was no time to deal with it now. Not if she was going to get herself and Sóley dressed and up to London by eleven o'clock. As she filled the kettle her pulse skipped forward. The gallery in Islington was tiny, but it was hosting her first solo show since giving birth.

Incredibly, some of the pieces had already sold and it was great to know that her work had an audience but, more importantly, the Barker Foundation wanted to talk to her about a commission. Getting funding was a huge step up. Not only would it allow her to continue working without having to teach in the evenings, but she might also be able to extend her workshop.

Glancing into the living room at the dark shape on her sofa, she imagined her brother's eye-rolling reaction to her pragmatism.

Ever since she'd bought the cottage he'd been teasing her about selling out, joking that getting a mortgage was the first step towards the dark side. As far as he and their mother Izzy knew the money had come from a private commission, and Lucas had a very dim view of private clients believing they were only interested in buying art as an investment rather than out of aesthetic appreciation.

She bit her lip. She hated lying to them, but telling the truth—that the deposit for the cottage had been given to her by her biological father, a man who up until two years ago hadn't even known she existed—was just not an option.

Having tested the milk on her tongue, she handed the bottle to Sóley and they both retreated upstairs. Pulling open drawers, she thought back to the moment when she had finally met Alistair Bannon in a motorway service station.

Her stomach clenched. She'd spent so many hours as a child staring into a mirror, trying to work out which of her features came from that man, but even before he had opened his mouth it had been obvious that he was not looking to reconnect with a fully-grown daughter. It wasn't that he didn't accept her as his child—just that he felt no urgency to know her, and their meeting had been strange and strained and short.

From downstairs, she heard the clump of boots hitting the floor. Lucas was up.

She wondered how her brother would react if she showed him the letter her father had sent afterwards. It was polite, carefully worded to offer no obvious rejection but no hope either, basically saying she was a remarkable young woman and he wished her well. Enclosed with the letter had been a cheque for an amount that he hoped would cover his financial contributions for the years he had missed.

Staring at his signature on the cheque, she had felt sick, stunned that she could be reduced to a four-digit sum, and she'd been tempted to tear it up. Only then she'd got pregnant.

Stripping off, she gazed down at her naked body, at the silvery stretch marks that were still faintly visible on her stomach.

Becoming a mother had been so far away in her future plans that she hadn't even suspected she was pregnant but, having been unable to shift a persistent stomach upset she had gone to the doctor, and three days and one urine sample later she had officially been having a baby.

A baby who, like her, was going to grow up never knowing her father. She still wasn't entirely sure how it had happened. They had used protection, but that first time had been so frantic, so urgent, somehow it must have failed.

Shivering, she pulled on her clothes, trying to ignore the sudden thumping of her heart.

She could still remember the night her daughter was conceived. She doubted she would ever forget it. It was like a fever in her blood. The heat and the frenzy had faded, but the memory remained in her bones and on her skin, so that sometimes she'd catch sight of the back of a blond head and a pair of wide shoulders and would have to stop and close her eyes against the urgency of wanting him.

Ragnar Steinn.

She would never forget him either.

It would be impossible.

It would be like trying to forget the sun.

But, despite having the muscular body and clean-cut profile of a Norse god, he had shown himself to be depressingly human in his behaviour. Not only had he lied about where he was staying, and about wanting to spend the day with her, he'd sneaked off before she'd woken up.

And yet together they had made Sóley, and no amount of lies or hardship or loneliness would ever make her regret her beautiful daughter.

'Looks like we've got snow coming,' Lucas said as she walked into the tiny sitting room, holding Sóley on her hip and munching a piece of toast.

He had switched on the ancient television and was wolfing down the remains of his bacon sandwich.

Catching sight of her expression, he grinned sheepishly. 'Sorry about the mess. Look, I'll tidy up, I promise, and I'll chop that wood today. Get it all stacked before the temperatures drop. Do you want me to have little Miss Sunshine?'

She shook her head. 'No, but you could give us a lift to the station.'

'Okay—but only if I get a cuddle.'

He held up his hands and Sóley leaned towards him, grabbing at his shirt collar. Watching her brother's face soften Lottie felt her anger and resentment fade as he pulled the little girl into his arms, wincing as she reached for his hair and grabbed it tightly in her fist.

Unpeeling her fingers, he handed his niece a piece of banana and glanced up at his sister. 'You couldn't put the kettle on as you're up—?'

Glancing at the clock on the wall, Lottie did a quick calculation in her head. There was time before she had to leave. She sighed. 'I'll make some tea.'

Rinsing out the teapot, she put the kettle on the stove.

'You know, I think Sóley is a lot more with it than most kids her age,' she heard Lucas say.

'You do?' Smiling, she poured water into the pot. For someone so laid-back, her brother was extremely partisan and competitive when it came to his niece.

'Yeah—I mean, she's watching the news like she knows what's going on.'

'Good. That means we can outvote you when the football's on.'

'No, seriously, she's completely transfixed by this guy—Lottie, come and look.'

'Okay, I'm coming.'

Walking back into the sitting room, she looked over to where her daughter had pulled herself up in front of the television.

Lucas was right, Sóley did seem to be fascinated. Pulling her gaze away from her daughter's plump cheeks, Lottie glanced at the screen.

The interviewer—a woman—was gazing at the man opposite her with the same fascination as her daughter, so that for a moment Lottie only registered his blond hair and eyes that were the cool, clear blue of a glacier. Then slowly his features came into focus and she felt her mouth slide open.

It was him.

It was Ragnar.

She had wanted to find him after she'd found out she was pregnant, and then again when their daughter was born. But both of them had shut down their profiles on the dating app they'd used to meet up, and there had been no trace of any Ragnar Steinn—or at least none that looked like him—on any internet search.

Her jaw tensed. Not that it would have changed anything if she had managed to get in touch. His clumsy lies had made it clear enough that he'd only been interested in her for one night only, so he was hardly going to jump at the news that he'd fathered a child with her.

She watched mutely, ice working its way up her spine, as Sóley began patting the screen. Her heart was jumping in her chest.

'Who is he?' she asked. 'I mean, why is he on TV?'

She had been aiming for offhand, but her voice sounded thin and breathless.

Thankfully, though, Lucas was too distracted to notice.

'Ragnar Stone. He owns that dating app. Apparently he's launching a VIP version.'

'Dating app?' she said woodenly. It felt as if she had stopped breathing.

She was about to ask which one, but there was no point. She already knew the answer. Only she'd thought he was like her—someone using the app to meet people. She hadn't known that he owned it—in fact, thinking about it, she was certain that he hadn't mentioned that to her.

'You know—*ice/breakr*?'

Lucas glanced up at her, and she watched his face still as his brain caught up with his mouth.

'Course you do…' he said quietly.

It had been Lucas who had signed her up to the app. Lucas who had coaxed her into replying to the 'ice breaker' question. It could be on any topic from politics to holidays. Not all of the questions were profound, but they were designed to spark an instinctive response that apparently helped match couples more accurately than a photo and a list of likes and dislikes. She knew he felt responsible for everything that had happened, but she was too stunned and angry to dismiss his obvious guilt.

Ragnar *Stone*!

So he'd even lied about his name.

And he hadn't just been using the app—*he owned it*.

She breathed out unsteadily, trying to absorb this new version of the facts as she'd known them, grateful that her brother's attention was still fixed on the TV and not on her face. Grateful, too, that she hadn't shown him Ragnar's profile at the time.

Her skin was trembling.

'Is he in London?' she asked.

'Yeah, for the launch. He's got an office here.' Lucas wiped Sóley's mouth with the hem of his shirt and met her gaze. 'One of those converted warehouses in Docklands. You know Nick?'

She nodded. Nick was one of Lucas's cohorts. He played drums in their band, but in his day job he was a graffiti artist.

'He did this huge old-school design the whole length of Ragnar Stone's building. He showed me some pictures and it looks really sick.' He nodded his head approvingly.

Lottie cleared her throat. 'Did he meet him?'

Lucas frowned. 'Nah. Best you can hope with a guy like Stone is that you catch a ride on his slipstream.'

She blinked. Yes, she supposed it was. That was basically what had happened twenty months ago in her hotel room. If she hadn't understood that before, her brother's words made it clear now that she and Sóley were not permanent features of that ride.

'So what time do you want me to drop you off?'

Taking a shallow breath, she looked over at her brother, but her eyes never reached his face. Instead she felt her gaze stretch past him to the TV screen, like a compass point seeking the magnetic north. She stared at Ragnar's face, the artist in her responding to the clean symmetry of his features and the woman in her remembering the pressure of his mouth. He was so beautiful, and so very like his blonde, blue-eyed daughter in every way—except the dimples in her cheeks, which were entirely her own.

She felt something twist inside her. What if it was more than just looks? Growing up not knowing where half her DNA came from had been hard when her mother and brother were so alike in character. It had made her feel incomplete and unfinished, and even finally meeting her father hadn't changed that. It had been too late for them to form a bond and get to know one another.

But would it have been different if he'd found out about her when she was a baby? And, more importantly, could she consciously deny her own child the chance of having what she had so desperately wanted for herself?

The seconds ticked by as she wondered what to do. He would have a PA for sure—only she couldn't tell them why she was ringing. But would they put her through to him without a reason? She bit her lip. More importantly, could she honestly go through with it? Tell him over the phone that he was a father?

She cleared her throat. 'Actually, Lucas, could you have Sóley for me after all?' she said, glancing over at her daughter. 'There's something I need to do. In person.'

* * *

Being interviewed was probably his least favourite part of being a CEO, Ragnar Stone decided, as he stood up and shook hands with the earnest-faced young man in front of him. It was so repetitive, and most of the answers could easily have been given by even the most junior member of his PR department. But, as his head of media Madeline Thomas had told him that morning, people were 'in thrall to the personality behind the brand', so he had dutifully worked his way through twenty-two interviews with just a half-hour break for lunch.

And now he was done.

Shrugging off his jacket, he loosened his tie and pulled a black hoodie over his head as his PA Adam came into the room.

'What time is the car coming to pick me up in the morning?' he asked, reaching down to pick up a slim laptop from his desk.

'Six-thirty. You have a meeting with James Milner at seven, you're seeing the graphics team at eight, and then breakfast with Caroline Woodward.'

'I'll see you tomorrow.' Ragnar smiled briefly at his PA. 'And thanks for keeping it moving today, Adam.'

Stepping into the lift, he ran his hand over his face. Only one more week and then, once this final round of publicity was over and the new app went live, he was going to take some time away from all this.

He knew he'd left it too long. His annual two-week recharge ritual had dwindled to a couple of snatched days, but since launching *ice/breakr* two years ago life had been insane.

Working long hours, eating and sleeping on the move in a series of hotel rooms, and of course in the background his gorgeous, crazy, messy family, acting out their own modern-day Norse saga of betrayal and blackmail.

Glancing down at his phone, he grimaced. Three missed calls from his half-sister Marta, four from his mother, six texts from his stepmother Anna, and twelve from his step-brother Gunnar.

Stretching his neck and shoulders, he slipped his phone into the pocket of his hoodie. None of it would be urgent. It never was. But, like all drama queens, his family loved an audience.

For once they could wait. Right now he wanted to hit the gym and then crash out.

The lift doors opened and he flipped his hood up over his head, nodding at the receptionists as he walked past their desk and out into the dark night air.

He didn't hear their polite murmurs of goodnight, but he heard the woman's voice so clearly that it seemed to come from inside his head.

'Ragnar.'

In the moment that followed he realised two things. One, he recognised the voice, and two, his heart was beating hard and fast like a hailstorm against his ribs.

As he turned he got an impression of slightness, coupled with tension, and then his eyes focused on the woman standing in front of him.

Her light brown hair was longer, her pale face more wary, but she looked just as she had twenty-odd months ago. And yet she seemed different in a way he couldn't pin down. Younger, maybe? Or perhaps she just looked younger because most of the women in his circles routinely wore make-up, whereas she was bare-faced.

'I was just passing. I've got an exhibition up the road…' She waved vaguely towards the window. 'I saw you coming out.' She hesitated. 'I don't know if you remember me…?'

'I remember.'

He cut across her, but only because hearing her voice was messing with his head. It was a voice he had never forgotten—a voice that had called out his name under very different circumstances in a hotel room less than a mile away from where they were standing.

He watched her pupils dilate, and knew that she was thinking the same thing.

For a second they stared at one another, the memory of the night they shared quivering between them, and then, leaning forward, he gave her a quick, neutral hug.

Or it was meant to be neutral, but as his cheek brushed against hers the warm, floral scent of her skin made his whole body hum like a power cable.

Stepping back, he gave her a small, taut smile and something pulsed between them, a flicker of corresponding heat that made his skin grow tight.

'Of course I remember. It's Lottie—Lottie Dawson.'

'Yes, that's *my* name.'

Seeing the accusation in her eyes, he felt his chest tighten, remembering the lies he'd told her. It wasn't hard to remember. Growing up in the truth-shifting environment of his family had left him averse to lying, but that night had been an exception—a necessary and understandable exception. He'd met her through a dating app, but as the app's creator and owner, anonymity had seemed like a sensible precaution.

But his lies hadn't all been about concealing his identity. His family's chaotic and theatrical affairs had left him wary of even the hint of a relationship, so when he'd woken to find himself planning the day ahead with Lottie he'd got up quietly and left—because planning a day with a woman was not on his agenda.

Ever.

His life was already complicated enough. He had parents and step-parents, and seven whole and half-and step siblings scattered around the world, and not one of them had made a relationship last for any length of time. Not only that, their frequent and overlapping affairs and break-ups, and the inevitable pain and misery they caused, seemed to be an unavoidable accompaniment to any kind of commitment.

He liked life to be straightforward. Simple. Honest. It was why he'd created *ice/breakr* in the first place. Why make dating so needlessly confusing? When by asking and answering one carefully curated question people could match their expectations and so avoid any unnecessary emotional trauma.

Or that was the theory.

Only clearly there been some kind of glitch—a ghost in the machine, maybe?

'So it's not Steinn, then?'

His eyes met hers. She was not classically beautiful, but she was intriguing. Both ordinary and extraordinary at once. Mousy hair, light brown eyes… And yet her face had a capacity for expression that was mesmerising.

And then there was her voice.

It wasn't just the huskiness that made his skin tingle, but the way she lingered over the syllables of certain words, like a blues singer. Had he judged her simply on her voice, he might have assumed she had a lifestyle to match—too many late nights and a history of heartache, but their night together had revealed a lack of confidence and a clumsiness that suggested the opposite. Not that he'd asked or minded. In fact it had only made her feverish response to him even more arousing.

Feeling his body respond to the memory of her flowering desire, he blocked his thoughts and shrugged. 'In a way it is. Steinn is Icelandic for Stone. It was just a play on words.'

Her eyes held his. 'Oh, you mean like calling your dating app *ice/breakr*?'

So she knew about the app. 'I wanted to try it out for myself. A dummy run, if you like.'

She flinched and he felt his shoulders tense.

'I didn't intend to deceive you.'

'About that? Or about wanting to spend the day with me?' She frowned. 'Wouldn't it have been fairer and more honest if you'd just said you didn't want to spend any more time with me?'

Ragnar stared at her in silence, gritting his teeth against the sting of her words. Yes, it would. But that would have been a different kind of lie.

Lying didn't come naturally to him—his whole family played fast and loose with the facts and even as a child he'd found it exhausting and stressful. But that night he'd acted out of character, starting from the moment he'd played games with his American father's name and booked a table as Mr Steinn.

And then, the morning after, confronted by his body's fierce reaction to hers, and that uncharacteristic and unsettling need he'd felt to prolong their time together, the lies had kept coming.

'I didn't—'

'It doesn't matter.' She swiped his answer away with a swift jerk of her hand. 'That's not why I'm here.' She glanced past him into the street. 'There's a café open down the road...'

He knew it. It was one of those brightly lit artisan coffee shops with bearded baristas and clean wooden counters. Nothing like the shadowy, discreet bar where they'd met before.

His heartbeat stalled. He could still remember her walking in. It had been one of those sharply cold March evenings that reminded him of home, and there had been a crush of people at the bar, escaping the wind's chill.

He'd been on the verge of leaving.

A combination of work and family histrionics had shrunk his private life to early-morning sessions with his trainer and the occasional dinner with an investor when, finally, it had dawned on him that his app had been launched for nearly three months.

On a whim, he'd decided to try it out.

But, watching the couples dotted about the bar, he had felt a familiar unease clutch at his stomach.

Out of habit, he'd got there early. It was a discipline he embraced—perhaps because since childhood any chance to assemble his thoughts in peace had always been such a rarity. But when Lottie had walked through the door rational thought had been swept away. Her cheeks had been flushed, and she'd appeared to be wearing nothing but a pair of slim-heeled boots and a short black trench coat.

Sadly she'd been clothed underneath but he'd stayed sitting down. If using his own dating app had been impulsive, then not leaving by another door had been the first time he'd done something so utterly unconsidered.

'And you want me to join you there?'

Her eyes met his and there was a beat of silence before she nodded.

His pulse accelerated.

It was nearly two years since that night.

He was exhausted.

His head of security would be appalled.

And yet—

His eyes rested on the soft cushion of her mouth.

The coffee shop was still busy enough that they had to queue for their drinks, but they managed to find a table.

'Thank you.' He gestured towards his *espresso*.

His wallet had been in his hand, but she had sidestepped neatly in front of him, her soft brown eyes defying him to argue with her. Now, though, those same brown eyes were busily avoiding his, and for the first time since she'd called out his name he wondered why she had tracked him down.

He drank his coffee, relishing the heat and the way the caffeine started to block the tension in his back.

'So, I'm all yours,' he said quietly.

She stiffened. 'Hardly.'

He sighed. 'Is that what this is about? Me giving you the wrong name.'

Her eyes narrowed. 'No, of course not. I'm not—' She stopped, frowning. 'Actually, I wasn't just passing, and I'm not here for myself.' She took a breath. 'I'm here for Sóley.'

Her face softened into a smile and he felt a sudden urge to reach out and caress the curve of her lip, to trigger such a smile for himself.

'It's a pretty name.'

She nodded, her smile freezing.

It *was* a pretty name—one he'd always liked. One you didn't hear much outside of Iceland. Only what had it got to do with him?

Watching her fingers tremble against her cup, he felt his ribs tighten. 'Who's Sóley?'

She was quiet for less than a minute, only it felt much longer—long enough for his brain to click through all the possible answers to the impossible one.

He watched her posture change from defensive to resolute.

'She's your daughter. Our daughter.'

He stared at her in silence, but a cacophony of questions was ricocheting inside his head.

Not the how or the when or the where, but the *why*. Of course he'd used condoms but that first time he'd been rushing. And he'd known that. So why hadn't he checked everything was okay? Why had he allowed the heat of their encounter to blot out common sense?

But the answers to those questions would have to wait. 'Okay…'

Shifting in her seat, she frowned. '"Okay"?' she repeated. 'Do you understand what I just said?'

'Yes.' He nodded. 'You're saying I got you pregnant.'

'You don't seem surprised,' she said slowly.

He shrugged. 'These things happen.'

To his siblings and half-siblings, even to his mother. But not to him. Never to him.

Until now.

'And you believe me?' She seemed confused, surprised?

Tilting his head, he held her gaze. 'Honest answer?'

He was going to ask her what she would gain by lying. But before he could open his mouth her lip curled.

'On past performance I'm not sure I can expect that. I mean, you lied about your name. And the hotel you were staying at. And you lied about wanting to spend the day with me.'

'I didn't plan on lying to you,' he said quietly.

Her mouth thinned. 'No, I'm sure it comes very naturally to you.'

'You're twisting my words.'

She shook her head. 'You mean like saying Steinn instead of Stone?'

Pressing his spine into the wall behind him, he felt a tick of anger begin to pulse beneath his skin.

'Okay, I was wrong to lie to you—but if you care about the truth so much then why have you waited so long to tell me that I have a daughter? I mean, she must be what…?' He did a quick mental calculation. 'Ten, eleven months?'

'Eleven months,' she said stiffly. 'And I did want to tell you. I tried looking for you when I was pregnant, and then again when she was born. But the only Ragnar Steinns I could track down weren't you.' She shifted in her seat again. 'I probably would never have found you if you hadn't been on the TV.'

He looked at her again, and despite the rush of righteousness heating his blood he could see that she was nervous, could hear the undertone of strain beneath her bravado.

But then it was a hell of a thing to do. To face a man and tell him he had a child.

His heart began to beat faster.

Years spent navigating through the maelstrom of his family's dramas had given him a cast-iron control over his feelings, and yet for some reason he couldn't stop her panic and defiance from getting under his skin.

But letting feelings get in the way of the facts was not going to help the situation. Nor was it going to be much use to his eleventh-month-old daughter.

Right now he needed to focus on the practical.

'Fortunately you did find me,' he said calmly.

'Here.' She was pushing something across the table towards him, but he carried on talking.

'So I'm guessing you want to talk money?'

At that moment a group of young men and women came into the café and began noisily choosing what to drink. As the noise swelled around them Lottie thought she might have misheard.

Only she knew that she hadn't.

Ever since arriving in London that morning she'd been questioning whether she was doing the right thing, and the thought of seeing Ragnar again had made her stomach perform an increasingly complicated gymnastics routine. Her mood had kept alternating between angry and nervous, but when he'd walked out into the street her mood had been forgotten and a spasm of almost unbearable hunger had consumed everything.

If she'd thought seeing him on TV had prepared her for meeting him again then she'd been wrong. Beneath the street lighting his beauty had been as stark and shocking as the volcanic rock of his homeland.

And he was almost unbearably like the daughter they shared. Only now it would appear that, just like her own father, Ragnar seemed to have already decided the terms of his relationship.

'Money?' She breathed out unsteadily. The word tasted bitter in her mouth. 'I didn't come here to talk to you about money. I came here to talk about our daughter.'

Her heart felt suddenly too big for her chest. Why did this keep happening? Why did men think that they could reduce her life to some random sum of money?

'Children cost money.' He held her gaze. 'Clearly you've been supporting her alone up until now and I want to fix that. I'll need to talk to my lawyers, but I want you to know that you don't need to worry about that anymore.'

I'm not worrying, she wanted to scream at him. She wasn't asking to be helped financially, or fixed. In fact she wasn't asking for anything at all.

'I've not been alone. My mother helps, and my brother Lucas lives with me. He works as a tattooist so he can choose his own hours—'

'A tattooist?'

Glancing up, she found his clear blue eyes examining her dispassionately, as if she was some flawed algorithm. She felt slightly sick—just as she had in those early months of the pregnancy. Only that had been a welcome sickness. A proof of new life, a sign of a strong pregnancy. Now, though, the sickness was down to the disconnect between the man who had reached for her so frantically in that hotel room and this cool-eyed stranger.

She stared at him in silence.

What made this strange, unnerving distance between them a hundred times harder was that she had let herself be distracted by his resemblance to Sóley. Let herself hope that the connection between Ragnar and his daughter would be more than it had been for her and her own father—not just bones and blood, but a willingness to claim her as his own.

But the cool, dispassionate way he had turned the conversation immediately to money was proof that he'd reached the limit of his parental involvement.

She cleared her throat. 'I know you're a rich man, Ragnar, but I didn't come here to beg.' She swallowed down her regret and disappointment. 'This was a mistake. Don't worry, though, it's not one I'll make again—so why don't you get back to the thing that clearly matters most to you? Making money.'

Ragnar reached across the table, but even before he'd got to his feet she had scraped back her seat and snatched up her coat, and he watched in disbelief as she turned and fled from the cafe.

For a moment he considered chasing after her, but she was moving fast and no doubt would already have reached the underground station on the corner.

He sat back down; his chest tight with an all too familiar frustration.

Her behaviour—having a child with a complete stranger, keeping that child a secret, turning up unannounced to reveal the child's existence and then storming off—could have come straight from his family's playbook of chaos.

Glancing down, he felt his pulse scamper forward as for the first time he looked at what she'd pushed across the table. It was a photo of a little girl.

A little girl who looked exactly like him—Sóley.

Reaching out, he touched her face lightly. She was so small, so golden, just like her name. And he was not going to let her grow up with no influence but her chaotic mother and whatever ragtag family she had in tow.

He might love his own family, but he knew only too well

the downside of growing up in the eye of a storm and he didn't want that for his daughter.

So arrangements would have to be made.

Picking up the photo, he slid it into his wallet and pulled out his phone.

CHAPTER TWO

Hitching her sleeping daughter further up on to her shoulder, Lottie glanced around the gallery.

Groups of people were moving slowly around the room, occasionally pausing to gaze more closely at the sketches and collages and sculpted resin objects before moving on again. It wasn't rammed, but she was pleased—she really was. She was also exhausted.

'Nearly over.'

She turned, eyes widening, and then began to smile as the woman standing beside her gave her a conspiratorial wink. Slim, blonde, and with the kind of cheekbones that grazed men's eyes as they walked past, Georgina Hamilton was the gallery's glamorous and incredibly competent co-owner, and despite the fact that she and Lottie were different in as many ways as it was possible to be, she had become an ally and fierce supporter.

Lottie screwed up her face. 'Do I look that desperate?'

Her friend stared at her critically. 'Only to me. To everyone else you probably just look artistically dishevelled.' She glanced at the sleeping Sóley. 'Do you want me to take her?'

Their eyes met and then they both began to giggle. They both knew that Georgina's idea of hands-on childcare was choosing baby clothes in her cousin's upmarket Chelsea boutique.

'No, it's okay. I don't want to risk waking her.' Lottie looked down at the top of her daughter's soft, golden-haired head. 'She's been really unsettled the last couple of nights.'

And she wasn't the only one.

Her cheeks were suddenly warm, and she tilted her head away from Georgina's gaze. It was true that Sóley was struggling to fall asleep at night, but it was Ragnar who had actually been keeping her awake.

It wasn't just the shock of seeing him again, or even his disappointingly predictable reduction of their daughter's life to a financial settlement. It was the disconcerting formality between them.

She pressed her face into her daughter's hair. The disconnect between her overtly erotic memories of the last time they'd met and his cool reserve in the coffee shop had made her feel as if she'd stepped through the looking glass. He had been at once so familiar, and yet so different. Gone was the passion and the febrile hunger, and in their place was a kind of measured, almost clinical gaze that had made her feel she was being judged—and found wanting.

Her heartbeat twitched. And yet running alongside their laboured conversation there had been something pulsing beneath the surface—a stirring of desire, something intimate yet intangible that had made her fingers clumsy as she'd tried to pick up her cup.

She blinked the thought away. Of course what had happened between them had clearly been a blip. After all, this was a man who had turned people's need for intimacy into a global business worth billions—an ambition that was hardly compatible with empathy or passion.

Her jaw tightened. What was it he'd said about that night? Oh, yes, that it had been a 'dummy run' for his app. Well, *she* was a dummy for thinking he might have actually wanted to get to know his daughter.

From now on she was done with doing the right thing for the wrong people. She was only going to let the people she could trust get close—like the woman standing in front of her.

'Thanks for staying, Georgina, and for everything you've done. I honestly don't think I would have sold as well if you hadn't been here.'

Swinging her cape of gleaming blonde hair over her shoulder, Georgina smiled back at her. 'Oh, sweetie, you don't need to thank me—firstly, it's my job, and secondly it's much better for the gallery to have a sold-out exhibition.'

'Sold out?' She blinked in confusion. 'But I thought there were still three pieces left—those sketches and the collage—?'

Georgina shrugged. 'Not any more. Rowley's contacted me at lunchtime and bought all of them.'

Lottie felt her ribs tighten. Rowley's was a prestigious art dealer with a Mayfair address and a client list of wealthy investors who flitted between Beijing, New York, and London, spending millions on houses and cars and emerging artists.

They also had an unrivalled reputation for discretion.

She opened her mouth, but Georgina was already shaking her head.

'No, they didn't give me a name.' She raised an eyebrow. 'You don't look very pleased.'

'I am,' Lottie protested.

After finding out she was pregnant, working had been a welcome distraction from the upheaval in her life, but it had quickly become much more.

She glanced at the visitors who were still drifting around the gallery. 'I just prefer to meet the buyers directly.'

'I know you do—but you know what these collectors are like. They love to have the cachet of buying up-and-coming artists' early work, but they love their anonymity more.' Georgina tutted. 'I know you hate labels, but you are up-and-coming. If you don't believe me then believe your own eyes. You can see all the "Sold" stickers from here.' Watching Lottie shift her daughter's weight to her other arm, she said, 'Are you sure I can't take her?'

Lottie shook her head. 'It's fine. They must be on their way. I mean, Lucas was supposed to meet Izzy at the station and then they were coming straight back.'

Georgina sniffed. She was not a huge fan of Lottie's family. 'Yes, well… I expect they got "distracted".' She smoothed the front of her sculpted nip and tuck dress, and then her eyes narrowed like a tigress spotting her prey. 'Oh, my…' she said softly.

'What's the matter?' Lottie frowned.

'Don't look now but an incredibly hot guy has just walked into the gallery. He has the most amazing eyes I've ever seen."

Lottie shook her head. No doubt they were fixed on the woman standing beside her.

'Ouch.' She winced as Georgina clutched at her arm.

'He's coming over to us.'

'To you, you mean—and of course he is,' Lottie said drily. 'He's male.'

Georgina had the most incredible effect on men, and she was used to simply filling the space beside her.

'He's not looking at me,' Georgina said slowly. She sounded stunned. 'He's looking at *you*.'

Lottie laughed. 'Perhaps he hasn't put his contact lenses in this morning. Or maybe he—'

She turned and her words stopped mid-sentence. Her body seemed to turn to salt. Walking towards her, his blue eyes pinning her to the floor, was Ragnar Stone.

She stared at him mutely as he stopped in front of her. He was dressed more casually than when she'd stopped him outside his office, but such was the force of his presence that suddenly the gallery seemed much smaller and there was a shift in tension, as though everyone was looking at him while trying to appear as though they weren't.

His blue eyes really were incredibly blue, she thought weakly. But Georgina had been wrong. He wasn't looking at her. Instead, his eyes were fixed on his daughter. For a few half-seconds, maybe more, he gazed at Sóley, his face expressionless and unmoving, and then slowly he turned his head towards her.

'Hello, Lottie.'

She stared at him silence, her heartbeat filling her chest, her grip tightening around her daughter's body. In the café there had been so much noise, but here in the near museum-level quiet of the gallery his voice was making her body quiver like a violin being tuned.

It was completely illogical and inappropriate, but that didn't stop it being true.

'Hello, Ragnar,' she said stiffly. 'I wasn't expecting to see you.'

She wasn't sure what kind of a response he would make to her remark, but maybe he felt the same way because he didn't reply.

'So you two know one another, then?' Georgina said brightly.

'Yes.'

'No!'

They both spoke as one—him quietly, her more loudly.

Lottie felt her cheeks grow warm. 'We met once a couple of years back,' she said quickly.

'Just shy of two years.'

Ragnar's blue eyes felt like lasers.

There was a short, strained silence and then Georgina cleared her throat. 'Well, I'll let you catch up on old times.'

Clearly dazzled by Ragnar's beauty, she smiled at him sweetly and, blind to Lottie's pleading expression, sashayed towards an immaculately dressed couple on the other side of the room.

'How did you find me?' she said stiffly. Her heart bumped unsteadily against her ribs. She was still processing the fact that he had come here.

He held her gaze. 'Oh, I was just passing.'

Remembering the lie she'd told, she glared at him. 'Did you have me followed?'

Something flickered across the blue of his pupils. 'Not followed, no—but I did ask my head of security to locate the exhibition you mentioned.'

A pulse was beating in her head. His being here was just so unexpected. Almost as unexpected as the feeling of happiness that was fluttering in time to her heart.

'Aren't you going to introduce me?'

For a moment she gazed at Ragnar in confusion. Was he talking about Georgina? A mixture of disbelief and jealousy twisted her breathing. Was he really using this moment to hit on another woman?

'Her name's Georgina. She's—'

'Not her.'

She heard the tension in his voice before she noticed it in the rigidity of his jaw.

'My daughter.'

Her heart shrank inside her ribs.

In the twenty-four hours since she'd left Ragnar, and his unsolicited offer of financial help, she'd tried hard to arrange her emotions into some kind of order. They hadn't responded. Instead she had kept struggling with the same anger and disappointment she'd felt after meeting her father. But at least she had been able to understand if not excuse Alistair's reluctance to get involved. Meeting an adult daughter he hadn't even known existed was never going to be easy, but Sóley wasn't even one yet.

Okay, at first maybe she would have been a little cautious around him—although remembering her daughter's transfixed gaze when Ragnar had come on the television screen maybe not. But even if she had been understandably hesitant it would have passed, and he could have become a father to her.

Only he'd immediately turned their relationship into a

balance sheet. Or that was what she'd thought he'd done. But if that was the case then what was he doing here, asking to be introduced to his daughter?

There was only one way to find out. She cleared her throat. 'What do you want, Ragnar?'

'Exactly what I wanted yesterday evening,' he said softly. 'Only instead of giving me the chance to explain you used the moment to have some kind of temper tantrum.'

She stared at him, a pulse of anger hopping over her skin. 'I did give you a chance and you offered me money,' she snapped. 'And if that's why you're here then you've wasted your time. I told you I didn't want your money and nothing's changed.'

'That's not your choice to make.' He held her gaze. 'I mean, what kind of mother turns down financial help for her child?'

She felt her cheeks grow hot. He was twisting her words. That wasn't what had happened. Or maybe it was, but it hadn't been about her turning down his money as much as proving him wrong about her motive for getting in touch.

'I wasn't turning down your money—just your assumption that it was what I wanted,' she said carefully. 'You made me feel cheap.'

His face didn't change. 'So what did you want from me?'

His question caught her off-guard. Not because she didn't know the answer—she did. Partly she had wanted to do the right thing, but also she knew what it had felt like to grow up without any knowledge of her father, and she had wanted to spare her daughter that sense of always feeling on the outside, looking in.

Only it felt odd admitting something so personal to a man who was basically a stranger.

'You're her father. I wanted you to know that,' she said finally. 'I wanted you to know her.' Her voice shook a little as she glanced down at her still sleeping daughter. 'She's so happy and loving, and so interested in everything going on around her.'

'Is that why you brought her to the gallery?'

She frowned, the tension in her stomach nipping tighter. 'Yes, it is,' she said defensively.

He might simply have been making polite conversation, but there was an undercurrent in his voice that reminded her of the moment when she'd told him that Lucas was a tattooist. But how could a man like Ragnar understand her loving but unconventional family? He had made a career of turning the spontaneity of human chemistry into a flow chart.

'I'm an artist *and* a mother. I'm not going to pretend that my daughter isn't a part of my life, nor do I see why I should have to.'

His eyes flickered—or maybe it was the light changing as a bus momentarily passed in front of the gallery's windows.

'I agree,' he said, his gaze shifting from his daughter's sleeping face to one of Lottie's opaque, resin sculptures. 'Being a mother doesn't define you. But it brings new contours to your work. Not literally.' He gave her a small, tight smile. 'But in how it's shaping who you are as an artist.'

Lottie felt her heart press against her ribs. The first time they had met they hadn't really discussed their careers. It felt strange to admit it, given what had happened later in the evening but they hadn't talked about anything personal, and yet it had felt as though their conversation had flowed.

Perhaps she had just been carried along by the energy in the bar, or more likely it had been the rush of adrenalin at having finally gone on a date through the app Lucas had found.

She'd had boyfriends—nothing serious or long-lasting, just the usual short-term infatuation followed by disbelief that she had ever found the object of her affections in any way attractive. But after her meeting with Alistair she had felt crushed, rejected.

Unlovable.

Perhaps if she'd been able to talk to her mother or brother about her feelings it would have been easier, but she'd already felt disloyal, going behind their backs. And why upset them when it had all been for nothing?

Her biological father's panicky need to get back to his life had made her feel ashamed of who she was, and that feeling of not being good enough to deserve his love had coloured her confidence with men generally.

Until Ragnar.

Her pulse twitched. Her nerves had been jangling like a car alarm when she'd walked into the bar. But when Ragnar had stood up in front of her, with his long dark coat curling around his ankles like a cape, her nerves had been swept away not just by his beauty, but his composure. The noisy, shifting mass of people had seemed to fall back so that it was just the two of them in a silence that had felt like a held breath.

She had never felt such a connection with anyone— certainly not with any man. For her—and she'd thought for him too—that night had been an acknowledgement of that feeling and she'd never wanted it to end. In the wordless oblivion of their passion he had made her feel strong and desirable.

Now, though, he felt like a stranger, and she could hardly believe that they had created a child together.

Her ribs squeezed tightly as Sóley wriggled against her and then went limp as she plugged her thumb into her mouth.

'So why are you here?' she said quietly.

'I want to be a part of my daughter's life—and, yes that includes contributing financially, but more importantly I want to have a hands-on involvement in co-parenting her.'

Co-parenting.

The word ricocheted inside her head.

Her throat seemed to have shrunk, so that suddenly it was difficult to breathe, and her heart was leaping erratically like a fish on a hook.

But why? He was offering her exactly what she'd thought she wanted for her daughter, wasn't he?

She felt Sóley move against her again, and instantly her panic increased tenfold.

The truth was that she hadn't really thought about anything beyond Ragnar's initial reaction to finding out he was a father. The memory of her own father's glazed expression of shock and panic had still been uppermost in her mind when she'd found out she was pregnant, and that was what she'd wanted to avoid by getting in touch with Ragnar while their daughter was still tiny.

But had she thought beyond the moment of revelation? Had she imagined him being a hands-on presence in Sóley's life? No, not really. She'd been so self-righteous about Ragnar's deceit, but now it turned out that she had been deceiving herself the whole time—telling herself that she'd got in touch because she wanted him in her daughter's life when really it had been as much about rewriting that uncomfortable, unsatisfactory scene between herself and Alistair.

And now, thanks to her stupidity and short-sightedness, she'd let someone into her life she barely knew or liked who had an agenda that was unlikely to be compatible with hers.

'I don't know how we could make that work—' she began.

But Ragnar wasn't listening. He was staring as though mesmerised at his daughter's face. And, with shock, she realised that Sóley was awake and was staring back at her father. Her heart contracted. Their blue eyes were so alike.

'Hey,' he said softly to his daughter. 'May I?'

His eyes flickered briefly to hers and without realising

that she was even doing so she nodded slowly, holding her breath as he held out his hand to Sóley.

Watching her tiny hand clasp his thumb, she felt the same pride and panic she'd felt back in the cottage, when her daughter had been transfixed by Ragnar's face. Whatever *she* felt for him they were father and daughter, and their bond was unassailable.

His next words made it clear that his thoughts were following the same path.

'We need to sit down and talk about what happens next.'

'What happens next…?' she repeated slowly.

He nodded. 'Obviously we'll need to sort out something legal, but right now I'd like us to be on the same page.'

From somewhere outside in the street a swell of uncontrollable laughter burst into the near-silent gallery. As everyone turned she glanced past Ragnar, feeling the hairs on the back of her neck stand to attention as she spotted the hem of her mother's coat and her brother's familiar black boots stomping down the steps of the gallery.

Panic edged into her head, pushing past all other thought. This wasn't the right time or place for Ragnar to meet her family. She wasn't ready, and nor could she imagine their various reactions to one another. Actually, she could—and it was something she wanted to avoid at all costs.

Her mother would walk a tightrope between charm and contempt. Lucas would probably say something he would regret later.

'Fine,' she said quickly. 'I'll give you my number and you can call me. We can arrange to meet up.'

'I think it would be better if we made a decision now.'

Watching Lucas turning to flirt with the gallery receptionist, Lottie felt her jaw tighten with resentment. Ragnar was pushing her into a corner. Only what choice did she have?

She glanced despairingly as the inner door to the gallery

opened. She couldn't risk them meeting one another now, but clearly Ragnar wasn't leaving without a date in place.

'Okay, then—how about tomorrow? After lunch.'

He nodded. 'Would you prefer me to come to you?'

'No—' She practically shouted the word at him. 'People are always dropping in. It'll be easier to talk without any distractions.'

'Fine. I'll send a car.'

'That won't be—'

'Necessary? Perhaps not.' Frowning, he reached into his jacket and pulled out a card. 'But indulge me. This is my private number. Text me your address and I'll have my driver collect you.'

There was a pulse of silence. She disliked the feeling of being treated like some kind of special delivery parcel, but no doubt this was just how his life worked, and refusing seemed childish given what was really at stake.

'Fine—but right now I need you to go. The exhibition will be closing in ten minutes and I want to get Sóley home,' she said, watching with relief as Georgina sped across the gallery to intercept her mother and her brother. 'So if you don't mind—?'

His gaze shifted to her face. 'Of course.' He gave her a smile that barely curved his mouth. 'I'll see you tomorrow.'

Gently he released his grip from Sóley's hand. For a moment he hesitated, his eyes locking with his daughter's, and then he turned and strode towards the door. She watched, her heart in her mouth, as he skirted past her mother and Lucas.

'Sorry we're late!' Her mother ran her hand theatrically through her long dark hair. 'We bumped into Chris and your brother insisted on buying him a drink—'

'I felt awkward.' Lucas shook his head. 'The poor guy practically lost his mind when you dumped him.'

'But never mind about *him*.'

Lottie winced as her mother grabbed her and kissed her on the cheek.

'Who was *that*?' Pivoting round, Izzy gazed after Ragnar with narrowing eyes.

Lottie shrugged. 'He was just passing,' she said quickly.

Lucas frowned. 'I feel like I've seen him before…'

'Unlikely,' Lottie said crisply. 'I don't think you move in the same circles—and don't try and distract me.' She raised an eyebrow accusingly. 'You were supposed to be here an hour ago. But now that you are here, do you think you could take Sóley for me?'

She watched with relief as Lucas reached out and scooped Sóley into his arms. It wasn't quite as terrifying as the thought of Ragnar meeting her family, but her brother making any kind of connection was something she didn't need. He might just put two and two together and come up with four—and then she would have to lie to his face or, worse, admit the truth to their mother.

There was no way she was getting into all that in public. She'd already over-complicated everything enough by letting a cool-eyed stranger into her life.

But if Ragnar thought her hasty acquiescence to his demands meant that he could set the boundaries for his relationship with their daughter he was wrong—as he was going to find out tomorrow.

Were they her family?

Mounting the steps from the gallery two at a time, Ragnar felt the onset of a familiar unease—that same feeling of being sucked towards a vortex that usually went hand in hand with spending time with his own family.

The scruffy-looking man with Day-of-the-Dead skulls tattooed on his neck and the dark-haired woman wearing an eye-catching red faux-fur coat must be Lottie's brother and mother—and the thought was not exactly reassuring.

He knew from dealing with his own family that eccentricities might appear charming to an outsider but usually they went hand in hand with a tendency for self-indulgence and melodrama that was exhausting and time-consuming.

But at least with one's own family you knew what to expect.

Remembering his daughter's hand gripping his thumb, he felt his jaw tighten. Had he been in any way uncertain as to whether he had a role to play in Sóley's life that doubt had instantly and completely vanished as her hand gripped his. Children needed stability and support from the adults in their lives, not drama, and it wasn't hard to imagine exactly what kind of circus those two could create.

No wonder Lottie had been so desperate for him to leave. The sooner he got this matter in hand the better.

Yanking open the door to his car, he threw himself into the back seat. 'Take me home, John,' he said curtly.

Home. He almost laughed out loud. What did he know about the concept of home? He'd lived in many houses in numerous countries, with various combinations of parents and step-parents. And now that his wealth had become something managed by other people he owned properties around the globe. Truthfully, though, despite their scale and glossy interiors, none was somewhere he felt relief when he walked through the front door.

No, there was only one place he'd ever considered home, and ironically the person who owned it was not related to him by either blood or marriage.

But he would make certain his child had the home he'd been denied.

The next morning Ragnar woke early.

It was still dark when he got up, but he knew from experience that he wouldn't get back to sleep. He dressed and made his way downstairs to the gym, and worked the machines until his body ached.

An hour later, having showered and changed, he lay sprawled on a sofa in one of the living rooms. There were eight in total, but this was the one he preferred. He let out a long, slow breath. Outside it was raining, and through the window all he could see was the dark glimmer of water and the occasional crooked outline of antlers as the red deer moved silently across the lawns.

The deer had come with Lamerton House, the Jacobean mansion and forty-acre estate that he used as a stopover when he was meeting bankers and investors in London. His gaze narrowed. They were less tame than reindeer, but the grazing herd still reminded him of home.

Home—that word again.

He stared irritably out of the window into the darkness. Normally it was a word that just didn't register in his day-to-day vocabulary, but this was the second time in as many hours that he'd thought it. His refocused his eyes on his reflection—only it wasn't his face he could see in the glass but his daughter's, so like his own and already so essential to him.

He might only have discovered her existence forty-eight hours earlier, but his feelings about Sóley were clear. She deserved a home—somewhere safe and stable. Somewhere she could flourish.

His fingers clenched against the back of the sofa. If only his feelings about Lottie were as straightforward. But they weren't.

At first he'd wanted to blame her for so carelessly unbalancing his life, and then for keeping the truth from him, only how could he? He was as much to blame on both counts. Nor could he blame her for resenting his heavy-handed offer of money. Having managed alone for the best part of two years, of course she'd feel insulted.

But acknowledging his own flaws didn't absolve hers. She was stubborn and inconsistent and irrational. His mouth thinned. Sadly acknowledging her flaws didn't change the facts. Being near Lottie made his body swell with blood and his head swim. He had felt it—that same restless, implacable hunger that had overtaken him that night. A hunger he had spent his life condemning in others and was now suppressing in himself...

Six hours later he stood watching the dark blue saloon move smoothly along the driveway towards the house. From the upper floor window he watched as his driver John opened the door. His heart started a drumroll as Lottie slid from the car and, turning, he made his way downstairs.

As he reached the bottom step she turned and gazed up at him.

There was a moment of silence as he took in her appearance. She was wearing jeans and a baggy cream jumper. Her cheeks were flushed and her hair was tied back with what looked like a man's black shoelace. For no accountable reason he found himself hoping profoundly that the owner of the shoe in question was her brother. Raising his eyes, he turned towards John and dismissed him with a nod, so that his voice wouldn't give away the sharp, disconcerting spasm of jealousy that twisted his mouth.

'You made good time,' he said.

She nodded, her soft brown eyes locking with his—except they weren't soft, but tense and wary. 'Thank you for sending the car. It was very kind of you.' Her gaze moved past him and then abruptly returned to his face. 'So what happens next?'

It wasn't just her voice that upped his heartbeat. Her words reverberated inside his head, pulling at a memory he had never quite forgotten.

So what happens next?

Twenty months ago she had spoken the exact same sentence to him in the street outside that restaurant, and briefly he let his mind go back to that moment. He could picture it precisely. The tremble of her lips, the way her hair had spilled over the collar of her coat, and then the moment when he had lowered his mouth to hers and kissed her.

His body tensed. It had been so effortless. So natural. She had melted into him, her candid words, warm mouth and curving limbs offering up possibilities of an intimacy without the drama he had lived with so long. But of course he'd been kidding himself. Whatever it was that had caused that flashpoint of heat and hunger and hope, it had been contingent on the preordained shortness of its existence.

With an effort he blocked out an image of her body gleaming palely against the dark, crumpled bedding...

'We talk,' he said simply. 'Why don't we go and get something to drink?'

In the kitchen, his housekeeper Francesca had left tea and coffee and some homemade biscuits on the granite-topped breakfast bar.

'Take a seat.' He gestured towards a leather-covered bar stool. 'Tea or coffee? Do you have a preference?'

'Tea. Please. And I prefer it black.'

He held out a cup and, giving him a small, stiff smile, she took it from him.

She took a sip, her mouth parting, and he felt his body twitch in response. It felt strange—absurdly, frustratingly strange—to be handing her a cup of tea when part of him could still remember pulling her into his arms. And another part was hungry still to pull her into his arms again.

He cleared his throat. 'So, shall we get on with it?'

He heard the shift in her breathing.

'I accept that Sóley is my daughter, but obviously that isn't going to satisfy my lawyers, so I'm afraid I need to establish paternity. It's quite simple—just a sample from me and you and Sóley.'

There was a short silence, and then she nodded. 'Okay.'

'Good.' His gaze held hers. 'Long-term I'll be looking at establishing custody rights, but initially I just want to spend a bit of time with my daughter.' And provide a structure and a stability that he instinctively knew must be lacking in her life.

'Meaning what, exactly?'

The flicker in her gaze held the same message as the rigidity in her jaw but he ignored both.

'Since everything took off with the app I've tried to take a couple of weeks off a year—three at most—just to recharge my batteries.'

'And...?' Her eyes were fixed on his face.

'And now seems like a good time for that to happen. Obviously it's just a short-term fix, but it would give me a chance to get to know Sóley and find out what's in her best interests.'

Her expression stiffened. 'I think *I* know what's in her best interests.'

'Of course. But circumstances have changed.' He waited a beat. 'This is just a first step. I understand that there's going to be a lot to work through, and naturally any future arrangements will take into account Sóley's needs—her wellbeing comes first.'

Lottie stared at him in silence. 'In that case, it's probably easier if you come to me,' she said finally. 'Coming here is quite a long way for a day trip.'

He frowned. 'I wasn't expecting you to come here, and I wasn't talking about a day trip.'

'I don't understand...' she said slowly.

'Then let me explain. The whole point of these weeks is to give me time to think, to unplug myself. That's why I go back to Iceland. It's a less hectic, more sedate way of life, and it's easier to take a step back there. I'd like Sóley to go with me.'

Her eyes slipped across his face, once then twice, as though searching for something. 'You're joking, right?'

'About getting to spend some time with my child? Hardly.'

He watched his put-down meet its target, as he'd intended it to. Colour was spreading over her cheeks.

'She doesn't have a passport,' she countered tonelessly.

'But she has a birth certificate.'

Her single, reluctant nod looked almost painful.

'Then it won't be a problem. I have people who can expedite the paperwork.'

Her face seemed to crack apart. 'No, this is not happening. She doesn't know you—and she's never been anywhere without me.'

He could hear the tension in her voice and unaccountably felt himself respond to it. How could he not? She was scared. Of him. Not physically, but of his claim, both moral and legal, on their daughter, and he couldn't help but understand and empathise with her. She had carried Sóley for nine months and cared for her on her own for another eleven. Now he was here in her life and everything was going to change.

His back stiffened. He knew exactly how that felt—the dread, then the confusion and the compromises—and for a few half-seconds he was on the verge of reaching out to comfort her. But—

But it was best not to confuse what was actually happening here. Lottie would adapt, and what mattered was agreeing the best possible outcome for Sóley.

'Clearly I was expecting you to join us.' He spoke patiently, as though to a confused child, but instead of calming her his words had the opposite effect.

'Me? Go away with you?' She shook her head. 'No, that isn't going to happen.'

'Why not? I spoke to the woman at the gallery and you have no upcoming exhibitions.'

'You spoke to Georgina?' The tightness in her face broke into a spasm of outrage. 'How dare you? How dare you talk to people behind my back?'

The note of hysteria in her voice made his shoulders pinch together. 'You're being ridiculous.'

'And you're being overbearing,' she snapped. 'You can't just expect me to drop everything.'

'Oh, but I can—and I do. And if you won't then I will have to apply a little pressure.'

'And do what, Ragnar?' She pushed up from the bar stool, her hands curling into fists, two thumbprints of colour burning in her cheeks. 'Are you going to send round your head of security? Or maybe you could kidnap us?'

How had this spiralled out of control so quickly?

He felt a familiar mix of frustration and fatigue.

'This is getting us nowhere—and in case you've forgotten, you got in touch with me.'

He stared at her in exasperation and then wished he hadn't. Her hair was coming loose and he had to resist the urge to pull it with his fingers and watch it tumble free.

He waited a moment, and then tried again. 'Look, Lottie. You go where Sóley goes. That's a given. And by pressure I just mean lawyers. But I don't want to escalate this. I just want to do what's best for our daughter. I think you do too, and that's why you came to find me the other day.'

There was a small beat of silence.

'I do want what's best for her, but...' She hesitated. 'But going away with you... I mean, three weeks is a long time for two strangers to spend together.'

There was another pulse of silence. His heart was suddenly digging against his ribs.

'But we're not strangers, are we, Lottie?' he said softly.

The silence was heavy now, pressing them closer.

Her pupils flared like a supernova and he felt his breathing stall in his throat. A minute went by, and then another. They were inches apart, so close that if he reached out he could touch her, pull her closer, draw her body against him…

And then above the pounding of his heart he heard her swallow.

'Okay. Sóley and I will come to Iceland with you.' Her expression hardened. 'And then she and I will go home. Without you.'

CHAPTER THREE

Lottie and Lucas started their walk, as they always did, by climbing over the stile in the wall at the back of the garden. After days of rain, not only was the sun shining but it was unseasonably warm.

'Usual route?' Lucas said, steadying himself on the top of the stile.

She nodded. 'But maybe come back by the river? There might be some ducks for Sóley.'

She glanced up to where her daughter sat, clapping her hands triumphantly in the backpack on Lucas's shoulders. She was wearing a lightweight purple all-in-one and a tiny knitted hat shaped like a blackberry, complete with leaves and a stalk, and in the pale lemon sunlight her skin looked as smooth and luminous as a pearl.

They trudged around the edge of the field across short, stubby tufts of grass to the lane that skirted the farmland. Instead of the usual hum of machinery, or the pensive bleating of sheep, it was still and peaceful, but Lottie didn't mind—her head was noisy enough as it was.

Ragnar had been on television again last night, on some panel show and, watching him talk about global expansion and emerging markets, she had felt a little sick. He had sounded cool, driven and utterly focused on his goals. Of course he'd been talking about his business, but she could easily imagine him applying the same focus and determination to getting what he wanted when it came to his daughter. Plus, he had all kinds of resources at his disposal. Look at how quickly and smoothly he'd acquired a passport for Sóley.

She felt her pulse jerk forward. So quickly, in fact, that

this time next week all three of them would be flying to Reykjavik.

It was difficult to say which was more terrifying. The future when her adult daughter would be able to travel outside of England without her made her skin grow tight with panic, but thinking about spending three hours with Ragnar, let alone the three weeks she had agreed to, set off a pinwheel of alarm in her chest.

To say that she didn't want to go was the mother of all understatements—only what choice did she have? She could refuse, but then he would simply make good on his threat to escalate matters through the courts. Or she could go into hiding. Izzy knew loads of people who lived off-grid in houseboats and artists' communes. Only she couldn't stay hidden for ever.

Her stomach tightened.

She was just going to have to accept that it was happening.

But it was all moving so much more quickly than she'd expected.

It wasn't that she blamed Ragnar for wanting to get things rolling. If she'd been in his position she would have felt just the same. And nor did she really regret her decision to tell him about Sóley. But even though she knew she'd done the right thing, seeing him with Sóley, feeling the imperative weight of the connection between them, was making her head spin.

She felt a longing to snatch her daughter away and hold her close, and yet at the same time a longing to be part of the golden warmth of their inner circle. It was so confusing. She wanted to feel happy for her daughter, not panicky and envious, and she knew that she was being illogical, but she still couldn't stop herself from feeling just a tiny bit jealous of their blonde, blue-eyed bond.

A bond that would never include her.

A bond she had so spectacularly failed to achieve with her own father.

'I thought we might take Sóley into town next week. They're switching on the Christmas lights.'

It was suddenly hard to breathe. As Lucas's voice reverberated inside her head she looked up at her brother's face. It was so familiar, so reassuring, and yet she still hadn't worked out a way to tell him what was happening.

In the distance she could see the broad expanse of the marshes. Above their heads the sky was pale grey, silent and immense. It felt overwhelming, and yet in another way it was liberating, for it put everything into perspective. In comparison to something so infinite and enduring, surely her problems were puny and trifling and her secrecy superfluous?

She glanced across at her brother, seeing the scuffed patches on his leather jacket and the tiny points of stubble along his jawline, and suddenly she knew that this was it. The turning point. The moment she had been waiting for and both hoping and dreading would happen.

Up until now it had all been just in her head. It had felt safe, contained, indefinite. But telling Lucas would make it real.

'That would be lovely,' she said carefully. 'Only I'm not going to be here.'

'Really?' Lucas frowned. 'I thought you were clear up until Christmas.'

She swallowed, or tried to, but the truth was blocking her throat, making it ache.

'I am—I was. But I'm…we're going to Iceland.'

He was staring at her now, his dark brown eyes trying to make sense of her words.

'Iceland? Wow, really?' He shook his head. 'That's pretty random. What brought that on?'

For a moment she was too busy trying out various sentences in her head to reply, but the need to share the truth was swelling inside her.

'We're going away with Sóley's father,' she said quickly. 'Just for a couple of weeks,' she added. 'So he can get to know her.'

Whatever Lucas might have been expecting her to say, it wasn't that. Her brother was difficult to shock. He was tolerant and easy-going. But she could tell that he was stunned by her words.

'I thought you didn't know who he was?' His eyes searched her face, trying to guess at the truth of what she'd told him in the past.

'I didn't. But then I found out by accident and I went to his office and told him about Sóley. Then he invited me to his house, and we talked.'

Lucas cleared his throat. 'When was this?'

'A couple of days ago.'

His eyes narrowed with disbelief. 'What? And he just invited you to go away with him?'

'Yes.'

'And you agreed to go?'

As she nodded a slick of heat spread over her skin. Put like that it sounded crazy, but what was she supposed to say? *Actually, he didn't so much as invite me as issue a directive.*

She could imagine her brother's reaction. He would be furious—and understandably so. From his perspective it would seem she had been backed into a corner. Only his anger wasn't going to change the facts. Ragnar was Sóley's father, and he had a right to know his daughter.

Her heart skipped forward guiltily and she felt a slow creep of colour stain her cheeks. Ragnar's desire to know his daughter was not the only reason she had agreed to go to Iceland with him. That involved a different kind of desire.

Her mind went back to that moment in the kitchen,

when the anger and tension between them had slipped into
something else, and the intensity of their emotions and the
nearness of their bodies had resurrected the ghost of their
unfinished connection with impossible speed.

Here in the cool November sunlight she could dismiss it
as the result of nervousness or an overactive imagination,
but alone with Ragnar it had been impossible to deny. In
that moment the truth had been irrefutable. She wanted
him—wanted him more than she had ever wanted any
man.

But the suffocating force of that longing was one truth
she wouldn't be sharing with her brother.

She glanced up at his profile. He looked calm, but she
could read the confusion in the lines around his eyes and
the tightening along his jaw.

'You think it's a bad idea,' she said slowly.

She watched with a mix of regret and relief as he shook
his head.

'No, I'm just sulking because you didn't talk to me about
it.'

Reaching out, she took hold of his hand and gave it a
quick, apologetic squeeze. 'I wanted to but I was worried
about what you'd say. What you and Mum would say,' she
corrected herself. 'I didn't want to let either of you down.'

Lucas frowned. 'Let us down? Sóley is your daughter,
Lottie. It's up to you, not me or Mum, if you want her to
know who her father is.'

'I know, but you've always been so definite about it not
mattering—you know, about our dads not being around—
and Mum's the same.'

She thought back to her childhood, the hours spent
watching Izzy's casual intimacy with men, the cool way
she seduced and then discarded them without so much as
a backward glance. To a child it had seemed both shocking, and eye-wateringly brutal, but as she'd grown older she

had seen it as something else—something that underlined a fundamental difference between herself and her mother.

She felt his fingers tighten around hers.

'I do feel like that, but I know you don't—and that's okay. You're just not programmed that way, and I know that makes you feel left out sometimes. But you're my sister and I'm here for you and nothing can change that.'

Feeling the knot of tension in her shoulders loosen, Lottie nodded. It was a relief to tell Lucas the truth, but his fierce affirmation of their sibling bond mattered more. It was nothing new. She'd always needed reassurance of her place in her family. But since being confronted by Ragnar and Sóley's kinship she'd felt even more precariously placed than before.

'But that doesn't mean you have to rush into anything with Sóley's dad.'

They had reached the river now, and Lottie stared down into the water, her brother's words replaying inside her head as Sóley began to crow excitedly at a group of mallards sifting through the mud for insects and seeds.

'I can totally see why you'd want to,' he said slowly. 'But it's not like there's a time limit on paternity.'

Except there was, she thought. And at a certain point time ran out.

The blood pulsed inside her head as she thought back to her meeting with her own father. She had left it too late. So late that there hadn't been any room left for her in Alistair's life.

'In theory, no,' she agreed. 'But every day that passes is a day that tests that theory, and that's why I don't want to wait with Ragnar.'

As the silence stretched out between them she could hear the booming of her voice inside her head. Lucas was staring at her, and she could sense that he was replaying her words, mentally tracing back over the last few days.

Finally, he said slowly, 'Ragnar Stone is Sóley's father.'

It wasn't a question but a statement of fact, and there was no point in pretending otherwise.

She nodded.

He tilted his head back and whistled soundlessly. 'At least now I get why you're going to Iceland.' Hesitating, he looked her straight in the eye. 'Unless there is some other reason you and Mr Stone want to spend a few weeks together.'

Her face felt hot and tight. 'Of course there's no other reason.' She knew she sounded defensive and, remembering how her body grew loose with desire whenever she thought about Ragnar, she knew why. 'There's nothing between us,' she said quickly. 'This trip is about Sóley getting to know her father.'

It was hopeless. The tangle of her thoughts might just as well be written in huge letters across a billboard by the side of the road. But that was the problem. She didn't know how she felt or how she should feel—not about Ragnar, nor about going away with him and having him in her life. But if anyone could help her make sense of her feelings, it was Lucas.

'So you still like him?' Lucas said gently.

'No.' She shook her head, hesitated. 'I don't know. Maybe—but it's not conscious. I mean, I don't actually like him as a person.'

There was a small beat of silence.

'Okay…' Lucas raised an eyebrow. 'So what *do* you like about him?'

Her heart shivered.

His skin. The curving muscles of his arms and chest. His smell. The way his hair fell in front of his eyes when he was gazing down at her. The fierce blueness of his gaze.

'I don't know,' she lied. 'It just felt good with him, that

night.' She could admit that much—although that too was a lie, or perhaps an understatement.

It had felt glorious. An ecstasy of touch and taste. She had never wanted it to stop. Never wanted to leave that hotel room. Never felt so complete or so certain. Every fibre of her being, every atom of her consciousness, had been focused on the pressure of his body and the circle of his arms around her. Nothing else had mattered. And in the flushed, perfect aftermath of that night she had been so blazingly sure of him.

But now she knew she had made hasty and hungry assumptions. And by agreeing to go to Iceland was she making them again?

'Do you think I'm being stupid?'

Much as she loved her brother, they were different in so many ways. Like Izzy, Lucas was a serial monogamist. He was single-minded, and not subject to any need for permanence or emotional bondage, but he liked women and, probably because he was always so honest, they liked him. It was one of his strengths, that unflinching honesty, and she needed him to be honest with her now.

His forehead creased, and then he shook his head. 'You made Sóley together, so something was good between you.' He hesitated. 'But you need to be careful and clear about where you fit into all this. Don't complicate what's already going to be a fairly tricky situation with something that's out of your hands.'

He was right, Lottie thought as they turned away from the river. However fierce and real it might feel, letting something as fickle and cursory as physical attraction take centre stage was a risk not worth taking. Giving in to her hunger would rob her of perspective.

She and Ragnar had had their chance and they'd failed to make it work—and nothing, including the fact that they had an eleventh-month-old daughter, would change that.

* * *

As his private jet hit a pocket of what felt like hollowed-out air Ragnar felt his pulse accelerate. But it wasn't the turbulence that was making his heart beat faster. Over the last year he'd racked up enough air miles to have overcome any fear of flying. What was making his pulse race was the tiny shift in the drone of the engines.

They were making their descent. In less than half an hour they would land in Reykjavik. Then it would be a drive out to his estate on the Troll peninsula, and then finally he would be able to start getting to know his daughter.

Daughter.

The word still felt so unfamiliar, but then he hadn't expected to become a father for a long time. Maybe not ever. Only then he'd met Lottie, and in that moment when they'd reached for one another in that dark London street his life had changed for all time.

His eyes drifted across the cabin to where she sat, gazing out of one of the small cabin windows. Opposite her, Sóley lay across two seats, with some kind of frayed cuddly toy clamped against her body, her thumb in her mouth. She was asleep and, watching the rise and fall of her tiny body, Ragnar felt his chest ache.

As predicted, his lawyers had insisted on a paternity test, and as predicted it had come back positive. But as far as he was concerned no proof had been required. Sóley was his—and not just because they were so physically alike. There was an intangible thread between them, a bond that started with DNA but went way beyond it. He might have only found out about her existence a couple of days ago, but he already felt an unquestioning, all-encompassing love for her, and a sense of responsibility that was nothing like he'd ever felt before.

He felt his heart contract. She looked so small, so vulnerable, so ill-equipped to deal with the relentless chaos of life.

For chaos read *family*.

He thought about the complicated layers of parents and children—some related by blood, some by marriage—that made up his family. They were wilful and self-absorbed and thoughtless, but he loved them—all of them. How could he not? They were a force of nature, so full of life, so passionate and vital.

But ever since he could remember they had seemed to him like whirling storm clouds battering a mountain top. Oblivious to the damage they caused, they kept on twisting and raging, and in order to survive he'd chosen—if you could call it a choice—to sit out the storm. To be like the mountain and just let the winds carry on howling around him.

That had been his response as a child. Now, as an adult, he'd embraced the role of mediator and umpire. It was exhausting, often thankless, and always time-consuming. The swooping melodrama of their day-to-day disputes and dramas required the patience of a bomb disposal expert and the diplomacy of a trained hostage negotiator, but it was the only way, for it allowed him to live a life of calm and order on the sidelines.

He shifted in his seat, pressing his spine against the leather to relieve the tension in his back.

Now, though, he felt as though he was being sucked into a new vortex—a vortex that was the unavoidable trade-off for getting to know his daughter.

Across the cabin Sóley shifted in her sleep, losing her grip on her toy, and he watched as Lottie leaned forward and gently tucked the bear back underneath her arm.

By vortex he meant *Lottie's family*.

That glimpse in the gallery had been enough of an incentive for him to call his head of security and instruct him to make some discreet enquiries. The slim folder that had arrived on his desk less than twenty-four hours later had made for depressing reading. Both Izzy, Lottie's mother, and her brother Lucas seemed to live off-grid, rarely staying in one place longer than a couple of years and with no regular partners or jobs.

At least Lottie had an address, and she owned a house, but the idea of his daughter being raised in the eye of *that* particular storm made Ragnar suddenly so tense that before he knew what he was doing he had stood up and was walking across the cabin.

'May I?'

He gestured towards the empty seat opposite Sóley.

Lottie looked up at him, her light brown eyes not exactly contradicting the slight nod of her head but reserving judgement. He wondered why he had thought her eyes were boring. Right now, in the softly lit interior of the cabin, they were the same colour as the raw honey produced on his estate.

'Of course. It's your plane.'

She spoke politely, and it was tempting to take her words at face value. But, although her voice was free of any resentful undertone, he could sense she was still chafing against what she took to be his high-handed manner.

His gaze was drawn to his daughter and he felt his own stab of resentment. Sóley was so small, and yet he'd already missed so many of the imperceptible changes that had marked her growth from birth to now. So Lottie's indignation would have to wait—just as he'd had to wait to find out he was her father.

'I thought it would be simpler and more comfortable for you both to travel this way.'

He glanced around the cabin. There was space to move around and no other passengers, but Lottie's stony expression suggested she was unconvinced.

'I just want to spend time with her,' he said mildly.

She frowned. 'I'm not saying you don't, but you have a

house in Surrey. I don't understand why we couldn't just visit you there.'

'As I told you—I like to take a couple of weeks off to recharge.'

'So we're working around your business schedule?' Her gaze narrowed. 'I thought this was supposed to be about our daughter and her wellbeing.'

He stared at her steadily, noting the paleness of her face and the dark shadows beneath her eyes. Clearly she'd been having trouble sleeping, and without meaning to he found himself diverting his thoughts away from the evidence to the cause.

Was her insomnia solely a result of this disruption to her life? Or was something else keeping her awake?

His pulse stalled. Since she'd door-stepped him in front of his office his own nights had been uncharacteristically unsettled. Either he struggled to fall asleep, his head filling with images of Lottie's pale naked body as soon as he tried to close his eyes, or he dozed off only to wake exhausted after a night spent twitching restlessly through feverish, erotically charged dreams.

Blanking his mind of everything but the here and now, he met her gaze. 'It was and it is. Iceland is my homeland. I want my daughter to understand her connection to the country where I was born.'

'But she's not even a year old,' she protested. 'She won't know where she is.'

She was angry—and suspicious. He could hear it in her voice, see it in the set of her shoulders. But did she have to escalate her irritation into a full-blown confrontation? Was this how it was going to be every time they talked?

He felt a twinge of frustration. 'But *I* will know.' He shook his head. 'Tell me, is this you being deliberately bloody-minded? Or is it just impossible for you to accept that I might have a genuine motive for bringing my daughter here?'

'I'm not being bloody-minded,' she snapped. 'Cynical, maybe. In my experience your motives seem to have a habit of being a little shaky at best.'

'Meaning...?'

This conversation was pointless. He should be shutting it down. But he could feel his control slipping. It was something that had never happened before with any woman, but Lottie got under his skin. She made him lose the thread of his thoughts so that he felt off-balance and irresolute when normally he would be all cool, level-headed logic.

'You lied to me that night,' she said flatly. 'You had a whole agenda—all to do with test-driving your app—only you forgot to mention that to me. Just like you forgot to tell me that it was *your* app—the one *you* created. So forgive me if I don't find you or your claims very genuine.'

His jaw tightened. 'You think what happened between us that night was some kind of Research and Development exercise?' He shook his head. 'Then you're right—you *are* cynical.'

Her eyes were suddenly blazing, frustration and fury lighting up their pupils. 'And you're manipulative and cold-blooded.'

He wanted to stay angry, and her absurd unjustifiable accusations should have made him see red, but as her gaze locked on his all he could think about was turning the fire in her eyes into a different kind of heat...a heat that would obliterate the tension and mistrust between them...the same white heat that had fused them together that night.

His heartbeat stalled and slowly he shook his head.

'Not with you. Not that night,' he said softly. 'You had all the power, Lottie, believe me.'

Her eyes widened and a flush of colour spilled over her

cheekbones. They stared at one another, caught in the unbidden simmering spell of those remembered moments.

'Mr Stone, Ms Dawson, we'll be landing soon.'

His heart jump-started. It was his stewardess, Sam.

'If you could buckle up...?' She smiled apologetically. 'And I'm afraid that includes this little one too.'

'Of course.' He smiled coolly—more coolly than he felt.

His blood was still humming in his ears, and with an effort he forced his mind away from those taut, shimmering seconds of madness. The strength and speed of his unravelling was not admirable, but it was understandable. He was tired, and he had let his imagination run away with him, but in some ways that was a good thing.

The overwhelming, uncontrollable desire that had led him to act so carelessly twenty months ago was still there, and he loved his daughter. Only this was a reminder that those feelings were two opposing forces that could never and would never be reconciled.

How could they be when his body's response to Lottie might unleash the kind of emotion and disorder that was incompatible with the serenity he was so determined to give his daughter?

CHAPTER FOUR

ICELAND WAS NOTHING like Lottie had imagined.

Since their arrival two hours ago the sky had changed colour so many times she had lost count. Swollen lead-grey clouds had given way to a dazzling sunlight that turned everything golden, and then moments later the sun had been swallowed up by diaphanous veils of mist.

But if the weather was capricious, the land itself was otherworldly.

Through the helicopter window, the countryside rushing beneath her looked like another planet. Huge, smooth boulders that might have been used by giants in a game of football sat in a field that appeared to be covered in what looked like bright yellow moss, and carving a path several metres wide through the field was a thundering river.

It was beautiful and alien and intimidating.

A bit like Ragnar himself, she thought, gritting her teeth and hugging her daughter closer to her chest beneath the lap strap. Except that rocks and rivers didn't continually leave you second-guessing their actions.

Gazing through the glass, she tried to concentrate on the scenery, but the feeling of apprehension that had started low in her stomach when they'd landed in Reykjavik was now pushing up into her throat.

She had assumed—naively, as it now turned out—that Ragnar's home would be near Iceland's capital city. He hadn't said as much, but nor had there been any indication that it would be at the edge of the known earth, or at least the solid part.

A panicky furtive check on her phone had confirmed the worst. His home was on the Tröllaskagi—the Troll Peninsula. Beyond the peninsula was only the sea, until you reached the archipelago of Svalbard, with a roughly equal ratio of humans to polar bears, and then there was nothing but open water until you arrived in the Arctic.

He might just as well be taking her to the moon.

She glanced swiftly across the cabin to where Ragnar sat, his blue gaze scanning the skyline. He was wearing slouchy jeans, some kind of insulated jacket, and a pair of broken-in hiking boots—the kind of ordinary clothes worn by an average man taking a break in a winter wilderness. But there was nothing ordinary about Ragnar—and she wasn't talking about his wealth or his glacial beauty. There was a concentrated intensity to his presence so that even when he was sitting down she could sense the languid power in the casual arrangement of his limbs.

He was not always so languid or casual.

Her pulse stuttered.

They had spent such a short amount of time together, and yet the memory of those few feverish hours had stayed with her.

She clenched her hands against the curl of desire stirring inside her.

Even before they'd left England the idea of being alone with him for three weeks had made her feel off-balance, but now that she was here his constant nearness was playing havoc with her senses. She didn't want to be affected by him, but unfortunately her body didn't seem to have got that particular memo.

She thought back to that moment on the plane. One minute they had been arguing and then the air had seemed to bloom around them, pushing them closer, holding them captive, so that for a few pulsing seconds there had been nothing except their mutual irresistible fascination.

She shivered. And now they were going to be stuck in

the wilderness together, with nothing to hold them in check except their willpower.

It was tempting to throw his 'invitation' back in his face and tell him that she was going home—or at least back to civilisation in Reykjavik. But she doubted he would listen. And anyway, she didn't want to give him the opportunity to accuse her of having another temper tantrum.

Her gaze returned to the window. The land was growing whiter and the sky darker—and then suddenly they had arrived.

Clutching Sóley against her body, she stepped out onto the snow and gazed mutely at the house in front of her. Without the frenetic noise of the helicopter, the silence was so huge it seemed to roar inside her ears.

'Welcome to my home.'

She glanced up at Ragnar. He was standing beside her, his blond hair snapping in the wind, a slab of sunlight illuminating his face so that she could see the contours of his bones beneath the skin. He looked impassive and resolute, more returning warrior than CEO.

His eyes held hers for a few endless seconds, and then he said quietly, 'Let's go inside. I'll show you your rooms.'

'Home' didn't seem quite the right word, she thought a moment later, pressing her face against her daughter's cheek, seeking comfort in her warm, sweet smell. This was a lair—a secluded hideaway miles from anywhere— its white walls and bleached wood blending perfectly into the snow-covered landscape.

The interior did nothing to reduce her panic.

Partly it was the sheer scale of the rooms—her whole cottage would fit into the entrance hall. Partly it was the minimalist perfection of the decor, so different from the piles of baby clothes hanging above the stove and the stack of newspapers waiting to be recycled in her home. But mostly it was having her earlier fears confirmed.

That now she was here she wasn't going anywhere.

She was effectively trapped.

Back in England, when she'd acquiesced to coming to Iceland, she had assumed that if she changed her mind she could simply call a taxi.

Of course there was a helicopter sitting outside, like some squat snow-bound dragonfly, but she certainly couldn't fly it, and nor could she walk all the way back to civilisation with a baby.

Her eyes darted towards the huge expanse of glass that ran from floor to ceiling in the main living area. In the distance jagged snow-covered slopes stretched out towards an empty horizon. There was no sign of any habitation. No other buildings, no roads or telegraph poles. Just sky and snow and a sense of utter solitude.

'This is Sóley's room.'

They were upstairs now.

'The light is softer this side, and there's a beautiful view of the mountains.'

She turned to where Ragnar was holding open a door and stepped past him, trying to ignore the ripple of heat that spiralled up inside her as she momentarily brushed against his arm.

It was a beautiful room—the kind of pastel minimalist nursery that would feature in one of those upmarket baby magazines. There was a cot and a rocking chair, and a wicker basket piled high with soft toys. Unlike the rest of the house, it wasn't painted in a muted shade of off-white but in a delicate lilac, exactly the same colour as the lavender that grew in the fields beyond her cottage.

But it wasn't the unexpected reminder of home that made her body and brain freeze as though she'd fallen through ice—it was the two framed prints on the wall.

'They're mine,' she said slowly.

For a minute she was too stunned to do anything more than stare, but then slowly her brain began working again.

'You bought these through Rowley's?'

Ragnar nodded.

She stared at the prints, her heart beating out of time. It felt strange, seeing her work here in this house. Stranger still that he should have bought them unseen. But that must be what had happened, because he hadn't arrived at the gallery until later that day.

Georgina's voice floated up from somewhere inside her head. *'You know what these collectors are like. They love to have the cachet of buying up-and-coming artists' early work.'*

And she was right. A lot of wealthy buyers treated art as a commodity, and got a buzz from seeing the price of their investment soar, but…

Her arm tightened around her daughter's reassuring warmth as a chill ran down her spine.

But those buyers hadn't had a one-night stand with the artist and got her pregnant.

Her skin was suddenly too hot and too tight, and she knew without question that Ragnar hadn't bought her work as an investment. It was something far more subtle, more insidious. He had wanted to give her money, she had refused, and so he had found another, more circuitous but less overt method of getting his own way. And he got to own a little piece of her too.

'I'll pay you back.'

Her voice sounded tense and raspy with emotion, but she didn't care. What mattered was making him understand that she was not going to be outmanoeuvred by him or his wealth.

'Maybe not right at this moment, but when we get back to England.'

His gaze skimmed her face, a muscle pulling at his jaw. 'Excuse me?'

'For the prints. I told you before that I didn't want your money—well, I don't need your charity either. Whatever it might suit you to think, I'm not some starving artist living a garret.'

As she finished speaking Sóley twisted against her, arching her back and reaching out towards the floor. She had noticed a brightly coloured octopus peeking out of the toy basket and wanted to get closer. Grateful for a reason to break eye-contact, Lottie leaned forward and let her daughter scrabble forward onto the floor.

'I see.'

There was a short silence, and then he said quietly, 'Can I ask you something? Is this how it's always going to be? Or is there the slightest chance that you can imagine a future where I can say or do something innocuous and you won't immediately put two and two together and make five?'

She looked up, her stomach swooping downwards in shock. 'What do you mean?'

'I mean,' he said softly, 'that I didn't buy your work out of charity. I came to the gallery in the morning, only you weren't there and so I had a look around. I wasn't planning on buying anything, but then I saw these, and the collage, and I changed my mind.'

Lottie stared at him in silence, her mind replaying the events of that day. There had been some kind of signal failure affecting the train on her way in and she hadn't got to the gallery until mid-morning. And when she'd arrived Jem, the gallery's co-owner, had been frantic. Georgina had swanned off to meet her latest boyfriend for a champagne brunch and he was supposed to be on the other side of London meeting a client...

As though sensing the route of her thoughts, Ragnar gave her a brief, wintry smile. 'I called Rowley's on the way back to the office,' he continued remorselessly. 'And then I was in meetings all day until I came back to the gallery in the afternoon.'

He glanced down at where Sóley sat clutching the octopus triumphantly, her mouth clamped around one furry leg, her fists clenching and unclenching with undisguised joy.

'Not that I expect you to believe me, but I bought your work for two reasons. I think they're beautiful and, more importantly, I wanted Sóley to have something of you here. I know she probably doesn't recognise your work now, but I thought that in time she will and it will mean something to her.'

Her face was burning. A hard lump of shame was sitting heavily in her stomach and she felt slightly nauseous. She had been so certain that his motives were self-serving, only now it appeared that the complete opposite was true.

But how was she supposed to guess that he would do something so unselfish? So far their interaction had amounted to one night of feverish passion and several tense stand-offs, and from those encounters she had learned what? That the man standing in front of her was a generous, intuitive lover, but that he also had a resolve as hard and cold as the ice gullies that ran through the granite hills of his homeland.

It was all so contradictory and inconclusive. But either way it didn't change the facts. She had jumped to conclusions and she'd been wrong.

Taking a breath, she made herself meet his gaze. 'I'm sorry, and you're right. I overreacted. It was a kind impulse.' She cleared her throat. 'And I'm not deliberately trying to make things difficult between us—ouch!'

Twin hands were gripping her leg and, glancing down, she saw that Sóley had discarded the octopus and was now trying to pull herself upright.

'Is she walking yet?'

She shook her head, relieved at the sudden change of subject. 'Nearly. She has a walker at home—you know, with wheels—and if I help her she can push it for a couple of steps.'

As though to prove the point, Sóley lifted up her foot and, holding it aloft, she stood wobbling unsteadily on one leg, before lowering it carefully onto the rug like a pony doing dressage. She tried the other leg but this was less successful, and she slid down onto her bottom, her lower lip crumpling.

'Come here then.' Lottie reached down, but her daughter had other ideas, and she watched, her heart bumping against her ribs, as Sóley crawled over to Ragnar and wrapped her arms around his legs.

'Here, let me,' she croaked.

'It's fine,' he said softly. 'May I?'

As he reached down and picked up his daughter she felt a mixture of panic and pride. For a moment Sóley looked uncertainly at Ragnar, and then, reaching forward, she buried her face against his neck, her chubby hands gripping the blond hair that curled down his neck.

Lottie felt a quick head-rush, and then her heart fluttered upwards like a kite caught in a breeze. It was the moment she'd imagined for so long—the father embracing his daughter for the first time—but nothing could have prepared her for the conflicting tangle of emotions inside her chest or the expression of fear and awe and eagerness on Ragnar's face.

Or the fact that she recognised how completely it mirrored her own reaction that first time she'd held her daughter.

'Through here is your room.'

She nodded dumbly as Ragnar gestured towards another door.

'I thought you'd want to be close to her at night.'

'Thank you.'

She managed to speak with a gratitude she knew she ought to feel—even with the briefest of glances she could see that it was a beautiful, spacious room, with the same jaw-dropping view of the mountains—and yet she was struggling to feel anything except a mounting anxiety.

His eyes were fixed on her face. 'And I'm only just down there if you need me.'

Her throat tightened and the floor seemed to tilt sharply. But why? It was a point of information, nothing more, and yet there was something in his unwavering gaze that made her pulse accelerate—a few spun-out seconds of shimmering shared memories of a different kind of need.

Terrified what her eyes would betray if she didn't move, she nodded briskly, her heart leaping with relief as Sóley made a grab for her.

'That's good to know,' she said crisply, and she stepped neatly past him, her body loosening in relief at having temporarily evaded his cool, assessing gaze.

The rest of the tour passed without any further awkward moments—partly because she was too speechless with shock to say much. She could hardly take it all in, and she hadn't even seen the indoor-outdoor geothermal pool yet, or the several thousand acres of land that made up the estate.

Pleading tiredness from the journey, she retreated to her bedroom and let Sóley explore the contents of the toy basket as she watched the light fade from the sky. It was a relief after their constant enforced proximity on the long journey to be free of that churning undercurrent of sexual tension.

But all too soon it was time for Sóley's dinner.

With all the other changes going on in her life, she wanted to keep her daughter's routines as regular as possible—particularly meal times. But venturing downstairs required a concentrated effort of will.

The cool grey kitchen was large and immaculate. Signy, Ragnar's housekeeper, showed her where everything was kept, and how to work the gleaming professional standard cooker.

'If there's anything you can't find, just tell me and I'll order it in,' she said in faultless English, beaming at Sóley.

'Thank you, but I think you've got everything already,' she said, picturing her own sparsely filled cupboards and comparing them unfavourably with the well-stocked shelves of Signy's larder.

Sóley was far less intimidated by the upgrade in her surroundings than her mother. Thrilled by her brand-new highchair, she behaved just as she did at home, thumping out a drum solo with her beaker and laughing uncontrollably as she blew peas out of her mouth.

Lottie was laughing too, so that she didn't notice Ragnar had joined them until he said quietly, 'I didn't know vegetables could be that much fun.'

She felt her heart jolt forward. Lost in the familiar rhythm of spooning peas and mashed potato into her daughter's mouth, she'd started to feel calmer. She had overreacted, but obviously being thrown together like this in a new environment, with a man she barely knew, was going to be confusing and unsettling. It was no wonder she'd got mixed up about what she was feeling.

And so what if Ragnar looked like Thor's body-double? Once she got used to having him around he would soon lose the power to make her blood catch fire.

She gave him a quick, stiff smile. 'Neither did she until last week. It's her latest trick.'

It was harder than she would have liked to shut him out. He was just so *there*—not just his actual physical presence, but that inner stillness he possessed, a self-contained sense of certainty that she lacked entirely except in her art.

Her fingers felt thick and clumsy as he watched her pick up the empty bowl.

'Does she have dessert? Or is that not allowed?'

'Yes, it's allowed.'

There was a small pause and, nodding reluctantly to his unspoken question, she tried not to feel resentful or, even more ridiculously, betrayed as he picked up a spoon and her daughter obediently swallowed every mouthful of the yoghurt she gave him.

They were bonding, and that was what she'd wanted to happen, so why did it hurt so much? Maybe seeing them together was a reminder of how she'd failed to connect with Alistair. Or perhaps, having been briefly the sole focus of Ragnar's gaze, it stung to be in the shadows.

Her chest felt tight.

She hated herself for feeling like this—and him too, for stirring up all these ambivalent, unsettling emotions. Suddenly she wanted to be somewhere far away from his orbit. Reaching down, she undid Sóley's safety harness and lifted her out of the chair.

'I'm going to take her up now and get her ready for bed.'

She sensed that he was waiting for an invitation to join them, and she knew that she was being mean-spirited by not offering him one, but she couldn't make the words form in her mouth. For a moment she thought he would challenge her, but instead he just nodded.

'I'll come up and say goodnight in a bit.'

Normally Sóley loved bathtime, but tonight her eyes were already drooping as Lottie started to undress her, and she had barely finished half her regular bottle of milk before falling asleep.

Turning down the lights, she carefully transferred her sleeping daughter to the cot. But where was her bear? Lottie frowned. Mr Shishkin had been a gift from Lucas—Sóley couldn't sleep without him. Quickly she reversed her steps, but he wasn't in the bathroom, or on her bed.

As she walked back into her daughter's bedroom her feet faltered. Ragnar was leaning over the cot.

'What are you doing?' Her heart was beating like a snare drum.

He straightened up, his eyes meeting hers in the semi-darkness. 'I found him downstairs.' He held something out to her, and she realised what it was. 'I noticed she was pretty attached to him on the flight and I thought she might need him to sleep. Or is it a her? I didn't actually look.'

She hesitated, and then saw a faint smile tug at the edges of his mouth, and even though she knew that there were no actual butterflies in her stomach, she finally understood what people meant by that phrase, for it felt as though hundreds of them were fluttering up inside her, each beat of their wings triggering a warm, tingling pulse of pleasure.

'No, it's a he. He's called Mr Shishkin.'

Feeling his curious gaze, she felt her face grow warm.

'After Ivan Shishkin, the Russian artist.' Her eyes met his. 'It's a long story, but when I was about fourteen Lucas went to Russia with some mates and he sent me this post-card of a painting of some bears climbing in a wood by Shishkin. And then he gave Sóley the bear when she was born, so...' She cleared her throat. 'Anyway, thank you for bringing him up.'

Smiling stiffly, she edged past him and, leaning forward, tucked the bear under her daughter's arm.

'You don't need to thank me. In fact, I should probably be thanking you.'

She looked up at him in confusion. 'For what?'

He held open the door, then closed it gently behind her.

'For letting me in. I know it can't be easy for you—sharing her with me, letting me get close to her—so thank you. And, if I didn't say so before, thank you for telling me about her. If you hadn't done that…if you hadn't put your personal feelings to one side… I would never have known about her.'

He meant what he was saying. She could hear it in his voice. But that wasn't what was making her skin tingle.

'What do you mean, my personal feelings?' she asked slowly.

He studied her for a few half-seconds. 'I mean that you don't like me very much.'

'I— That's not— It's not that I don't like you. I just don't…' She hesitated.

'You don't trust me?' He finished the sentence for her.

There was a small, strained pause. 'No, I suppose I don't.'

He waited a moment. 'I can understand that. But if this is going to work—you and me and Sóley—I want that to change, and I'm going to do whatever it takes to make it change, to make you trust me. And I think the best way to achieve that is by talking and being honest with one another.'

She stared at him mutely. The blue of his eyes was so clear and steady that she could almost feel her body leaning forward to dive into their depths.

'Why don't we make a start over dinner?'

Her pulse twitched, and she took an unsteady step backwards.

Dinner. The word whispered through her head, making her think of soft lights and warm red wine, and his fingers moving through her hair, and his mouth tracing the curve of her lips, stealing her breath and her heartbeat…

'I was planning on getting an early night,' she said carefully. 'It's been a long day.'

His eyes fixed on hers.

'Not for Iceland,' he said softly. 'Please, Lottie. We can eat and talk at the same time. And Signy has already prepared the food.'

Lottie hesitated, but who could resist an invitation offered up so enticingly?

An hour later, with the entire uninspiring contents of her suitcase lying on the bed, she was starting to regret her decision. It wasn't that she cared what Ragnar thought—not really—it was just hard working out what to wear. At home in her draughty cottage with Lucas she just put on more layers, but Lucas was her brother. Then again she didn't want to look as if she was trying too hard.

In the end she settled for pale grey skinny jeans and a black cable-knit sweater, smoothing her hair into a slightly more glamorous version of her usual low ponytail.

She had thought they'd eat in the kitchen, but instead she found a table set for two in the dining area of the huge living space. The table was striking, made of some kind of industrial material—carbon fibre, maybe. It looked more like a piece of an aircraft than something you would dine around. But clearly it was a table, and it was set for dinner.

She breathed out unsteadily.

Dinner for two.

Only not some heavy-handed, candlelit cliché.

There was a soft, flickering light, but it came from a huge, slowly rotating, suspended black fireplace that she didn't remember seeing before, although obviously it must have been there. But maybe her mind was playing tricks on her, because the furniture looked different too—less angular and stark, more enticing...

She shivered. Of course everything familiar looked a little different in the shadows.

Ragnar was standing at the edge of the room. He looked like a monochrome portrait, his black jeans and sweater contrasting with the bleached gold of his hair and stubble, and she felt her body loosen with desire as he walked slowly towards her.

'Are you hungry?'

She stared at him, dry-mouthed, her unspoken hunger for him blocking out the ache in her stomach, and then she nodded. 'Starving.'

His eyes met hers, the pupils black and the irises blue like bruises. 'Then let's eat.'

The meal was simple but delicious.

Mussels with butter and birch, lamb with caramelised potatoes, and a burnt bay leaf ice-cream. She wasn't usually bothered about wine, but Ragnar's wine was exceptionally drinkable.

They both made an effort to avoid conversational pitfalls, so that despite her earlier reservations she found herself relaxing. Ragnar really wasn't like any other man she'd ever met. In her experience men either had no small talk at all, or pet subjects which they returned to again and again like homing pigeons. But, although his responses were brief, Ragnar was happy to talk about anything.

Mostly, though, he wanted to talk about their daughter.

As Signy cleared away the plates, he leaned back against his chair, his blue eyes resting on her face. 'It must have been hard, bringing up a baby on your own and being a professional artist at the same time. But I want you to know that you're not alone any more. I'm here to support you in whatever way I can.'

Trying to ignore the prickle of heat spreading across her skin, she met his gaze. An hour ago she had been feeling threatened by how easily Ragnar had been accepted by their daughter, but now it felt good to know that he would be there beside her.

'Thank you. But please don't think it was all bad. Like I said before, my family have been great, and Sóley's very easy going. She's more like Lucas than me in that way.'

His face stiffened, and her stomach clenched as briefly she wondered why, but before she had a chance to speculate he said softly, 'So how is she like you?'

She felt her face tighten. It was a question that had never occurred to her. Raising Sóley as a single parent, she'd never thought about her own genetic input. It had been a given. Now, though, she could feel that certainty slipping away. *How was her daughter like her?* Physically Sóley looked just like Ragnar, and character-wise she seemed to have Lucas's sunny, open temperament.

'I don't know,' she said slowly, flattening her hands against the table to stop them from shaking.

Her heart was beating too fast, and she felt a slippery sense of panic, as though she was looking through the wrong end of a telescope, watching herself shrink.

'I do.'

She glanced up, Ragnar was staring at her steadily.

'She has your focus. She even has the same little crease here…' reaching across the table, he touched her forehead lightly '…when she's concentrating.'

Her heart was still beating too fast, only this time not in panic but in a kind of stunned happiness. Ragnar was right. She did screw up her face when she was concentrating. And the fact that he'd made the connection made her breath catch in her throat.

'She doesn't just look at things, or people, she really gives them her whole attention. It's like she's already realised that there's something else there—some kind of "other" that she can't see.'

His fingers moved gently through her hair, then lower to her face, and his touch felt so warm and solid and irresistible that suddenly she was pressing her cheek against his hand.

She felt his hand tremble and, looking up into his face, she saw herself in the black of his pupils, saw her need and want reflected in his eyes and the same desire reflected back into hers, so that it was impossible to separate her hunger from his.

Her pulse scudded forward.

Behind her and around her the lights seemed to be spinning like a carousel, and she felt both warm and shivery. She must have drunk too much wine. But, glancing down, she saw that her glass was full. And then she looked up at Ragnar and felt her breathing change tempo as she realised that he was the source of her intoxication.

She reached shakily for the carafe of water but he was too fast.

'Here let me.'

He handed her a glass and she took it, being careful not to let her fingers touch his.

'I'm sorry… I think I must be tired.'

'We can leave dessert if you want.' As she nodded, he reached into his pocket and pulled out an envelope. 'I want to give you this. It's not urgent, but I'd like you to take a look at it when you've got a moment.'

She stared dazedly at the envelope. 'What is it?'

His eyes were a chilling, glacial blue. 'It's a letter from my lawyers—a kind of synopsis of my future relationship with Sóley.'

Her lungs felt as though they were on fire. Slowly she gazed across the room, seeing the soft lighting and glowing log fire as though for the first time.

She was such an idiot. All that talk about her seeing beneath the surface and here she was, oblivious to what was going on in front of her nose.

Her hands clenched around the stem of the glass. He'd even told her his plans.

'I'm going to do whatever it takes to make you trust me.'

And, like all successful businessmen, he'd identified her weak spot and then used the most effective weapon he had to exploit it and so achieve his goal. It just so happened that they were one and the same thing. *Himself.*

She felt numb. She had let her guard down, and all the

time he'd been cold-bloodedly pursuing his own agenda. He might have talked about support, but he wanted control.

She thought back to when he'd showed her Sóley's bedroom. Distracted by the sight of her own artwork, she'd missed the bigger picture.

The beautifully decorated room had been a message, spelling out the future—a future in which her daughter would be picked up by a chauffeur-driven car and taken by private jet to spend time with her father. Trips that would not include her.

Her heart contracted. Why did this keep happening? She had gone to meet her father and found she was superfluous. And now, having introduced her daughter to Ragnar, he was trying to push her out of Sóley's life.

Her heart began to beat hard and high beneath her ribs.

Well, he could think again.

Plucking the envelope from his hand, she stood up. 'I'll pass it on to my own lawyer.'

She was bluffing, of course. She didn't have a lawyer. But she wanted him to feel what she was feeling—to experience, if only for a moment, the same flicker of panic and powerlessness.

Watching his face darken, she turned and walked swiftly out of the room, trying to stifle the jerky rhythm of her heart, wishing that she could walk out of his life as easily.

CHAPTER FIVE

WATCHING LOTTIE STALK out of the room, Ragnar felt as though his head was going to explode. Had that just happened? He couldn't quite believe that it had, but then it was all a completely new experience for him.

Not someone flouncing off like a diva. That had been practically a daily occurrence during his childhood. Only back then, and even more so now, he had never been a participant in the drama.

Although with Lottie he kept getting sucked in and dragged centre stage.

And now she'd walked off in the middle of everything, leaving him mouthing his lines into thin air.

A part of him was desperate to go after her and demand that she act like the grown-up he and their daughter needed her to be—but what would be the point if he didn't know what he was going to say? And he didn't.

What was more, he had no idea how an evening which had started so promisingly had ended with her turning on him like a scalded cat.

Leaning back in his chair, he rubbed his hand over his face. Her reaction made no sense.

Earlier, outside their daughter's bedroom, when they'd talked about the future, he'd made it clear that he wanted to be honest with her and she'd seemed completely on board. In fact it had been the first time since their lives had reconnected that the conversation had felt ordinary and less like the verbal equivalent of a boxing match.

Agreed, his timing with the letter could have been better, but he had thought that she'd actually started to relax a little over dinner.

He glanced across to her empty chair. He had liked it that she had started to relax, for it had reminded him of the evening when they'd first met.

His pulse quickened.

It was strange. In real terms they had spent such a short time together—so short, in fact, that it could be comfortably counted in hours. And yet the memory of it had been imprinted in his head, so that it already felt as if he'd known her a lifetime.

His mind went back to the moment he'd first seen her. She had looked just like her profile picture on the app, and yet nothing like it. Her hair was a kind of mid to light brown, but the camera lens hadn't picked up all the lustrous threads of gold and copper, and nor had it caught the softness of her eyes or the sweetness of her tentative smile. But mostly, because of course it was only a photo, it had failed to capture that mesmerising husky voice.

Frankly, she could have been reading the phone book backwards to him and he wouldn't have noticed. And it had been the same earlier, as she'd talked about their daughter.

He hadn't wanted to break the spell. In fact, he hadn't been able to break it. Truthfully, he had been fighting himself all evening not to lean across the table and kiss her. But there was no point now in imagining how it would feel to have those soft lips part against his and, picking up his wine glass, he drained the contents.

Standing up, he switched off the lights and made his way upstairs. As he reached the top step he hesitated.

His rooms were to the right, but from where he was standing he could see a thin line of light beneath Lottie's door. Instantly he felt his breath clog his throat. She was awake, and they definitely had unfinished business. Before he had a chance to finish that thought, he was turning to the left and walking towards her room.

He reached her door in three strides and raised his

hand—but as he did so he caught sight of the illuminated numerals of his watch and something…a sharp memory of nights spent listening to the sound of raised voices and doors slamming…stayed his hand. Instead of knocking, his knuckles brushed soundlessly against the wood.

It was after midnight. The house was in darkness.

More importantly, this wasn't him. He watched, he waited, but he didn't participate. He certainly didn't ever walk into a storm of his own volition, and there was nothing to be gained by doing so now.

Restarting their tense conversation in the more intimate setting of her bedroom had 'bad idea' written all over it in mile-high letters. It would be far better to wait until the morning to confront her—not least because their strongest motive for any reconciliation would be awake and eating breakfast in her highchair.

Turning, he walked to his room. It was late, and he was tired, and his body was aching as though it was going through some kind of withdrawal.

He needed a quick shower and a long sleep—not some protracted debate with someone who was just going to argue that black was white.

Besides, she was probably already in bed.

He breathed in sharply, his groin hardening in the time it took his brain to jump from thinking the word 'bed' to picturing a near naked Lottie between the sheets.

Was this his fault?

He couldn't see how. The evening had been going so well. They'd eaten and talked, and watching the way her eyes shone with eagerness when she talked about Sóley had made his breathing lose rhythm. Only when he'd asked her how she was like her daughter the joy had faded from her voice and her fingers had started to shake as if someone was pressing a bruise on her heart.

He hadn't thought about what he was going say or do—

in fact he hadn't been thinking at all. He had felt her pain, and he'd wanted to make whatever it was that was hurting her stop, and so he'd reached out and touched her face, half expecting her to pull away.

Only she hadn't. And then, watching her eyes soften, he had been lost, falling back to that night when the softness in her eyes had stripped him not just of his clothes but of all sense and inhibition.

His body tensed—not at the memory of Lottie's hands pulling at the buckle of his trousers, but at the dull, insistent hum of his phone.

Glancing over to where it lay on the bed, he cursed softly. It would be Marta, his nineteen-year-old half-sister. She was the youngest member of his family and for the last two months had been holding off all rivals in a crowded field to take the title of most demanding sibling in his life.

His jaw tightened. He loved his sister, but since the acrimonious breakdown of her parents' marriage her life had been spiralling out of control. She had been stopped by the police and given a warning for reckless driving, and then she and her now ex-boyfriend Marcus had been involved in an argument with some photographers, after his twenty-first birthday party. And all of it had been gleefully reported in the media.

What she needed was guidance and reassurance.

What she had was a father—Nathan, who had already moved on to a new actress-model wife, and was wrapped up in the imminent birth of their first child.

She also needed her mother—who also happened to be *his* mother. Except Elin was far too busy being placated by her entourage of hairdressers and personal trainers to deal with her difficult daughter.

Only why did that make Marta his problem?

But he knew why. He couldn't turn his back on his family, and nor could he live like them, so the only way he could make it work was by taking a step back—just as he'd done outside Lottie's door.

He thought back to when Marta was a little girl. She had always been bringing him some necklace or bracelet that was so snarled up it was impossible to see where it began and where it ended, but he'd always sat down and patiently untangled it for her. It was just what he did—what he was still doing. Only now it was her life that he was untangling.

'Marta—'

He heard her quick breath, like a gasp, and then she was speaking incoherently, fat, choking sobs interspersing every other word.

'Ragnar—Ragnar, I hate her! She won't listen to me. It's not my fault. I can't stand living with her. You have to speak to her.'

She burst into tears.

Pushing back against the surge of tiredness swirling around him, Ragnar walked slowly across the room and stopped in front of the window, wondering exactly what had triggered this latest set-to between his mother and half-sister, and whether she had even considered the possibility that he might be sleeping.

Almost certainly not, he thought, gazing up at the sky. It was a clear night, and his brain ticked off the constellations as he waited for her to stop crying. When, finally, she let out a juddering breath he said calmly, 'Better? Okay, tell me what's been going on.'

It was a fairly straightforward story from Marta's point of view. In her telling, she was the innocent victim, her mother and father were twin evil villains, and he, Ragnar, had been drafted in to play the role of rescuer.

'She's horrible all the time and I'm sick of her acting like it's all about her.'

'It's not all about her—but she has just lost her husband,' he said mildly.

His sister's tears slid into resentful fury. 'He's not dead,' she snapped. 'He's just shacked up with that hideous stick insect in Calabasas. And anyway, it's hypocritical of her to be so upset. It wasn't as though she cared when she left Frank.'

To a certain extent that was true, Ragnar conceded. Elin had discarded her fourth husband, Frank, without so much as a backward glance, but perhaps she had expected her fifth husband to be her last. Although perhaps not. His mother had the kind of blonde ethereal looks that laid waste to any man who crossed her path, and she was rarely satisfied with anything or anyone for long.

But, putting aside Marta's tears and rage, what mattered was brokering peace between her and their mother.

'I think what you both need is a bit of space from one another.'

He hesitated. Lamerton would be empty for three weeks, and in his family three weeks was the equivalent of a decade in terms of drama. Quite possibly the whole thing would have blown over by then, but in the short term getting his sister and mother on different continents would stop them killing one another.

He cleared his throat. 'Look, if you need somewhere to stay you can use Lamerton. I'm sure you'll find something to amuse you in London.' Or more likely *someone*, he thought dryly. 'And if you don't want to see anyone you can just chill out on the estate.'

'Oh, Ragnar, really? You're an angel.'

Hearing her squeal of excitement, he nearly changed his mind. An empty house miles from anywhere and an unsupervised and excitable Marta were not a good combination—but, having planted the seed, he knew that it would be impossible to dislodge the idea from her mind. He would just have to hope that her fear of getting on his wrong side would curb her worst instincts.

'This doesn't mean I don't have rules, Marta,' he said firmly. 'You will be polite to John and Francesca. They are not there to put up with your mess or your tantrums.' He paused. 'Of course ordinarily I'd tell you to treat the place as your own, but in your case—*in your case*,' he repeated over her squawk of protest, 'I would ask that you don't. And do not—I repeat, *do not*—even think about having a party. And by "party" I mean any gathering of people numbering more than you and one other person.'

There was a small sulky silence from the other end of the phone, and then he heard her sigh.

'Okay, fine. I'll be polite, and I won't make a mess, and *obviously* I wouldn't dream of having a party in your house.'

Catching sight of himself in the window, Ragnar was tempted to roll his eyes at his reflection. Instead he said calmly, 'I just don't want there to be any confusion.' Glancing down at his watch, he grimaced. It was nearly a quarter past one. 'Right, I'll leave you to talk to Elin. Just let me know when you're going over and I'll send John to pick you up.'

'Thanks Ragnar.' Her voice softened and she hesitated. 'Actually, do you think you could call her? I think she'll take it better from you.'

After he'd hung up he stood with the phone in his hand, thinking. As usual Marta hadn't asked him one question about himself, but at no point had it occurred to him to tell his sister that she was an aunt. Nor was he planning on telling her until it was absolutely necessary. He wanted to keep his daughter to himself for a while—keep her from being absorbed by his family.

He'd talk to his mother later. Now he really was going to bed.

He showered quickly, towelled himself dry and then pulled on the loose cotton trousers he wore to sleep in.

As he unfastened his watch, he heard it.

A baby crying.

He paused, his body turning instinctively towards the sound.

The wail faded and, flicking off the light, he closed his eyes and rolled onto his side, his mind sliding smoothly into sleep.

He woke with a start.

Reaching out, he found his watch in the darkness. It was just gone half-two in the morning.

But why had he woken?

And then he heard it—the same unmistakable wail as before. For a few half-seconds he lay in the darkness, listening to his daughter cry. Only this time it didn't falter. Instead it seemed to be escalating.

Had she cried like that before?

Not really. A little on the plane, but that had been more like a kind of fussing.

His chest felt suddenly leaden with tension, and he sat up and switched on the bedside light.

It was ten to three now.

Was that a long time for a baby to cry?

Why wasn't she stopping?

He tried to remember his half-brothers and sisters at Sóley's age, but all the adults in his life had always been more than happy to let a crying baby or toddler disappear with a nanny.

His pulse sped up as the baby carried on wailing. She had seemed fine earlier, but she didn't sound fine now. Her cry was changing, intensifying in pitch, so that even at this distance he could feel her distress resonating inside his chest.

And suddenly he was moving—rolling out of bed and walking swiftly out of his room.

The noise grew louder and louder as he got closer. For a

moment he stood outside the door to his daughter's room, but when the crying began again he pushed it open.

Lottie was standing in the centre of the room with her back to him, wearing some kind of robe, her hair spilling over her shoulders. She was rocking the baby gently, making soothing sounds, and as he spoke her name she turned, her eyes widening with shock.

'Is everything okay?'

It wasn't. He didn't need to be a childcare expert to see that Sóley was upset and so was Lottie.

The baby's cheeks were red and tear-stained and she was burrowing against her mother's shoulder like some little mammal, then abruptly rearing backwards, her small face scrunched up in inconsolable fury.

Lottie looked pale and exhausted. 'She's teething.'

She winced as Sóley jerked her head up and banged into her chin, and then immediately began crying again.

As her ear-splitting crescendo of rage and frustration filled the room, Ragnar took a step forward. 'Here, let me.'

'No—' Her eyes flared, and she half turned away, clutching her struggling daughter. 'I didn't ask for your help and I don't want it.'

He could hear the fatigue in her voice—and something like fear.

Only why would she be scared?

He stared at her back in silence. He didn't know the answer to that question, but he did know that he didn't like the way it made him feel.

'Lottie,' he said again. 'I know you don't need my help. Of course you don't. You've managed without it for eleven months. I'm not trying to interfere—really, I'm not. Just tell me what to do and I'll do it.'

'You can leave.' She turned, her eyes fierce. 'That's what you can do.'

He stared at her, biting down on his own corresponding

rush of anger. Earlier she'd got upset about the letter from his lawyers, and now she'd turned on him like a cornered lioness with her cub—so what exactly was the right way for him to be a part of his daughter's life?

As though Sóley had heard his thoughts she lifted her head, her blue eyes fixing on his face, and then without warning she reached out for him. Shocked, he caught her, intending to return her to Lottie, but her tiny hands were already grasping his neck and he felt his heart swell against his ribs as she tucked her face against his shoulder, her sobs subsiding.

Her body felt hot and taut, but after a moment he felt her grow heavier and automatically he began to rock her in his arms, shifting slowly from side to side, holding his breath, his entire consciousness fixed on the softness of her cheek against his skin and its confirmation of his in-contestable role in her life.

'Here.' Lottie was laying a blanket over her daughter's back. 'When you put her in the cot she needs to go on her side,' she said flatly.

He leaned over and placed the baby carefully on the mattress. As he slid his hands out from under the weight of her body she shifted in her sleep, her fingers splaying out like tiny pink starfish, but then she gave a small, juddering sigh, and as he tucked her bear underneath the blanket her breathing slowed and grew steadier.

He felt a rush of relief and exhilaration and, straightening up, he turned towards Lottie. It wasn't quite a team effort, but it was the first time they had worked together as parents. He wanted to share the moment with her and, stupidly, he had assumed, or hoped anyway, that she might feel the same way.

If anything, though, she looked drawn and distant, and desperate for him to leave.

His jaw tightened.

Obviously they had parted on poor terms earlier in the evening, and he would have to be emotionally tone-deaf not to see how annoying it must have been to watch Sóley settle in his arms, but surely she could take a step back and meet him halfway.

He glanced over at her small, still face.

Apparently not.

'So, I should—we should probably get some sleep,' she said stiffly.

There could be no mistaking either her tone or the implication of her words. She was dismissing him.

The skin of his face was stretched so tight he thought it might crack, and he was having to physically restrain his temper as though it was a wilful horse.

But he'd reached his day's quota of conversations with irrational childish women, and without saying a word he turned and left the room.

Watching the door close closed behind him, Lottie breathed out unsteadily.

She wanted to scream and rage like her daughter. Her whole body was jangling, aching with misery. She knew she was being unreasonable and petty, and that she should be happy that Ragnar wanted to be a hands-on father. But she hurt so badly that there wasn't room for any other feeling.

It had been such a shock, seeing Sóley reach out for him like that. Her daughter had always wanted *her*, before anyone else. Watching him settle her, she'd told herself that it didn't matter. That it was what was meant to happen and what she'd wanted to happen and that she didn't mind.

Except that she did mind.

It made her feel empty and cold, as though a huge dark cloud was blocking out the sunlight.

You're being stupid, she told herself. *You're just tired and*

it's making you think crazy thoughts. Sóley was exhausted.
If he hadn't been there she would have settled with you.

But that wasn't the point.

She had been there and her daughter had still chosen Ragnar. If he'd been in her life from birth she would never have questioned it, or cared. Only having grown up without a father herself, she'd assumed that she took precedence and that his role was secondary…inferior. Optional.

She bit her lip. But those were her mother's values, not hers, so why was she behaving like this? Why invite his involvement and then keep him at arm's length?

It was all such a mess.

If only she was at home. She would go downstairs, where the range would be warm, and she would lean against it, absorbing its heat while she waited for the kettle to boil. And maybe Lucas would wake up and come and sit at the table and tell her some crazy story about his day…

She pushed back against the swell of homesickness in her throat. Thinking about family and her cottage wasn't going to help. She needed to sleep, but the thought of lying in the darkness and just waiting for her body and brain to relax was appalling. Maybe if she made herself some tea? It would mean going downstairs, but it was what she would do at home and right now she needed something familiar.

Clutching the baby monitor and using her phone as a torch, she made her way to the kitchen. Thankfully, she remembered where the light switches were.

Signy had shown her how to use the stainless steel state-of-the-art coffee machine. But coffee was the last thing she wanted or needed.

'What are you doing?'

An electrical current snaked down her spine and her head snapped round. Ragnar was standing at the other end of the kitchen, watching her steadily.

She stared back at him, her heart bumping against her

ribs. Upstairs, with Sóley screaming and her nerves in melt-down, she had not really noticed what he was wearing—or rather not wearing. Now, though, in the quiet intimacy of the kitchen, it was difficult to drag her gaze away from his smooth, muscular chest, and the trail of tiny golden hair that disappeared into the waistband of his trousers.

But never mind what he was wearing, what about her? She glanced down at herself, her skin suddenly prickling. Had her robe shrunk or did it always show this much leg?

'I'm trying to find tea bags. Signy did show me, but I can't remember.'

'I know where they are.' He walked across the kitchen. 'Any particular flavour?'

She shrugged. As soon as his back was turned she jerked the robe tighter, tugging the hem lower over her thighs. 'Chamomile. Or peppermint. I can make it myself.'

There was a moment's silence.

'I'm sure you can,' he said.

She watched as he filled a teapot with boiling water from the coffee machine.

'Here we are.' He slid a teapot onto the counter. Her eyes darted to the cups—the *two* cups.

'I thought I'd join you.' His eyes rested on her face. 'Unless you've any objections?'

Taking her silence as consent, he slid onto one of the bar stools and she jerked her eyes away from the flex of his stomach muscles. 'Would it matter if I did?'

He held her gaze. 'That would depend, I suppose, on your objection.'

She swallowed. 'You sound like a lawyer.'

He didn't flinch. 'You're not on trial here, Lottie.'

'Really?' She shook her head. 'That's not how it feels to me.'

He leaned backwards, his arm draped casually against

the counter, but she caught a flash of blue and knew that he was watching her intently. 'I disagree.'

She blinked. 'Right. So you're telling me how I'm feeling?' she said slowly.

Her fingers twitched against the handle of the cup. There was something about his words that made a veil of red slide in front of her eyes. His arrogant assumption that he knew better than her. That he knew her better than she knew herself.

'That's not what I said.'

'And yet that's exactly how it sounded.' She glared at him.

He sighed. 'You know, if anyone's on trial here it's me— although I have to admit I'm not exactly sure what it is you're accusing me of doing.'

She was suddenly simmering with anger. Surely he was joking? 'Other than backing me into a corner and threatening me with lawyers at every opportunity.'

'There was nothing threatening in that letter—which you would know if you'd bothered to read it. But then why read it when you've already made up your mind?'

He spoke quietly, but she could hear a thread of exasperation weaving through his voice.

What did he have to be frustrated about?

She was the one losing control of her life and her daughter. And it was disingenuous of him to say that the letter wasn't threatening. Maybe it wasn't, but the fact that he had lawyers on call who worked out of office hours to protect his interests was intimidating, and he knew it.

'You said that you didn't want to escalate things,' she said accusingly. 'That you just want what's best for Sóley—'

'I don't.' He cut her off. 'And I do.'

'Well, I disagree.' She met his gaze, feeling a small rush of satisfaction as she threw his words back at him. 'You want what's best for you. Everything is on your terms.

Where we met, *when* we met. *This holiday.* You even went behind my back to Georgina.'

'Out of courtesy.' His blue eyes were like chips of glacial ice. 'And if I hadn't—if I'd left it to you—I'd still be waiting to meet my daughter.'

She stared at him, open-mouthed, a beat of anger leapfrogging across her skin. He was unbelievable. How could he be so unfair? So self-righteous?

'In case you've forgotten, I was the one who got in touch with you.'

'I haven't forgotten,' he said tersely. 'I just don't understand why you bothered.'

Her hands balled into fists. 'You know why. So you could get to know Sóley.'

'Except you don't want me to get to know her.' He shook his head, his blue eyes hard and uncompromising. 'What exactly is it you want from me? You gave me such a hard time for even suggesting that I help you financially, but every time I so much as offer to hold my daughter you can't get away from me fast enough. Look at tonight,' he carried on remorselessly, 'I wanted to help and you kept pushing me away.'

Her heart was pounding. He was right. She *had* pushed him away, and from his perspective it probably didn't make sense. But why did she have to see anything from his point of view? It wasn't as though her needs were high on his agenda.

She took a deep breath. 'Do you think that was the first time she's been like that?'

'No, of course not. And I'm not questioning your parenting skills. I know you can cope, but I don't know why you think you need to cope alone.'

She felt a buzzing in her ears. Out of any question he could have asked, it was the one that hurt the most. How could she explain to this cool-eyed stranger who didn't need anyone how she felt?

Her daughter's birth had made her feel whole and necessary. It had taken the sting out of her father's rejection and eased her ever-present sense of being 'other' to her mother and brother's dark-eyed autonomy.

And then she had seen Ragnar on television and, prompted by guilt and a desire to do the right thing, she had got in touch. Maybe it had been the right thing to do, but it felt like a mistake—only it had taken until tonight for her to see how big a mistake.

'It doesn't matter.'

Her throat tightened and she pushed back her chair. Her voice was shaking…her hands too. She wanted to leave, to crawl somewhere quiet and dark and hide from the terrible ache of loneliness that was swallowing her whole.

'It does to me.'

He was standing too now, but that wasn't what made her hesitate. It was the sudden fierceness of his words, as though they had been dragged out of him against his will.

'I have to go,' she said.

She felt his hand brush against hers.

'What is it?' he asked.

'It's nothing.' She shook her head. 'I'm just tired.'

'Tired of what?'

The gentleness of his voice as much as his question itself surprised her. 'I don't know,' she lied, lowering her face.

She couldn't tell him the truth. How could she explain the convoluted, chaotic journey that had brought her here, to this kitchen, to this man who lived his life by numbers?

But if she'd thought her silence would answer his question she'd been wrong. Glancing up, she saw that he was waiting, willing to wait for however long it took, and the fact that he was prepared to do that for her seemed to ease the tightness in her throat.

'It's stupid really…and unfair.'

'What is?' he said softly.

'It's not their fault. It's not my mum and Lucas's fault that I feel like an outsider when they're together.'

He studied her face. 'I thought you were close to them?'

'I am.' Her mouth trembled. 'I love them, and they love me, but we're so different.' She frowned. 'I know it sounds ridiculous, and I'm not expecting you to understand, but it feels like even though they're my family I don't fit in.'

For a moment he didn't reply, and then his eyes met hers. 'No, I do understand.'

She took a breath. 'I thought for a long time that I must be like my dad. My mum never told him she was pregnant with me, and I was convinced that if I met him there would be this moment of recognition, this connection between us.'

Her voice faltered, the memory of that stilted meeting catching her unawares, the feeling of failure and disappointment undimmed by time.

'But it didn't?' he asked.

She shook her head. 'It was too late. There was nothing there. We were like damp firewood.' Clenching her hands, she forced her mouth into a stiff smile. 'That's why I wanted you to meet Sóley now, when you still had room for her.'

'It wouldn't have mattered when you told me. I would always have made room for her,' he said simply, and her heart thudded hard as he caught her hands, uncurling her fists and slotting his fingers through hers. 'But that doesn't mean there isn't room for you too.'

She was about to protest, to pretend that he'd misunderstood, but then she thought back to how it had felt when her daughter had reached out to Ragnar. 'I don't want to lose her.'

'You won't.' Letting go of her hands, he gripped her shoulders. 'You can't lose her. She loves you and needs you more than anyone else in the world. You're her mother.'

'And you're her father.' Her face tightened. 'And I'm sorry that I've pushed you away.'

His gaze was the clear deep blue of an Arctic sky. 'I'm right here. And I'm not going anywhere.'

'But I've made everything so difficult—and that's not what I wanted to do…not what I want to do—'

She broke off, her insides tightening as they both listened to her words reverberate around the silent kitchen.

A minute passed, and then another.

'So, what is it, then?' he said hoarsely. 'What do you want to do, Lottie?'

She stared at him dazedly. Her tongue was in knots and she couldn't seem to breathe right. The air around her was shifting and swelling, pressing closer. She was losing her balance.

Reaching out to steady herself, she laid the palm of her hand against his chest. He breathed in sharply, his shoulders tensing, and the sudden acceleration of his heartbeat made her whole body tremble.

'What do I want?' she whispered.

For one intense, dizzying second they stared at one another, and then she took a small, unsteady step towards him.

'I want this,' she said and, leaning forward, she kissed him lightly.

His mouth was warm and firm, and she felt her limbs turn to air as he wrapped a hand around her waist and pulled her closer, moulding her body against his.

Heat was seeping through her robe, spreading out beneath the insistent pressure of his fingers, and she moaned softly, her arms circling his neck, her hands grasping his hair as he parted her lips, deepening the kiss. She felt his hands sliding smoothly over the bare skin of thighs, and then he was lifting her up onto the counter.

The granite was hard and cold, but she barely noticed. She could feel his lips moving over her neck, his tongue circling the pulse beating at the base of her throat, and then his hands cupped her breasts, and as his fingers pushed aside the thin fabric and found her nipples she gasped into his mouth.

Her head was spinning, her abdomen aching with a tension that made her stir restlessly against him. She was so tight and damp and, grabbing his arms, she curled her legs around his thighs, drawing him closer, pushing against the solid length beneath his trousers, trying, wanting, *needing* to appease the ache—

The sudden burst of static was like a thunderclap.

They both froze, jerking backwards from one another as though they'd been stung.

Lottie clutched at the counter as the kitchen swam back into focus. What were they doing? *What was she doing?*

'Lottie—'

Ragnar was standing beside her, but her eyes were fixed guiltily on the baby monitor.

'I have to go.'

She glanced up at him. His eyes were narrowed and he was breathing unsteadily. He looked as dazed as she felt, but right now she wasn't up to sharing anything with him— particularly her shock at their sudden mutual loss of control.

She shook her head. 'I can't.'

And, still shaking her head, she snatched up the monitor and fled.

CHAPTER SIX

STANDING IN FRONT of his bedroom window, Ragnar gazed unblinkingly into the lemon-coloured light. At some point it had snowed heavily, and an eiderdown of sparkling untouched whiteness stretched away from the house as far as the eye could see.

He had woken late—so late, in fact, that in the first few seconds after he'd opened his eyes he'd struggled to remember where he was, even when it was. The last time he'd slept in late he'd been about fourteen years old.

He breathed out against the dull ache in his groin. And that wasn't the only similarity with his fourteen-year-old self. His body hardened as he rewound his mind back through the early hours of the morning, pressing 'pause' at the moment when Lottie had reached out and touched his chest and then leaned in to kiss him, or had he lowered his mouth to kiss her?

She had been wearing some kind of soft cotton robe and, catching a glimpse of her trying to smooth the fabric so that it covered more of her thighs, he had completely lost track of what she saying, for it had been all too easy to imagine those same hands smoothing and caressing his body.

But had he known what was about to happen?

He considered the question. Not in terms of seconds and minutes maybe. And yet it had been out there waiting to happen since the moment their lives had reconnected outside his office.

They'd both been fighting it, using anger to deflect their desire, but each time they'd quarrelled their hunger had edged out their anger a little more, until finally it had been too tempting, too inevitable, too impossible to resist.

Their unfinished connection was like that feeling when you found a loose tooth and couldn't leave it alone and kept probing and jiggling it with the tip of your tongue. Hardly surprising then, that they had ended up kissing.

The kiss had been fierce and tender and beyond any conscious control. A kiss driven by a need and hunger that had burned like a molten core deep inside him.

It had lasted sixty seconds at most, and yet it had felt like an admission of everything that had gone on between them. And everything that was still pulling them together now.

He breathed out unsteadily. It was the first time he'd really acknowledged that fact—that this pulsing thread of longing was as much about the present as the past. Although why it had taken him so long to figure that out was a mystery, given that he seemed to think about Lottie in all the pauses in his day and in the dark silence of the night.

To put it in its simplest terms, he wanted her—and she wanted him. But where would that wanting take them?

His heart thumped lightly against his ribs. Sex was supposed to be simple, and at its most simple it was just bodies connecting and intertwining.

He felt his body harden more.

But, of course, in reality sex was rarely that straightforward. How could it be? There were billions of people on the planet. Even if you eliminated vast numbers of them on the grounds of age, geography, or mutual attraction, that still left a lot of potential hook-ups out there—and, realistically, what were the chances of two people who felt exactly the same way about sex and commitment finding one another and then continuing to feel the same way until death parted them?

He grimaced. Judging by his family's track record: slim to none. But he already knew that. It was the reason he'd created *ice/breakr* in the first place. To mathematically optimise the odds of couples finding a match. And the numbers clearly worked. According to the latest data from his team, the app was making about twelve million matches a day.

There was just one small problem. According to his own algorithm, one night should have been enough to satisfy both himself and Lottie—and they'd already shared a night. Yet just hours ago, the strength and speed of their desire had been mutual and irresistible.

So what happened now?

He sighed. He was back where he'd started and no nearer to finding an answer.

The dull, insistent ring of his phone made him glance away from the window and the confusing, circuitous path of his thoughts. Walking over to his bed, he picked up the phone and looked down at the screen, his face stilling. It was his mother.

He'd called her earlier and left a message, suggesting that Marta should go over and stay at Lamerton. No doubt she was returning his call. He was about to answer her when something pulled at the edge of his vision—a movement, the shape of a person, a woman...

His pulse began to beat faster, his heart leaping against his ribs as though trying to reach her.

It was Lottie, holding Sóley in her arms. Maybe it was her clothes—she was dressed for the weather in a black fur-trimmed parka and dark jeans—or maybe it was her loose ponytail and chunky dark boots, but she looked more like a student than a professional artist and mother.

He stared at her, transfixed. In the margins of his brain he knew that his phone was still ringing, but for the first time in his life he ignored it.

There was something so beautiful and tranquil about the scene outside his window, and he didn't want to risk spoiling it by letting an episode of his family soap opera play out in the background.

He felt his phone vibrate in his hand as his mother left a message. But that was fine. For once, she was going to have to wait.

His shoulders tightened. Outside the window, Lottie was holding out a handful of snow for his daughter to inspect.
His daughter.

He frowned. He should call his mother back, tell her about Sóley. Forming the words inside his head, he tried to imagine saying them to his mother. But, just as when he'd been talking to Marta, he checked himself—and immediately felt guilty, but relieved.

At some point he would tell everyone, but right now he wanted to keep his daughter to himself for a little longer—to defer the moment when she would be absorbed by his chaotic, wonderful, exhausting family.

He walked slowly beside the window, shortening his strides to mirror Lottie's as she picked her way slowly across the snow-covered lawn like one of the deer at Lamerton.

She stopped, and he stopped too. Holding his breath, he watched her lean forward and lower the little girl onto the snow. Sóley was wearing an all-in-one snowsuit, and her bright golden curls were hidden beneath a tiny hat shaped like some kind of fruit. Holding both her mother's hands, she teetered unsteadily on the spot, but even at this distance her excitement was tangible, and he felt a smile pull at the corners of his mouth as she tugged one mittened hand free and crouched down to pat the snow.

It might be the first time she'd ever seen it, and he felt a buzz of elation at witnessing her delight.

He stared intently through the glass, enjoying this unexpected opportunity to observe mother and daughter together, all the more so because Lottie had no idea that she was being watched.

His mouth twisted.

That made it sound like he was spying on her—but was it really so bad to want this one small moment to himself? Obviously it wasn't the first time he'd seen the two of them together, but he knew his presence set Lottie's teeth on edge.

Although maybe that had changed now, he thought, remembering how she had opened up to him in the early hours of the morning.

When she'd first started talking about feeling tired he'd assumed she was referring to all the sleepless nights involved in having a small baby, but then she'd told him about her father's rejection, and her feeling of being different from her mother and brother.

Her honesty had surprised and touched him—the more so because he still regretted the lies he'd told her that first night.

But it was not just her honesty that had got under his skin.

His sisters and brothers, even his parents, poured out their hearts to him on a regular basis, but always his first instinct was to blank out the emotional drama and concentrate solely on the facts. Only with Lottie there had been no drama. She hadn't wept or raged, and yet he'd found it impossible to block out the quiet ache in her voice as she'd told him her story.

It was an unsettling discovery to meet someone who could slip beneath his defences, and for it to be Lottie was even more unnerving. Only wasn't it completely understandable for him to feel that way? Logical, even?

Lottie was the mother of his daughter, so of course he cared. He hadn't liked knowing that she was upset, or that in some clumsy way he had contributed to her distress. And it had been only natural for him to want to comfort her.

Glancing back down at the woman standing in the snow, he felt his body still, remembering the feverish kiss they'd shared. Truthfully, comforting her had been low, low down on his agenda when the blood had been pounding through his veins and he'd lowered his mouth to those sweet, soft lips.

He wanted her and she wanted him, and his heartbeat stumbled as the question came back to him—the one he'd turned away from earlier. *But where would that wanting take them?*

He wasn't a fool, and he knew that giving in to this ache, this hunger, this pull between them, would end badly. How could it not? There was too much at stake—too much to lose or damage or both. Having sex with Lottie, no matter how badly he wanted it or she wanted it, would introduce too many random elements into their relationship, and he didn't do random.

He felt his shoulders stiffen.

More to the point, he didn't do relationships.

And here in his home, the home he was sharing with her and their daughter, sex was never going to feel like just some casual hook-up. There would be consequences— tempting to ignore now, in the face of the urgency and pull of their desire, but as he knew from personal experience of unpicking his family's destructive, impulsive affairs, they were consequences that ultimately neither of them would be able to outrun.

Consequences he didn't want to take on.

Not now, not ever.

Taking her eyes off her daughter for a moment, Lottie raised her face and gazed up at the sky. She had been hoping that it would have the same effect that it did in Suffolk, and that the feelings of inadequacy and mortification she'd been carrying on her shoulders since waking would magically melt away in the face of its vast indifference.

It might have worked if the sky had been the washed-out grey of yesterday. Unfortunately she was in Iceland, and today the sky was the same brilliant blue as Sóley's eyes—Ragnar's too.

Her heart gave a thump and she felt a thumbprint of heat on both cheeks as she thought back to what had happened and what might so easily have happened in the early hours of this morning.

She still couldn't quite believe that she'd told Ragnar about her father, and about how she felt about Lucas and her mum. But that wasn't even the worst part. As if blurting out all that wasn't mortifying enough, she'd then completely lost her mind and kissed him.

Driven by the restless ache that had been turning her inside out, she hadn't been able to hold back—and she hadn't wanted him to hold back either.

She'd crossed the line. Not in the sense of winning a race, but by stepping into a no-man's land where anything could and might happen.

It was just a kiss, she told herself firmly. And yet if the baby monitor hadn't interrupted them, what then?

Short answer: nothing good.

Her skin twitched as her brain silently offered up a slideshow of herself and Ragnar, their naked bodies a perfect fit as they moved together, breath quickening in a shuddering climax.

Okay, that was a lie.

Sex with Ragnar would be fierce and tender and utterly unforgettable, but that was exactly why she should never have kissed him.

Her heart began beating a little faster. It was tempting to blame her behaviour on tiredness, or the stress of the last few days—to argue that the simmering anger between them had blurred into another kind of intense emotion and so struck a different kind of spark.

And, yes, some of those arguments were plausible, and

others were true, but none of them was the reason she had kissed him. That was much more simple.

He had been standing in front of her, close enough that she could feel the heat coming off his skin, close enough that his gaze had made her think of choices, and possibilities, and a never-forgotten night of peerless pleasure.

In other words, she had kissed him because she'd wanted to.

But then he had kissed her back, his mouth parting hers, pressing her closer, until their bodies had been seamless, until she had been frantic and twisting in his arms—

Her face felt hot, the skin suddenly too tight across her cheekbones. She knew she should regret what had happened, and yet she couldn't—not quite. But that didn't mean it was going to happen again.

Clearly she and Ragnar had 'chemistry'. It seemed like such a boring word for the astonishing intensity of their attraction, for the ceaseless craving that made her breathing change pace. But, after struggling even to be civil to one another, they had finally achieved a fragile symbiosis based on what was best for Sóley. Having sex was only going to put that in jeopardy. Whatever her body might want to believe.

Sex was never simple.

Her daughter was proof of that.

She and Ragnar had used logic and mathematical certainty to select one another, on the basis that they both wanted the same thing, only that certainly hadn't included having a baby together.

But, even without putting Sóley into the equation, she knew from her own limited and unremarkable experience that for most people, most of the time, sex was more than just bodies. There was always some kind of emotional response—regret, hope, doubt, excitement—and that response was often complex and confusingly contradictory.

Right now she didn't need any more confusion in her life, and she was going to have to find a way to express that to Ragnar.

She swore silently, and Sóley looked up at her, her eyes widening in confusion as though she had actually heard and understood the word.

'Let's go and get your lunch,' she said, and quickly, guiltily, swung her daughter up into the air and held her close, burying her face in her daughter's neck until the soft pressure of Ragnar's mouth was just a dull memory.

For the moment anyway. But she was going to have face him sooner or later.

She turned towards the house—and froze.

Ragnar was walking towards her, smoothly and steadily, his blond hair shining like bronze in the sunlight. Unlike her, he wasn't wearing a coat, just a dark jumper with jeans and boots, and suddenly her breath felt hot and slippery in her throat. He was so heart-stoppingly handsome—and, in comparison to the flickering images inside her head, as solid and unwavering as a long ship.

'Hello.'

He stopped in front of her, his eyes meeting his daughter's, his face softening in a way that made her stomach crunch into a knot of pleasure and pain.

'How was the rest of your night?'

'It was fine. She didn't wake up until nearly nine.'

Should she say something now? She hesitated. Words were not her thing, but she couldn't exactly sketch or sculpt what she needed to say to him.

His blue gaze shifted to her face. 'And what about you? Did you manage to get any sleep?'

There was a small beat of silence. Then she nodded, still tongue-tied as he stared at her impassively. And then, with relief, she saw that Signy was hurrying towards them.

'I didn't realise you were out here.' The older woman's

unruffled smile cut effortlessly through the awkward silence. 'Lunch is ready. Or I could feed Sóley if you and Mr Stone are talking? I'd be more than happy to,' she added as Lottie started to protest.

But it was too late. A hungry and determined Sóley was already reaching for Signy with her arms outstretched and, heart pounding, Lottie watched helplessly as her daughter disappeared into the house.

She had no excuse now not to say something.

But before she could open her mouth he said abruptly, 'Would you like to come and have a look at the horses with me? They're out in the paddock. I thought maybe—' He frowned and stopped speaking mid-sentence, as though he'd said more than he'd intended.

She hesitated. Yesterday she would definitely have made up some excuse and refused, but today it was easier to nod and say, 'Thank you, that would be lovely.'

The horses were beautiful, and incredibly friendly. They were all different sizes and colours, from piebald through to palomino, and their coats were thick and shaggy like reindeer fur. Peeling off her gloves, she leaned over the wooden fence to touch their velvety faces. As a beautiful chestnut put his face forward for her to rub, she realised that she was enjoying herself.

Her stomach tightened. So maybe she didn't need to talk to him after all.

Here, in the bright sunlight, with the crisp air on her skin, their kiss felt distant and dreamlike. Perhaps if they stood here for long enough the brilliant blue sky might part like the sea and swallow up the memory of it entirely.

'Do you ride?'

His voice jogged her thoughts and, glancing up, she instantly realised the stupidity of that notion.

It was nearly two years since she and Ragnar had slept together and yet she could still remember every second.

And not just his hard-muscled body or the careless beauty of his face. He had an aura, a disruptive, sensual energy beneath his stillness, and it separated him from every other man she'd ever met. And right now that aura was pinning her to the frozen ground and making her limbs flood with heat.

She nodded. 'I used to. When I was younger we lived in a converted farm building and the farmer's wife had horses. She let me and Lucas ride them in exchange for mucking them out.'

She felt his gaze on her profile and, looking over, found that he was staring at her intently.

'And now?'

She shrugged. 'I don't really have the time.'

His expression shifted infinitesimally, in a way that she couldn't pinpoint—a kind of tensing in anger, but not quite.

'But you'd like to?'

As she nodded, he seemed to relax a little.

'I'll make it happen,' he said softly.

'Thank you,' she said. 'And thank you for yesterday... well, I mean this morning. For listening to me. I'm sorry to throw all that drama at you.'

'Drama?' He seemed amused or maybe surprised by her choice of word. 'You were very dignified—not dramatic at all. And I'm sorry that I made you feel excluded. Truly it wasn't and isn't my intention to push you out of Sóley's life.'

'I know. I understand that now.'

She glanced past him. There was nobody around. If she waited until they went back into the house she might have to seek out another private moment, and the thought of being alone with him inside was the spur she needed to speak.

'About what happened after we talked...'

She looked up, jolted by hearing the words she had been about to say come out of his mouth.

'You mean when I...?' She hesitated.

He gazed at her steadily. 'I mean when we kissed.'

For a second her vision blurred. It felt significant, him choosing those particular words, for he could have made it sound like her sole responsibility. Instead he was admitting his own desire had played a part.

'I thought you might want to pretend it hadn't happened,' she said.

There was a small silence, and then he shook his head. 'I don't want to do that—and even if I did I'm not sure that I could.'

His gaze fixed on her face and she felt her blood thicken and slow at the hunger in his eyes...a hunger that seemed to reach through the layers of her padded jacket so that she could feel heat spiralling up inside her.

'I know I haven't given you much reason to trust me, but trust me on this: I wanted to kiss you every bit as much you wanted to kiss me. I was just waiting for permission.' He gave her a small, taut smile. 'Look, Lottie, there's something I need to say to you. I want you to know how sorry I am for lying to you the night we met. I hope that maybe one day you'll believe that's not who I am.'

She stared at him in silence, processing his statement. He made it sound as though he'd acted out of character—but then why had he lied to her?

It was on the tip of her tongue to ask, but what had happened early this morning had to take precedence over the past. 'Why are you telling me this now?' she asked.

'I want us to be honest with one another,' he said simply. 'About what happened and why.'

'I don't know why it happened.' She paused. He had been open with her, so he deserved honesty in return. 'Or maybe I do...' Her face tightened. 'I know it's been twenty months since we—'

There was a small silence.

'I thought you might have forgotten,' he said quietly.

She wanted to laugh. Forget him? Forget that night? 'No, I didn't forget you, Ragnar. I can't.'

'You mean Sóley—?'

The sun was in her eyes, making his face unreadable. But she hadn't been talking about her daughter, she thought with a mix of shame and panic. She had been talking about *him*, and about how he had made her feel, and the soft, urgency of his mouth, and her own quickening gasp as she arched against him.

'There hasn't been a day when I haven't thought about you,' he said.

Looking up at him, she let her gaze search his face and, seeing the heat in his eyes, she nodded, acknowledging the truth of his words and the fact that they were true for her too.

His hand came up and she breathed in sharply as his fingers traced the curve of her cheekbone. Without knowing it was what she wanted to do, or that she was going to do it, she rubbed her face against his hand.

'I thought it would pass,' he said simply.

She stared at him, hypnotised by the ache in his voice—an ache she shared. 'Me too.' With an effort she slid her head away from his hand. 'And it will… But in the meantime I don't think acting on it would be—' She stopped.

'A good idea?' he finished for her.

'It would be a very bad idea,' she agreed.

She could hardly believe she was talking to him like this, but what were the alternatives? To pretend that it was a figment of their imaginations? To listen to their libidos?

Of course she could see the appeal of both—but, while she didn't know the limits of the man standing beside her, she knew her own limits, and there was no way she could play happy families with Ragnar and have no-strings sex with him at the same time.

'We're here to be parents and I think we should concentrate on that,' she said.

'I'm glad we're on the same page,' he said quietly.

Her fingers tightened against the fence and she winced as something small and sharp dug into her skin. It was just a splinter, but it stung more than it should, and she welcomed the pain—for it gave her something to focus on other than the hollowed-out feeling in her stomach. But however much it hurt, she knew her regret at stopping things before they got started would be inconsequential compared to the fallout from a self-indulgent affair.

Straightening up, she met his gaze. 'I think we should probably get some lunch.'

'Then let's go and see what Signy has cooked for us,' he said slowly.

Lunch was a beautiful fish soup with fresh sourdough bread and the most delicious butter she had ever eaten.

After lunch, Sóley almost fell asleep in her highchair. Transferring her smoothly into his arms, Ragnar took her upstairs to bed.

Lottie watched him go. It was getting easier to let him be involved now, and it was also a relief to have a few minutes without her body being so intensely aware of exactly where he was in relation to her.

She glanced around the empty kitchen, and then wandered into the huge living space. It was a beautifully proportioned room, and the light was truly incredible. As it shifted in depth and colour it was like a kind of ever-changing art installation that perfectly complemented the striking mobile spinning and shifting in the invisible air currents.

Her pulse twitched. Mobiles were supposed to be calming, and yet she felt anything but calm.

Restlessly she moved around the room. Ragnar's taste was minimalist. Everything was pared back to its essence, each piece selected on the basis that its beauty equalled its functionality.

Surprisingly, given its stark beauty, it was still a comfortable, welcoming space—perhaps because it so clearly embodied the personality of its owner. She glanced over to the amazing rotating suspended fireplace. The room certainly didn't feel cold. She could feel the heat from the fire seeping into her blood.

Collapsing onto one of the huge leather sofas, she leaned back against the cushions and gazed upwards—straight into Ragnar's blue eyes.

'Are you tired?'

He dropped down beside her, and instantly his nearness made her breathe out of time.

'A little bit.'

The light from the fire was playing off his face and for a moment she stared at him in silence, transfixed by the shifting shadows. And then her pulse tripped over itself as he put his hand on her shoulder and pressed down lightly.

'You're tense here...'

Was she? She didn't feel tense. In fact her body felt as though it was melting.

Pull away, she told herself. *Move.*

But her limbs wouldn't respond. Instead—and completely unforgivably, given what she'd said to him at the stables—she could feel herself wanting to arch against him like a cat.

'You need to relax...'

His voice vibrated through her shoulder blade and a prickling heat spread over her skin.

'Have a bit of down-time. Maybe unwind in the pool. We could take a dip after dinner.'

Her head was spinning. There were so many dangerous words in that sentence. *Relax, unwind, pool, dip, after dinner*... And yet the idea of a relaxing swim in a hot pool was so tempting. Her eyes roamed briefly around the exquisite room. Really, when was she ever going to get a chance to live like this again?

'That sounds lovely.'

'You won't regret it.' His gaze met hers. 'In fact, your body might even thank you.'

There was no moon but it was a cloudless night and, staring up through the glass ceiling of the pool house, Ragnar allowed himself a moment to tick off the constellations in the dark sky before wading into the steam-covered water.

He breathed out slowly. It was like slipping into liquid velvet. It was incredibly warm—blood-hot, in fact—and as he lowered himself down he felt his body grow heavy with a languid, almost boneless weight.

On any other night he would have simply floated on his back and watched the stars. Now, though, he moved slowly through the water, his narrowed gaze tracking the progress of the woman making her way along the edge of the pool like a nervous gazelle at a watering hole.

His heartbeat accelerated as she slipped off the thick towelling robe and dropped it onto one of the fur-covered loungers at the side of the pool. Underneath she was wearing a caramel-coloured swimsuit, a shade darker than her eyes, which hugged her body in a way that was completely understandable.

Watching her step down into the pool, he mentally thanked Signy for reminding him to suggest that she bring one.

As the water closed over her shoulders he felt a sharp twinge of regret that no amount of geothermal heat was going to fix but, ignoring his quickening pulse, he swam towards her.

'How does it feel?'

'It feels wonderful.' Her gaze followed the steam rising up from the water. 'And a bit crazy.'

'Why crazy?' He swam a little closer, drawn in by the surprise and excitement in her face.

'I don't know—it just seems mad for there to be snow everywhere and yet the water in here's so hot.'

'Well, it is the land of fire and ice.'

'The land of fire and ice?'

She repeated his words slowly and, feeling his body respond to the eagerness in her voice, he cursed himself silently. If anything was crazy it was his suggestion that he and Lottie take a dip together beneath the stars. But of course he'd been slowly going crazy for days, his feverish brain torturing his body with images of a naked, gloriously uninhibited Lottie.

They swam slowly in silence. He usually swam alone, and when he was away from Iceland he craved his solitary moments in the pool, but with Lottie beside him he felt an entirely different kind of craving, and he was shocked by how badly he wanted to give into it.

His stomach clenched. It made no sense after what he'd said earlier, and what she'd said, and yet it was there—a need, a hunger, a heat that had nothing to with any geothermal activity.

'Do you use the pool a lot?' she asked softly.

He nodded. 'Usually once a day. Sometimes twice. During the day you can see the sky reflected in the water and it's like you're swimming among the clouds.'

She turned towards him, her eyes wide and unguarded, and he felt something squeeze in his chest at the surprise he saw there.

'I didn't have you down as a poet,' she said.

For a moment, he was captivated by the softness in her voice, and then he felt an almost vertiginous rush of panic.

Glancing upwards, he felt his body loosen with relief.

'I know my limits. If you want real poetry, you just need to look up.'

She gasped. Above them, the sky seemed to be melting. Colour was suffusing the darkness, lighting up the night, and swathes of green and amber and amethyst were swirling and shifting like oil on water.

It was the Aurora Borealis—the Northern Lights—but Ragnar barely noticed the dazzling display. He was too busy watching Lottie.

He breathed out unsteadily. His body was alive with need, worse than before, and his heart hammered in his ears so that thinking was impossible. But he didn't need a conscious brain to know that he still wanted Lottie.

And then, just like that, the show was over.

'We should go in,' he said quietly.

She nodded, following him reluctantly out of the pool. 'Did you know that was going to happen?'

He held out the robe. 'Only in that it's a clear night and it's the right time of year.'

He hardly knew what he was saying, but what he did know was that he still regretted those lies he'd told her that first night. And if he didn't tell her what he was thinking now, wasn't that just a different kind of lie? One he would regret for ever?

So tell her the truth. Be honest, like you said you wanted to be.

He met her gaze, felt his pulse stilling. His home here in Iceland was his sanctuary. A place of calm and order. If he said what he was thinking then he ran the risk of unleashing chaos and passion here.

But if he didn't, what then?

The chaos would still be there, underneath the surface, and it wasn't going anywhere.

And now, finally, he understood why. Ever since that night in the hotel room he hadn't felt whole. The panic that had led him to slip away while she slept still haunted him, and only by owning this hunger was he going to restore balance to his life.

'Earlier…when I talked about what happened… I think I was wrong. Actually, I *know* I was wrong.' He frowned. 'What I'm trying to say is this thing between us, I know it's complicated and confusing…but it's also real, and pretending it isn't would be a lie. I think you feel the same way. But if you don't, that's okay. I just need you to tell me and then I'll never—'

'I do.' She swallowed. 'I do feel the same way.'

His eyes dropped to her mouth. Had she spoken or had he just imagined it?

'Are you sure?' he said hoarsely.

'About wanting you? Yes.'

She looked away and, reaching out, he gently framed her face with his hands. 'We don't need to have all the answers, Lottie.' He was surprised to find that he meant what he said. 'We can work it out together.'

She breathed out shakily and his own breath stalled in his throat as she let the robe slide from her fingers to the floor. For a few pulsing half-seconds she stared at him in silence, and then she took his right hand from her cheek and pressed the palm against her breast.

He felt his pulse accelerate, his body hardening with a speed that almost made him black out, and then, leaning forward he kissed her. Only not in the way she'd kissed him in the kitchen. This was a raw and urgent kiss, a kiss without restraint, a kiss designed to satisfy the hunger in both of them.

'You have no idea how much I want you,' he murmured against her mouth. 'I haven't been able to get you out of my mind.'

'Me too,' she whispered. She was leaning into him so

that their foreheads were touching, their warm breath mingling. 'It's like you're in my head…'

Her voice, that beautiful husky voice, made his body loosen with desire. Beneath his hand he could feel her nipple tightening through the damp fabric of her swimsuit and, breathing raggedly, he began caressing the swollen tip with his thumb, liking the way it made her arch into him and the sudden quickening of her breath.

Her hands were clutching him and tugging him closer, pulling at the waistband of his shorts, and then she pressed her hand against the hard ridge of his body and he groaned.

'Let's go upstairs—' He was fighting to get the words out.

'No.' Her voice was husky with need.

He tried to protest, but it turned into another groan as her fingers slid beneath the waistband. Recognising defeat, he picked her up and dropped her onto the nearest lounger. As she sprawled backwards on the fur he took a step away and, keeping his eyes trained on her face, he slid down his shorts.

CHAPTER SEVEN

HIS HEART WAS slamming against his ribs like a door in a gale.

Had any woman ever looked sexier? She was sprawled against the fur, her eyes wide and feverish, her damp hair spilling over her shoulders. Like the ice in spring, he felt his blood start to melt as his gaze dropped lower. The wet fabric of her swimsuit looked so much like melted caramel all he could think about was how it would feel to lick it off the curves of her body.

It was suddenly difficult to swallow past the hunger swelling in his throat, and without even really knowing that he was doing so he moved swiftly to join her.

Her skin was hot to touch, and dotted with drops of water like tiny transparent pearls. Leaning forward, he touched the one closest with the tip of his tongue and then, keeping his eyes fixed on her face, he traced a path to the next one, and the next, feeling her tremble at his touch.

'Ragnar...'

She murmured his name, and it was the sweetest sound he'd ever heard. He stretched out over her and kissed her hungrily. She cupped his face with her hands and kissed him back. They broke apart to catch their breath, and then without a word he reached out and slid first one and then the other strap away from her shoulders, peeling the damp costume away from her body until she was naked.

He breathed out unsteadily, staying his hunger to admire her high, firm breasts and slightly rounded stomach. 'You're so beautiful,' he whispered and, lowering his face, he ran his tongue over her nipples, tasting the salt from the water as she arched upwards, pressing against him, offering herself to the heat of his mouth.

And then she was jerking free, her eyes dark and fierce, and he breathed in sharply as she reached for him, wrapping her fingers around his hard length. His hand gripped hers but she batted him away, bending over him to brush her lips against him. And then she was taking him into her mouth and he was groaning, his fingers grasping her hair, his body gripped by a pleasure so intense it was almost painful.

He was fiercely aroused, his body tight to the point of breaking. The feel of her mouth was turning him inside out. He was so close, *too close*—

Clenching his teeth, wanting, needing, to be inside her, he pulled away, moving with panicky suspended hunger to fit his body against hers.

'Ragnar…'

Her fingernails dug into his back, but it was the urgency in her voice that cut through his heartbeat.

'I'm not protected.'

Not protected.

He stared down at her, blood roaring in his ears. His preoccupied overheated body was making it hard to think clearly and her words were bouncing off his dazed brain like hailstones on a roof.

And then he swore silently—not just at the implied consequences of that statement, but at his own near-adolescent loss of control. Had he really been so caught up in the moment that he'd forgotten all about contraception?

Catching sight of her small set face, he put his shock and shame to one side and, blanking out the relentless ache in his groin, captured her face between her hands and kissed her gently. 'It's okay…we don't have to—'

He breathed out against her cheek, fighting to contain the desperation in his voice. He would rather wait than put her under pressure.

Her fingers tightened against his arms. 'I want to, only I don't have any condoms.'

'It's okay,' he said again. 'I don't either—well, not here, anyway.'

He didn't want her to think that he wasn't careful, and nor did he want it to look as if he'd made assumptions about what would happen here tonight.

She bit her lip. 'There hasn't really been anyone since… That's why I'm not…why I haven't…'

He didn't know why but her words made a warm ripple of relief spread over his skin, and without meaning to, he said softly, 'There hasn't been anyone for me either.'

Her eyes widened. He wasn't sure if she believed him. Hearing it out loud, he found it difficult to believe too, but it was true. After what had happened with Lottie he'd buried himself in work, too unnerved by the failure of his mathematical certainties to test them again in person.

She breathed out unsteadily. 'We should probably go inside.'

The prospect of returning to his room alone made his body tense—with hunger, not misery—but he managed to nod. 'Yes, we should.'

He felt her lean into him, and hesitate, and then she said shakily, 'My room or yours?'

The air swelled around them, swallowing up her question and retreating. He stared down at her in confusion. 'I don't— We don't— I'm not—'

Her wide-eyed, panicky gaze met his. 'Have you changed your mind?'

Hope fought with fear, and he gripped her tightly. 'You know I haven't. I can't. There's nothing inside my head except you.'

He heard her slow intake of breath.

'My room then,' she said quickly, and this time his relief was swift and sharp.

* * *

They dressed and he led her back into the house, moving purposefully through the darkness. Her heart was beating out of time and too fast, the aftershocks of their feverish almost-coupling mingling with a leaping panic. She was scared of leaving the starlit heat of the pool house, scared that the shift in mood and pace might introduce a change of perspective.

But as they walked upstairs she felt his hand tighten, and then he was pulling her against him, his mouth blindly seeking hers, kissing her with such blazing urgency that she forgot where she was and who she was, and there was nothing but the darkness and their staccato breathing and the insistent pressure of his mouth.

They made it to her bedroom—just. She had left the curtains open and, using the light from the pool house, they stripped again and kissed their way to the bed.

And then any fears she'd had about coming upstairs were forgotten as he raised her hips and gently nudged her legs apart. She felt his breath on her skin, and then her own breath seemed to stick in her throat as his tongue found the pulse between her thighs and began to move with slow, sure precision.

A moan of pleasure rose to her lips and her eyes slipped backwards. And then she was clasping his head, pushing him deeper, then pulling back, wanting more, but not wanting it to end. She felt weightless and her head was spinning. Heat was spilling over her skin in waves, each one faster and stronger than the last, so that her whole body was vibrating. And then she was tensing, pressing against his quickening tongue, her hands jerking through his hair.

She felt him move up the bed and then his mouth was on hers, pushing and parting her lips, probing her mouth and then dropping to lick her throat, her collarbone, her nipples.

Her breath caught in her throat. He felt solid, harder and bigger than before. Was this how it worked? It had been so long she couldn't remember.

'It's okay,' he whispered, his lips brushing her mouth, his fingers sliding inside her, oscillating back and forth until her skin was tightening, her body melting against him.

She found her voice. 'Do you have the—?'

'Are you sure?' He spoke through gritted teeth and she knew he was holding himself in check.

'Yes, I'm sure.'

He rolled off the bed and moved swiftly to the door. Watching him leave, she curled her fingers into the sheet. His absence felt like an actual physical loss—like the sun dropping behind cloud—but suddenly he was back, tearing open the packet and rolling on the condom with smooth, precise care, then sliding back down beside her.

He pulled her against him, and as his mouth found hers she pulled him closer still, her hands pressing against his back, reaching down to hold his hips, and then she was guiding him into her body.

His eyes were rapt and unblinking in the half-light, his face taut with concentration and a need that mirrored her own as he moved against her in time to her accelerating heartbeat. And then she felt him tense, and he was thrusting into her, filling her completely, his groan mingling with her soft cry as her muscles tightened sharply around his hard, convulsing body.

He collapsed beside her, pressing his face into the curve of her collarbone, and she clung to him weakly. They were both breathing raggedly, their bodies slick with sweat, but she wanted to lie there for ever. Finally, though, he shifted his weight and pulled out of her. For the briefest half-second she thought he'd pull away completely. Instead, though, he drew her back against him.

'I was careful...'

'I know,' she whispered, surprised but grateful that he had understood her nervousness about contraception.

His arm curved around her back, and he kept it there as his breathing slowed.

And that was how they must have fallen asleep.

She wasn't sure what woke her, but even before her eyes were properly open she was aware of the solid warmth of his body beside hers and her body's instant and unqualified response to it. Her heartbeat slowed. For a moment she kept her eyes shut. She just couldn't bring herself to open them, for to do so would mean having to return to reality, to clothes, and to being composed and civilised. She wanted to stay here in his arms for ever—to be the woman she had become in his arms.

Her body felt loose and languid, and yet she had never felt more alive, more at one with herself and the world and her place in it. If only she could freeze time…just until she was ready.

She shivered. But ready for what?

There was only one way to find out.

Opening her eyes, she felt her pulse scamper forward. Ragnar was watching her, his gaze more grey than blue in the predawn half-light.

'Morning,' he said softly.

Her eyes had adjusted to the light now, and she gazed up at him, trying to read his expression. Not once during the night had she felt that he was regretting their decision, and nor did she feel any regret for what they'd done. But cocooned in darkness, sheltering in one another's arms, it had been easy to feel as if they were in their own little world, outside of time and answerable to no one.

'What time is it?' she asked quietly.

'About six.' He hesitated, his face stilling as though he

was working something through in his head. 'Sorry, did I wake you?'

Shaking her head, she met his gaze. 'No, I'm nearly always awake by six.' She gave him a small, swift smile. 'Sóley doesn't really do lie-ins yet.'

There were three beats of silence.

Her right leg was curled over his left, and she could feel the prickle of his hair against her skin, but what did this physical closeness really mean?

Inside her head, a nervous round of questions began firing off like party poppers. What was he thinking? Had the night changed things for him as it had for her?

The questions, or maybe the thought of his possible answers, made her stomach tighten.

Was having sex really that big a deal?

She felt her face grow hot at the stupidity of her words. Yes, it was—and not because there had been nobody since that first time with Ragnar. Last night had been about more than satisfying her hunger. It had felt like an admission of something other than sex.

Her heart began to pound. Or was she just doing what she'd done with Alistair? Building castles in the air? Letting her imagination play fast and loose with the facts?

'About last night—'

They both spoke at the same time.

Her chest tightened as his eyes lifted to her face. 'You think it was a mistake?' he said.

'Do you?' she prompted. Her heart was beating so loudly now she felt sure that it must have moved from her chest into her head.

He stared at her for what felt like half a lifetime and then he shook his head. 'No, I don't.'

'I don't either.' She spoke quickly, relief making her words run into one another like a runaway train's coaches hitting the buffers.

There was another beat of silence, and then he reached out and pulled her close, kissed her with the same urgency he had in the darkness. Her heart was still pounding, but with his lips on hers the tightness in her chest began to ease.

Finally, he raised his mouth and rubbed his face against hers, so that she could feel his warm breath on her skin. 'So, what happens next?'

It felt strange, hearing her own words come out of his mouth, for asking him that question had been a defining moment in her life. It was as if they had come full circle.

Only back then everything had been possible. Standing outside the restaurant, pressed up against the heat of his body and with his blue gaze resting on her face, she had felt as though they had a limitless number of futures, some too distant to fully imagine, others too fragile to be considered seriously, but all of them had been out there.

Now, though, too much reality had come between them—good and bad—for her to feel like that.

But what was she feeling? Did she even know?

Closing her mind to the confusion of her thoughts, she let her eyes drift over the hard muscles of his chest and stomach, then lower to where the hair grew most thickly.

What she did know was that she didn't want to walk away just yet.

'Lottie?'

His blue gaze was searching her face, only she didn't know what to say. She was more confused than ever, but it seemed incredibly important not to offer up something less than the truth.

She looked up at him and swallowed. 'I want this. I want you.'

His eyes locked with hers. 'And I want you too. Emphatically. Completely. Shamelessly.'

His fingers traced the curve of her hipbone as he spoke, so that suddenly she was squirming against him.

'And I don't want to turn away from this thing between us. Not yet.'

The certainty in his voice was captivating, and she stared at him spellbound.

'Let's give ourselves these three weeks.'

He was spelling it out for her, making it simple for both of them in a way that had been beyond her, and she was grateful that one of them had managed to put it into words.

'And afterwards you'll still be Sóley's mother and I'll still be her father—just like we agreed.'

'So we just carry on as we are?' she said slowly.

He nodded. 'Until we stop.'

His blue eyes were clear and calm and irresistible. Breathing in his warm scent, she nodded slowly, and as she leaned into him they began to taste one another all over again.

'How do you feel about taking the horses out after lunch? I'd like to show you the estate while you're here.'

Keeping his eyes fixed on Lottie's face, Ragnar leaned forward and refilled her water glass. They were having lunch alone today. Sóley had already eaten and gone upstairs for her nap, and they were eating in the dining area.

It was a glorious room, with a glorious view, and normally he simply sat back and enjoyed the contrast between the restrained luxury of the interior and the stark wilderness outside the glass. Today, though, his gaze kept returning to the woman sitting opposite him.

It was easier between them now. She was still quieter than any woman he'd ever met—certainly quieter than any in his family—but her quietness no longer felt like a show of defiance. Now that he wasn't so on edge himself, he realised that if she was quiet it was because she was concentrating, really listening to what he said.

And not just listening. When her gaze was on his face it felt as if her soft brown eyes were reaching inside him.

'What about Sóley?'

He stared at her blankly. Caught in the honeyed trap of her eyes, he'd lost track of the conversation.

With an effort, he refocused his thoughts. 'We'll only be out for an hour or so at the most before we lose the light, and Signy is desperate to spend some time with her.' Sensing her uncertainty, he changed tack. 'But if Sóley isn't happy to be left then we won't go, obviously.'

'I'd really like to see the estate, and I'd love to go riding.' She glanced longingly through the glass, and then her face creased. 'But I don't have any jodhpurs or boots or a helmet.'

'That won't be a problem. When you said you liked to ride I had one of my people pick up everything you need.'

She frowned. 'But how did you know my size?'

He held her gaze, feeling his body respond in about fifty different ways to her words. 'I know how you fit against me, so I just scaled down.' His eyes flickered over the high curve of her breasts. 'With a few adjustments.'

Signy chose that moment to come and check their plates and find out if they wanted coffee or tea, and he took the opportunity to make sure she was happy to look after Sóley.

When they were finally alone, he looked back across the table at Lottie. The curve of her cheekbones was still pink and, watching her fingers slide up the stem of the glass, he felt his body stiffen to granite hardness. It was all too easy to remember her hand moving in just such a way but for a very different purpose.

Picking up his own glass, he drank some water. It was refreshingly chilled, but unfortunately its cooling effects ended at his stomach and didn't extend to his blood. He was starting to think that where Lottie was concerned nothing was going to change the way his body felt about her.

Earlier, as her hot skin had fused with his, desire as raw and potent as moonshine had driven all conscious thoughts and most unconscious ones from his head. He'd never been so perfectly out of control in his life, and Lottie's unrestrained, passionate response had left him craving more.

Only, was that *all* he was craving?

His heartbeat accelerated.

At any other time in his life, with any other woman, his answer would have been an unequivocal yes. But, remembering how he had felt when finally he'd forced himself to leave her bed that morning, he felt his chest grow tight.

Whatever he had said to Lottie, did he really believe that they could just stop and go back to their own lives at the end of three weeks? More importantly, did he want them to?

He tensed. The answer to that was an unequivocal no. And it wasn't just sex. Living with Lottie and Sóley felt right; they were a family now.

And that was great—except he already had a family, and the idea of introducing one to the other was just not something he could handle right now.

Maybe not ever…

Thirty minutes later Ragnar zipped up his jacket and gazed at the sky. The sun was rising at a shallower angle every day, and today it was barely visible behind a low, bleached grey bank of cloud, but at least it wasn't raining or snowing.

There were any number of possible routes he could have chosen for today's ride, but he'd said that he wanted Lottie to see the estate, and that meant heading up the hillside.

He might have made a different decision if Lottie had been a less experienced rider but, although it was true that she was a little rigid at the start, once she'd relaxed on Orvar, the beautiful chestnut gelding he'd chosen for her, he could see that she had perfect balance and an easy, open riding style.

Turning his own horse—a bay mare called Camille—away from the jagged iced-up edge of a stream, he moved steadily with her towards the ridge, letting the horses choose the pace, trusting them to pick their way across the uneven ground.

Feeling his phone vibrate inside his jacket, he gritted his teeth. The ongoing saga between his mother and half-sister had now sucked in his ex-stepfather Nathan and his other half-sister Freya, and he was desperate to find a resolution.

Glancing over at the expression of unguarded sweetness on Lottie's face, he felt his heart beat faster. Right now, they could wait.

'How are you doing?' he asked.

'Fine.' She smiled shyly. 'I think that's more down to Orvar than me. I mean, he's a strong horse, but I just have to switch my weight a little and he does exactly what I want. He's so quick to react, so responsive.'

He turned to look across at her, a pulse beating down his spine. 'Not with everyone. He is a strong horse, but you're not fighting his strength. Your hands are gentle, and that's why he's not pulling.' His eyes locked with hers. 'Like a lot of powerful males, he just needs the right handling. I think he's okay with you being the boss.'

He watched her fingers curl against the reins.

'Probably because he knows it's only going to be a short ride,' she said quietly.

His phone vibrated again and, watching the curiosity in her eyes, he realised that he would have to answer it after all.

'Sorry. I'm going to have to take this,' he said and, unzipping his jacket, he pulled out his phone.

Watching Ragnar edge his horse away, Lottie breathed out unsteadily.

She had thought that getting away from the house and out into the cool air would be a good idea. Obviously it was going to be difficult to make sense of how she was feeling

in Ragnar's home, and with Ragnar himself so distract-
ingly close.

Mounting Orvar, it had been easy to persuade herself
that the way she was feeling was normal for someone who
had just had sex after nearly two years of celibacy. Not
just take-it-or-leave-it sex, either. Ragnar made her head
swim. And, after thinking about it for so long, it was only
natural that she was going to have some kind of emotional
response to his relationship with Sóley.

But now, out here in the pale grey light, with the cool
wind in her face, they weren't having sex, and Sóley was
back at the house, and yet the feeling of her world turning
upside down persisted.

She glanced over to where Ragnar was talking. It was
impossible not to catch occasional snippets of his conversation and it was clear that he was comforting someone—
someone female.

'Okay, I will talk to Nathan, but you have to apologise.
Because she's our mother—'

Her pulse jumped a beat.

Not just someone—his sister.

Her head was spinning. So was this Nathan his brother?

Shifting against the saddle, she breathed out slowly. She
didn't even know he *had* a sister or a brother—in fact, given
the lack of any photos around the house and his reclusive
lifestyle, she'd assumed he didn't have a family. But clearly
he did, and clearly he cared about them—a lot. So why
hadn't he said anything about them before?

Her pulse jumped again. Probably because he hadn't
trusted her any more than she had trusted him.

It was a disconcerting thought, but before she could pur-
sue all its implications she realised that Ragnar had hung
up and was riding towards her.

'Sorry about that.'

His face was unreadable, probably intentionally so, but

now that she'd got past the shock of discovering he had a family she wanted to know more—for the obvious reason that Ragnar's family was also Sóley's.

'Is everything okay?'

For a moment she thought he wasn't going to answer her, and then he stared past her, his eyes fixed on the horizon. 'It will be.'

She took a breath. 'So was that your sister?'

His hesitation was so brief she might not have noticed it but for the slight tensing along his jaw.

'Yes—Marta.'

Holding her breath, she waited.

Finally, he said stiffly, 'She's had a row with our mother. It's nothing really… It's just my mother has rules and Marta pushes back. But it'll blow over—it always does.'

She nodded slowly. 'At least she can call you if she needs someone to talk to.'

'Yes, I suppose she can.' He nudged Camille forward. 'Come on, it's not far now.'

And that was that.

They reached the top of the ridge ten minutes later.

Pulling up her horse, she stopped and stared. It was an incredible view.

In the distance, she could just see the blue glint of a glacier. Closer than that, snow-covered fields bumped up against twisting towers of haphazard jagged rocks in every shade of grey and silver, and then, nearer still, twin one-hundred-foot waterfalls cascaded down black basalt cliffs.

'Can we get closer?' she asked.

He nodded. 'We can walk underneath them, if you want.'

It took them another fifteen minutes to reach the waterfalls. They left the horses by the edge of a small geothermal pool. Steam from the water had melted the ice, revealing some surprisingly green grass, and both horses instantly lowered their heads and began to graze.

Behind the falls the noise of the water hitting the rock was ear-splittingly loud, and after a moment of neck-tilting admiration they moved far enough away that they could speak without having to shout.

She frowned. 'I should have brought my camera.'

'Here.' He handed her his phone. 'Use this.'

'Thank you.'

Clambering up onto a rock, she took her time to frame the picture, conscious of his gaze and of the questions building up inside her head.

'So, how many siblings do you have?' she asked as she slithered off the rock.

She felt him tense at her question. Then, 'Seven.'

'Seven!'

She turned towards him, not bothering to hide her surprise. As a child she'd desperately wanted to be part of a big family—mainly because she hadn't always felt as if she belonged in her small one—and she could feel herself falling for a different version of the same fantasy now.

'Wow, you're so lucky. And do they all live in Iceland?'

'Sometimes.' A muscle ticked in his jaw.

'So why did you choose to live out here miles from anyone?'

He shrugged. 'Why does anyone choose to live anywhere?'

Ragnar let out an uneven breath. His chest felt as though a band of steel was wrapped around it, getting tighter and tighter.

He always found it stressful talking about his family, but here, now, with Lottie, and with that stupid conversation about giving themselves three weeks still ringing in his ears, he felt as though he might fly into a thousand pieces.

But it was ridiculous to feel that way. She was only asking him what any normal person would ask, so why was he reacting as if she was conducting an inquisition?

His shoulders tensed. He was making such a mess of this. Why didn't he just tell her what he was thinking? Why didn't he just say that he'd got it wrong? That, waking this morning—no, even before that, holding her last night—he'd felt something shift inside him, so that now he didn't want her to disappear from his life at the end of three weeks.

Shoving his hands into his pockets, he felt his knuckles bump into his phone and he felt the tension in his shoulders spread to his spine.

What was he supposed to do?

He only knew one way of managing his life, and that was to keep all the different parts separate—and up until now it had worked just fine. His family had nothing to do with his business, and his private life was private. But Lottie and Sóley would have to meet his family, and then what?

His brain felt as though it might explode. He didn't know the answer to that. But it was impossible to see the hurt expression on Lottie's face and not know that he was the reason for it. And he didn't like how that made him feel. Or the fact that she'd had exactly the same expression when she'd been talking about her useless father.

She deserved to know the truth, or at least an edited version of the truth, but he couldn't explain the messy, melodramatic dynamic of his family out here on this beautiful, tranquil day. And nor did he want to expose her to the mesmerising pull of their drama just yet. He knew what would happen if he did. Lottie and Sóley would be absorbed into the chaos and he couldn't bear for that to happen.

Only he wanted to give her something.

He couldn't change the past, or give her the father she deserved. But he could give her a part of himself he'd never shared with anyone else.

'My mother's family had a house not far from here. We

used to come every holiday and one summer, when I was about eight, I met a boy about my age—Daniel. He was with his father, fishing in the lake over there.'

It had been the holiday before his parents had divorced—six months before his father had found out about his mother's affair—and the rows had been volcanic in their scope and ferocity, and seemingly endless in those long days of summer.

'They taught me how to fish and I caught a salmon—my first.' He grinned at the memory. 'Then we went back to their house and cooked it. It was the best meal I'd ever eaten.'

And not just because of the freshness of the fish or the fact that he'd caught it. Daniel's house had been small and simply decorated, but his parents had been so calm and patient, and it had been so relaxing he'd actually fallen asleep.

'And that's why you like coming here?'

She looked confused, and something in her soft brown gaze made him reach out and pull her against him. He could see how his words would make no sense to her, but there was no way to recreate his childish astonishment at discovering there was another way to be a family—a way without drama.

He couldn't reveal how, sitting in that quiet, ordinary little house, he'd made up his mind to live his life in just such a way, and how living that kind life meant never giving in to the unnamed feeling in his chest.

Already he'd let her get too close—closer than he should. He'd felt her happiness and her pain as his own, and he couldn't let that keep happening. He couldn't risk being swamped by emotions he couldn't handle and didn't want to feel. He needed to keep his feelings under wraps and then everything would be fine.

And if that was what he had to do to keep Lottie and Sóley in his life then that was what he would do.

What other choice did he have?

CHAPTER EIGHT

LEANING FORWARD OVER the banister, Lottie felt her heart jump guiltily against her ribs. Sóley had decided to pull her socks off and push them into her breakfast cereal, and she'd only come upstairs to grab a clean pair for her. But as she'd been walking back along the galleried landing she'd heard an irresistible squeal of laughter, and then a deeper, definitely male laugh, and she'd had to flatten her body into the cool brickwork to even out her breathing.

Now she was smiling. In the living area below, Ragnar was playing hide and seek with their daughter, and she watched, transfixed, her smile widening, as he allowed himself to be found, much to Sóley's giggling, appreciative amusement.

A week ago she would have found it impossible to enjoy this moment. She would have wanted to, only her fear of being pushed out would have overridden her good intentions. Now, though, she felt differently. She knew that the father-daughter bond wasn't a threat to her own relationship with Sóley.

She inched backwards, concealing herself in the shadows, feeling a knot of nervous uncertainty tightening beneath her diaphragm.

She felt differently about other things too.

Instead of feeling as if she was trapped in a villain's lair, out in the wilderness, she felt almost as much at home as she did in Suffolk. And, rather than counting down the days until she could leave, she was trying to stretch out every minute.

Mostly, though, she felt differently about Ragnar.

Oh, she could remember her resentment and her scepticism, but they seemed to have broken up and melted away like spring ice on a lake.

She thought back to their conversation the morning after that first time they'd yielded to the burning, incessant pull of their desire. It had been a little nerve-racking, waking in *his* arms in *her* bed. She'd had no idea of what to expect, knowing only that she didn't regret what had happened.

But then they'd talked—or rather he'd talked—and she'd agreed with him that she didn't want it to be just that one night and that they should give themselves these three weeks.

Only down by the waterfalls she'd started to realise that wasn't what she wanted either—or at least not *all* she wanted.

That phone call from his sister had made her want to learn more about this man who was Sóley's father, whose touch turned her inside out but about whom she knew next to nothing.

The knot in her stomach tightened. But, judging by his terse, oblique answers to her questions, and the shuttered expression on his face, he clearly didn't trust her enough to give her more than a glimpse into his life—a glimpse that had confused more than clarified her understanding of him.

But could she blame him for being reluctant to open up?

Even her decision to tell him about Sóley had been framed as much by her failed relationship with her own father as by a need to do the right thing.

She'd been so preoccupied by her fears of being pushed out that she'd relegated his feelings, and his family, to second place—to the point of never even actually asking him a single question about them.

Her stomach muscles clenched. He was clearly the pole-star of his family. Marta had called again twice, and his mother once, and listening to him talk to them, patiently and calmly, she had felt both moved and almost envious that they had a permanent right to his attention, and she—

She pushed the words away, letting them be pulled into the swirling centrifuge of emotions she couldn't seem to unpick or understand.

Downstairs in the living area, Sóley was gratifyingly excited to see her. Kneeling down on the rug, she let her daughter climb into her arms.

'She missed you.'

Turning towards where Ragnar sat, slouching against one of the huge leather sofas, she felt her heart slip sideways. He was wearing a thin blue V-neck sweater a shade darker than his eyes, and a lock of blond hair was falling across his forehead. He looked calm and relaxed and incredibly sexy.

'Sorry for taking so long.'

He shifted against the sofa, stretching his leg out so that his thigh was next to hers, and instantly the heat and pressure of his body made her breathing change rhythm.

'You really don't need to keep apologising to me every time I look after her. Otherwise I'm going to have start retrospectively apologising to you for the last eleven months.'

'I just don't want to take you for granted.'

His eyes rested on her face, the blue suddenly very blue. 'How *do* you want to take me?' he said softly.

Behind the sudden insistent thud of her heartbeat she heard her phone vibrate on the sofa. It could be her mum, or Lucas, or even Georgina to say that the gallery had burned down, but she couldn't seem to make herself care enough to pick it up and find out.

'Here.' He reached across and handed her the phone. 'It might be a commission. Just because I'm on holiday it doesn't mean you have to be too.'

Thankful for being given a reason to lower her face,

away from his steady stare, she glanced down at the screen as her mind nervously tried to interpret his words.

He was talking about being on holiday from his job, not commenting on their affair. Or was he?

She wanted to ask him so badly that words filled her throat and mouth. *Is this just a holiday romance? Is that why you don't want to tell me anything about your family?*

But she wasn't brave enough to find out for sure.

Glancing down at the screen, she saw that it wasn't a commission—just a message from Lucas telling her that he'd fixed the leak in the workshop and asking if she thought a swing would be a good idea for Sóley's birthday.

She laid her phone down on the rug, pushing Lucas's question to the back of her mind. It should be the biggest date in her calendar, but right now she didn't want to think about her daughter's first birthday, for that would mean planning for the future—a future in which she would no longer wake to find Ragnar's warm body beside hers or fall asleep in his arms.

'All okay?'

Blocking the hollow ache in her stomach, she looked up and nodded. 'Yes, it's just Lucas.' Afraid that he might read her thoughts, she turned towards her daughter. 'Right, you, let's get these socks—'

But before she had a chance to finish her sentence Sóley had wriggled off her lap, snatched the phone off the rug and begun crawling across the floor at great speed.

'You little monkey!' Laughing, Lottie chased after her, scooping her daughter into her arms and burying her face in her stomach until Sóley was squirming and giggling uncontrollably.

Having retrieved her phone, she lowered her still giggling daughter to the rug. She could feel Sóley straightening her legs, steadying herself as she had been doing for last few weeks, pulling impatiently against her mother's restraining hands.

'Okay—you can stand by yourself.'

For a few seconds or more her daughter swayed on the spot, finding her balance, and then she raised her arms, cooing breathlessly towards where her father was kneeling in front of the huge suspended fireplace.

Watching him toss in a couple of logs, Lottie felt her heart begin to pound.

'Ragnar…' She spoke his name softly, and as he turned towards her, her eyes met his and she smiled. 'She wants you,' she prompted.

He started to get up, but she shook her head. 'No, say her name.'

A flicker of understanding passed across his face and he stayed crouched down, his eyes fixed on his daughter as Lottie lifted her phone.

'Sóley.'

His voice was raw-sounding, and she could tell that he was struggling to hold on to his composure.

'Sóley, come to Daddy.' He hesitated and then repeated himself in Icelandic.

Holding her breath, Lottie watched as Sóley teetered towards his outstretched hands, taking one wobbly step after another like a tiny astronaut, and then she stopped, weaving unsteadily on the rug. And as she tipped forward he caught her in his arms.

Lottie switched off her phone camera, tears burning her eyes as Ragnar got unsteadily to his feet, still holding his daughter close, pressing his face into her loose blonde curls. And then suddenly he was walking across the room and pulling her into his arms, pulling her close.

Burying her wet face against his shoulder, still clutching her phone, she breathed out unsteadily.

'Thank you,' he said softly.

Her hands gripped his sweater. 'For what?'

'Her first steps.'

She felt his emotion in her own chest. 'I'm just sorry it took me so long to let you be her father, and for being so wrapped up in myself. I should have asked you about your family before—especially after burdening you with what happened with my father—'

His arms tightened around her. 'You didn't burden me with anything. I'm glad you told me. And, just for the record, I think your father made the biggest mistake of his life giving up the chance to know you. You're an incredible person, Lottie.'

She shook her head. 'I'm not. I've been selfish and self-absorbed.'

'And I've been overbearing and manipulative and cold-blooded.' His eyes were gleaming, but his voice was gentle.

Recognising her own words, she smiled. 'Did I say that?'

He smiled back at her—a sweet, slow smile that made her insides loosen.

'I probably deserved worse.'

Lottie laughed. 'I definitely *thought* worse.' She took a breath. 'I'll send you that video and you can share it with your family.'

Maybe her daughter's first steps might be *her* first step towards making amends.

'I've got other videos,' she added. 'I can send those too.

He was silent for a moment, and then he said, 'I'd like to see them.'

Her eyes flicked to his face. There was something different about his voice… Only before she had a chance to consider what had changed, or why, Sóley leaned forward and grabbed her shoulder, pulling all three of them into an embrace.

Her heart was suddenly thumping hard inside her chest, as she pictured the three of them in her garden in Suffolk:

she and Ragnar were taking turns to push their daughter in her swing, their eyes bright, their faces flushed with the chilled air and with something less tangible that she couldn't name—

She cleared her throat. 'I was thinking... I know you're already taking time off work now, so don't worry if you can't,' she said quickly. 'But I was just wondering if you'd like to come to Suffolk for Sóley's birthday? It's not a party, or anything, but I know she'd love you to be there.' She hesitated. 'I'd love you to be there too.'

He was staring at her steadily, and she felt heat rise up over her throat and curl around her neck like a cashmere scarf.

'I'd like that very much.'

'Excuse me, Mr Stone— Oh, I'm so sorry—'

It was Signy.

Lottie felt her cheeks grow warm. She had no idea whether or not Ragnar's housekeeper had detected a change in their relationship, but she didn't want to make the older woman feel in any way uncomfortable.

'No need to apologise, Signy,' Ragnar said calmly. 'Sóley just started walking and we were celebrating.' He hesitated. 'In fact, why don't we celebrate properly? We have champagne, don't we, Signy?'

'Yes, we do, Mr Stone.'

'Good.'

Lottie watched as he gently kissed his daughter's forehead, and then the air was squeezed from her lungs as he lowered his mouth and brushed his lips against hers.

'Then let's celebrate.'

Leaning back in his chair, Ragnar stared down at his laptop, watching the cursor blink on the pitifully blank screen. On the desk beside him he had a neatly stacked pile of unread business plans and magazines. But it didn't matter how neatly they were stacked—he already knew they were definitely going to stay unread.

Two years ago, when his business had been starting up and he'd felt as if a hosepipe filled with data was pumping non-stop into his head, he'd followed the example of other successful CEOs and taken a couple of 'think weeks' out of his schedule.

He found them incredibly productive, and now he was following the same rules as he always did. Web-browsing was forbidden, he could only check emails once a day, for no more than fifteen minutes, and he could take no business calls whatsoever. The idea was to remove all distractions from his life and allow his mind the space and freedom to reset his goals, so that when he did return to work he would hit the ground running—and in the right direction.

He glanced again at the blinking cursor.

But clearly some distractions were just way more distracting than others, he thought, his body hardening as a slow-motion replay of the morning shower he'd shared with Lottie slid unprompted into his head.

He gritted his teeth. No wonder he was finding it difficult to focus his thoughts.

Except that wasn't true. His thoughts *were* focused— only not on the future direction of his business but on the woman who had managed to get so far under his defences that he'd actually told her about that fishing trip with the boy Daniel.

He flipped his laptop shut, moving his eyes involuntarily to the window and through the glass, to the fractured outline of a small, wooden cabin that was just visible from where he was sitting.

His shoulders tensed. When Lottie had asked him about his family he'd told her part of the truth.

Maybe he hadn't expressed it very eloquently, but he'd wanted her to know that meeting Daniel and his family had been a transformative moment for him. Like falling down a rabbit hole into Wonderland, except in reverse, for in his family there had been no end of mad tea parties and pools of tears.

In Daniel's family cabin he'd found a bolthole from the drama, and every minute he'd spent there had only made it clearer to him that one day he would need a separate space, away from his family. He loved them, even when they exhausted and infuriated him, but he couldn't live with them.

His fingers tapped impatiently against the desktop.

But he could *live with Lottie and Sóley.*

He was already doing so, and he wanted the situation to continue—even more now, after what had happened yesterday.

Suddenly he felt as if some invisible force was squeezing his chest. Watching his daughter take her first steps towards him, then catching her as she fell, he had felt something crack inside him as the swell of pride at her reaching the milestone of walking had battled with panic that one day he might not be there to catch her when she fell.

Three amazing, overwhelming, unrepeatable minutes of his life—Lottie's gift to him.

Only he hadn't wanted it to be his alone. He'd needed to share it with her. As he'd pulled her into his arms he'd been on the verge of asking her to stay longer, but then she'd offered to send him the video of Sóley walking, so that he could share it with his family, and something had held him back from speaking his thoughts out loud.

And it was still holding him back now.

Fear.

The word tasted sour in his mouth.

He didn't like it that fear was dictating his actions, but truthfully he was scared of what would happen if he asked her to stay on. Maybe if it had just been sex, as he'd told himself it would be, or if he simply respected her as the mother of his child it would be okay, but as he'd watched, felt, listened to her quiet devastation as she talked about her father's rejection his anger had been monumental.

Only what if, like the rest of his family, his emotions got too big to be contained?

He pushed the thought away uneasily.

They won't, he told himself firmly. He had a lifetime of experience in separating himself from his feelings—why should dealing with Lottie be any different?

His eyes snagged on the title of the topmost document in the pile on his desk. Even without the double distraction of Lottie and his daughter, he would find it perilously hard to be distracted by a report on *Strategic Pre-interaction Behaviours Using Emerging Technologies*. But it was the suggested date of a meeting to discuss the report that made his fingers stop tapping against the smooth desktop.

December twenty-first.

Sóley's birthday.

His gaze returned to the view outside his window. This time, though, his eyes were drawn upwards to the sky.

After days of pale grey silvery cloud today the sky was a limitless ice-blue, stretching out above the snow-covered fields like the ceiling of a Renaissance cathedral.

It was a perfect day.

He breathed out slowly. Maybe he had found a way to reset his goals after all. It would be a first step for him—a different kind of icebreaker from the one they'd first shared, but something he could give to Lottie.

With the determination of having finally made a decision, he pulled out his phone and punched in a number. 'Ivar. I need you to be ready in about an hour. No, just a short trip. Thanks.'

Hanging up, he glanced at the watch. Now all he needed to do was talk to Signy.

* * *

Pressing her face closer to the curved window, Lottie gazed down at snow-covered land, half-heartedly trying to imagine what it might look like in summer.

It was her second flight in a helicopter, and once again she had no idea where she was going, but this time, with Ragnar's fingers wrapped around hers, her feelings were very different. Instead of being tense with nervous apprehension, her stomach was tingling with excitement.

She watched as Ragnar leaned forward and tapped Ivar on the shoulder.

'Just over the ridge will be fine, if that works for you.'

The pilot nodded. 'Yes, sir.'

The sound of the helicopter made normal speech impossible and both men were having to raise their voices.

Dropping back into his seat, Ragnar gave her hand a quick squeeze, and then her heart picked up speed as he bent closer and she felt his warm breath on her throat.

'Just another couple of minutes.'

She felt her body soften as his mouth found hers. Her head was swimming, and she had to lift her mouth from his to stop herself from deepening the kiss and tearing at the layers of padding that separated them from one another.

'Until what?'

'Wait and see.'

Ivar landed the helicopter exactly three minutes later.

Flecks of snow whipped up by the rotor blades whirled around them as Ragnar climbed out and then lifted her down. As she pulled her hood up over her hair she looked up at him questioningly.

'So where now?'

He took her hand. 'This way.'

They crunched steadily through the snow, up a curving bank, and then abruptly the snow ended and she felt her feet stall. She pushed her hood back from her face. In front of her a lead-grey sea stretched out to a horizon that looked as though it had been drawn with a ruler.

And next to the sea was the beach.

Only this beach was nothing like the pale, biscuit-coloured sands of home—it was black.

Lottie let Ragnar lead her down the shifting dunes.

'It's lava,' he said as she reached down and picked a handful of tiny black pebbles. 'When it reached the sea it stopped and cooled instantly. That's the dull, scientific explanation, anyway.' His mouth curved up. 'But I still can't stop myself from looking for dragons every time I come here.'

The pull of his blue gaze was intoxicating and irresistible. She smiled back at him. 'So what are we waiting for? Let's go see if we can find one.'

It was the most amazing place, Lottie thought as they made their way across the gleaming wet sands. Apart from the noise of the waves hitting the shore at regular intervals, the only other sound was the occasional seabird crying as it swooped above the water far out at sea.

'Do you like it?'

His blue eyes rested steadily on her face and she nodded, her vocal cords suddenly paralysed by the intensity of his gaze.

'Enough to stay for lunch?' he said softly.

Lunch? She frowned. 'Where are we going to eat lunch?'

And then she saw it.

At the back of the beach, where the white snow met the black stones, was a huge fire pit filled with burning logs. Around it, fat kilim-covered cushions were spread out invitingly over a collection of shaggy sheepskin rugs, and a picnic basket was sitting on top of what appeared to be a table made out of snow.

Lottie breathed out unsteadily. Something was wrong

with her. A shard of ice seemed to be lodged in her throat, but her eyes felt as though they were burning.

'I don't understand...' she whispered.

He pulled her against him, brushing the tears from her cheeks. His jacket was quilted, hers was too, but she could still feel his heart beating through the layers of fabric and insulation.

'It's my way of saying thank-you for yesterday. For letting me share Sóley's first steps.'

Cupping her face with his hands, he kissed her fiercely and she kissed him back, relieved to have an outlet for the dizzying intensity of her longing for him.

Finally, they drew apart.

'How did you do all this?'

He glanced away. 'Signy and Ivar did all the hard stuff.'

She swallowed. There was a fluttering fullness in her chest she didn't understand, like happiness mixed with nerves—only she didn't feel nervous.

'But it was your idea?'

'I didn't just want to say what I was feeling, I wanted to show you,' he said.

Taking his words into herself, she leaned into him and kissed him again, until he groaned against her mouth and pulled away from her. Catching sight of the expression on his face, she smiled.

'Later,' she said softly, catching his hand. 'Come on— let's eat.'

There were soft rolls filled with sticky pulled pork or buttered lobster, and a creamy artichoke dip with crisp vegetable *crudités*. To follow there was hot mulled cider and some delicious *kleinur*—an Icelandic pastry that was like a twisted cinnamon-flavoured doughnut.

'Signy is a genius,' Lottie said when finally she couldn't eat another mouthful. 'Are you feeling better now?'

She spoke playfully, liking the way his eyes gleamed

in response to her teasing, but liking the weight of his arm around her waist more.

He pulled her closer. 'No.' His eyes locked with hers. 'But *you* feel wonderful.'

Her heart skipped forward. She felt wonderful too. Lighter, calmer. Happier. For the first time since her father's rejection she didn't have the nagging sense of being inadequate. Ragnar made her feel special and secure. He made her feel differently about herself.

A tic of uncertainty beat in time to her pulse.

But it wasn't just *her* feelings that mattered—her father had taught her that—and right now Ragnar had given her no reason to think this was anything more than just a thoughtful gesture.

'Is it always this empty here?' Glancing across the deserted beach, she frowned. 'Where I live there's always someone on the beach. Dog walkers, or teenagers having a bonfire party, or windsurfers.'

He took a moment to reply. Then, 'People don't come here because it's a private beach.'

It took a moment for his words to sink in. 'Is it *your* beach?'

He nodded. 'It came with the estate. There's a lot of protected wildlife up here, so it's probably for the best that there aren't hordes of people traipsing all over it.'

His eyes met hers, and she could see he was weighing up something in his head.

'Actually,' he said slowly, 'you're the first person I've ever brought here...and you and Sóley are the first people to stay at my house.'

She stared at him in confusion. Was that true? And if it was, why were they the first? And why was he telling her now?

His skin was taut over his cheeks, and she could feel a tension in him that hadn't been there before—a kind of rigid pose, as though he was bracing himself before jumping off a high-dive board.

Her own stomach tensed, but the question was waiting to be asked. 'Why hasn't anyone stayed at the house before?'

He stared past her. 'I didn't want anyone else before you,' he said finally. 'I come here to escape.'

Of course—he came to recharge, to rethink his business goals. Only she knew from the forced steadiness in his voice that he wasn't talking about work, and she thought back to when she'd asked him about living here.

'Was that why you went to Daniel's house when you were a child? Because it was an escape.'

His eyes were still watching the horizon. 'Pretty much.' His mouth twisted. 'It was difficult at home. My parents were arguing a lot. They got divorced shortly after that holiday.'

It seemed to Lottie that her head had never been so full of questions. She picked one at random. 'What happened then?'

'They remarried—both of them—quite a few times, actually. I have four stepfathers and three stepmothers, two full sisters and one brother, and the rest are halves and steps. It's all quite complicated and full of drama.'

He'd used that word before. 'What kind of drama?' she asked.

He shrugged. 'Oh, you know…the usual hallmarks of a good soap opera. Jealousy. Infidelity. Power. Pride.'

She stared at him in silence. His voice was calm and even, but for some reason it jarred with the mocking smile that accompanied his statement.

'But you love them?' Watching his eyes soften, she felt the same fluttering fullness in her chest as earlier.

'Very much. But this place—' he glanced back down the beach to the dark, jutting rocks '—is dramatic enough as it is.' His gaze returned to her face. 'Does that make sense?'

She nodded.

Truthfully, she didn't fully understand what he was trying to say, but she did understand how hard it could be to try and express yourself. Just like her, words weren't his thing—but the fact that he'd opened up to her was what mattered.

'I do understand.'

His arm tightened around her. 'I was hoping you would.' He hesitated. 'And I was hoping, too, that you might consider staying on here with Sóley a little longer.'

Her heart was thumping against her ribs. 'How much longer?'

His eyes were suddenly very blue. 'I thought maybe you might consider staying here for Christmas.'

'Christmas?'

He misread the shake in her voice. 'I know it's a lot to ask, and you've probably got other plans, but I really want to spend it with—' His face tensed into a frown and he paused. 'I really want us to spend it together. The three of us...as a family.'

His admission made the breath slip down her throat . Beneath the jerkiness of her heartbeat she felt a fluttering moth's wing of hope, even though she knew it was ridiculous to wish for something she could never have.

'You don't have to make up your mind now.'

He was right. She should give it some thought, but there was no point. It was what she wanted.

'I'd like that. A lot,' she said simply.

His fingers pushed through her hair, tipping her face up to meet his lips. 'I don't know where this is going with us, but I don't want it to be over yet.'

Something stirred inside her chest, moving stealthily, swelling against her ribs so that breathing was suddenly a struggle. She pushed against it, but this time it wouldn't go away.

'I don't either,' she said.

Not yet, not ever.

Her pulse was pounding in her head. He wasn't offering her permanence. He wasn't offering her a future beyond Christmas. But that didn't seem to matter to her heart.

She had fallen in love with him anyway.

She grabbed the front of his jacket to steady herself. Of course she was in love with him. Somewhere deep inside she knew that she'd always been in love with him—ever since that first night in London. But closer to the surface she felt panic.

She was unbearably conscious of being in love. But there was no need to tell him what she was feeling. She'd done that before—told a man what she was thinking and feeling too quickly, without filters—and she wasn't going to do it again. She couldn't risk the swift sting of rejection.

Right now what mattered was that incredibly, miraculously, he wanted her to stay.

But with Ragnar so close, and with his words echoing inside her head, the urge to blurt out her feelings was almost overwhelming.

She was desperate for the oblivion of his mouth on hers and, pulling him closer, she kissed him fiercely, losing herself in the heat of his response, letting the synchrony of their desire stifle her need to confess her love.

CHAPTER NINE

'ARE YOU COLD?'

Tilting her face, Lottie gazed up at Ragnar and shook her head. They hadn't made it into the bed—instead were lying on top of a luxurious white fur throw, her limbs overlapping with his, his arm around her waist.

'No, I'm not,' she said truthfully.

Heat was radiating from his body into hers, and the fur beneath them was incredibly warm and soft. Only...

She twisted against him, pressing closer. 'Actually, I was going ask you, just out of interest, what exactly am I lying on?'

In the heat of passion the sensation of fur against bare skin was intensely erotic, and usually she was too spent afterwards to speak, much less formulate a question. There had always been a kind of frenzied intensity to their lovemaking—maybe because they both knew that there was a time when this would end, and their imminent separation was at the back of their minds. But now they had given themselves more time they could allow themselves to savour these moments of exquisite easy intimacy.

She thought back to yesterday's conversation on the beach. It still didn't feel quite real, but it *was* real—it had happened, Ragnar had asked her to stay on with him in Iceland, and even though she knew it was just a couple more weeks, his hesitant words were making her dream of something she'd always thought life would deny her.

He shifted against her and, dragging her attention back to the present, she met his gaze—or tried to. But he was looking anywhere but at her.

'I was hoping you wouldn't ask that.' His gaze met hers.

She stared at him uncertainly. 'Why? What is it?'

He sighed. 'It's fake.'

'Oh, you.' She punched him on the arm. 'I thought you were going to say it was a polar bear, or a seal or something.'

But she wasn't angry with him. She couldn't be. Not when she could hear the smile in his voice. Shaking her head, she moved as if to roll away, but he grabbed her and, pulling her beneath him, he stretched her arms above her head, capturing her wrists with his hands.

A beat of heat ticked through her blood as he stared down at her, his blue eyes gleaming. 'I'm not a complete barbarian.'

Her body twitched as she met his gaze. They were teasing each other, using the intimacy of sex to test their relationship. 'And you're happy to say that lying naked on a fur rug?'

His lips curved upwards and she felt her heart begin to beat unsteadily. Now she couldn't just hear his smile, she could see it. Her breath caught in her throat. He might not smile much, but when he did it was as miraculous and warming as the first rays of midwinter sunlight on her face.

'I'm not lying on a fur rug,' he said softly. 'I'm lying on you.'

He shifted against her, and as the hard muscles of his chest brushed against her nipples she felt her body stir. 'Yes, you are...but I'm not sure how that disqualifies you from being a barbarian.'

Holding her gaze, he drew the tip of his tongue softly over her bottom lip, pulling at a thread somewhere deep inside her.

'What are you thinking?' he asked.

She stared at him dazedly. 'That I want you,' she said hoarsely.

His eyes narrowed, the pupils flaring, and he rolled over

taking her with him so that suddenly she was on top. Her eyes drifted hungrily over the muscular contours of his chest and she felt his hands move from her waist to her hips, his fingers biting into her skin as she pushed down against him.

He gritted his teeth and his hand caught hers. 'Give me a minute.'

His eyes were dark and glazed, and she felt his fingers tighten around hers as he fought to gain control. Glancing down, she saw that he was watching her, and his blunt expression made heat unspool inside of her. She started to move against him, wanting, needing to still the insistent ache between her thighs.

Her body was losing its bones…she could feel herself melting… Leaning forward, she clasped his face in her hands and kissed him frantically. He kissed her back deeply, licking her mouth until her body was shaking and hollowed out with desire.

'I want to feel you inside me…' she whispered.

His jaw clenched tight and, taking a breath, he rolled off her on to the fur and reached into the drawer by the bed. She watched impatiently as he rolled on a condom, and then he took her face in his hands again and kissed her fiercely, catching her hair as her searching fingers closed around him.

He sucked in a breath as she began to stroke, and then he was moving against her hand, his dark, glazed gaze watching her steadily as he reached down and lightly touched her breasts. Her nipples tightened and she moaned softly, and then his hand moved from her breast to her stomach, then lower still, his fingers tangling through the triangle of hair, easing a path between her thighs so that she was raising her hips, seeking more of his tormenting touch.

'No…not this way—'

His fingers found hers and he freed himself from her

grasp. Then he turned her gently but firmly so that she was facing away from him. Leaning into her, he reached under her stomach to caress her nipples, his fingers pulling at the swollen tips, and then he was parting her thighs, stroking the slick heat, making sure she was ready for him.

'Yes,' she whispered. 'Yes...'

Pushing back, she guided him inside her and began to move against him in time with the pulsing urgency of her heartbeat, heat spreading through her like a fever as he thrust up inside her, his body jolting into climax in time with hers...

Breathing out softly, Ragnar inched backwards, making sure that he didn't wake the woman sleeping beside him. It was early—too early to get up—but his brain was brimming with unasked and unanswered questions.

Away from the distracting warmth of her body it would be easier to think straight—or at least think instead of feel.

His phone was on silent, but he picked it up anyway, in case its vibrations or flickering screen inadvertently disturbed Lottie.

Closing the bedroom door softly behind him, he made his way quietly through the silent house, moving instinctively in the darkness. Downstairs in the living room he made his way across the rug to where the still glowing embers of the fire spread a soft red light across the walls.

Crouching down, he picked up a couple of logs and pushed them into the amber-tinged ashes. Watching the flames creep over the dry wood, he leaned back against the sofa, stretching his legs out towards the fire's reviving warmth.

It had been long time since he had woken so early, and more specifically woken with his eyes feeling so heavy in his head that it was as though he hadn't closed them at all. Nearly twenty years, in fact, since that day when he'd gone to Daniel's house and realised that he could step back from his parents' explosive marriage.

His spine tensed against the sofa cushions.

Maybe it would have been different if he'd been the second or third child, but as the firstborn there had been no diluting the impact of their relationship on him, and his parents had been fiercely in love. Every encounter for them had been an emotional collision. Even their kisses had looked like a form of fighting to him, and as a child he'd often wake early, with his head still ringing in the aftermath of yesterday's feuding.

Going downstairs, he would huddle up in front of the remnants of the fire from the night before. It had been cold and dark, but it had been the only time of the day when he could find the silence and solitude he craved.

And now he was here, in his own home, doing exactly the same thing.

His phone screen lit up and, picking it up, he glanced down automatically to check his notifications.

It was a text from his mother, and there were four missed calls from Marta. His mouth twisted into a reluctant smile. He could imagine his sister's outrage at being asked to leave a message. She wasn't used to such treatment—particularly from him—but he didn't have his phone on at night now that he was with Lottie.

The words echoed inside his head. *Now that he was with Lottie.* It was a simple sentence, but what did it mean?

He let out a long, slow breath.

He knew what it meant now and up to Christmas. It meant the three of them living as a family, eating meals together and playing in the snow, and it meant that at night he and Lottie would retreat to her room, moving inside and against each other's bodies until that dizzying mutual moment of swift, shuddering release.

But what would it mean after Christmas?

He swore softly. That was what had woken him this morning.

Out on the beach it had seemed to make perfect sense. Of course he wanted to share Sóley's first birthday and spend Christmas with her as a family, and inviting Lottie to stay on had felt like an obvious step. Now, though, he couldn't understand why it had felt like such a big deal—or why he'd chosen to make it about his daughter's birthday instead of what it was really about.

His hand tightened around the phone.

He'd told Lottie that he would be honest with her, but how could he be when he wasn't even being honest with himself.

So be honest!

This wasn't just about playing happy families for the sake of their daughter—in fact it wasn't really about Sóley at all. He had a relationship with his daughter now, a bond that would endure beyond any fabricated deadline, and he wasn't going to let anything come between them.

But what about Lottie?

Where did she fit into his life in the long term?

Leaning forward, he picked up another log, and edged it carefully into the embers.

If he'd asked himself that question at any point up until the night in the pool house, when he'd handed her the robe, his answer would have been *nowhere*—except as Sóley's mother, of course.

He'd had casual affairs throughout his twenties, but no serious relationships, and he'd never wanted anything more—never wanted anyone for more than sex. To do so would mean getting out of his depth and too close for comfort.

But he wanted Lottie.

Maybe at the beginning their hunger had just been an

urgency from which neither of them could turn away. Only now it was different.

Now, after the shortest time, she felt essential to his life—and yet he was still shying away from what that meant.

He gazed into the red core of the fire. Given what he knew about people's behaviour when they went from casual to committed, that was completely understandable. To him, relationships were unpredictable and challenging. His family had proved that time and time again. There were so many risks—so many unknowns for which there was no neat algorithm.

His mouth twisted. Or perhaps it wasn't the unknown that scared him but the acknowledgement of his own shortcomings that was making him hold back.

The fact that his parents and siblings acted as though they were living in a modern-day Asgard had never impacted on anyone but himself before now, but Lottie was unsure of her place in the world—could he really risk introducing her into the chaos of his family life?

He had no right to expect or ask that of her.

More importantly, he couldn't introduce her to them because he hadn't actually told his family about her or Óley yet.

His spine tensed.

Telling them was not as simple as it sounded. Not because his family would judge—they wouldn't—but because they would want to be involved, and being involved on their terms would mean being consumed. In an instant he would be fighting for control.

He would tell them soon. But on his terms. Calmly, quietly, individually. But for now he wanted to keep Lottie and Óley to himself, for just a little longer.

Maybe that thought had been in his head when he'd asked her to spend Christmas with him. At the time, on the beach, with panic swirling up inside him like spindrift off a snow-covered mountain, he'd justified it to himself as a first small step, a baby step...

His mouth curved upwards and he felt the rise of fierce pride and happiness as he pictured his daughter moving towards him with slow, unsteady certainty. His smile faded.

Except he wasn't a baby.

He was a grown man, and he needed to start acting like one—because for the first time in his life he was more scared of losing someone than of letting them get close to him.

Rolling onto her front, Lottie lowered her face and closed her eyes. Sóley was having her nap and Ragnar was holed up in his office, reading through business proposals. She hadn't felt like sketching today. Instead, she had sneaked out to the pool house and, after a quick dip in the steaming water, she made her way to the sauna and was now stretched out on one of the slatted wooden benches.

Beneath the towel she felt warm and weightless.

Of course that was due in part to the voluptuous heat of the sauna. But it was Ragnar's invitation—and this time it *was* an invitation—to stay on in Iceland that had wiped all tension from her body.

Her heart swelled against her ribs.

It wasn't a big deal, she told herself for perhaps the tenth time since waking. It was just a couple of weeks. Only she could sense that the words hadn't come easily to him. And he hadn't had to say them at all, so surely that did make it into some kind of deal.

They would be together, properly together, so his inviting her to stay must mean that he liked her. The thought made her pulse dart forward and she allowed herself a moment of pure, incredulous happiness.

She was growing drowsy now. And as her limbs grew

heavier she felt the air currents shift and knew that some-one had come into the sauna. Even without looking she knew it was Ragnar.

Opening her eyes, she looked sleepily up at him. He was wearing a towel, knotted low around his hips, and as her gaze skimmed his powerful body her sleepiness vanished instantly and her nerves started to hum like an electricity substation. Against the soft fabric the lean muscles of his chest and stomach looked like burnished bronze, and as he walked towards her she felt her insides tighten around a ball of hard, pulsing heat.

'I thought you were working.'

'I was.' Sliding onto the bench beside her, he dropped a kiss on her half-open mouth. 'I got through it quicker than expected.' His eyes slipped slowly over the bare skin of her shoulders. 'But then I had an incentive…'

She bit her lip. Her skin was prickling, and she could feel the tips of her nipples pressing into the towel. 'Incentive? Is that how you see me? As some kind of carrot on a stick?'

His long dark lashes flickered up and, blue eyes narrow-ing, he reached out and hooked a finger under the knotted towel above her breasts. 'That's not what I was picturing in my head, no.'

Pulling her closer, he tipped up her head and ran his tongue lightly along her lips. She moaned against his mouth, arching her body upwards, blindly seeking more contact.

'Have you got a condom?'

'No…' He groaned softly and kissed her hard, his lips parting hers, and then slowly he released her. 'I was so des-perate to get down here I didn't think.'

Her stomach flipped over at the sweet look of regret on his face. It was flattering to know that she affected him so strongly, but there was a tension beneath his skin as though he was bracing himself, or building up to saying something that was on his mind.

Her heart began to thump inside her chest. 'Let's just go upstairs,' she said quickly.

'No. I don't want to go upstairs.' His voice was hoarse, but it was the tension in his arms that made her stop talking and stare at him uncertainly.

'I didn't mean that.' Gritting his teeth, he reached out and touched her cheek. 'I do. It's just there's something I want to say to you. About you and Sóley staying on for Christmas. When I asked you on the beach I made a mistake—'

In other words he'd changed his mind.

She stared at him miserably. Beneath her legs the solid bench felt suddenly as though it was made of paper. He'd had time to think and of course he'd changed his mind—but she wasn't going to let him know about the stupid hope in her heart.

'It's okay—I get it,' she said woodenly. 'You're a busy man and you've already taken three weeks off.'

'No, that's not what I meant.' His face was taut. 'I asked you to stay on here, but what I really meant to ask—what I should have asked you—was will you move in with me when we get back to England?'

She stared at him in mute disbelief, stunned by his unexpected miraculous question.

He stroked her face gently. 'I'm not good with words and I didn't make myself clear yesterday, so I'm going to try a little harder this time. I want *you* to move in with me Lottie. Sóley too, of course, but I'm asking *you*.'

Lottie pressed her hand against her mouth. Everything was spinning out of reach, her breath, her heartbeat, her thoughts. He wasn't saying that he loved her, but he wanted her—and not just for sex, but for herself. And right now that was enough.

'I want that too, but are you sure?'

His hands tangled in her hair and he drew her forward. 'More sure than I've ever been.'

And, tilting her face up to his, he kissed her.

Warmth flooded her body and she felt her bones start to soften. He was wrong, she thought. He was good with words—but he was even better at kissing.

For Lottie, the rest of the day passed in a kind of bubble of invulnerable happiness. At first she could hardly believe what had happened, but then Ragnar told Signy, and she'd finally allowed herself to accept that for once the hopes and expectations of her imagination had matched up with real life.

The following morning they woke early, reaching for one another in the darkness, making love slowly, taking their time. Afterwards Ragnar held her close to him, so that it felt as though his blood was pulsing through her veins.

As the sun started to ease into the room they could hear Sóley, gabbling to herself from next door. Lottie inched away from Ragnar's warm, solid body.

'No, I'll get her,' he said.

She shook her head. 'I want to—you always get up first.' Leaning forward, she kissed him softly on the mouth. 'Why don't you grab some more sleep?'

His gaze drifted slowly over her naked body and she felt her breasts start to ache.

'I'm not actually feeling that sleepy...'

They stared at one another, a pulse of desire rebounding between them—and then there was a short, imperious shout from the other side of the wall.

His eyes locked with hers and then the corner of his mouth curved upwards. 'It's fine. I'll go and hit the gym for an hour.' Shifting against the bedding, he grimaced. 'Maybe two.'

Lottie fed Sóley her breakfast and then had a piece of

toast herself. Signy had taken the morning off to visit her sister, so it would be a treat to cook breakfast for both of them. Imagine cooking breakfast being a treat. She smiled. It was just one small example of how her life had changed over the past few weeks.

The biggest and best change was that she and Ragnar had both managed to overcome the false start they'd made twenty months ago in London. Okay, he hadn't said that he loved her, but then she hadn't said it either—and besides, she smiled, neither of them were good with words.

Picking up Sóley, she glanced down at her daughter's cereal-splattered dungarees. 'How did you get so mucky?' She sighed. 'Come on, then, let's go and clean you up.'

They were less than halfway up the stairs when she heard the sound of a car in the driveway.

It must be Signy. Except Signy would let herself in, she thought, frowning as there was a sudden frantic knocking on the door, followed almost immediately by someone pressing the doorbell insistently.

She stared at the door uncertainly.

Ragnar hadn't said anything about visitors, and the house was so off the beaten track it couldn't be anyone looking for directions. It was probably just another delivery of work papers for him.

She glanced up at the discreet security video screen in the wall and felt her spine stiffen. That didn't seem very likely. Standing in front of the camera was a young, very beautiful woman with white-blonde hair, wearing ripped jeans and some kind of shaggy astrakhan coat.

A young, beautiful, weeping woman.

Heart pounding, Lottie punched in the security code and opened the door.

'Oh, thank goodness—I thought there was no one here.'

Storming past her without a word of explanation or even a nod of acknowledgement, the young woman pulled ou her phone and with tears still pouring down her face began frenetically typing.

'You can bring that in,' she called shakily over her shoulder.

Lottie watched in stunned silence as a slightly apologetic-looking taxi driver carried in an expensive, monogrammed suitcase.

'Oh, you need to pay him. You *do* understand English, right?'

Still too stunned to speak, Lottie nodded.

After paying the driver, she closed the door and turned to face the young woman. She had stopped typing into her phone, but she was still crying, and yet her smudged mascara and swollen eyes didn't detract from her quite extraordinary beauty.

Lottie stared at her in confusion. *Who was she?*

The question was barely formed in her head when the woman finally looked at her straight on and her arresting blue eyes instantly and unequivocally provided the answer.

'You must be Marta.'

The woman frowned. 'Yes, I am.' Despite her tears she spoke disdainfully, as though her identity should be a matter of common knowledge. 'Is Ragnar here?'

Lottie nodded. 'He's in the gym.'

Marta sniffed. 'He must be in holiday mode.' Her eyes narrowed on Sóley, as though seeing her for the first time. 'I'm surprised he lets you bring your baby to work.'

'Oh, I don't work for Ragnar,' Lottie said quickly. 'I'm Lottie—Lottie Dawson. And this is Sóley.'

She hadn't been expecting to meet Ragnar's sister, so she hadn't given much thought to how Marta would react to her words, but blank-eyed bewilderment probably wouldn't have been high on her list—or on her list at all.

'Who?' Marta stared at her, her lip curling.

'Lottie…' She knew there was a slight tremor in her

voice, but there was something unnerving about Marta's cool, dismissive gaze, so like her brother's and yet not. More unnerving still was the stinging realisation that Ragnar's sister had no idea who she was, or what she was to him.

The happiness and certainty of earlier fell away. She felt as though she was gripping on to a cliff-edge.

Breathing in against the feeling of vertigo filling her head, she held her daughter closer, taking comfort in the tight grip of her arms.

What should she say? Even if she had the right words, the thought of saying them out loud was just too daunting—for how could she reveal what Ragnar had so clearly decided to keep secret? Only why would he keep his daughter a secret from his sister? And was it just his sister or his whole family?

'Marta—'

Lottie turned, her heart pounding. Ragnar was walking down the stairs and clearly he'd dressed in a hurry. His hair was wet from the shower and his shirt clung to his body, where his skin was still damp.

'What are you doing here?' he said softly.

Bursting into tears, Marta bolted towards him and, watching his arms pull her close, Lottie felt suddenly like an intruder. Whatever it was she needed to ask Ragnar, right now he needed to take care of his sister.

'I'll leave you two to talk,' she said quietly and, side-stepping Marta's sobbing back, she forced herself to walk upstairs.

For the next two hours she tried hard to distract herself from what was going on downstairs. It helped that Sóley was extra demanding, refusing to be put down for a moment and wanting her mother's full attention. Probably she'd been upset by Marta's distress, but thankfully she was too young to have understood Ragnar's deceit by omission.

Lottie shivered. A lump of ice was lodged in her stomach and she could feel its chill spreading outwards. Why hadn't he told his sister about their daughter? It didn't make any sense. He'd spoken to Marta countless times—how could he not have mentioned her?

Maybe he hadn't wanted to tell her when she was so upset. Then again, he had a big family, so maybe he was telling them one at a time.

Glancing down, she saw that Sóley had fallen asleep. Even with her blue eyes out of the equation, the family resemblance between her daughter and Marta and Ragnar was unmistakable. It was there in her jawline and the shape of her mouth.

Turning, she felt her heart stutter. Ragnar was standing in the doorway, his gaze resting on her face. He looked tired. Instantly she forgot her own fears and, walking across the room, she pulled him against her. She felt him breathe out, and the lump of ice in her stomach started to melt.

'Shall I put her down?' he asked.

She nodded and, lifting his daughter up, he laid her gently in the cot.

'Let's go downstairs,' he said quietly.

The hall was empty and silent, the kitchen too.

Lottie watched as Ragnar poured two glasses of water and handed her one.

'Is Marta okay?'

He nodded. 'She will be.'

'She probably needs some food. I can make her some lunch—'

'You don't need to do that.'

'Oh, I don't mind—'

'No,' he said firmly. 'You don't need to do that. She's not here.'

She frowned. 'Not here. Where has she gone?'

'To Reykjavik. To a hotel.'

'But she was so upset. She shouldn't be on her own—you should go after her.'

His face stilled. 'That would be a little absurd as I was the one who sent her there.'

She stared at him, not understanding. 'You sent her away? But why?'

'This is my home. I have rules. And Marta broke those rules. She knows I don't have people to stay here.'

His answer both irritated and confused her. 'She's not "people". She's your family.'

He shrugged. 'I know—and I particularly don't have my family here. This is a place of calm and order. I don't want their drama under my roof.'

Rules. Drama. What was he talking about? She could feel panic clawing up her throat. 'But you love them.'

'Yes, I do. And I show that love to them in many different ways, twenty-four-seven. All they have to do in return is follow my rules, and the first and most important rule is that they don't turn up unannounced.'

He sounded as though he was explaining a scientific law, like gravity, not talking about his family.

'But love doesn't have rules…' she said slowly.

'Which probably explains why so many people are unhappy.'

She felt a chill as his blue gaze met hers. His eyes were hard and unreachable.

'I love my family but I can't—I *won't*—live with them. I keep everything separate and contained. That's how it works. That's how I live.'

The hurt in her chest was spreading like a blizzard.

'Is that why you didn't tell Marta about me and Sóley?'

She saw the truth in his eyes before he even opened his mouth, and it hurt so badly she had to grit her teeth against the pain in her heart.

'Yes.'

'Have you told *anyone* in your family?'

This time he shook his head.

She breathed out unsteadily. It had happened again—just like with her father. They had met too late. Ragnar, the man she loved, the man she so badly wanted to love her, was someone who couldn't be what she wanted or give her what she needed. Only she'd been too busy painting pretty pictures in her head to see what was actually in front of her nose.

'What if I tell you that I love you?' she whispered. 'Would that change anything?'

As he shook his head the distance in his eyes made her almost black out.

'I want to go home.' The words left her mouth before she knew they were there. 'I want to go back to England—now.'

He glanced away, and there was a long, strained silence.

'Then I'll go and speak to Ivar,' he said finally. 'I'll leave you to pack.'

And without meeting her eyes he turned and walked out through the door.

CHAPTER TEN

STANDING BESIDE THE fire in the middle of the living room, Ragnar breathed out unsteadily. This was his home, and yet he felt adrift—disconnected and dazed.

He didn't know which was more unbelievable. The fact that Lottie and Sóley were gone or that he had stood and watched them leave.

He fumbled with the equation in his head but nothing he did would balance it.

He shivered. He felt cold, and the house was so quiet. No, not just quiet—it was silent. The silence of reproach and regret.

His eyes flicked across the empty room to something square and yellow, poking out from beneath a cushion on the sofa. Slowly he walked towards it, his heart pounding as he saw what it was.

Lottie's sketchbook.

He picked it up, his hand shaking as he turned the pages, an ache flowering like a black orchid inside his chest.

What had he done?

Or rather what hadn't he done?

Why hadn't he stopped her leaving?

Why had he just stood and waited while she packed?

It made no sense. He'd only just asked her to move in with him, and she'd agreed, and for the first time ever he'd been thinking about a future that offered something other than lives lived separately with clearly defined borders. For the first time ever he'd been looking at a hazy rose-gold sunset of a future, with Lottie and his daughter.

And then Marta had arrived, crashing into his ordered, tranquil life, trailing snowflakes and suitcases and disorder in her wake, and instantly the sunset had been blotted out by the need to act quickly and decisively.

Of course he'd taken care of her, but there had been no possibility of her staying. And he'd tried to explain that to Lottie. Tried to explain that he couldn't let his family into his home with all their tears and traumas.

Only she hadn't understood, and she'd kept on pushing and pushing, and then—his breathing faltered—then she'd told him she loved him.

He could still see her face now—the expression of shock and hurt when he'd more or less told that her love didn't change how he felt. He gritted his teeth. Except he hadn't said anything. He'd just shaken his head like a robot.

But he hadn't been able to make his voice work. Marta's random appearance was such an unsettling reminder of what would happen if he allowed the separate strands of his life to overlap, that her astonishing words and his own feverishly joyous response to them had been silenced.

Of course, seeing Lottie upset had hurt—badly—but not enough to blank his mind to the fear, so that when she'd told him she wanted to go home he'd told himself that it was for the best.

But it wasn't.

It was the biggest mistake he'd ever made.

The next few days were interminable, and he realised that time was *not* a great healer. Being alone in the house—or worse, in his bed—was like pressing against an open wound, and after one more day of agonising solitude he went down to the stables and led Camille out into the yard.

He rode blindly, seeing nothing, caring about nothing, just trying to put as much distance between himself and his silent home as he could. But when they reached the top of a hill Camille slowed and, leaning back in his saddle, he gazed down at the waterfalls. His eyes blurred—and not because of the freezing wind.

The sky was dark and low and the wind was bitterly cold against his face. Any rational, sane person would be happily sprawled out on the sofa in front of a log fire. But he didn't feel rational or sane or happy. And that was why he was here, roaming the freezing hills.

It was ridiculous and illogical to act like this.

Signy certainly thought so.

Probably Camille, too, but thankfully horses couldn't talk.

Only he didn't know what else to do.

For years he'd relished coming here. Even before *ice/ breakr* had gone global it had been a place of sanctuary— somewhere he could take a breath before the next storm hit.

His hands tightened against the reins.

But not any more. Now his house was an empty, echoing reminder of his stupidity and cowardice. For so many years he'd had to fight to keep his life orderly and tranquil, and now he had succeeded in achieving his ideal. After expelling Marta from his home, even his family were keeping their distance—only instead of relishing his solitude he hated it.

He missed Lottie and Sóley.

Without them life had no purpose, no value.

But she deserved a better man than him.

So be that man, he told himself. *Be the man she needs you to be. Find her and fight for her.*

And, turning away from the waterfall, he pushed Camille down the slope towards the only future he wanted—a future he was not going to let slip away again.

Looking up at the Suffolk sky, Lottie flinched as a few flakes of snow landed on her face. She was standing in the back garden of her cottage, supposedly trying to decide where to put Sóley's swing. All week it had been threatening to snow, but of course it had to wait until today, her daughter's birthday, to actually make good on its promise.

As if she didn't have enough reminders of Ragnar Stone already in her life.

All the shops were filled with fur throws and cushions for Christmas, and when Lucas had finally managed to drag her to the pub one evening she'd caught sight of a blond man crouching in front of the open fire and, ignoring her brother's exasperated protests, had simply reversed back out through the door.

But of the man himself there had been nothing.

Not a word in nearly three weeks.

No phone call.

No text.

She swallowed against the ache building in her throat.

Not even a birthday card for their daughter.

A mixture of misery and anger flared inside her. She still couldn't accept that he was acting like this—punishing Sóley for what had happened between the two of them. It seemed so small-minded and cruel, so not like Ragnar.

Or maybe it *was* like him.

Remembering the cool, almost clinical expression on his face when she'd told him she loved him, she shivered. After hearing him talk so dispassionately about his family, and his ruthless dismissal of Marta, she'd been mad to tell him that. But then she'd naively been assuming that her words would mean something to him, that they would matter—that *she* mattered.

Her mouth twisted. But they hadn't—and she didn't.

And now she was here, back in Suffolk, it was difficult to see why she had ever thought he cared about love *or* her.

Truthfully, she barely knew him—she'd just made herself feel that she did, letting the intoxicating power of their lovemaking weave a spell not just over her body but her mind too. She'd been so flattered, so desperate to believe in the story she'd told herself in her head of two people separated by circumstance but destined to be together.

She bit down on a sudden choking swell of tears. She was stupid. And selfish. For it was her fault that her daughter—her beautiful, sweet daughter—would never have a father in her life. But clearly Ragnar had meant what he said about keeping his life separate and contained.

'Lottie—'

Hearing Lucas's voice, she swiped the tears from her cheeks and took a quick, calming breath. If she could take one positive away from this whole mess it was that it had made her realise how close she and Lucas and Izzy were as a family.

Her brother and her mother were fundamentally different from her in so many ways, but she understood now that it wasn't just nature that mattered. Ragnar had taught her that nurture was just as important. Since she'd stumbled into the cottage, with tears pouring down her face, both Lucas and Izzy had been utterly amazing.

Those first few days back in England she had felt adrift from everything—like the survivor of a sinking ship, she had only been capable of clinging to the wreckage. Then, when the shock had faded, she had been ill, stricken with cramps, immobilised by the crushing weight of failure and disappointment.

And all the time, despite everything that had happened, she'd missed Ragnar. The nights were bad, but waking was worse, for each morning she had to work through her grief and her loneliness all over again.

It was her family who got her out of bed, and dressed, and she was so lucky to have them.

Forcing her lips into a smile, she turned towards Lucas. He sighed. 'Oh, Lottie, we agreed. No crying today.'

'I'm not crying.' She met her brother's sceptical gaze. 'Honestly. It's just the cold. I'm fine, really.'

'So, did you decide where you want it?'

She gazed at him blankly still lost in thoughts of Ragnar. 'Want what?'

He groaned. 'The swing, Lottie. Remember? I said I was going to put it by the vegetable patch and you didn't want it there—'

Without warning, she felt her face crumple. 'Sorry, I forgot.'

'No, I'm sorry.' Reaching out, he pulled her against his battered leather jacket. 'I'm just feeling cranky, but I shouldn't take it out on you.'

She pressed her face into her brother's chest, breathing in his familiar smell. 'You didn't—you've been great, Lucas.'

Looking up at him, she watched his jaw tighten.

'I want to kill him, you know. For how he's treated you and Sóley.'

'Well don't.' She smiled up at him weakly. 'We need you here—not in prison.'

His face creased into a reluctant smile. 'Is that your way of telling me you know where you want the swing?'

It took over an hour to make the frame and fix it into position but, despite the numerous setbacks, Lottie found it strangely relaxing. At least trying to make sense of the comically inadequate instructions took her mind off Ragnar, and the swing was lovely. Made of wood, it had two seats—one for a baby and one for an adult.

Lucas took hold of the frame and tried to jiggle it. 'Look at that.' He grinned at Lottie. 'Rock-solid.'

'Oh, well done, darling.' Izzy was standing by the back door, holding Sóley in her arms. 'It looks fantastic. Shall we give it a try?'

But as she tried to put Sóley into the baby seat her bottom lip protruded and began to wobble.

'Here, let me try, Mum.' Reaching out, Lottie took her daughter.

'Look what Lucas has made. Isn't he clever?' she said softly.

She felt Sóley relax at the sound of her voice but when she tried to lower her into the seat the little girl just grabbed her neck and refused to let go.

'I'm sorry, Lucas.' Looking over at her brother's disappointed face, Lottie felt her stomach twist with guilt.

Since getting home, Sóley had stopped being the easy-going baby she had always been. She was clingy, and often woke several times in the night. It was tempting to tell herself that it was just her age, or her teeth, or even the change in routine, but she knew that Sóley was missing Ragnar as much as she was, and that only added to her feelings of guilt.

'You'll be okay, you know…' Her mother leaned forward and kissed her cheek. 'You're stronger than you think. Strong enough to survive this. And Sóley will be okay too. Children are very resilient.'

'I don't *want* her to have to be resilient,' she said hoarsely.

'I know, darling.' Izzy smiled. 'But that's nature's way. You have to be tough to survive. Look at everything I put you and Lucas through. No father figures, let alone actual fathers, and all those different homes and schools, and always having the wrong clothes.'

Her mother was looking straight into her eyes, and in that moment, the calmness of her expression made Lottie realise that she had focused too much on their differences instead of how much they were alike.

She shook her head. 'It wasn't that bad.'

Lucas caught her eye and grinned. 'It was pretty bad—especially the clothes.'

Lottie smiled. 'But whatever happened you were always there, Mum. And we were lucky to have you.' As she spoke, she wondered why she had never said that to Izzy before and why it felt true now. 'I'm lucky to have you, then and now.'

'Me too,' Lucas said, his eyes gleaming. 'Only don't go getting the wrong idea and start thinking that this love-in means you get to wear any of your weird kaftans to the party.'

Izzy and Lottie both laughed.

'Right, darling,' said Izzy. 'I'm going to take my grand-daughter home with me so she can have a nap. No.' She held up her hand imperiously as Lottie started to protest and then gently pulled Sóley into her arms. 'She needs a nap and you need a little time on your own to make your peace with today. Come on, Lucas.'

After the car had driven off Lottie went and sat on the swing. It was starting to snow again, but it wasn't that cold, and it was calming just to sit and let her feet scuff against the ground. Glancing up at the sky, Lottie breathed out, try-ing to find the peace her mother had mentioned.

Her emotions were not out of control now. She felt sad—but not the crushing misery of those early days, just a lin-gering emptiness that she couldn't seem to shift. And that was okay, because her mother was right. She was strong and she was going to survive.

And because she was strong she was going to put her sadness aside this afternoon for the sake of her family—especially her daughter.

Ragnar Stone was not coming to this party so she cer-tainly wasn't going to let the memory of him ruin it for her or anyone else.

Her body stilled. From beyond the hedge she could hear the sound of a car making its way up the lane. No doubt her mother had forgotten something crucial, and sent Lucas to retrieve it. As she swung gently back and forth she heard the car stop in front of the cottage, and then the crunching sound of footsteps on the path. Then the click of the garden gate. Definitely Lucas, then. Her mother could never open it without a huge tussle.

'So what did you forget?' she called out. 'I'm going to go with either your phone or Mum's bag.'

'Actually, I didn't forget anything. I let it slip away.'

Her heart turned to stone. She stared across the garden, her breath dissolving in her lungs. Ragnar was standing at the edge of the path, his clear blue eyes fixed on her face. He looked just as he always had, and the pain of seeing him again made her feel lightheaded.

'What are you doing here?' Her voice sounded small and unfamiliar in the sudden echoing silence.

'I came to talk to you.'

Her throat tightened. He made it sound as though he was just dropping in, when the reality was that he hadn't been in touch for weeks. Two weeks and six days, to be precise.

She swallowed, pushing back against the ache in her chest. 'In case you've forgotten it's our daughter's birthday, so I don't really have time for a chat.'

He didn't move. 'I know it's her birthday, and I want to see her. But I have something I need to say to you first.'

'I don't want to listen to anything you have to say, Ragnar.' She stood up abruptly, letting go of the swing so that it banged into the back of her legs. 'Do you really think you can just turn up here for her birthday? It's been nearly three weeks.'

'I know. And I'm not proud of myself.'

'Well, that makes two of us.'

He sucked in a breath as though she'd slapped him. 'You have every right to be angry with me.'

Angry? *Angry?* She stared at him, the word spinning inside her head like the ball in a roulette wheel.

'You think I'm angry?' She shook her head. 'I'm not angry, Ragnar. I'm hurt.'

Crossing her arms in front of her chest, she clenched her teeth. She was not going to cry in front of him.

But as he took a step forward she felt her eyes fill with tears.

'I'm sorry,' he said softly, and the softness in his voice hurt more than anything else, for that was what she missed most. 'I'm sorry,' he said again. 'I never meant to hurt you. I would never hurt you.'

'You're hurting me now.' Her arms tightened around her ribs. 'You had no right to come here. I was just starting to feel okay.'

'I had to come. I had to come and see you.'

'And now you have—so you can go.'

He didn't move. He just stood there, with snowflakes spinning slowly around him.

'Ragnar, please.' The hurt broke through her voice, and as she pressed her hand against her mouth he was walking towards her and pulling her close. She pushed against him. 'You have to leave.'

'Please give me a chance.'

'To do what? Throw my love back in my face?' She shook her head. 'It's too late, Ragnar. Whatever you think is going to happen here, it isn't.'

'I love you.'

'No.' She shook her head. 'You don't get to say that. That's not allowed.'

'I thought love didn't have any rules?' he said quietly.

His voice was strained, and now that he was closer she could see dark smudges under his eyes, and he looked as if he'd lost weight.

Blanking her mind to the idea that he might be suffering too, she shook her head again. 'You don't love me,' she whispered. 'And more importantly I don't love you. Not any more.'

His eyes were steady on her face.

'I don't believe you. I think you do love me, Lottie. And
I know that I love you.'

Reaching out, he caught her hand, but she pulled it away

'You think that's all it takes? Just three little words
Well, I've got three words for you. Separate and contained

'But I don't want to be separate from you.' He took her
hand again, and this time the fire in his voice stopped her
pulling away. 'I can't be separate from you. I thought
could—I thought that was what I wanted, what I needed
But I need *you*.'

'So why did you let me leave?'

Leaning forward, he pressed his face against her. 'Be
cause I was stupid and scared.'

'Scared of what?'

She was holding her breath.

'Of feeling. Of how you made me feel.'

The shake in his voice made her eyes burn.

'My family feels everything so intensely, and when
was kid it used to scare me, being around that kind of in
tense emotion. And then, when I met Daniel that summer
I realised there were other ways to live. All I needed to d
was take a step back, keep my distance.'

She felt him breathe out unsteadily.

'I shouldn't have let you go. It hurt so much, but I kep
telling myself that I was doing it for the right reasons. Tha
I couldn't be the man you needed and so I'd just end u
hurting you.'

Remembering his tense expression when he'd foun
Marta in his house, she thought her heart might burst wit
understanding and relief. So it had been fear that had mad
him put his sister in a taxi. Fear, not indifference, that ha
stopped him from telling her what was in his heart.

'So what's changed?' she said softly.

His hands were shaking. 'I did. I realised that I didn

ave a choice. I can't live without you or Sóley. I'm going
razy without you.'

He was laying his heart bare, saying the words she'd
onged to hear, and yet she was scared to hope, scared to
elieve that they were true.

She felt his fingers tighten around hers.

'I didn't believe it could happen to me. I didn't think I
ould fall in love. And then it came so quickly and com-
letely—and that scared me, because I didn't think I was
apable of giving you the love you deserve.'

His eyes softened.

'My family are crazy when they're in love, and I didn't
vant to be like them. And then I realised that I'd been so
ixated on all the ways I didn't want to be like them that
'd stopped seeing all the ways I did. Like how brave and
enerous and loving they are.'

'I know what you mean,' she said slowly. 'I did the same
hing with my mum and Lucas, reading too much into our
ifferences.'

He stared at her uncertainly. 'Did you mean what you
aid? About not loving me.'

She shook her head slowly. 'I want to mean it, but I
an't.'

Sliding his arm around her waist, he kissed her. She felt
im breathe out shakily against her mouth.

'I love you,' he said.

'I love you too.'

His eyes locked onto hers. 'Enough to be my wife?'

Looking down, she felt her heart swell. He was holding
ring with a sapphire as blue and clear as his eyes.

'Let me try that again,' he said hoarsely. 'Will you marry
ie, Lottie Dawson?'

She was nodding and smiling and crying all at the same
me.

'That *is* a yes, isn't it?'

She nodded again. 'Yes, it is.'

As he slid the ring onto her finger she pulled him close. 'So what happens next?'

He smiled. 'This…' he said softly.

And, tilting her face up to his, he lowered his mouth and kissed her.

EPILOGUE

Six months later...

GLANCING OUT OF the window, Lottie bit her lip. Why was it taking so long? Surely they must nearly be there.

But the scenery scudding beneath the helicopter's whirling rotor blades was no help at all—mainly because it looked nothing like it had the last time she'd seen it, just over six months ago. Then, it had been covered in snow, but now the snow was gone, and the land was a patchwork of colours and textures—a bit like her sixth form art project, she thought, a bubble of laughter squeezing out of her chest.

'What's so funny?'

Meeting her brother's gaze, she shook her head. 'Nothing, really. I was just thinking about an art project I did at school.'

'Okay...' He raised an eyebrow. 'You did eat breakfast, didn't you?'

'Yes, I did. I had muesli and yoghurt and fresh fruit.' She poked him gently in the ribs. 'So, what do you think?'

It was Lucas's first visit to Iceland, and she was desperate to hear his thoughts—to find out if he felt the same way as she did about this incredible country that was now like a second home to her.

'Of your breakfast?' He grinned. 'Oh, you mean of all this.' Shaking his head, he blew out a breath. 'What can I say? It's right out there... I mean, look at this place!' He leaned forward, his eyes widening as they flew over a huge vivid green field of moss. As he looked back at her, his face softened. 'I can see why you love it so much.'

She smiled. 'It's just so beautiful and rugged and remote.'

His eyes gleamed. 'Are you talking about Iceland? Or Ragnar?' he said softly.

Looking down, she stared at the sapphire ring on her finger. 'You do like him now, don't you?'

She thought back to the moment when she and Ragnar had walked into her mother's garden together, after he'd proposed. Lucas hadn't liked him at all then, but thankfully Sóley's babbling open-armed excitement at seeing her father had meant that his disapproval had been limited to a stiffness of posture and a murderous scowl.

Her pulse skipped forward. It had been a shock, seeing her normally easy-going brother like that, but it hadn't lasted. Ignoring her panicky protests, he and Ragnar had gone for a walk the next day, and when they'd returned they hadn't been brothers-in-arms, exactly, but Lucas had welcomed him as a brother-in-law.

She felt him shrug beside her.

'Yeah, he's not the worst. I mean, I wouldn't ask him to join the band, but he's pretty handy with a pool cue.' As she looked up to meet his gaze, he rolled his eyes. 'I like him, okay? He knows a lot of stuff but he's not boring about it, and he's generous with money but not flash.' His mouth twitched. 'Oh, and he's got some *extremely* hot sisters.' He hesitated, his face suddenly serious. 'But mainly I like him because I can see how much he loves you, and I know that he makes you happy.'

She swallowed against the lump in her throat. 'He does...he really does.'

Her heart contracted. Ragnar had worked so hard these last six months to turn his life around. He'd started by introducing her and Sóley to his family, and he hadn't stopped there. He'd talked to each of them in turn, explaining how he'd felt as a child and then as a man. It had been really difficult for him, but he'd been determined to deal with his fear and committed to their future—his and hers and heir daughter's.

She'd been scared of meeting his family, and it had been errifying. They were all so glamorous and emphatic. But almost immediately she'd realised that beneath all the drama there was a solid core of unbreakable love and, even though they'd been at loggerheads for months, the first ime she'd met Ragnar's mother, her ex-husband Nathan, his new wife Kim and their new baby had been there too.

It had been surreal, but kind of wonderful.

A bit like his family.

The family who had welcomed her into their hearts.

Lucas frowned. 'Hey, you promised no crying.'

As Lottie swiped at her eyes she felt the helicopter start o slow. 'We're here,' she said softly.

Her heart gave a thump as they landed, and then he was sliding back the door and climbing out, holding up his hand o help her down.

'Here.' He took her hand and slid it through his arm. 'Let's go find your man.'

Her man. Her Ragnar.

Her chest squeezed tight and, gripping Lucas's arm to steady the trembling of her heart, she started to walk towards the beach, to find the man she loved without limits.

The man she was going to marry today.

'She's here.'

Glancing up, Ragnar felt the twist in his stomach muscles loosen. Behind him, his brother and best man Rob gave his shoulders a reassuring squeeze.

'Shall I get the bridesmaids?'

Ragnar glanced over to where a giggling Sóley was holding hands with his sister Marta. Their blonde hair was gleaming in the sunlight, their faces tipped back as they led from his brother, Gunnar, across the black sand.

'No, it's okay. They're having fun.'

Turning his head, he gazed at the rest of his family. They were standing in a casual semi-circle, and his eyes moved slowly from one smiling face to the next.

It was true—everyone was having fun. There had been no arguments or tears or sulking. He felt an ache around his heart. They were all trying so hard, because they loved him. And he loved them as he always had, only now it felt so much easier to love and be loved.

He felt his gaze pulled back across the sand to where Lottie was walking towards him.

And that was down to her.

Lottie had made this happen.

She had made him stronger. And kinder. She and Sóley had made loving as simple and natural for him as breathing, so that now he found it difficult to understand how he'd survived for so long living as he had.

But everything was different now—particularly him. He no longer kept those he loved most at arm's length—and, incredibly, now that they could come and go at will, his family seemed like different people too, less intense, less demanding.

More fun.

That word again.

It was so not what his life had been about before, but now he had fun every day.

A flicker of heat skimmed over his skin. He had passion too. And tenderness. But most of all he had a love that was as warm and bright and unending as the summer solstice—and that was why he'd wanted Midsummer's Day to be their wedding day.

Straightening the cuffs of his dark suit jacket, he breathed out unsteadily.

Lottie stopped in front of him, her hand trembling against her brother's arm, her face soft and serious.

He stared at her, his pulse beating in time to the waves curling onto the beach.

She looked amazing. Fitted to her waist and then spilling out in layers of tulle, her white dress was perfectly offset by the black of the sand beneath her feet. She was holding a bunch of wild flowers picked by Sóley and Marta from the fields surrounding the house, and her hair was loosely caught up at the base of her neck.

She had never looked more beautiful. And, meeting her gaze, he felt the ache in his chest intensify.

Her eyes were shining with tears of emotion, and the same emotions that were shining in his eyes were filling his heart. A happiness like no other, and a gratitude that life had let them find one another not once but three times—a statistic that had no basis in logic and was just the beautiful, disorderly, topsy-turvy mathematics of love.

'You look beautiful,' he whispered.

The celebrant stepped forward and smiled. 'Shall we begin?'

As they spoke their vows tears were sliding down his face—tears he would never have allowed to fall before meeting her.

Finally, they exchanged rings, and the celebrant smiled again. 'And now you may kiss, as husband and wife.'

They each took a step forward and then, as he lowered his mouth to hers, she leaned towards him and they kissed, softly at first, and then more deeply, to the appreciative applause of their watching families.

'I can't believe we're married,' she whispered, gazing at the gold band on her finger.

'I can't believe I made us wait so long.' Cupping her face in his hand, he brushed his mouth against hers. 'But it had to be this day.'

Her heart swelled with love as she looked up at him curiously. Ragnar had chosen the day, and at the time she'd assumed he'd picked it because Midsummer was a day of celebration for Icelanders. But the shake in his hand now told a different story.

Reaching up, she stroked his cheek. 'Tell me why you chose it?'

'It's the summer solstice.' He hesitated, struggling to contain the emotion in his voice. 'That means the sun will never set on our wedding day. I just liked the idea of that.'

'I like it too.' Tears filled her eyes and throat and, pulling him closer, she kissed him softly. 'I love you.'

'And I love you. So very much.'

For a moment neither of them could speak, but as Ragnar lowered his mouth and kissed her again Lottie knew it didn't matter. Sometimes words were irrelevant.

* * * * *

COMING SOON!

We really hope you enjoyed reading this book. If you're looking for more romance, be sure to head to the shops when new books are available on

Thursday 12th December

To see which titles are coming soon, please visit

millsandboon.co.uk/nextmonth

MILLS & BOON

Coming next month

BILLIONAIRE'S WIFE ON PAPER
Melanie Milburne

'But you don't want to get married.' It was a statement, not a question.

A shadow passed through his gaze like a background figure moving across a stage. He turned back to face the view from the windows; there might as well have been a 'Keep Away' sign printed on his back. It seemed a decade before he spoke. 'No.' His tone had a note of finality that made something in Layla's chest tighten.

The thought of him marrying someone one day had always niggled at her like mild toothache. She could ignore it mostly but now and again a sharp jab would catch her off guard. But how could he ever find someone as perfect for him as Susannah? No wonder he was a little reluctant to date seriously these days. If only Layla could find someone to love her with such lasting loyalty.

'What about a marriage of convenience? You could find someone who would agree to marry you just long enough to fulfil the terms of the will.'

One of his dark eyebrows rose in a cynical arc above his left eye. 'Are you volunteering for the role as my paper bride?'

Eek! Why had she even mentioned such a thing? Maybe it was time to stop reading paperback romances and start reading thriller or horror novels instead. Layla could feel a hot flush of colour flooding her cheeks and bent down to straighten the items in her basket to disguise it. 'No. Of course not.' Her voice was part laugh, part gasp and came out shamefully high and tight. Her? His bride of convenience? Ha-di-ha-ha-ha. She wouldn't be a convenient bride for anyone, much less Logan McLaughlin.

A strange silence crept from the far corners of the room, stealing oxygen particles, stilling dust motes, stirring possibilities…

Logan walked back to where she was hovering over her cleaning basket, his footsteps steady and sure. Step. Step. Step.

Step. Layla slowly raised her gaze to his inscrutable one, her heart doing a crazy tap dance in her chest. She drank in the landscape of his face—the ink-black prominent eyebrows over impossibly blue eyes, the patrician nose, the sensually sculpted mouth, the steely determined jaw. The lines of grief etched into his skin that made him seem older than he was. At thirty-three, he was in the prime of his life. Wealthy, talented, a world-renowned landscape architect—you could not find a more eligible bachelor...or one so determined to avoid commitment.

'Think about it, Layla.'

His tone was deep with a side note of roughness that made a faint shiver course through her body. A shiver of awareness. A shiver of longing that could no longer be restrained in its secret home.

Layla picked up her basket from the floor and held it in front of her body like a shield. Was he teasing her? Making fun of her? He must surely know she wasn't marriage material—certainly not for someone like him. She was about as far away from Susannah as you could get. 'Don't be ridiculous.'

His hand came down to touch her on the forearm, and even through two layers of clothing her skin tingled. She looked down at his long strong fingers and disguised a swallow. She could count on one hand the number of times he had touched her over the years and still have fingers left over. His touch was unfamiliar and strange, alien almost, and yet her body reacted like a crocus bulb to spring sunshine.

'I'm serious,' he said, looking at her with watchful intensity. 'I need a temporary wife to save Bellbrae from being sold or destroyed and who better than someone who loves this place as much as I do?'

Continue reading
BILLIONAIRE'S WIFE ON PAPER
Melanie Milburne

Available next month
www.millsandboon.co.uk